THE
30th
CANDLE

ALSO BY ANGELA MAKHOLWA

THE
30th
CANDLE

ANGELA
MAKHOLWA

LAKE UNION
PUBLISHING

Text copyright © 2009, 2013, 2023 by Angela Makholwa
All rights reserved.

Published by Lake Union Publishing, Seattle

www.apub.com

Amazon, the Amazon logo, and Lake Union Publishing are trademarks of Amazon.com, Inc., or its affiliates.

First published as *The 30th Candle* by Pan Macmillan in South Africa in 2009. This edition contains editorial revisions.

ISBN-13: 9781662504327
eISBN: 9781662504310

Cover design by The Brewster Project

Cover image: © Reinhold Leitner / Shutterstock; Mstock / Alamy Stock Photo

Printed in the United States of America

THE
30th
CANDLE

Chapter 1

LINDA

'Linda, who is this? I can't believe what I'm seeing,' gasped Lehumo. He was standing transfixed at the door, his light complexion ripened to red, his hands shaking and his mouth trembling, as if he were suddenly stuck in below-freezing temperatures. At that moment, his giant frame did nothing to make him look any less vulnerable. Linda just looked at him, then at the half-naked man lying next to her in bed. She cast her eyes down for a split second, perhaps feigning a modicum of remorse for the mortifying scene that she and her lover had set out for Lehumo to stumble upon.

For an eternity, they all froze in their positions: Lehumo planted firmly at the door, holding his phone as if it were a gun that was about to go off; the stranger lying in bed next to Linda, shamefaced and trapped, as helpless as a little rabbit; and the Jezebel herself, now sitting upright in a stoic position, as if refusing to plead guilty to any indiscretion.

'*Broer*, what are you doing with my fiancée? Aren't there enough women in Gauteng for you to be banging on other people's beds?' A deathly silence.

Then: 'Well, technically speaking this is not your bed,' said Linda, her characteristic bluntness staying with her in this of all moments.

'Hey, *wena*, I'm not even talking to you right now . . . you . . . you . . .'

'Okay, okay,' said the stranger, an older man, holding out his hands in a conciliatory gesture. 'This is a very uncomfortable situation for all of us, but I think there's a way we can handle this without causing anyone any further pain.'

Lehumo took three giant strides towards the bed, grabbed the man by what little clothing he still had on and hurled him onto his back.

'Fuck you, arsehole. Don't you dare try and act like the hero here. I find you in bed with my fiancée and you have the audacity to think you have a say in all this? Take your stinking Vasco da Gama pants and your fucking phone and get out of my face now!'

The stranger quickly grabbed his clothes, cast a last glance at Linda, then picked up his wallet, keys and phone, and vanished from the room in a flash.

As a parting shot, Lehumo spat the words, 'You fucking pensioner!' Slowly, he marched towards the bed like a wounded soldier.

'Now tell me, Linda, why, why do you keep hurting me? What is it you want from me? Why is nothing ever enough for you?' he pleaded, tears rolling down his face as his heavy frame slumped next to her.

Linda stayed seated, as still and as quiet as if she had turned to salt.

Lehumo grabbed her by the shoulders in exasperation. 'Talk to me! Talk to me, you witch! Don't you feel anything? Are you even human?' he yelled in desperation, his big eyes bulging, searching her face hopefully for something: guilt, remorse, regret – *anything*.

Linda shook him away from her and stood up, revealing that other than the white vest, she was wearing absolutely nothing else. She walked to her closet, took out her red satin gown and wrapped it around her curvaceous body. 'Listen, baby, I think you've had enough drama for one day. If the engagement is off, I fully understand, trust me. You don't deserve this. You deserve better,' she said, with an eerily calm expression on her face.

Lehumo gave her an incredulous look. 'Whatever happened to you? I once thought you were the perfect woman,' he said quietly, as if to himself.

She looked at him with pity in her eyes. 'Humo . . . I think that's the most valuable lesson you've learned today. I'm not the perfect woman, at least not for you. To be honest, I'm not even sure how you managed to stick it out this long with me. I don't even think I'm wife material,' she said, calmly folding her hands as she went to sit next to him on the bed.

There were tears in Lehumo's eyes again. Shaking his head in shock, he said, 'But why did you lead me on like this? Why did you accept my proposal?'

Now she was massaging his shoulders. 'Baby, I never accepted or rejected your proposal. You just forced me – not literally forced me, but in that persuasive way of yours, where you only hear what you want to hear. You orchestrated this whole romance, the engagement . . . everything. I had no major role to play in this relationship. In fact, this is probably my one cameo appearance.'

'What the hell are you talking about? Excuse me, but I don't believe I was having a relationship with myself all these months! You were always there, and I never forced you into anything you didn't want!'

She sighed, shaking her head. 'Lehumo, if you just allow yourself to think back, I'm sure you'll see that the main actor here has always been you. It was always your friends' houses we went to, it was your colleagues I met with, and it was you, always you, who was making plans for the two of us. I was merely tagging along because I didn't have anything better to do.'

'Well, thanks for making something I thought was a great relationship sound like a one-man show featuring a puppet called Linda,' replied Lehumo.

She looked at him. 'I probably deserve that, but I did try to explain my feelings . . . you just refused to hear me. You'd change the topic, talk about something else. So, what was I to do? I'm twenty-nine years old, pushing thirty. Everybody says thirty's the pits, especially if you're not in a stable relationship, so I just went along with it.

'But,' she added dramatically, standing up as if to put ice on whatever warmth or empathy she had almost induced, 'I never really reached the depth of commitment you were seeking. For some reason I was too afraid to face up to that reality. You were just so . . . so certain about us that I thought if I gave it enough time, I'd be able to give you the kind of love you deserved. I just never got there. I'm sorry,' she said, shrugging resignedly.

'Oh, and Grandpa, in those ridiculous eighteenth-century pyjamas, is more your type? I can't believe you betrayed me with another man, and all you can give me are some pitiful excuses about commitment! I've been here all along. Why couldn't you have shared your feelings with me before leading me on like this? You've stolen my pride. Shit, couldn't you at least do this with someone younger or something?'

Suddenly Linda looked angry. The fact that this was the first time she'd shown any emotion about the situation did not escape Lehumo's attention.

'Lehumo, maybe you should start looking at things from another point of view, because I swear that would save you a lot of trouble,' she said, trying to regain her composure. 'If you hadn't walked in on me like you did, it was probably going to be something else. Maybe not as awful as this, but the truth is, I think I was acting out. I've been very frustrated because I feel like I've been living a lie.'

'Yeah, at least we agree on one thing: you're a whore.'

'No. If I were in love with you, none of this would have been possible. It's just . . . I've been trying to let you know how I feel but you've not been listening. Don't you see this was my cry for help? All of a sudden, I found myself wearing an engagement ring without remembering when exactly my heart said yes to you . . . if ever. I swear, sometimes I'd look at my finger and wish that ring would fall off!'

Lehumo shook his head disbelievingly. He could not bring himself to look at her.

'The past few weeks have been hell for me,' she said. 'I've been having sleepless nights imagining myself trapped in some rambling house with forty kids and you, with a giant pot belly, coming home smelling of beer. I just couldn't handle it. It was freaking me out.'

'You honestly think being married to me would be that pathetic?' he asked, still in shock. It was as if he were talking to a stranger.

Linda looked like she was mulling over the question. Slowly, eyes downcast, she nodded.

'Well, then I guess I made a big mistake,' he said, standing up. 'I should have listened when people told me not to date Xhosa women – nothing but a bunch of bitches! One thing's for sure – I'm never doing that again!' Lehumo took his keys, his wallet and his mobile phone, and left.

He hoped never to see Linda Mthimkhulu's face again, and Linda hoped he would not hold her individual actions against her entire tribe. Did he have to make that comment about Xhosa women?

Chapter 2

Nolwazi

Nolwazi looked at her watch. A quarter to twelve. Great. This is perfect, she thought, her skinny legs struggling to keep up with the urgent business at hand. 'I'm gonna get fired, I'm gonna get fired,' she chanted mentally. This was the third time she would be late to a meeting with their most demanding, most difficult, bitchiest client.

The client's name was Aldo Mabuza. She owned a mining company, three butcheries in the township, and was on her way to buying a stake in an advertising agency. Everybody knew this was Aldo's big night, and the company that Nolwazi worked for, The Style Surgeons, was responsible for dressing her, as well as other hotshot businesswomen and high-profile personalities. Aldo did not like to be kept waiting and Nolwazi had kept her waiting not just once but three times now; at least that was the score that Aldo would keep in her mental calculator.

As Nolwazi passed the security guard, she pleaded with him to allow her entry without signing in.

'Sorry, *sisi*. Rules are rules,' said the smiling security guard. Nolwazi felt like punching the smile right off his face.

Why was it that she had not been born with the gift of punctuality? What did others do with their clocks that she was not doing?

Which shortcuts did they take that she had yet to discover? Why, why, why did she choose a career involving egotists and bitches?

In a month she would be turning thirty. Wasn't she supposed to be doing something better with her life? Saving the world, maybe?

Her despairing thoughts had brought her to the sixth floor – with the three outfits, designed specifically for Aldo by none other than Ephry Modibe, safely tucked under her arms. Ephry, the head designer at The Style Surgeons, had perfected the art of dodging difficult clients while still managing to make them feel that they were the very centre of his universe.

Humph, that's one skill I would love to master, thought Nolwazi, though deep down she knew it would take decades for her to be nearly as good as Ephry at anything. Being good enough to dodge difficult clients without raising an eyebrow was an art form in itself.

She entered the reception of Aldo's stylish office. Ornate gold everywhere and high ceilings with two slightly over-the-top chandeliers – which instantly gave the feeling of a classy hotel instead of an office – welcomed visitors to Aldo Empowerment Holdings, the name emblazoned in gold on the antique oak reception desk. Aldo's receptionist looked Nolwazi up and down, her eyes settling on her slightly scuffed shoes.

The receptionist, known only as Ivy, was as poisonous as her name. Nolwazi dreaded these visits as they literally had her trembling with fear. She could tell that Poison Ivy enjoyed the torment. The fact that Ivy was related to Aldo Mabuza clearly spared her from some of Aldo's outbursts, but it seemed she could never get enough of seeing them inflicted upon lesser mortals. With one of her long red talons, she pointed at a gleaming maroon leather couch in the reception area. 'There,' she commanded with a cat-like tone.

'I'm sure Ms Mabuza has been anxiously waiting for these outfits. I'll just leave them here quietly so she can have ample time to try them on,' said Nolwazi, hoping for a quick escape.

As she turned towards the lift, she heard, 'Not so fast.'

'Wha-what?' Nolwazi asked.

'I'm not going to be stuck with the dirty job of explaining why those garments got here late, missy. Madame Mabuza is a very busy woman. She had set aside eleven thirty till twelve thirty for the fittings. She's got a very hectic schedule that includes accessories, hair and make-up to ensure everything blends together. You've ruined her day. She has a meeting with the president at one o'clock. How on earth do you expect her to explain to the president of this country that she was made late by some boutique secretary? Hmm?'

Nolwazi wished she could yank all the horsehair off this coldhearted minx's head! She drew a quick breath, slowly walked towards the reception desk and said, 'All right then, Ivy, can you call Ms Mabuza out so I can explain to her why I'm late?'

'My pleasure,' said Ivy with a big smile.

Her mind working in overdrive, Nolwazi remembered that Aldo despised Lerato Molefe, another fiery businesswoman who was going to the same function. She recalled how her colleague and fellow fashion warrior, Tshepang, had said that Ms Molefe's garment, which she had chosen weeks before, had been set on fire by Ms Molefe's unruly ten-year-old son, along with the wig that Ms Molefe was to wear to the event. This had meant that Ms Molefe had been detained at their studio for half the day trying to find something suitable to wear on her head and ample body. Surely sharing this piece of news would add some shine to Aldo's day?

Suddenly, Aldo appeared, as if she had materialised from nowhere. 'Well, I hope that the stupid grin on your face is not a sign of satisfaction for all the failures you've managed to accomplish in your miserable, short life so far, miss.'

'Umm . . . no, ma'am . . . I mean, I apologise profusely for the delay with your garments. We had a huge crisis at the office because Ms Molefe – you know, of African Merchants Mining – her son burned her dress for the evening and, worse still, all of her wigs and accessories as well. So we were stuck all day trying to fix the disaster.'

'Hmm, really?' said Aldo, enjoying a giggle. 'You mean he burned everything for tonight?'

'Yes, shame, she's in quite a state.'

'How are you going to find anything for her to wear? I mean, she does have a rather large frame. A bit of a *biiiiig* unit, don't you think?'

'I'm sorry, I don't think it's my place to say . . . although it has been a bit of a struggle,' Nolwazi conceded.

Still chuckling, echoed obediently by Ivy, Aldo said, 'Well, run along now. I'm sure you have your work cut out for you . . . go, go.'

The laughter that Nolwazi left in her wake was enough to make one think Trevor Noah was in the house.

Chapter 3

DIKELEDI

Dikeledi placed the phone back on the receiver and shivered involuntarily. Then, out of nowhere, tears washed over her face. Worried that her five-year-old daughter would bear witness to this shameful display of emotion, she ran a hot bath. Pouring in a generous amount of herbal foam, she watched the bubbles responding to the warm running water. She perched herself on the edge of the bath, allowing the tears to run freely down her face.

'Why am I crying?' she said out loud to the empty bathroom. 'My best friend is about to get married and all I can manage is to cry? Am I really that pathetic? *Nkosi yam* . . . I'm turning thirty in October, and I'm still stuck with the tag of single mother! I never wanted to be a single mother! Nobody in my family is a single mother! Why doesn't he propose?'

She turned off the water, took off her black linen suit, carelessly tossing it on her bed, and slid into the bath. But no matter how hard she tried to focus on the warmth of the water and the embracing scent of the herbal foam, all she could think of was how her best friend, Sade, had managed to bag an engagement ring after dating a man for eight months, while she had been lugging along the same piece of baggage (and garbage) that she had unfortunately adored for no less than ten years. Ten years! It was a bloody lifetime! In those ten years she could have been married, had two kids and had a big fat joint mortgage on a plot somewhere, maybe with livestock.

She looked at the bubbles as they multiplied in the water and oddly, she started thinking of all the useless sperm cells that Tebogo had floated into her body. Just like the bubbles, they'd all vanished into nothingness.

She sighed, reflecting on their umpteenth argument about the state of their relationship. The last argument about the property he had bought had been their worst.

To think that Tebogo had had the gall to put down a deposit on a larger space without consulting with her.

'It was meant to be a surprise,' he'd said. Yet he still had not taken her to see it. He'd always argued that he wanted to first pay for the traditional 'damages' that were expected in Sesotho culture before he could officially claim paternity of Phemelo, as was customary for a child born out of wedlock. Tebogo's great 'plan' was a study in financial management.

First would be the damages paid to her parents so that Phemelo could take his surname. Then he would pay *lobola*, or the bride price, and only then would they be able to stay together as a family.

Payment of *lobola* is the first step to sealing the union between couples in most South African cultural groups. Tebogo insisted that only once they'd passed this rite of passage could they live like a married couple.

He'd insisted that he wanted to do things 'the right way', which needed time and money, but she did not care about culture, time nor money. She just wanted to have a solid family life with the man she loved. She doubted that all these noble ideas about culture and 'doing the right thing' were the real motivations behind Tebogo's delays.

11

Why couldn't he commit? They'd met at varsity and, as far as she knew, all the varsity couples had either tied the knot or called it quits by now. Why were they still stuck in limbo? 'Maybe I'm stupid . . . maybe he stopped loving me long ago. Next time I talk to that bastard I'm gonna have it out with him,' she murmured, as if the words came from another, disconnected source.

At that moment her phone rang.

'Pheme, please bring my phone in here,' she howled at the top of her voice. Less than a minute later, their adorable five-year-old daughter Phemelo was in the bathroom, phone in hand.

'Here, Mommy. You interrupted me. I was playing with my doll.'

'Sorry, love. Thanks. Go back to spoiling Lolo,' she said, smiling.

'Hello,' she breathed into the phone once her daughter had left.

'How's my favourite girl in the whole wide world?' asked Tebogo.

'Ooh . . . I thought Phemelo was your favourite?' she replied, suddenly all smiles. In spite of herself, she could never resist him when he sounded even mildly affectionate.

'Well, you two will always be at the top of my list, you know that. Speaking of which, what are you guys doing next weekend?'

'Hmm, nothing special.'

'How would you like to join me in Durban? Just us, sun, sea and . . . soccer?'

'*Eish wena*. You're following Pirates cross-country again? Okay. Us girls will do sun and sea with you, but the soccer . . . brother, you're on your own.'

'I'll have you know Phemelo does a mean header, so, *wena*, we'll leave you to lounge around in the hotel while we enjoy the Happy People's thrilling performance.'

'I don't even know why they call Pirates "Happy People". That club gets hammered every weekend!'

'Baby, do you want me to drop the phone?'

'Okay, okay, sorry my love. I'm only joking. Phemelo and I would love to join you next weekend.'

'Looking forward to it. Love you, *nana*.'

'Love you too.'

Dikeledi put the phone down. 'Oh, I just love that man!' she said aloud, merrily kicking splashes of water into the air.

Chapter 4

SADE

Sade looked at her reflection in the mirror once more before preparing to leave for her date with Winston. Hmm, Winston . . . he was too good to be true! And to think he landed in her lap just like that at that dreary conference. What a blessing he'd turned out to be. The perfect man: principled, exciting, loving and sensitive. God had truly listened to her prayers. She loved the fact that they were both born-again Christians, and that they shared the same values through and through. She was glad that she had saved herself for him. Of course, technically speaking, she was no virgin, but surely not having sex for two years qualified for something? It was certainly the closest one got to virgin status in a city like Johannesburg.

Secretly, she could not wait for their wedding day. She and Winston had agreed to save the consummation of their union for the big day. Quite frankly, it was driving her crazy! She knew she was doing the right thing according to her and Winston's values and the vow she had made to God, so that part made her feel immensely proud, but . . . she was only human.

She recalled the previous night when Winston sprang the proposal on her. She had never been happier! Everything about last night felt dream-like, picture-perfect, so wonderful. That was why they had decided to meet again tonight. They were incredibly happy and could not get over the fact that they were both ready to take such a leap.

'"If you believe in me, all good things shall come to you" says the Bible, and I say amen to that!' she uttered, looking at the gorgeous diamond ring on her finger. She could not wait to tell the other girls in her church cell group. Her mom had been ecstatic. She and Winston planned to go over to Umlazi, her hometown in KwaZulu-Natal, for the weekend to formally announce the news to her parents. Then there was all the planning to do. They wanted to get married in October, on her birthday. Oops! Poor Dikeledi. It was their joint birthday, and usually they spent it doing some girly, self-indulgent activity like going to a spa or spoiling themselves rotten by going shopping. She had forgotten to tell her about that. *Ag*, she would do something special with her before or after that date, if time allowed.

Her mom had told her that everything changes when a woman gets married, and she instantly picked up that she was referring to her friends. It was common knowledge that once a woman was married, her husband, and later the family they shared, would take centre stage. A marriage while devoted to friends never lasted. Hmm, this was not only exciting but also really quite frightening, but she was ready for it. All of it.

When she had decided to change her ways two years ago, she knew that she had crossed a line and she never wanted to look back. Her varsity and early career days had been filled with wild debauchery. She could hardly recognise that girl anymore. She sighed and hoped that Winston would never find out about that part of her life. Gosh, he'd probably bolt out of the door immediately!

The sound of a text message brought her out of her reverie.

Am at Browns. Can't wait to see you, Mrs Gumede.

She smiled, then replied.

Will be there in a minute, my hubby!

She dashed to her red Mini Cooper. She loved this little baby. She had just been promoted to accounts manager at the management consulting firm she worked for and had acquired this red hottie a month ago. Winston had helped her choose it because she had been torn between the Mini and a baby Beemer. As she slid her tiny, curvy frame into the car, she nodded. This was definitely the perfect choice.

She and Winston had so much in common; it was crazy sometimes. They both enjoyed the finer things in life and this was definitely going to be a marriage made in heaven. Soon they would be looking at real estate. She could just see herself on a beautiful equestrian estate with graceful horses and perfectly manicured lawns. Ah, the beauty of a joint income! After all, as Pastor Franks always said, 'God does not want you to be poor, my brothers and sisters.' To that, Sade said another big, resounding amen. She and Winston understood the principle of tithing. If you want abundance in your own life, you must give to the Lord what is rightfully His!

As she sped along the N1, Winston called.

'Aw, baby, what's happening? You know I don't like being kept waiting, hey,' he said, sounding rather edgy.

'I know, love. I'm going as fast as I can. Order yourself some passion fruit, and I'll be right there next to you in no time,' she said, a smile spreading over her lips.

'Okay, okay, but make it quick, please,' he said.

She revved the car up to 180 kilometres an hour. One thing about a Mini Cooper is that when it goes, it really goes, she thought, though she still felt slightly under pressure.

When she eventually pulled into the parking lot next to the upmarket Browns Restaurant, she glanced at herself in the mirror, put her lipstick on and half ran in to meet her future husband. She did not want to do anything to spoil this evening, and she knew how impatient Winston could get sometimes.

There he was, looking tall and confident, even though he was sitting down. The way he looked at her sent her heart into a little flip-flop. No man had ever looked at her like that, not even when she was Miss Fresher at varsity. Winston's eyes carried a warm, fiery intensity.

She smiled, feeling self-conscious as he eyed her from across the room. When she finally completed the dance to his table, she kissed him lightly on the cheek and sat next to him. Sade could not resist the urge to lean into his shoulder, to soak in his smell and feel the assurance of his masculine presence.

'Oh, my sweetheart, I hope I wasn't snapping at you,' he said, taking her hand in his. 'I just missed you. I wanted to see what you looked like with my ring on your finger.'

She looked into his eyes. 'This is the closest I've felt to heaven, you know. Every time I look at this ring, I thank the Lord that He somehow managed to make our paths cross. I must be the luckiest girl in Joburg.'

'*Woman*, baby; luckiest *woman*. I'm marrying a beautiful woman, not just any old girl,' he said, with the same edginess he had had in his voice earlier.

Sade decided not to make too much of it. Sometimes Winston could be quite serious; she'd noticed that he didn't really understand her sense of humour so she had consciously cut down on her off-beat but well-meaning comments.

A few minutes later, the restaurant violinist came to play at their table and a flower hawker, recognising the perfect romantic opportunity, sprang on them.

'Sir, would you like to buy a red rose for the beautiful lady?' asked the bohemian-looking trader.

She hated the tackiness of these hawkers. Being hassled to buy a flower for a woman just because she'd been leaning against a man had previously caused her, and whichever partner she'd been dining with, countless embarrassing incidents. Sometimes she would be on a first date with someone, and out of the blue one of these itinerant merchants would appear with their flowers, and the poor guy would be trapped in a veritable catch-22. She'd decided, at the height of her cynical dating stage, that a guy who bought a rose from these romance con artists was a definite no-no, or, at best, nothing but a wet blanket. She drew in her breath in anticipation of Winston's response, confident that he would know her enough not to fall for such a ploy.

'Umm, let me have one,' he said, as he fished out a ten-rand note from his pocket, much to Sade's disappointment.

Chapter 5

NOLWAZI

'Rise and shine, birthday girl! Hmm, let me clear my throat. One, two, three, here goes: *Min' emnandi kuwe, min' emnandi kuwe*, happy birthday, dear Nolwazi, happy birthday to you,' sang a chirpy Linda into Nolwazi's ear.

'Oh no, what time is it?' Nolwazi said drowsily.

'It's six o'clock, girly, better rise and shine! Part of the package, I hear, when turning the big three-oh.'

'Oh, man, please don't remind me,' sighed Nolwazi.

'*Hhawu*, what's wrong with you, *wena*? It's not a crime any-more to turn thirty, you know. In fact, I heard it's legal in all but one of the nine provinces,' Linda said.

Nolwazi chuckled. 'Well, tell me where it's illegal, cos I'd rather be in jail than be thirty.'

'For real?'

'Yes . . . I mean, my twenties are gone and I've got nothing to show for it!'

'Oh please, Nolwazi, no pity party today of all days! It's your—'

'Birthday. I know, quit saying that please.'

'Okay, let me remind you what you have achieved at the ten-der age of thirty, milady. Number one: a perfect little frame that most models would kill for; number two: a degree in Fine Arts from the University of Cape Town; number three: a delicious secret boyfriend that no one knows much about – that alone makes you dark and interesting, an essential trait for the "mature" woman; and number four: a job at one of the top fashion-design companies in South Africa. So there. I don't know what you are worrying about!'

Nolwazi listened patiently to her friend, trying to allow Linda's positive mood to take her over by some sort of crosswire osmosis. It was not working. 'Okay, okay, Linda. I'm wonderful, I have a great life and I shall repeat this throughout my day.'

'That's the spirit. Now, what are we doing after work to celebrate this momentous occasion? Shall I gather the girls and we can go paint the town red? Hmm?'

'Humph, I'm not sure. Let's play it by ear, okay?'

'Okay, darling. Enjoy your day, and don't let anyone spoil your mood, please, or else I'll personally come down to that snooty office and burn all those gorgeous frocks I can't afford.'

Nolwazi smiled. 'Thanks, *mngani wami*. You're wonderful. See you later then.'

'Bye!'

Chapter 6

Linda

Linda was feeling elated. Maybe it was because she really loved her friend and was looking forward to spoiling her, or maybe she was just in the mood for fun, with a capital F, even though it was only six thirty on a Thursday morning.

She took a quick shower and went to her study upstairs to check her email. She had worked late last night on a film shoot. Linda was producing a documentary on the 'invisible souls' of Johannesburg, and it was taking a lot out of her, although she did find the whole process highly stimulating and educational. It confirmed her philosophy in life that the privileged wasted far too much oxygen complaining about their lot, when in fact there were people out there who truly understood the concept of 'struggle'. Ironically enough, the homeless complained much less than those who had it all. It was the oldest story in the book, but she still found herself immensely drawn to this project.

She was waiting for an email from her cameraman who had said he would find time to view the shots from last night, because he had captured some incredible, never-to-be-repeated, spontaneous footage, and they were both keen to see how it had come out.

When she opened Outlook there was nothing except the usual spam, advertising Viagra.

Where had these Viagra people ever heard of a man called 'Linda'? If they were going to spend a lifetime trying to sell Viagra via the Internet, the least they could do was to target men. Maybe they thought there were enough women dealing with unresponsive units that they would order the Viagra themselves. She pondered this for a moment and decided that such matters were definitely not in her realm of experience.

She went back downstairs to her bedroom to fetch her phone so she could call the other two ladies to make arrangements for Nolwazi's birthday. She was not sure which call she dreaded the most – both women were dealing with some serious issues. With Sade, Linda had to steel herself against hearing, yet again, about the wonderful, perfect, amazing Winston; the amazing, perfect new car; and the amazing, perfect new job. What she wouldn't give for the old Sade. And then there was Kedi (her pet name for Dikeledi).

Dikeledi, literally translated as 'tears', was the most aptly named person Linda had ever met. Ever since her best friend Sade had been 'bagged' by Winston, Dikeledi had been calling Linda at odd hours of the day, agonising over Tebogo. Should she leave? Should she stay? Did he love her? Why was he not proposing?

Good grief. The worst part was that throughout varsity Dikeledi had been asking the same questions. Only differently. Despite the fact that Tebogo had gone out with two other girls in the same residence that Linda and Dikeledi shared, she'd still managed to overlook the man's flaws and stick it out for decades . . . at least, it felt like decades.

Frowning, Linda suddenly realised that Dikeledi had never been with anyone but Tebogo. Hmm, she still did not have the heart to tell her about the breaking off of her engagement to Lehumo. While Dikeledi would probably be relieved that at least another one of her friends was not about to get married before her, she knew the question, 'Why did you break it off?' would arise, and of course, the inevitable, 'How did you break up?' would follow.

She was ill-prepared to deliver the news, especially to those two.

She could just imagine Sade's reaction. Linda was sure Sade would bring her pastor to pray for her immediately . . . Then again, maybe she did need a prayer.

Linda waited until nine to make the calls. First, Dikeledi.

'Hi, Kedi. How are you, gal?'

'Is that you, Linda? I'm fine. Why are you calling from a private number? *Shoo*, my day is so hectic! I've just dropped Phemelo off at school and I have a lecture at ten . . . ah, the joys of raising a child by my damned self.' Linda knew what this meant. It was Dikeledi's most annoying trait – she was fishing for sympathy.

'Shame,' she murmured, as per obligation, while rolling her eyes.

If Dikeledi was so set on being with Tebogo, why couldn't she just show up on his doorstep with baby in tow? That's what Linda would have done if she were in her shoes. It's not like he'd turn Dikeledi and Phemelo away. He loved his daughter. And probably liked Dikeledi well enough . . . but then again, this was Tebogo they were talking about. Who knew what that man was capable of?

'Listen, Kedi, it's Nolwazi's birthday today. I was thinking maybe we should do something after work . . . you know, just us girls.'

'*Eish*, I'd clean forgotten, I feel so bad! Where am I going to get a babysitter at such short notice?'

'Oh, but you have a full-time maid.'

'She quit last week so I'm between maids. Maybe I'll ask Tebogo to take her after school. Let me confirm later, my dear,' she said.

'Okay, later then.'

Next, Sade. Linda just hoped she did not ask about Lehumo.

'This is Sade, hello?' Sade breathed into the phone.

Linda could not get over how seductive Sade's voice always sounded. No wonder men found her so attractive.

'Hi, Sade, it's Linda. Can you talk?'

'Hey, Linds. Of course I can talk. Being accounts manager means I get to be more in control of my time, believe it or not.'

Ah. Of course, Sade.

'Cool. So I gather you're enjoying the new job?' asked Linda.

'It's quite challenging, but I think it's what I need right now. As Winston says, "It's your attitude that determines your aptitude", you know.'

'Mmm hmm. Anyway, reason I called was to let you know that today is, of course, Nolwazi's birthday.'

'Oh, yeah I know that. I called her earlier to wish her a blessed one. Isn't it amazing that she's turning thirty? I wonder how she feels being stuck in that dead-end job. Apparently a lot of women go through some kind of breakdown just thinking about what might have been, especially at that age. Shame, I really feel sorry for her sometimes,' said Sade.

Linda was incensed. It seemed Sade had forgotten that she would also be turning thirty soon. She made it sound like some evil plague that only infected women like Nolwazi.

'Well, I don't think she feels sorry for herself. I mean, she has a degree in Fine Arts. She could have been a curator at some art gallery or something, if that's what her heart was after. Remember that Lwazi is not as materialistic as some of us.'

'Oh, are you now labelling me materialistic?'

Linda held her breath and let out a long sigh. 'You know, Sade, I didn't call you to pick an argument. All I wanted to find out is if you'd join me and Dikeledi to give Lwazi a nice outing tonight. That's all.'

'Hmm . . . my diary is chock-a-block this week. Winston and I still have so much to do for the wedding,' said Sade.

'Come on, please? Do a friend a favour. I mean, you and Winston practically live together. You see each other every day, and your friend for a decade does not turn thirty every day,' pleaded Linda, rolling her eyes.

'Okay, okay, I'll come. Let's meet at my house and then we'll all go out in one car.'

'That's my girl. Done deal. We'll be there at around seven, and I'll let Nolwazi know.'

'Okay. Cheers, love.'

'Bye.'

Chapter 7

Nolwazi

Nolwazi did not quite know what to make of the day. The first thing she noticed as she strolled into the tiny cubicle she called her office was a lengthy to-do list stuck on her computer in Ephry's illegible handwriting. She needed to pick up twenty metres of satin fabric in Chinatown, at some small shop owned by a Mrs Chang.

Problem number one: she did not have the faintest clue how to get to Chinatown. How Ephry managed to locate these strange spots only God knew. Next, she was supposed to meet with some of the seamstresses to give them specific instructions about designs that Ephry had on the go, which were to be completed in two days' time. This, she could do; and then she had to return a call from Aldo Mabuza, the bane of her existence.

Start with the unpleasant business first, she thought, picking up her phone to make the undoubtedly painful call.

'Aldo Empowerment Holdings, good day,' said Ivy.

If only she were half as nice as she sounded on the phone.

'Hi, Ivy, this is Nolwazi from The Style Surgeons. May I speak to Ms Mabuza please?'

A pause.

'Why do you need to speak to Ms Mabuza? She only talks to Ephry when she needs something from you people.'

'Well, she called me so I'm returning her call.'

'Are you sure? Let me check with her before I put you through,' she purred, catty as ever.

After a few moments, she was back on the line. 'You're going through,' she said sweetly.

'Hello,' barked Aldo.

'Hi, ma'am. I was returning your call.'

'Yes. I have an unscheduled meeting with the French High Commissioner tonight. I need you people to organise something simple yet elegant for me. Preferably in a flattering cream colour, and please don't allow Ephry to create anything with that horrid material he's started using. It's not flattering for my figure at all,' she lamented.

'But Ms Mabuza, Ephry's on deadline for Fashion Week. His schedule is impossible. There is just no way he can put something together at such short notice.'

'Make a miracle happen.' The line went dead.

'Hmm, what am I going to do?' thought Nolwazi.

She phoned Ephry.

'Darling, I can't talk to you right now. I'm busy-busy-busy. Anything you need to know is on that list I left on your desk. Bye.' Another dead line.

She called again.

'Ephry, this is an emergency. Aldo Mabuza is one of our most important clients and she needs a garment for this evening.'

'Well, I wish I had ten hands but even I'm not that special. Make it go away without making the client go away, *comprende*, darling?' He hung up on her again.

Suddenly a wild idea took shape. Nolwazi knew Ephry's design style; she would be able to place Ephry's work on any woman, big or small. She understood his lines, the specific understated elegance he maintained and his innate ability to flatter almost any figure under the African sun. More importantly, Aldo Mabuza had been the first client she worked with when she had arrived at the boutique three years ago. She knew her measurements off by heart, even though they kept changing every three months or so. Ephry had said to make a plan without losing the client, and knowing Aldo, if she demanded a miracle, then she expected a sorcerer to appear to bring the miracle to life.

Nolwazi switched off her phone and walked into Ephry's studio, making sure to lock the door behind her, to design her first creation. She grabbed the paint brushes that had become second nature to her while studying Fine Arts, and started playing around with different designs with her deft hands and precise eye for detail. Soon she was immersed in something she had desired to do for many years.

Four hours later she emerged with a sketch that she immediately took to the seamstresses to work on. She gave them specific instructions 'from Ephry' and alerted them of the urgency of the job. Then she set off to find Chinatown and found herself singing in her Toyota Conquest as she went to look for Mrs Chang.

For a brief moment, she managed to forget about the pregnancy test she had taken a week earlier.

Chapter 8

DIKELEDI

Dikeledi rounded off her last lecture. Her first-year psychology students seemed fascinated with Sigmund Freud, no doubt because of all the sexual content inherent in his theories. While some of them asked genuinely insightful questions, most were merely out to milk the psychology of sexuality for all it was worth. Feeling exhausted, she strode to the staff kitchen to make herself a cup of coffee before retiring for the day.

As she walked into the kitchen she bumped into Professor Kwame, who held a mug steaming with hot chocolate.

'Hi, Prof, how are you finding this campus so far?' she asked, with a friendly smile.

'It's quite pleasant, Dikeledi. Thanks for asking. I was hoping you guys would show me around the city. I've already run out of things to do by myself,' he replied.

Professor Kwame was a Ghanaian professor in his mid-to-late thirties who had joined the faculty three months previously. A tall man with a seductive voice and a strong British accent, he posed a major distraction to most of the female population on campus. His dark skin and solid physique gave him the sort of masculinity that few women could resist. Dikeledi was the only woman on the staff who was impervious to any of that.

Today she wore a silky peach blouse, which offset her ample bosom, and a pencil skirt to flatter what she called her non-existent waistline. She noticed that, for a split second, Professor Kwame stared at her breasts. For some reason she was not as annoyed as she often was when men did this – her 36DD bust usually garnered uninvited attention.

Sipping at her cup of coffee, she looked at him and noticed his large, oval-shaped eyes and long eyelashes. For the first time it struck her that this man was actually insanely attractive . . . but she was not one for foreign men. Foreign meaning not from Planet Tebogo.

'I was asking if you could find time in your busy diary to show me the city sometime,' he reiterated, interrupting her thoughts.

'Oh, Professor, I'm afraid I have my hands full. I'm a single mother, you see,' she said.

'Yes, and . . . ?'

'Well, between work and a child, I really don't have much time for anything else.'

'How old is your child?'

'She's five, but that's beside the point. I'm afraid my life is pretty frantic enough right now,' she said, nervously placing the now-empty cup of coffee on the kitchen table and heading for the door.

'Okay, didn't mean to put you on the spot,' he said to her retreating back.

Dikeledi went to her desk to pick up her belongings. Thankfully, Tebogo was spending the evening with Phemelo, so she was free to join the girls later. She called to confirm with Linda and promptly left to pick up Phemelo from nursery school.

As she drove to the school she recalled her conversation with Professor Kwame. Something about him unsettled her. She knew that everybody in the faculty was mad about him but he was a bit too charismatic for her. Too smooth for her liking. Like he could have any woman he wanted.

Gosh, she had to admit though, that velvety voice certainly made you want to . . . She laughed aloud. Was she getting the hots for the new lecturer? Her? Dikeledi? Never!

Nonetheless, it was nice to fantasise about someone else. Her life had revolved around Tebogo for so long, it made a change to think of someone new. She shrugged. No matter how magnetic the professor was, she would not dream of cheating on Tebogo. They had been through so much together. He was her first and, she hoped, last love. She had grown up with him, shared so many of life's triumphs and disappointments with him. He was the only one who understood her; even accommodating her self-esteem issues. He was her rock. She truly could not imagine how she would navigate her way through life without him. She felt like Tebogo was a giant on whose shoulders she sat and, as long as he was around, she would be able to survive. While she felt inadequate at tackling life's challenges, he seemed perfectly capable of taking life head on and, so far, Tebogo had always won, which was why she was so grateful to have him in her life.

Chapter 9

NOLWAZI

By seven o'clock that evening, Nolwazi had resolved the Aldo Mabuza situation. Ephry had left Fashion Week and driven to the office to inspect the garment before it was sent to Ms Mabuza. He was so impressed by the work that he could not stop gushing.

'My dear darling, you are a genius, you know that? I can't believe I had this gem right under my nose all this time and I didn't even know it! Oh, Ephry can be stupid sometimes, you know?' he said, arms akimbo, addressing Nolwazi and the seamstresses, who had not heard Ephry pay anyone a compliment in months.

Nolwazi was gobsmacked. It was the first time Ephry had addressed her without issuing an instruction.

He grabbed her by the shoulders. 'Listen, Khanyisile Mbali wants The Style Surgeons to design her bridal gown *and* to do her bridesmaids' dresses. How do you feel about designing the bridesmaids' dresses for me, hmm? After what you did for our local super-bitch, I'm sure you'll come up with a knockout. I might even make you my assistant designer. You just need to knock my socks off again!'

Nolwazi grinned. 'Um, of course. I'll do it.'

With one hand on his hip, he said, 'Well, you have no choice in the matter, my darling. Now go to Sylvia downstairs and grab the brief Khanyi sent us. I want you to start looking at it tonight so you can get inspired. Most of my best designs come to me in my sleep, you know.'

Nolwazi was so exhausted she felt like collapsing, but if Ephry wanted her to take some work home, she would definitely do that. Elated, she planned to share her triumph with the only person whose approval she sought. In all the excitement of putting together the high-pressure Aldo Mabuza job, she had decided to switch off her phone to ward off any distractions. When she turned it back on at seven fifteen that evening, she discovered that the only messages on her phone were from Linda, Sade and her mom. 'And this on my birthday . . .' she mumbled. Of course he still hadn't called. Why was she surprised? It was typical of him, especially since she'd dropped *that* bombshell.

She needed some fresh air, so she went to stand on the office balcony. Nolwazi wished she could smoke, but of course that was completely out of the question. She was tempted to do something very stupid. She had already left him two messages earlier that morning so maybe she could . . . no. That was so masochistic. She wouldn't do it.

A few seconds later, she was doing it. She hid the caller ID on her phone and dialled him again. After several rings he picked it up.

'Hello?'

'Hi, baby, it's me. I was just phoning to see how your day is going,' she said, grimacing at how pathetic she sounded.

'Oh, hi, Nolwazi, it's you . . . Umm, I'm fine. How's it going?'

'*Ag*, you know how it is. I pulled off a miracle dress for one of our most difficult clients and life as we know it has changed completely. Ephry's singing my praises and I really think things are going to start turning around for me here,' she said, remembering how he'd once mentioned that he was turned on by successful go-getters.

'Really? That's nice. That's really nice, but listen, I'm waiting for a conference call from our Washington associates. I'll chat to you later, okay?'

'Yeah. I hope you haven't forgotten that today's my—' She heard the click of his phone as the line went dead.

'—birthday,' she finished, to no one in particular.

Chapter 10

LINDA

Linda was the first to arrive. She parked beneath the carport next to Sade's Mini Cooper and grabbed her cell phone to check on Nolwazi and Dikeledi. To her distress, Nolwazi's phone was still off.

It was already six thirty. Was she with her secret lover? Linda hoped not. The man sounded like pure poison. There was a lot about Nolwazi's relationship with him that Linda did not understand, especially the fact that he was a secret in the first place. Linda was very bad at keeping secrets, but she had promised Nolwazi never to mention the man to Sade or Dikeledi. The sheer effort of it made her want to gag.

She tried Dikeledi, who confirmed that she was on her way.

As Linda walked up to the front door of Sade's classy, modern cluster, the door opened before she knocked.

'Hi, girl. Looking good,' said Sade, offering Linda a warm hug.

'Thanks, you too. This whole engagement thing agrees with you.'

As Linda made herself comfortable on one of Sade's cream leather ottomans, she noticed that Sade had changed her curtains. In place of her old, standard white linen curtains she had fitted glorious designer curtains made with a mixture of creamy organza and toffee-brown taffeta material. The results were quite impressive. The house looked elegant from every angle. Sade had always had good taste, and now, with the new job, she seemed to have launched into a serious style offensive.

'Your home looks really great, Sade. Do you have some Chardonnay for us while we wait for the girls?'

'Oh, wine is something that I don't stock these days. Winston is not much of an alcohol person.'

'Well . . . yes, but you are.'

Sade pursed her red lips. '*Ja*, but . . . you know how it is in a relationship sometimes.'

'What? Are you pretending to be something you're not?' asked Linda.

'Hey, *wena*, you're always jumping to conclusions. Let's go to Woolies quickly and grab some wine without an interrogation, please.'

'Cool. But, babe,' said Linda as she half rose, getting ready to go, 'I know how happy you are with Winston, but I don't think you should start changing who you are for any man. You're fucking amazing just as you are.'

Sade smacked her lips irritably. 'I know you mean well, Linda, but I'm really not taking relationship advice from you right now, okay?'

'What's that supposed to mean? Besides, I'm not giving rela-tionship advice. "Be true to yourself" is the stuff we've been taught since nursery school. Even the Cat in the Hat says that.'

'We're going to be late. Let's just go get the wine without moti-vational quotes, please, "Little Miss Cat in the bloody Hat".'

'Fine, fine, fine,' said Linda grudgingly as they went for the quick dash to the local grocery store.

Fifteen minutes later, Dikeledi joined them at the house, and immediately launched into a psychoanalysis session.

'So, ladies,' she said as she sipped her glass of white wine, 'do you think foreign men are better lovers than the local models?' The other two women just laughed.

'Hmm, Mrs Tebogo Makwetla is suddenly worrying about the merits and demerits of foreign men?' taunted a genuinely surprised Linda.

Dikeledi immediately switched to defensive mode. 'No, man, it's something I've been pondering for my psych one class. The whole question of how cultural perceptions impact on group behaviour,' she responded, not looking directly at either of her friends.

Linda laughed. 'Nice one, Kedi, but as much as you're devoted to behavioural studies, I very much doubt that you're sipping wine and worrying about your psych one class at seven o'clock on a Thursday night. Spill it. What *kwerekwere* man has got your heart aflutter, hmm?'

'W-well,' said Dikeledi, a dreamy look in her eyes, 'there's this new guy in the faculty . . . he's Ghanaian. The women on the staff have been making a fuss about him, but you know me; I don't go around ogling men. But he keeps passing these comments. I think he just enjoys flirting with me because he knows I'm unavailable.'

'Ha! I don't believe you! I think you like the guy. You know, Dikeledi, instead of moping around for Tebogo all the time you should consider having an affair with someone hot, like this guy. He sounds like someone who can give you just the sort of adventure to shake that man of yours out of his illusion of being the centre of the universe. And from what I've heard about our brothers up north, they are truly gifted, if you know what I mean.' Linda winked, an absurdly naughty look on her face.

Sade was standing up now, hands on her shapely waist. 'No, no, no. Linda, that stuff just doesn't work. It's juvenile and it's evil. Dikeledi, don't listen to this one. She never stops playing games with men. We're not twenty-two anymore,' she protested, shooting a dangerous look in Linda's direction.

Linda crossed her legs. 'I don't know. All I'm saying is, you can't expect to keep doing the same thing if you want different results. All these hundreds of years that you've been trailing around after Tebogo while he does God knows what. I'm sorry to point this out, but nothing in the way he treats you or his level of commitment to you has changed,' she said, folding her arms with conviction.

'*Eish*, can't we just change the topic? Where's Nolwazi anyway? It's her birthday we're celebrating. I'm not in the mood to discuss my relationship with Tebogo. Just because you guys are both engaged it doesn't mean I'm some kind of basket case that needs your wisdom to deal with my issues,' she said, fidgeting with her phone to find Nolwazi's number.

The other two looked at her in anticipation.

After a while, holding the phone to her ear, she said, 'It's going straight to voicemail. Maybe we should just go to her house. You know how Nolwazi is. She's probably locked herself in cos she's scared of facing thirty.'

Linda drained her wine glass. 'Okay, but just to clear the air, guys, I'm not engaged anymore, so, Dikeledi, you can stop feeling that we're being all superior on you. Your relationship with Tebogo has always sucked. You deserve better than what he's giving you and that's just a fact.'

They both stared at her, shocked.

After a lingering silence – because, with Linda, anything was possible, and they were not really sure whose fault it was that the engagement was off – Sade ventured: 'Shame, babe. What happened? I'm so sorry.'

Linda laughed. 'Oh no, don't be sorry. I think it was always going to turn out like this,' she said, with an air of nonchalance.

Dikeledi shot Linda a strange look. 'What happened?' she finally asked, curiosity getting the better of her.

'It's a long story. To be quite honest, I don't think I was ever really into it. I think I just said yes because I had nothing better to say.'

The two looked at her as if she were an alien that had just landed on Sade's ottoman and started sipping wine. 'What?' they both gasped.

Dikeledi hated her right now. Linda honestly thought life was some kind of chess game and that she was the little maestro, manoeuvring all the pieces. She really seemed to think that people existed purely for her amusement. It felt like a slap in the face. Here was Dikeledi, agonising over when her own eternal love would say the word, and crazy Linda just sat there smugly, making this out to be one of those trivial little episodes that just happen to people. What a bitch.

'Linda, you do realise that Lehumo possibly loves you more than anyone will ever love you, right? I mean, all you have to do is walk into a room and his eyes just soften up. He's sweet,' she said, holding up her pinkie finger to show that a list was coming, 'loving, caring, cute and responsible. What in the world do you want? What if nobody else ever proposes? You are not as young as you used to be, you know?' she said, choosing her words carefully.

Linda just looked at her, flabbergasted. 'Well, thanks for the vote of confidence, but I'm not going to marry some guy just because he's there,' she said, shrugging her shoulders dismissively.

Sade looked at her and shook her head. '*Ja*, now I've heard it all. *Wena*, Linda, you've got a big head on those shoulders of yours. Dikeledi's right. You just wanna keep sleeping with different men for the rest of your life, or what? I mean, did you even sit down and think about this? Why did you waste all that time with Lehumo if you knew he wasn't the one for you?'

Linda was becoming irritable. 'You know what? This is exactly what I was trying to avoid. It took me a whole month to tell you two, who I consider my best friends, about this, because you're so afraid. You go through life with these huge blinkers and a big sign saying, "I'm thirty, I'm terrified. Please come – anyone – come and rescue me cos I'm spoiled goods." Well, I'm not like that and I don't even want to entertain such bullshit!' She stood up dramatically and started to pour herself another glass of wine.

'Don't do that,' said Sade, upset. 'Let's go look for Nolwazi. I've had it with your self-righteous attitude for tonight.'

Outside, the trio climbed in awkward silence into Linda's black Jeep Wrangler. Sade and Dikeledi watched glumly from their seats as Linda sped off towards Nolwazi's apartment. Throughout the ride no one said a word.

When they got to the complex's security gates, they asked the guard to buzz number 45: Nolwazi's townhouse. After a while on the intercom, the guard returned.

'Sorry, nobody's answering,' he declared.

'But you know the owner, right? Lady with a small frame, light in complexion, short hair, and almond-shaped eyes? She drives a silver Toyota Conquest.'

The security guard nodded. '*Ja*, she came in a little while ago. I don't remember seeing her go out but she's not answering her intercom so maybe she's gone somewhere.'

Linda looked at the other two for advice.

'Let's go in anyway,' said Dikeledi. 'I know Nolwazi and her moods. She's probably hiding under her duvet, waiting for her birthday to go away.'

Linda nodded, then turned to the security guard. '*Baba*, you know what? She's our friend and it's her birthday, so can we go in anyway, please?'

The guy hesitated for a minute then smiled. '*Hhawu*, is it really her birthday? She didn't look that happy for someone celebrating such a special day. She's usually quite friendly and chatty but today she just zoomed past the gate. Anyway, I'll let you through. Tell her Samson said happy birthday,' he said as he opened the gate.

They meandered through the lanes of Nolwazi's townhouse complex, a maze of flats squeezed onto a piece of land that could have comfortably accommodated only half the number of houses on the site – a testament to the greed of suburban developers.

Once they got to her visitor's parking bay they started whispering, though none of them knew why.

'Why is she being so cagey?' asked Sade, spotting Nolwazi's car in her parking spot. 'It's just an additional candle on her birthday cake.'

'Very refreshing to hear you say that,' said Linda, who had categorised Sade as a serial worrier ever since Sade had 'changed her ways' two years back. She just wasn't the same person she'd met at varsity. Of course, Dikeledi understood Sade better, mostly because they'd both attended the same all-girls private school.

When they got to Nolwazi's upstairs apartment and pressed her doorbell, it did not ring. They resorted to knocking. It was already nine o'clock, Sade noticed, as she glanced at her wristwatch. The girl better open up because she was not about to fight with Winston for nothing.

After a few minutes they heard footsteps approaching the door. Nolwazi looked through the peephole and was shocked to see her three friends on the other side of the door. She had switched off her phone to ward off the temptation to call her man again and had finally left work at eight and collapsed straight into bed on her arrival home. Although she was excited about developments at work, she was still not up to celebrating her thirtieth birthday, especially since it was beginning to dawn on her that the man she considered to be her soulmate had not even bothered to wish her a happy birthday . . . if he even knew that it was her birthday.

She sighed. Well, here they were. Her three best friends. Gosh. They were relentless.

Reluctantly she opened the door for them and was accosted by hugs, kisses and birthday wishes.

'Guys, come on. You just don't let up, do you?' she asked, with half a grimace. Linda switched on the lights in Nolwazi's lounge and placed the bottle of Pongrácz on her coffee table before hopping to the kitchen to retrieve four champagne glasses.

'There's not enough champagne in the world to help me cope with turning thirty. In fact, I think I'm gonna start going easy on the stuff. Do you know how much alcohol ages you?' Nolwazi grumbled, to unexpected laugher from the other three.

'Prove it,' Linda challenged, now opening the bottle.

Sade whisked out a gift-wrapped package, seemingly from nowhere, and Dikeledi did the same.

They both wished her happy birthday again and hugged her, as if this would take away the panic she was experiencing. Linda switched on the home theatre system, located Nolwazi's U2 CD, and soon the birthday girl's favourite track, 'Beautiful Day', was playing.

Predictably enough, Nolwazi's spirits started to lift. She hesitated, then poured a glass of wine from the bottle that Linda had opened and they all started to relax.

'Nice to see you're finally coming around. It's an age, not a dress size,' Linda joked. 'We're all getting there soon anyway . . . in a few months, to be exact.'

'Yeah, but why did I have to be the first one?' Nolwazi asked plaintively.

'It's not really so bad, turning thirty, you know,' said practical Sade. 'I'm even looking forward to turning forty, when I'll have half the insecurities I have now, or so they say.'

'*Ja*, me too. I think forty is a pretty cool age for women,' enthused Linda. 'I've been reading *Woman & Home*. It's full of these old white ladies, but what I like about it is that it has great stories about people venturing out on new journeys at forty, fifty and even sixty. Most of them look great, which of course could just be down to plastic surgery, but I can't resist their joie de vivre. They really make you feel like growing old is this graceful, esoteric experience filled with all sorts of adventures.'

Nolwazi shrugged. 'I think it's easy for you guys to say because you've all found your footing in life. Me, I'm still kind of floating; although things are starting to look up at work a little, but it's nothing to write home about. With Ephry, Mr Head Designer, anything is possible. I think that's what terrifies me the most. I see people younger than me driving these expensive cars and bandying about these huge titles, and I just panic.' Nolwazi did not want to tempt fate by gloating about her earlier triumph. There had been precious few breakthroughs in her career, and she was not sure if Ephry's generous compliments signified anything concrete for her future.

Sade offered her a hug. 'Just pray to the Almighty and all your dreams will come true. Do you tithe?'

'What?' asked Nolwazi.

'I mean in church. Do you tithe?' Sade asked again. Nolwazi had a puzzled expression on her face.

'She means you must give something to God if you want something. You know, like the mafia do,' explained Linda sarcastically.

Nolwazi hesitated. 'I'm not sure if the God I know is like that. I mean, I pray, but I didn't know I had to pay to have my prayers realised.'

'Argh! Linda, I swear I could kill you sometimes,' Sade moaned. 'Why do you like twisting everything I say around? What is it with you? Do you have something against me and my beliefs, or what? Being evil is not going to get you anywhere in this world, I promise you!'

'Oh, so now I'm evil?' Linda retorted.

Dikeledi was getting tired of this. 'Cut it out, you guys. We came here to celebrate Nolwazi's birthday, not to watch another riveting episode of the Sade versus Linda boxing tournament,' she said, offering Nolwazi another glass of wine.

Sometimes she could swear the two were separated at birth. They were equally stubborn, equally fiery, yet at their core, they both had hearts of gold.

Nolwazi barely seemed able to finish the first glass. 'No thanks. I told you, this face is not going craggy before its time. Besides, I've got enough entertainment watching this cat fight. Let's bring out the sparring gloves,' she joked.

They all laughed and started to relax, reminiscing about the highlights of their ten-year friendship.

When Sade and Dikeledi began talking about their days in boarding school, giggling about some crazy science teacher, Linda suddenly made up an excuse about needing a new dress that required the expertise of her friend. She wanted a private chat with Nolwazi. 'I want something like one of those gorgeous cocktail dresses you have. Come, let's go to your room. I'll show you the one I'm talking about.'

As soon as they stepped into Nolwazi's room, Linda immediately shut the door.

'So, where's 007, the undercover lover?' she whispered conspiratorially.

Nolwazi regretted telling Linda about him, because now she had to deal with this. She shrugged. 'Things are not so great between us. He's busy at work, I'm busy at work . . . you know how it is.'

'So, did he get you some sexy lingerie, per the job description of any secret lover? Maybe he's planning to surprise you with some weekend getaway? Whisk you off to his latest spy mission? Hmm?'

Nolwazi shrugged. 'Let's not talk about him, okay? It'll only spoil my mood. Let's go and join the others,' she said, trying to hide her irritation.

By eleven o'clock, Linda, Sade and Dikeledi had polished off two bottles of wine and were ready to retire, all the while poking fun at Nolwazi's newfound fear of alcohol. Nolwazi thanked them for a great, spontaneous evening and walked with them to the door where Dikeledi assured Nolwazi that she looked exactly as she did in her first year of varsity. The fact that it was Dikeledi who said this brought back the day's dark clouds, which Nolwazi had been trying not to think about.

Chapter 11

SADE

Sade woke up with a mild hangover. She realised that she and her friends had not eaten anything while they'd guzzled down gallons of wine last night. Thank God it's Friday, she thought as she slipped into the shower, allowing the cold water to spray her body back to life. It was so refreshing it almost felt sensuous . . . Gee, she really needed to get laid if she was having sexual thoughts about water.

Soaping her body, she frowned, thinking about last night. Winston had been upset when she'd called him at eleven thirty in the evening to let him know she was home safe. He had petulantly declared that this was not the sort of behaviour he expected from the future Mrs Gumede. Of course he was right – even her cell group at church would concur. It was just that one could not afford to discard some friends. Even if you changed your ways and they stuck stubbornly to theirs.

This thought agitated her. She and Winston had begun discussing the wedding and Winston had made it abundantly clear that he did not expect any of her three oldest friends to play a major role in the planning or execution of it.

She had no idea how she was going to handle this contentious issue, but she understood where Winston was coming from. Their church was the apex of their relationship and she noticed the high regard with which Winston was held by the church community. It was clear that it would play a central role in their nuptials; something that she fervently hoped would build a strong foundation for their marriage.

Besides, she did not want Winston to be too exposed to the 'Terrible Trio' because then he might stumble upon some morsel of information from the past that she would rather keep private.

A crazy thought occurred to her as the image of a ghost from her past flicked through her mind for a split second. No, she did not want to think about him. Would not think about him.

Was she leading a double life? She laughed it off, thinking that Linda's acidic comments last night were probably getting to her. Besides, all of that was ancient history anyway. It wasn't as if anyone had a clean slate. *Tabula rasa*? Impossible. By the time anyone hit thirty they were bound to have done something they regretted.

Sade reasoned that she had made a healthy transition in life – a mature and inevitable one. The fact that someone like Linda refused to grow up would come back to haunt her, not Sade, when she least expected it.

It was strange that someone who had been so naive and off-the-wall at varsity would turn out to be so – what was the word? – brusque and reckless in later life. But, surmised Sade, underneath all that toughness, Linda was still the same girl who had arrived at university wide-eyed, virginal and innocent. Maybe all this toughness was just a defence mechanism to mask her vulnerability.

Chapter 12

Dikeledi

Tebogo hadn't been to see Dikeledi or their daughter since she'd met up with her friends for Nolwazi's birthday, which was three weeks ago now. He always had an excuse about work pressures and delivering some report. He was a consummate liar, hence he was a lawyer. The fact that he was defending a disgraced politician made him even more arrogant and inattentive than usual.

This irked Dikeledi because the scandal was a minor one – a child maintenance case. Hardly the stuff that shaped the destiny of the country, but one would never guess that from Tebogo's new, imperious attitude. What was up with him anyway? He was so distracted she could have sworn there was another woman, had she not been aware of the case. The fact that it was in the Sunday papers probably made Tebogo feel that his career was suddenly gaining some kind of glamorous allure. Whatever the reason, her man was as good as married to the bloody case.

She called him anyway. It was a Saturday, after all; he could not possibly claim to still be engrossed in the case.

'Hello, you've reached Tebogo Makwetla, attorney at law. Please leave a message and I'll return your call,' blurted the voicemail.

Shit! It was only ten o'clock in the morning. She decided to go out for some retail therapy with Phemelo, although her budget was seriously stretched. This month, in spite of his big-shot lawyer attitude, Tebogo had not deposited his maintenance check into her account, much to her annoyance. Maybe that was why he was so stuck on the politician. Maybe he was some kind of role model for bad behaviour. Typical bloody politician!

Chapter 13

Nolwazi

Nolwazi was bored. It was a Saturday, which meant no promise of anything rosy for her miserable existence. Although work was going well and Ephry had finally promoted her to assistant designer, she still felt torn by the new developments in her personal life.

For the umpteenth time she drew back her T-shirt to stare at her stomach. Why was it still flat? It must be about eight weeks now. Wasn't it supposed to be popping out by now? She felt tears run down her face. Oh no, not again. 'I'm such a pathetic mess,' she said to no one in particular.

Her secret lover, as Linda liked to call him, had called last night to say they needed to discuss the *options*. She hated that word because it epitomised who he was – a man of many options.

Why did men have to have it so easy? Growing up, she had watched them, these men. All sorts of them – fat men, skinny men, short men, tall men, gangly men – all prancing around with the confidence of princes. Always managing to score the prize, because regardless of what state they were in, they always got the women. Broke, rich, obese, whatever . . . they always managed to come up with the trump card. Why?

And if you were a woman? Oh no, you had to wait your turn. Always wait your turn. If you grew up skinny, like she had, you had to wait and wait until men started looking at you because you had finally, thankfully, developed breasts. Or rather, more realistically, it was because South African black men had suddenly bought into the European ideal of tall and skinny that Nolwazi had suddenly become more visible to them. *Shoo*, how close that was.

But, sadly for her, there was only ever one man – and he was an epic prick. And now she was pregnant with his child. She felt nauseous and unsure whether the dizzying wave of ill-health sprang from the effect of father or child.

Just then Linda called. Nolwazi did not have the stomach to tell her about the new developments, but in the way Linda had suddenly become so attentive, Nolwazi knew that she had sensed something was amiss. Linda was not the sort to call often, if at all. Not that she was a bad friend, but her mind seemed forever immersed in some or other new adventure.

'Hey, what's up, cuz?' Linda said, trying to be funny. This was reminiscent of a balefully stupid phase they had undergone at varsity; the pseudo-American period that had accosted most of their peers at some point or other in their lives. She and Linda had gone to the extent of wearing full black regalia for the whole week to commemorate Tupac Shakur's death. 'Tupac's Widows', they'd called themselves.

Tsk. Shameful.

'Nothing much. What do people do on Saturday mornings again?'

'According to most women's magazines, they go shopping,' Linda responded. 'Are you game? I need some equipment to jazz up my productions, so we don't have to gape at stockings and skirts if you're not in that kind of mood.'

Why was she being so nice? Nolwazi just wanted to be left alone. She certainly did not want any of her friends to know she was pregnant . . . at least not yet. Not until she had sorted it out with Mr Man.

'I'll pass,' she declared.

'No, no, no. You're acting all weird, like you're holding something back. I'm on my way. And please don't hang yourself or something. I'll be there in a minute,' promised Linda.

Within thirty minutes Linda was at Nolwazi's door.

'Geez, you're quite evangelical about this pursuit of happiness thing, aren't you?' Nolwazi said with an accusatory air.

Linda was not having any of it. She waltzed into the flat and said, 'Don't worry, I'm not possessed or anything. Just want thirty to be nice for you so that when I get there, it won't seem so awful. Young women need positive role models, you know.'

It was funny how all her friends were so fixated on turning thirty. If only they knew how convenient they had made it for her to hide her own, larger demons.

Chapter 14

DIKELEDI

Sandton City mall offered far too much. She had an enticing limit on her credit card, and she needed to vent. Maybe her house could do with a new garden suite? Maybe add something for Phemelo to play with? She could get that bastard to pay for it with his blood money. Protecting corrupt politicians, humph, honourable trade indeed! She fumed, thinking about Mr Practical Tebogo making fun of her 'psychological babble'.

She looked at garden equipment for a while. Phemelo kept insisting that they watch *the latest blockbuster cartoon* at the cinema. When did these kids get so smart? She didn't remember ever pressuring her mother to watch some movie or other, especially not at that age. Besides, weren't girls supposed to be more attuned to their mothers' quiet yet screaming sense of eternal suffering? Was the entire experience of being a mother – a single one *nogal* – not supposed to engender all the womanly instincts of sisterhood in females of all ages? Was she expecting too much?

Phemelo was spoiled, that much was certain. Sometimes Dikeledi wished she'd had a boy instead. They seemed more understanding. She caught herself, feeling guilty all of a sudden. How could she think that way?

Chapter 15

Linda

Linda hurled poor Nolwazi into the frightening landscape of conspicuous consumption that was Sandton City. Linda did not particularly like the mall because she reckoned that everybody who went there looked like a clone of someone beautiful from Hollywood. Black or white, all the women there were designer-label skinny. They had this controlled, perfected air about them, as if they were walking in some mass-produced Axe deodorant ad.

Yes, Sandton City bored the living daylights out of Linda, but since Nolwazi lived in Benmore Gardens, the mall's proximity won hands down. More importantly, it had a number of electronics stores that she wanted to browse through because she was scouting for video-editing software for her company. Her boss was away on vacation in Europe and had left her with the task of upgrading their technical equipment.

As they headed towards the escalators to one of the shopping floors, they bumped into a distracted Dikeledi with Phemelo in tow.

'Hey, funny running into you guys here,' said Linda.

Dikeledi did an about-turn. She had almost missed them. 'Hi, guys. Shopping this early too? How've you been, Nolwazi? Hope you've recovered from your birthday "event",' she said, using her fingers to show inverted commas.

Nolwazi looked bashful. 'Yeah, I guess I was being a bit of a baby about it, hey? What are you guys looking for here, anything specific?'

Phemelo said, 'Mommy's gonna buy me a new castle for my doll and new clothes and then we'll go to a pizza restaurant.'

'Wow, that sounds like fun,' said Linda enthusiastically. 'Mommy really likes to spoil you. Maybe we'll join you for that pizza later.'

All of a sudden, Nolwazi looked uncomfortable. 'No, no, Linda . . . remember, I have to go pick up something at the studio for Ephry.'

Linda gave her a strange look. She did not recall Nolwazi mentioning any such thing.

She shrugged. 'Guess we'll have to do it some other time. Enjoy your shopping spree, guys,' she said, giving Phemelo a peck on the cheek.

As they parted ways, Linda remarked, 'Phemelo's so cute, hey? Funny how she looks like that prick Tebogo but still manages to have that angelic quality about her.'

'She's a kid. They're supposed to look angelic,' said Nolwazi dismissively.

'*Wena!* You seem to be wearing this blanket of negativity lately. It's beginning to get to me.'

'What do you mean? Just because I said all kids are angelic?'

'No, you know exactly what I mean: like how you quickly bailed out on having lunch with Kedi. What's up with that?'

Nolwazi kept quiet. Then she suddenly said, 'Oh, look, Movie Madness. Isn't that the shop you're looking for?'

'Oh, *ja*. They're supposed to have some great stuff at affordable prices, if you believe the hype. So much of the filming equipment we use is exorbitantly priced. I just hope that these guys are as good as some of my colleagues say.'

An hour later, Linda still had not found what she was looking for, so they decided to stop for a quick bite at Smith & Wollensky. The restaurant was located in an open boulevard where shoppers shuffled either to the banking mall or went upstairs to exclusive clothing shops and bookstores.

'If Dikeledi sees us here after you turned down the chance to dine with her and her daughter, I'm not liable,' said Linda.

'Right, let's sit at the far corner then, where nobody will see us,' replied Nolwazi.

Linda shrugged and sat at the seat furthest back from the passing shoppers, safely tucked away in an enormous glass cubicle. She relaxed on the comfortable chair and looked pointedly at Nolwazi. 'Okay, spill it, Nolwazi. Why are you acting so dodgy?'

Nolwazi looked down and then squinted like a child trying to evade a tricky question. 'You mean it doesn't show?'

'What? You're not pregnant, right?' joked Linda, as she took off her woollen scarf.

When there was no response, she repeated, with rising alarm, '*Right?*'

Nolwazi nodded slowly.

'*Ag*, shit. Why? By whom? Your secret lover?'

Again, Nolwazi nodded.

'Okay, who is this guy? You said he's not married, so if you're knocked up, you have to tell me who he is,' Linda insisted.

Nolwazi raised her hand to gesture to the waiter. 'Can I have a bottle of mineral water?'

Linda placed her hands on the table and stared at her, impatiently waiting for an answer.

'Linda, I can't tell you who the father is, okay? Not right now. I just need some time.'

'Why ever not? You can't have this eating away at you like this. How are you going to cope, Nolwazi, carrying some big bad secret on your shoulders? I'm not the kind of friend who's judgemental, you know that. What, is it Ephry, your gay designer boss? Maybe you guys had one drink too many one day? It happens all the time. People accept that these things happen.'

Nolwazi almost fell off her seat laughing. 'Ephry!' She covered her mouth, spilling over with uncontained giggles. 'You, my friend, may be accused of a lot of things, but a lack of imagination is not one of them.'

Linda laughed along, glad to see Nolwazi's amused expression; it made a change. '*Ja*, well, what else am I supposed to think? I mean, it's great that you're pregnant . . . if you're ready for the responsibility. But the first question that's going to come up whenever you talk to anyone, is, "Who's the father?" This whole secret-lover thing is going to make things harder for you. You need to have at least one confidante.'

Nolwazi still shook her head. 'The first thing I have to figure out is whether I want to keep the baby or not.'

Linda reached out her hand to Nolwazi. 'Whatever decision you make, I'll support you. It's quite scary, though . . . the prospect of an abortion, isn't it? Most people deal with it in their early twenties. At our age, people expect you to know better . . . you know, than to get yourself pregnant and everything.'

Nolwazi looked at her disbelievingly. 'Well, so much for not being judgemental!'

'I didn't mean it like that! I just meant that's how people see these things. Nolwazi, I'm just trying to think you through your options, okay? I mean, your mom . . . have you told her yet?'

Nolwazi leaned on her elbow and looked down at the table. 'There are just too many things to think about. It's so complicated, Linda. I wish I could tell you but I'm so ashamed of myself. I mean, when it started, it felt like déjà vu. I was that skinny, shy girl with no self-esteem again, and there was this man whose attention I'd always desired who was suddenly interested in me. I was excited; it was like this personal, forbidden pleasure that I somehow always felt entitled to.

'At first, he would call me in the evenings to check how I was doing; he would sympathise with my daily grind at work. It felt so good to have someone care about me. Besides' – she shrugged – 'I guess I never stopped loving him.

'Linda,' she continued, her eyes glimmering with intensity, 'you remember when I first met you . . . it was during the second semester, at that party at the Old Vic? I told you that my boyfriend left with another girl, and I never spoke about him again . . . well, that person came back to me . . . in a way.'

Linda was dumbstruck. This was kind of romantic, in an old Hollywood flick sort of way. A boyfriend from first-year varsity rising up from the dead like that? Wow. She found the revelation highly intriguing.

'Are you telling me that all this time your secret lover is some dude from varsity? How did you guys hook up? Did he just call you out of the blue? Did he find you on social media? Damn, now I believe in fairy tales.'

'Well, it's not really that romantic . . . I mean, it is to me, but there's kind of a big snag about the whole thing . . .'

'Come on, you already said he's not married. So if he's engaged and has been seeing you all along, it means maybe he's having second thoughts about the other girl. I mean, you've not really given me much to go on, but if it's somebody from the past, you guys might actually have a chance.'

Nolwazi, as always when it came to her mystery man, wanted to believe anything that cast a rosy glint on her relationship. 'You really think so? Because he's not even engaged. I mean, this other woman was always around, and they have a kid together, but if he really loved her I think he'd have married her by now, right?'

Linda shrugged. 'Well, I don't really know the details about their relationship, but since you're so close to the guy, what do *you* think? Is he that serious about the other woman? Maybe there are family issues involved. Maybe his mom adores the girl, and the families have coffee every other Sunday as they wait to hear the "big announcement". I think you should just ask him what's going on. He has to choose between the two of you at some point.'

At that, Nolwazi suddenly looked very uncomfortable. 'I think I need another glass of water. This thing with Tebogo is really starting to drive me crazy. The fact that I can't even drink my troubles away is gonna make me start climbing walls,' she said, clearly exasperated.

Linda's jaw literally dropped. 'Did you just say Tebogo? As in Dikeledi's Tebogo? Please don't say it's him,' she said, looking pleadingly at Nolwazi.

'Oh shit! I said it, didn't I?' Nolwazi said, her hands shaking. Fortunately, the waiter arrived with her water at that moment.

'I'll have a double Scotch on the rocks, please,' said Linda, who suddenly could not bring herself to look at Nolwazi. For a while she remained speechless, trying to deconstruct their varsity life in the hope of picking up any nuances that may have suggested romantic undertones between Tebogo and Nolwazi, but she could not, for the life of her, come up with anything.

'Did you and Tebogo ever date – I mean back then? Cos I just can't seem to remember even seeing you guys together.'

Nolwazi gave her a pained grin. 'Thanks for reminding me, but Tebogo was actually my boyfriend first. I told you earlier about that day at the Vic, the boyfriend who left with another girl. That was Tebogo and the other girl was, and still is, the lucky Dikeledi. I don't know if you remember, but for a long time during first year I kept obsessing about the guy, but I never told you his name. It was so painful, watching them together all those years. Finding myself in a circle of friends with the woman who took my first love . . . Well, if that didn't kill me, I don't know what will.'

Linda was shocked and suddenly she felt a terrible pang of empathy for her friend. She could not imagine what it must have been like for Nolwazi all these years. She flashed back to when their friendship had begun but, this time, she tried to look at it through Nolwazi's eyes. Linda, Dikeledi and Sade had become firm friends from their first day on campus because they had met on the Greyhound bus on the way to UCT. They immediately struck up a good rapport. Two childhood girlfriends from Durban and this tall, imposing prankster from Johannesburg found themselves giggling most of the way to their newfound freedom as they shared secret fears and hopes about the glimmering, golden road that lay ahead.

Two months later Dikeledi had passed out at some third-year students' digs and was brought back to their shared residence by a tall, good-looking, if a little skinny, boy from North West Province with short little 'Rice Krispies' dreadlocks. The boy's name was Tebogo. From that day on, this skinny boy was constantly coming to check on Dikeledi, taking her out on dates to the local Spur, and generally hanging around like Dikeledi's shadow.

When Linda met the pretty, shy Nolwazi a few months later, she had never imagined that the boy Nolwazi spoke about so forlornly was none other than her friend Dikeledi's now firmly established boyfriend. Only now, more than ten years later, Nolwazi was able to confess this deeply lodged secret, and under the worst circumstances possible. Was she really saying what Linda thought she was? What was this magic power that the despicable Tebogo possessed over women anyway?

'So, are you telling me you're expecting Tebogo's baby? Oh my God. You poor thing . . . Geez, you poor thing,' was all Linda could manage.

'I don't know what to do, Linds. I mean, how do I look Dikeledi in the eye? Isn't it ironic though? All those years ago, when I got drawn into your circle, I harboured this huge ball of resentment for Dikeledi because she had what I wanted. When she fell pregnant it was the only time I started feeling for her because, even then, Tebogo was still cheating on her,' confessed Nolwazi.

Linda drank the last of her Scotch, then opened her eyes wide, as was her habit whenever she was about to impart what she hoped was some morsel of wisdom. 'Well, I'm glad you at least remember that. That man will never change. I'm not even sure what it is that you guys see in him. I mean, sure, he's good-looking, but so was Joseph Stalin, if you looked at him hard enough.'

At last, Nolwazi laughed. 'Hey, the guy may be bad, but there's no reason to compare him to Stalin, okay?' she said, a slow, sweet smile spreading across her face. 'What you don't know about Tebogo is that when he's with you, just the two of you together, he has this ability to make you feel like the most special, most beautiful person in the world. He can be very funny, irresistibly so . . . and he's one of those people who has the power to make you feel that as long as he's around, everything is going to be okay. I don't know how he does it,' she sighed, 'but I definitely understand why Dikeledi loves him so much.'

Linda was still trying to digest everything Nolwazi was saying. 'So, where do things stand now between you two?'

Nolwazi sighed again, still trying to make Linda understand where she was coming from. 'Tebogo has come to be more than just any man. He's the epitome of how the right man for me should look, act and laugh. When he started taking me out to elegant restaurants, I could finally pretend that he was mine again. It felt like I'd recovered a long-lost love.'

Linda looked at her friend and only barely managed to hide her revulsion. Tebogo was easily her least-favourite man on earth. 'You

61

mean you've been harbouring such intense feelings all this time? So how long did you guys go out for – before Dikeledi stepped in, I mean – back then?'

Nolwazi looked out of the window at the passing shoppers whose only concern, or so it seemed to her, was to max out their credit cards. If only she could be that carefree. She responded with a faraway look in her eyes. 'I don't know, Linda, maybe this is all a silly childhood fantasy gone wrong. We only dated for about three months. He was my first, you know . . . I guess I was infatuated with him, you know. We met during orientation week and clicked immediately. It was those kwaito days, remember,' she said with a sad smile, now looking directly at Linda. 'So there I was, with my skinny little legs clad in this blue denim mini skirt, a crisp white cotton halter top to show off my waist, and long braids – right down to my arse. I thought I looked like a real sexy varsity girl, you know. So anyway, this hot guy walks up to me and asks me to dance, then never leaves my sight for the whole night.

'We didn't do it right away, but it only took two weeks of Tebogo's smooth tongue for me to drop my panties for him. I thought it was special, although, I admit, I was in a hurry to get rid of my virginity after wearing it around my neck throughout high school.' Nolwazi shrugged. 'But I really thought that this was the guy I wanted to be with. At least for as long as possible,' she said, rolling her eyes and laughing in a self-deprecating manner. 'That's how naive I was . . .'

Linda ordered a cappuccino and watched as her friend cringed while telling a story she had, without a doubt, avoided for ten years.

'Look, Nolwazi. We all have our dreams and fantasies. We all have this idea in our heads of what the perfect guy would look like, and the thing is, once you meet someone who seems to fit the picture and, worse still, get to actually go out with him, it takes a while to let go of that perfect image. But you know what? Tebogo honestly does not deserve that. He's an arse and I never tire of saying that because he just is.

'The guy's a player, but I have to say that as many misdemeanours as he's committed towards Dikeledi, it seems she's the one woman who keeps going back for more of the torture. Another way of looking at it is that he keeps going back to her. Either way, it's a vicious cycle and you don't want to be part of that, I promise you,' said Linda.

Nolwazi sighed with a resigned air. 'Anyway, I'm meeting him tonight, and we'll decide from there where this goes.'

Linda suspected that Nolwazi was hoping Tebogo would plead undying commitment to her, but, to her knowledge, the chances were as slim as that of their dead 'husband', Tupac, coming back to life.

Chapter 16

Sade

Sade's nerves buzzed like a hive full of bees. She kept biting her fingernails absent-mindedly. Her mother had asked her to stay in her room and only come out when the elders asked her to. This felt so traditional. She could not believe it was really happening. So much for her feminist era. Thank God it came and went with those halcyon days at varsity – specifically when she was dating that British exchange student who kept telling her how much assertive women turned him on. Sade used to love men so much that Ian's declarations about liberated women were enough to turn her into a staunch (albeit fleeting) feminist. Now here she was, waiting for her bride price to be negotiated. Feminism would have proved rather impractical under these circumstances, she mused.

She had never cemented her views on *lobola* because it was only over the past two years that she'd considered getting married. Before the 'transition' she'd been much like Linda. She shuddered at the thought.

Her parents' eight-roomed house in Umlazi township was a hive of activity. She could hear a lot of shuffling noises as Winston's people were welcomed into the spacious living room that had been impeccably cleaned, sprayed and polished by her mother and sister earlier that day. They had even prepared traditional home-brewed beer to welcome the 'delegation'.

Since this morning, her Uncle Themba, who led the Khumalo delegation, had been in his element. As was usual during such ceremonies, he had the air of someone who was about to go in for the kill. Rumour had it that with the *lobola* negotiations for her cousin Xoliswa, he had managed to negotiate the highest bride price in Umlazi township's modern history.

She had warned Winston about her uncle's negotiation skills, that they would be sought after in any merger or acquisition, but Winston had assured her she had nothing to worry about; whatever bride price was required, he would make a plan. Besides, he assured her, his delegation was no collection of mice either. He also had pointsmen amongst the uncles who could sell you the socks you were wearing at a mark-up!

Sade was required to dress like a typical maiden in waiting – a long white skirt respectably covering her body, along with a loose-fitting lilac top and an elaborate lilac head wrap to show respect for those who had come to negotiate her *lobola*. She hoped her tweezed eyebrows and full, round lips would be sufficient to offset her looks, despite the drab regalia she was forced to wear.

Winston was not allowed to accompany the elders, as per custom, but she barely managed to resist sending him a text message to ask how he was feeling, and to share her own elation. She knew that Winston regarded such matters with grave reverence. He could not be humoured on matters traditional, so it was best to act equally reverential.

The elders from Winston's family asked to see the bride for whom they were there to negotiate, and when her mother peeked through the door to call her, Sade, who had walked on a number of catwalks during her beauty pageant days, felt nervous and self-conscious about making her debut appearance before Winston's family. Would they think her too old? Was she as pretty as she used to be? Was her beauty still striking enough to leave no doubt in these men's minds that she was a worthy bride for their son?

With a shy, graceful step, she emerged, looking radiantly beautiful. The delegation of uncles, who donned stern, stony visages, looked all the more serious with the heavy dark coats they wore. They merely nodded at her languidly, until her mother gestured to her to return to her bedroom.

After another hour or so, the delegation prepared to depart. Once they had left, Sade could not wait to hear the results of the negotiations from her mother and father. They both joined her in her old bedroom.

'Well, *mntanam*, I knew those men would have to abide by the Khumalo clan's wishes. Your Uncle Themba . . . he, he, he!' Her mom squealed with delight, clapping her hands with relish. Something about this gesture reminded Sade of the old English Mrs Bennet from her favourite classic novel, *Pride and Prejudice*. She had been just as anxious to ship her daughters off to the institution of marriage.

'He meant business. He told them, "This family has sacrificed a lot to get that young woman through good private schools and a reputable university. She has excelled at everything she has done and has carried herself with the grace and good manners typical of her breeding,"' her mother said, folding her arms across her ample chest. 'Ntombekhaya! He made you sound like Cinderella, I swear!'

Sade had always enjoyed being home and having her mother use her Zulu name. It made her feel like a child . . . young and innocent again.

'Those people would have been embarrassed to go back with a negative answer to Winston, I promise you. I was even tempted to claim that we're from royal blood. The way Themba described you, I promise you, they would have believed it!' Her mother chuckled.

'So how much did you ask for?' Sade asked, her lower lip trembling. She knew her mother too well and suspected she had brought out a large mafia-style briefcase 'to collect'.

Her father stroked his beard with a contented air. His name was Dingaan, after Shaka Zulu's half-brother who took over the throne from the great warrior. He bore the name with pride and often went about acting like a Zulu *induna*. Dingaan Khumalo even possessed the requisite pot belly of a chief for good measure. Sade's father, the local pastor at the neighbourhood Methodist church for more than thirty years, was the strictest man in Umlazi township. When Sade had decided to plunge into a period of wanton rebellion, her father had struggled to forgive her for the disgrace she had caused his family. They had been at loggerheads ever since, with the result being that Mr Khumalo still regarded Sade's born-again status with suspicion.

'Don't worry, Sade. We only asked for forty thousand rand, which is reasonable, considering all the toil it took to raise you. Thinking back on all those troubles you brought us during your high school and varsity days, even eighty thousand would have been reasonable,' he said tersely.

Sade hated it when he reminded her of that time. Had she not displayed enough remorse? She said a silent prayer that her father would never raise the subject of her hell-raising past to Winston at any time during what she hoped would be a long marriage.

Chapter 17

DIKELEDI

Dikeledi received a call from Tebogo just after she had clicked her remote to enter the gate of her townhouse complex. With one hand on the steering wheel, she quickly picked up the call.

'Hey, angel. Are you with Phemelo?'

'Yes, Tebogo. What's with all the unanswered calls? I hope you're not up to your usual shit, I swear!'

'Come on! Why am I being attacked? Didn't I tell you I'm busy with Ramathasela's case? *Lona basadi maar!* And I'd appreciate you not swearing in front of our daughter. It's unbecoming. Can you put her on the line now,' he commanded irritably.

'Sure, whatever, but I need to see you soon, Tebogo. This is not working,' said Dikeledi, before handing the phone over to Phemelo.

'Is that my daddy?' she asked.

Dikeledi nodded.

'Hey, Daddy. When are you coming to see me? I miss you so much.'

'I'll be there tomorrow at nine in the morning. Daddy can't wait to see you either, love. Tell your mom to have you bathed and pretty because I want to take you somewhere. Just the two of us, okay?'

'Okay, Daddy. I love you.'

'Love you too, angel.'

Chapter 18

Nolwazi

A mere fifteen kilometres from Dikeledi's residence, Nolwazi changed her outfit for the fifth time that evening. In spite of herself, she could not resist the compulsion to measure herself against Dikeledi. The first outfit, a striking blue dress that cinched her tiny waist, was chosen specifically to highlight her waif-like figure, something that Dikeledi definitely lacked. She knew it was unfair to be so competitive, but she really loved this man. She sighed, now trying on a pair of tight, hipster pants, chosen because they elongated her legs and gave her the silhouette of a model. Finally, she settled on a fitted tracksuit that emphasised all of the above, and which she knew someone like Dikeledi would never dare to wear – it just would not have the same effect.

With a tinge of guilt, she did herself up for the impending meeting – bit of lipstick; dusky sensuous perfume, which was commended as having the effect of 'driving him wild with desire', regardless of who he happened to be.

She checked the time. He was already late. She had texted him earlier to see if he was on his way. He had not responded, but she hoped that maybe he had not seen it. She bit her lip. It was already seven forty-five. He had said he would be there at seven. What if he just did not pitch? That would kill her.

With tears threatening to sting her eyes, she rushed to the fridge to fix herself a glass of Southern Comfort and lemonade. She sat down on the couch and stretched her legs, but found that she could not even bring herself to smell the whisky. Her Internet research about pregnancy had terrified her enough about the dangers of foetal alcohol syndrome to put her off drinking for life. She wished God could have arranged it that pregnant women could be on happy hour for nine months. This was easily the most difficult period of any woman's life. A little sympathy from up above would have come in handy.

The phone rang. She sprang up quickly to take it in the kitchen. Linda. Not exactly who she was looking forward to talking to.

'Hi,' Nolwazi answered with a dry tone.

'Hey. Just checking on you. Is he there already?'

Oh Linda, yes, go ahead and humiliate me by asking that question. 'Umm, no . . . but I'm sure he's on his way. Oh, actually, there's a call waiting. It's him!' she said, a bit too enthusiastically.

'Okay, good luck, girl,' said Linda flatly.

'Hi, Nolwazi, I'm at your gate,' Tebogo said, assertive as ever. Nothing about being late, just straight to the point. This man was annoyingly arrogant.

She opened for him through the intercom system and waited. She sat down, then stood up, then sat down and then rose and rushed to the mirror for a final check. By now he was already at the door.

Her mouth felt like hot pepper. She took a deep breath and swung the door open. He was leaning against the doorway. She could not discern the expression on his face, but she was nervous nonetheless. Once he was in, she asked if she could fix him a drink.

'Do you have whisky?' he asked.

'No, just Southern Comfort. It's a bourbon, right?'

'It'll do,' he said, sitting down slowly on the pink couch.

She took some time in the kitchen, trying to get the mix of Southern Comfort and lemonade just the way she would have liked it. She then changed her mind and decided that the situation was stressful enough for Tebogo to take his drink neat, so she opted to serve it straight up, with a few blocks of ice.

Handing him the drink, she sat on the couch opposite him. They were separated by the glass coffee table. He drank slowly, then rubbed his forehead.

'So, how've you been?' he asked.

She feigned a smile and shrugged. 'Okay, I guess. Under the circumstances.' Silence.

He stood up, glass in hand, and started pacing. 'I've been thinking about this . . . situation . . . a lot over the past few days, and the thing is . . . it is very bad timing, Nolwazi, for something like this. I mean, I assumed you'd taken care of everything. We're not kids here, you know. It's not entirely your fault but if you were not on something, why did you let me do it without a condom? Even then, there's still the morning-after pill. Girl, this is just . . . it perplexes me. How could this happen? I don't get it. I just don't get it.'

She looked up at him, trying to contain the rage building inside of her. 'Tebogo, I didn't just let this happen. If you recall, I went on the Pill the minute we stopped using condoms. I've been very careful! I honestly don't know why you'd even think to pin this on me.'

Tebogo was not backing down. 'But you're a woman. I have unprotected sex with Dikeledi all the time and we've never had an accident in years. Didn't you think about what this would do to her?'

At this, Nolwazi flew into a rage. 'How dare you pin this on me, you bastard? It's obviously an accident because I was using contraceptives. I don't know who the fuck you think you are, to assume that I'd give up everything I'm working for to get knocked up with your child! You're an arsehole, you know that? A real fucking arsehole!' She was sobbing now as she got to her feet and beat weak fists against his chest.

He took her arms and held her while she cried. He carried her towards the two-seater couch he'd occupied earlier and let her sob on his shoulder. He patted her gently, like a small child, and said, 'Listen, baby, I'm really sorry, but . . . we have to start thinking about how we're going to sort this out. I promise I'll be with you every step of the way, but we must just take care of this together.'

She stopped crying and looked up at him. 'You mean it?' she asked, wiping tears from her eyes.

'Of course I mean it,' he said, taking her by both hands. 'And the thing is, many couples have done this and still survived; still kept the relationship alive. It's all about maturity.'

She nodded. 'What are you going to tell Dikeledi?' she asked, not really believing her ears. He was actually embracing this. He was choosing her. It was too good to be true. Part of her felt wretched about what this would do to Dikeledi . . . and Phemelo? What a mess.

But maybe there was a way . . . maybe if she could take time to sit down with her friend and explain how she'd met Tebogo in those early days and share her feelings about the strong connection that they had established, it may even help Dikeledi understand why Tebogo had struggled so much to commit to her through all these years. Clearly, he'd always held a candle for Nolwazi. This could help her friend finally move on with her own life and find someone who would value her for all the wonderful qualities she had.

She knew that Tebogo had never stopped loving her. The past few months had proved it. The way he would get so excited to see her, how he was barely able to keep his hands off her, and the intensity with which he made love to her. The chats they'd have till dawn. It was as if time had compressed back to that first spark that had ignited when they first laid eyes on each other in her freshman year.

She sighed. Why did love have to be so complicated? Why did it have to hurt so much? She really hoped that Dikeledi would be able to pick up the pieces and move on. She certainly deserved the best in life. She really did.

In the meantime, she could not believe that the love of her life had finally come round to claiming her as his. Officially.

'I think we should make an extra effort to be gentle about how we break this to Dikeledi, babe. She's such an amazing person. I feel bad that we're doing this to her. Do you think it's best if you do it alone or if we do it together? It feels like we've both betrayed her.'

'What do you mean? I can't tell her about this. Nolwazi, I think, as her friend, you can appreciate that we have to protect her, right? She's the innocent party in all this.'

Nolwazi was confused. 'But how do we continue with such a big thing without letting her know? I mean this is a baby we're talking about, Tebogo. You can't just hide a big thing like that from someone, especially since you're saying we're going to do this together.'

He buried his head in his hands. Shaking his head, he said, 'You don't get what I'm saying, do you? I really think we should get rid of the baby. It's best for everyone. You're not ready to be a mother; your career is just about to take off. Come on, be reasonable here.'

'Get rid of the baby?'

Had he just said that? She felt dizzy. As if she'd been pushed off a cliff.

'But why, Tebogo? Why must I get rid of the baby? Did you say the same thing to Dikeledi when she was pregnant with Phemelo?

Don't you see? You wouldn't have had Phemelo otherwise. Don't you care at all about our baby?'

Tebogo looked irritated. 'Come on, Nolwazi, be reasonable. You can hardly compare this to my situation with Dikeledi. You're still young, you are stronger than Dikeledi, you are an incredible, beautiful, independent and headstrong woman. You don't need someone like me in your life. You don't need the kind of baggage I'd be bringing. Besides, you know how vulnerable Dikeledi is. She wouldn't survive if she were to lose me.'

She looked at him in incredulous shock. Did he really just say that? Did he think he could get away with playing her against her friend? Making Dikeledi seem like a pathetic wet blanket just so he could convince her to get rid of her baby?

'Fuck you, I know what you're doing.'

He regarded her with what he clearly hoped were doleful eyes. 'I'm serious, Nolwazi. You're different. You've always been level-headed. That's what I admire about you. Who would win in this scenario, huh? Not me, not Dikeledi, and certainly not you, nor an unwanted baby.'

'What? *What?* You're honestly trying to get my sympathy for you and Dikeledi when you're the one who initiated this whole mess in the first place? I was just living my life, having completely forgotten about your wretched arse when you started texting me out of the blue. Are you really this monstrous? Get out of my house, Tebogo. Get out! And I'm giving you twenty-four hours to tell Dikeledi, otherwise I'm telling her myself, you bastard!' she fumed.

Tebogo just looked at her and shook his head as he stood up slowly. 'Are you seriously blackmailing me right now? Can you hear what you're saying? That's low, Nolwazi, even for you.'

She rose and screamed at him, 'Get out!'

As he walked out the door, she repeated, 'I'm not bluffing. If you don't tell Dikeledi, I will let her know what a scumbag you really are.'

She slammed the door behind him and collapsed onto the sofa, feeling tremors of hurt and pain ride up her body till tears started running down her face.

She'd never hated herself as she did at this moment. What did he mean when he said that this was low, even for her?

Is that how he regarded her? Just a lowly excuse for a human being? Someone to be used for sex then discarded. So Dikeledi was the Madonna, and she was the Whore?

She hated that she was competing with her friend for a man's attention, but why could she not stop loving this poor excuse for a human being? Why?

They both deserved better. She needed to get over him . . . but Dikeledi *must* know who Tebogo Makwetla truly was.

Chapter 19

LINDA

Linda was feeling sick – not in a physical sense, but like someone who suddenly realised that she had committed an error of tsunamic proportions and nothing could turn back the clock. It was a Saturday night, and she was all alone. The best she could do on this singles-unfriendly night was babysit her friends' problems. This was unnatural. It was just not her. Had she made a mistake by dumping Lehumo? The world felt so quiet and uneventful without him. Good grief!

What if the universe had jinxed her and she was never going to be loved by any man ever again, like her friends had said?

Thinking about her friends and their various dramas, she shook her head. This thing with Nolwazi and Tebogo was an impending hurricane. Not only would it shake up things with the threesome of Dikeledi, Tebogo and Nolwazi, but it would also force her and Sade to take sides. And the two kids involved? Phemelo and this new package of Nolwazi's? They were the biggest losers in this drama. Why didn't Nolwazi at least insist on using protection? Was her friend so manipulative that she would deliberately fall pregnant by Tebogo? She shuddered at the thought.

Seriously though, was it an accident? She loved Nolwazi to bits. After all, it was Nolwazi with whom she had shared a flat for two years when they were both starting out, and they had had a blast – living on skimpy salaries, going through endless affairs and generally having a glorious party on their way to their appointment with 'growing up'. Growing up had meant turning thirty. Yup, this was it. No wonder everyone was messing up; they'd reached the crest of a wave. From here onwards they were all swimming downstream.

She had never suspected Nolwazi of having any designs on Tebogo, although she'd noticed the way Tebogo looked at Nolwazi sometimes. It was one of the reasons she hated him. He was such a womaniser that he left no skirt unturned, not even that of Dikeledi's friend. What an arsehole.

She breathed in. Okay, Linda, relax and get a life, she told herself as she took her phone and scrolled for a prospective gentleman-in-waiting she could call up. Maybe even an old boyfriend with whom she had unfinished business.

She went through all the As, a short list, then through the Bs in her phone book. 'Buster'. Oh no, God forbid. Buster, with the pimples and the halitosis. That must have been some kind of desperate period she'd gone through. Oh *ja*, she remembered. It was the time she'd gained weight and felt unloved. Buster came and went with the five extra kilos.

Now she was already on the Ls. 'Lehumo'. Lehumo? Should she call him? And say what exactly? 'Hey baby. About that break-up . . . sorry, man. I'd had a rough night. Let's get back together. The engagement is back on. Yeah! Party on!' Not quite. He would probably not even answer her call. Okay, skip Lehumo. On to the Ms. 'Moremi'. Oh yeah. He was kind of gorgeous. Why did they break up again? For the life of her she could not remember. Let me call him, she thought. Maybe he won't remember either. She dialled him immediately.

'Hey, Morems. It's Linda here. How's it going, man?' she asked in her bubbliest tone.

'Linda? Linda Mthimkhulu! Wow, to what do I owe the pleasure?'

'Well . . . I just wanted to see if you're still alive. It's been a while.'

'Yes, all of . . . a year . . . year and a half? Geez, so what are you up to these days, kid?'

'Nothing much. Actually, I thought maybe we could do drinks or something. Play catch-up,' she said boldly.

'Hmm, I'd love to but I'm on baby duty. My wife's out of town for the weekend. We have an eight-month-old baby; can you believe it, kid?'

Oh great. What is this, Instant Marriages Anonymous club? She hadn't seen him for maybe eighteen months and he'd got married and had a baby? How depressing.

'Oh, okay. That's nice. Well, I guess another time then,' she said, all the enthusiasm washed out of her voice.

'Cheers. Take care, kid,' he said.

She remembered why she'd broken up with him. It was the 'kid' thing. Hey kid! Bye kid! Love you lots, kid! Yawn. Let him babysit and find out what real kids are made of!

Hmm. Next.

Oh yes. Sifiso. Sweet, soft, swift Sifiso, the tea-drinking accountant. He was all right. A bit stiff, but he could loosen up sometimes. She remembered the time she'd taken him out dancing. After he'd consumed his requisite number of cups of tea at a restaurant, he had danced like he was in an eighties revival at the Sudada Lounge.

That had been fun.

After a few rings, Sifiso picked up.

'Hello,' he said, rather sternly.

'Hi, Sifiso. This is Linda Mthimkhulu. How've you been?'

He hesitated, then sighed. 'Linda, I can't believe you have the gall to call me after what you did to me. You're really unbelievable, you know that?'

Uh-oh. What had she done? Was he really still mad about that text?

'Let me tell you something, Linda. If you want people to still pick up your calls, you'd better start treating them with a little bit more decency. Dumping a guy who cared about you via text is not only childish but it's also very cruel and callous. Have a nice life!' Click.

Well, there goes sweet, soft, swift Sifiso.

She scrolled and scrolled and scrolled. Nothing. Either too much baggage or too little spark. The worst part was, she remembered that she was the one who had broken up with all these people. With some of them, not so nicely, either. She needed to go speed dating or something!

Chapter 20

DIKELEDI

Dikeledi woke up and instantly wished she had not overslept. She desperately needed to go to church. The situation with Tebogo had become insufferable and she was beginning to feel tempted into agreeing to go out with Professor Kwame. Somewhere within her soul, though, was this little girl who still believed in happy endings and good Christian values. The little girl who believed what her mother said about saving yourself for one man and staying the course.

Dikeledi's mother, a demure Mosotho woman, married Dikeledi's traditional Zulu father when she was seventeen years old. Although Dikeledi's father only stopped beating her mother when Dikeledi was at varsity, her mother held on to the marriage and stayed faithful to her father through both storms and sunshine.

As far as Dikeledi could discern, her father had stopped being abusive towards her mother. He was now a faithful old man who doted on all three of his children, although Dikeledi's eldest brother could never forgive him for how he had treated their mother when they were younger. In fact, Dikeledi suspected that her brother Mandla had something to do with the cessation of the abuse. She had gone back home from campus during her second year and, presto, her father was a changed man. Mandla had been staying with their parents throughout that period and Dikeledi noticed that there was a respectful distance between Mandla and the old man. This did nothing to cast a shadow on Dikeledi's chosen illusion of their family as being perfect.

What impressed Dikeledi the most was that whenever she and her siblings went back to their village home in Ixopo to visit their parents, they always enjoyed a solid family reunion. Their father would slaughter a cow and pick vegetables from his sprawling garden. Their mother would busy herself in the kitchen, preparing an elaborate family meal. When dusk came, their father would build a fire outside and regale them with tales of his days as a schoolmaster in the village. In his deep, gruff voice he would share humorous anecdotes about the naughty children at the school and their parents, who were constantly in denial about their children's delinquent behaviour. Her mother would laugh the loudest, holding on to her father's arm in possessive companionship.

Dikeledi had thought that that was what she wanted – to grow old gracefully with someone. She abhorred the thought of sharing her body with another man. Like her mother, she wanted to share herself with one man for eternity.

When she looked up at the clock on her bedroom wall, she was disappointed to see that, as usual, she had missed Mass. It was already nine thirty; the exact time that the Mass at the local Catholic church started.

Then she remembered that Tebogo would be coming to pick up Phemelo. When she walked into Phemelo's bedroom, she found the little lady already washed and dressed, sitting primly on the bed, waiting for her father.

'*Yoh*, you look so cute, baby,' she said, laughing quietly at Phemelo's little-madam demeanour.

'Yes, Mommy. I want to look nice for Daddy.'

'I'm sure you do, *sweetie*,' she said, kissing her on the cheek. 'Do you need me to fix you *ipapa*?'

'Yes, please,' she said, starting to play with her toys.

Dikeledi smiled as she went to the kitchen. She was proud of Phemelo. She knew that she would turn out to be a bright young lady, in spite of acting like a spoiled princess at times.

After handing Phemelo the bowl of soft porridge, she called Tebogo to check if he was on his way.

'Hey, baby. Listen, I'll be a few hours late. There's something I have to urgently take care of. But definitely by twelve o'clock, I'll be there.'

'No, Tebogo, you can't do this to her. She's been waiting for you since eight. She actually woke up and got all dressed up for you. Please don't do this to her too.'

He sighed painfully. 'Baby, I promise I'll be there. Just keep her busy. It's worth it, you'll see. Oh, and by the way, please fix yourself up too. I want this to be a nice family outing,' he said, and quickly hung up.

'Arsehole,' she murmured under her breath.

Chapter 21

SADE

Sade was standing outside the church entrance, watching while Winston spoke to the pastor and two of the church deacons. He looked authoritative in his navy-blue Armani suit and his square black glasses. He was laughing appreciatively at something the pastor said. Looking at him now, she knew she was the envy of most of the single women in her church. The pastor had announced after the sermon that one of the ushers in church, Mr Winston Gumede, was engaged to wed none other than the charitable Sade Khumalo. The applause was deafening. They were both very active and popular in the church community. Most of the congregants were certain to attend the upcoming wedding, which was now a mere two months away.

'He is quite a catch, isn't he?' said Palesa, a buxom, perky young lady who belonged to Sade's church cell group, as she caught Sade staring warmly at Winston.

Sade smiled. 'Gosh, am I gawking at him? I sometimes forget that he's mine,' she said, sounding boastful and possessive.

'My dear, I must say, I've known Winston since we were at Wits University together. I don't think I've ever seen him happier.'

Sade smiled sweetly. 'Oh, that's such a kind thing to say. Thanks, Palesa. By the way, I think I speak for Winston as well when I say we'd both love for you to help us with the arrangements . . . for the wedding, I mean.'

'You mean . . . you want me to be the maid of honour? I'd love to!'

Uh-oh. That wasn't exactly what she'd meant.

'I . . . um . . . I actually meant . . .'

At that moment, Winston came to join them. Palesa immediately gave him a gracious hug.

'Winston, your beautiful fiancée here just told me the good news, that you guys want me to be the maid of honour! I'm so touched; I did not expect it at all.'

Winston beamed at Sade. 'Well, I know my Sade. She never ceases to amaze, that's why I chose her,' he said, hugging Sade close with one arm.

Palesa flinched for a second, then said, 'Well, let me leave you two love birds. I really look forward to helping out. Praise the Lord!' she said as she trotted off.

'Honey,' he said, during the drive home. 'I'm really impressed that you chose one of the sisters at the church to play such a major role at our wedding, especially since I've known Palesa since varsity. She's like a sister to me. I can't tell you how much I'm touched by that gesture.'

Should she bother clearing up the misunderstanding? What was Dikeledi going to say? And her other friends? They would feel so betrayed. The bride's maid of honour is someone who knows her inside and out. She barely knew anything about Palesa, and vice versa. All she had meant was that she should be there and represent her from a church perspective. What a mess. How could she tell Winston what she really thought?

Oh, *nkosi yam'!* She was just going to have to find a way to explain everything to the girls. She did not want to upset Winston, especially at this crucial time in the wedding preparations. He could get moody at times, so she'd been enjoying the mellow mood he'd been in since the *lobola* negotiations. This was the Winston she'd hoped to spend the rest of her life with. She was determined to hold on to the dreamy atmosphere they'd maintained in the last few days. They usually said 'Happy Wife, Happy Life', but she equally felt that a happy husband would mean a blissful life for her, and that's all she'd ever wanted.

Chapter 22

DIKELEDI

Dikeledi kept looking at her watch subconsciously; she was calculating that if Tebogo were a minute later than twelve, then . . . then she was going to end this pathetic charade once and for all.

She was an adult, a seasoned soldier well accustomed to the bruises that came with the battle of loving Tebogo Makwetla, but she was not going to allow him to develop the same, poisonous relationship with Phemelo. It was bad enough that Phemelo had to explain to her friends why her mom and dad did not live together, but having to deal with the raw, bitter feeling of unfulfilled expectations was just too much. Her little daughter didn't deserve to suffer from excuses made by an adult who should know better.

As she poured herself a glass of orange juice, she calmly pondered that perhaps this was the ultimate lesson for her. After all the pain and the disappointment that Tebogo had inflicted on her, it was only through seeing her daughter suffer the same fate that she would finally wake up to the harsh reality. Tebogo was never going to change, she thought, as she slumped against her kitchen counter, sitting unsteadily on one of the high chairs around the granite top. Whether she liked it or not, Linda was right. In order to get different results, she had to change tack; it was foolhardy to continue in the same vein.

For the first time, Dikeledi opened a different window in the cluttered, confined spaces of her mind. She was not getting any younger and, quite frankly, neither was Tebogo. If she continued down this path she would doubtless turn out bitter at all the opportunities she had missed. She sighed heavily, surprisingly unafraid of confronting what she'd thought was the big bad *tokoloshe,* which she'd long swept under the carpet. Maybe there was another way. Maybe she should take a break; a week or two away on her own. She knew that the university owed her a lot of leave days, so organising this would certainly not be a problem. All she needed was to shut herself off from everything, get a fresh perspective on life, and then maybe she'd have the strength to walk away for good – if not for her own sake, then at least for Phemelo's. She thought of her stoic mother. She could see her gentle, lined face, steadily leaning against her father's ox-like shoulder as he rambled on about his eventful past. Shrugging, she said out loud: 'Maybe we're not all destined to find our perfect mate.'

At that moment there was a buzz on the intercom. Tebogo. He liked doing this: not calling to warn that he was on his way, despite knowing that he was the most unreliable person on God's good earth. She sighed again. Lord, give me the strength to stay true to myself, she thought.

A few minutes later he was at the door. When Phemelo eagerly went to open it, she was confronted with a large bouquet of sunflowers – Dikeledi's favourite because they reminded her of home – her father had a whole garden full of them. She steeled her heart from melting.

He hugged her, then Phemelo. He seemed different. She held her hand to her heart and looked at him curiously. Something about him looked urgent, as if he was bursting to say something but was fighting to keep it to himself.

'Baby, do . . . do you have plans for today? These are for you,' he stuttered, handing her the sunflowers. 'I think it would be nice for us to just take a drive to this beautiful place in the south. It's got a lovely stream that runs through it and they cook a mean Sunday lunch. I discovered it last year when our firm attended that "New Rights, New Laws" conference. You'll love it. I know I haven't been attentive of late but I really want to make it up to you – to both of you,' he said, scooping Phemelo up in one arm.

Promptly, Phemelo planted a big kiss on his cheek. 'Let's go, Momma, let's go!'

Dikeledi was speechless. Why did he always manage to do this? Was he a mind-reader? She shook her head helplessly.

'Sweetie, go get that nice red jacket that matches your dress. It might get a bit chilly where we're going, okay?'

Phemelo looked up at her parents. 'Okay, Mommy. Can't wait for Sunday lunch with Daddy!' she said as she hop-skipped to her room.

Dikeledi sometimes resented how Tebogo had such an adoring fan in Phemelo, despite his many faults. It was amazing how he managed to twist women of all ages around his crooked little finger.

'Look, Tebogo, it can't always be like this. I can't go on like this. I feel like I'm living on the edge of my seat, never knowing what to expect from you – whether it's ecstasy or disappointment. Whatever it is, I must just swing whichever way the Tebogo choo-choo train is going. It's exhausting. This can't be what my life's about, you know,' she said.

Tebogo kissed her tenderly on the cheek. 'I promise you, today is the beginning of a new chapter for us. Just believe in me, please, baby. Go get changed. Wear something comfortable and relax, just relax. I swear, things are going to be different.'

No longer armed with the strength of faith, or even trust, she trudged along in defeated spirits to her bedroom. She put on her favourite pair of jeans, and a burgundy top that outlined her generous bosom, then fastened her long, straight hair into a ponytail. She applied some dark eyeshadow, chocolate-brown lipstick and a pair of ox-blood-red, kitten-heeled shoes.

Dikeledi kept thinking that if this was the last outing she was to have with Tebogo, she wanted him to remember what he was leaving behind. Before stepping out, she looked at the reflection in the mirror, and practised her speech: 'Tebogo, I just can't stay in this relationship anymore. People's lives are moving along, progressing, while I'm stuck in limbo, waiting for my life to begin. It's been ten years, and you still haven't committed to me. This is it. For both our sakes, I think we should move on and see what else is out there.'

'Mom! We're waiting!' Phemelo screamed at the top of her voice.

With one last glance in the mirror, she took a deep breath and then came out of the bedroom to rave reviews from her audience of two.

'Mmm, Mom, you look really pretty.'

'Thanks, my angel. Okay, folks, let's go,' she said, clutching her maroon bag.

When they got into Tebogo's Mercedes C-Class, Dikeledi slumped on the seat and closed her eyes. This was going to be very difficult, she thought, tears starting to well up in her eyes. I mustn't show any emotion, she told herself. Lord, please don't let him see me crying.

But Tebogo was oblivious to all the drama going on in Dikeledi's head. He was humming happily, having inserted a George Benson CD, their favourite, and narrating to Phemelo for the umpteenth time how this was the song that reminded him the most of her mom.

90

Dikeledi noticed his upbeat mood and tried to join in the light-hearted atmosphere, but deep down, she felt a thick lump in her throat that she knew would only go away once she had expressed her resolve.

An hour and a half later they were thankfully at the Three Sisters Resort in southern Gauteng. A quaint, whitewashed building with an evergreen lawn and luscious plants in full bloom, it conjured up the dream of an ideal getaway in living colour. As soon as they stepped out of the car, Dikeledi began to relax.

'It's beautiful. I'm impressed,' she said softly.

Tebogo grabbed her by both arms and kissed her. 'I knew you would be, bunny bear,' he said.

She laughed out loud. She could not remember when last he had called her that.

Phemelo was already running ahead of them. She picked two white roses and gave one to each of her parents. 'At school they told us if you love someone you must give them a rose. So, here's one for you, and one for you!' she said, her dimples turning into deep smiles.

'You guys are really in quite a good mood today, aren't you?' observed Dikeledi.

They finally settled in the outside dining area, all the better to enjoy the greenery that was coming back to life with the whisper of spring in the air. Aside from them there were only two other couples outside. Five multi-coloured ducks kept waddling past the family of three, along with a tall, proud peacock.

'What's that, Mom? Is it a peacock?'

'Aha. And can you see those ducks and that guinea fowl there? Aren't they pretty?' Dikeledi said. As she looked up, she caught Tebogo looking at her with a gentle expression on his face.

'Hey, *wena*. Quit looking at me like that. We didn't just meet yesterday, you know,' she said, enjoying the attention.

'While you guys were admiring the wildlife, I ordered a bottle of champagne for us and a glass of juice for Pheme. Hope you're up to it.'

'Hmm, what are we celebrating?'

'Nothing.' He shrugged. 'Just life,' he said, kissing her on the back of her hand.

The drinks arrived and Dikeledi passed the glass of juice to her daughter, while Tebogo took the champagne from the waiter and poured for the both of them.

'Here's a toast to the first and the second best things that have ever happened to me. You guys are the apples of my eye,' he said as he raised his glass.

Phemelo, who loved all manner of ceremonious gestures, raised her glass to her parents and said, 'Cheers to apples!'

They both laughed until Dikeledi suddenly stopped, screwing up her face in a puzzled expression. She felt something chunky in her mouth.

'Mommy, Mommy, are you okay?'

Dikeledi spat out the ring.

'You could have killed me!' she said, gasping.

Phemelo started crying.

'Mommy, are you okay? Did Daddy really try to kill you?'

Suddenly realising the hilarity of the disastrous situation, Dikeledi burst into laughter. She took Phemelo by the hand.

'No, sweetheart, Daddy didn't try to kill Mommy. I think he was actually trying to do something really sweet.'

Tebogo picked up the ring, which was now lying inelegantly on the floor. He asked the waiter to bring a napkin and then carefully wiped it, gently treating it like the precious stone it was. When he was done, he looked into Dikeledi's eyes, then went down on one knee.

'Dikeledi Langa, would you take me, Tebogo Makwetla, as your wedded husband?'

She read his lips, for she could barely hear anything as she nodded in wondrous disbelief. Then she hugged him, laughing and crying at the same time. 'Yes, yes, yes!' she exclaimed.

Phemelo jumped up with joy as she went over to kiss both her parents.

It was certainly an unforgettable marriage proposal.

Chapter 23

SADE

When Sade got home she started preparing lunch for herself and Winston while ruminating over the maid of honour debacle. Why was she so terrified of disappointing Winston? Was she really so desperate for his approval? Each chop of the carrots she was preparing on the cutting board reminded her how her loyalties were being gradually torn to pieces. Is this what they meant about marriage involving a lot of sacrifices? No, she was really taking it too far. Acting desperate. She should be open and honest with him. After all, these were the hallmarks of a good marriage. Palesa what's-her-name was hardly worth destroying a friendship that had spanned almost two decades! That's how long she'd known Dikeledi.

'Baby,' she said to Winston, who was reading the Sunday papers in the lounge. 'I need to talk to you about something.' Just then, her phone rang. 'Hello,' she answered.

'Sade, it's me. Guess what? I'm at this beautiful little restaurant in the south, and I'm wearing a brand-new, sparkling, diamond-encrusted ring. Tebogo's just proposed!'

'Oh my gosh! Wow!' screamed Sade.

By now, a curious Winston was in the kitchen, staring at her.

'It's Dikeledi,' she mouthed to Winston. 'Wow! I'm so happy for you, sweetie. I can't believe it. That Motswana man finally came to his senses. This is great! I'm so happy. At least now I'll have someone to share wedding tips with. Have you guys started discussing possible dates?'

'Oh, Sade, you're so pragmatic. We still need to go to the elders and discuss *lobola* issues and stuff. I'm just over the moon that Tebogo didn't let this drag out for any longer. I swear, I'd reached the end of my tether. You won't believe I was thinking of leaving him just earlier today.'

'Well, you know what they say: the Lord may not answer your prayers when you want, but he'll always be at your door right on time! I really hope your marriage is blessed and I pray that Tebogo will be true to you, Dikeledi. You've been so good to him, you really deserve the best.'

'Oh, thanks, Sade. You know you've always been like a sister to me. I'm glad you're the first one to hear the news. Let me get back to my family before they start wondering where I disappeared off to. Bye then, I'll talk to you later tonight, okay?'

'All right. Bye, babes,' Sade said, and hugged the phone to her chest.

She jumped on Winston and kissed him all over.

'Did you hear that? Isn't it fabulous? That little twit finally proposed. I was feeling so sorry for Dikeledi. She's probably been looking forward to this for the past ten years.'

'Serious? But this guy can't be the most honourable person in the world. Dikeledi's a sweet woman. Why did he take this long? He should have married her the minute he found out she was pregnant,' Winston replied.

'Honey, not every man is like you. Tebogo's a bit of a cold-hearted brute. He used to cheat on her on campus and get up to all sorts of mischief. Although I'm happy for her because this is what she wants, I worry this guy might continue with his ways into their marriage. I actually wonder why he decided to pop the question out of the blue like this,' she said, as she went back to preparing lunch.

'Do you need some help?'

'Um, *ja*. Maybe you could peel those potatoes for me and then just throw them in the oven to roast with the chicken.'

'Yes, ma'am,' he said, rolling up his sleeves. 'So you think she could be making a mistake?' he asked.

'I don't know. Sometimes the heart wants what it wants. If she's making a mistake, I don't see how it could alter his behaviour towards her. She's been with this guy for ten years. Can a man really change?'

Winston took the potato peeler and started working briskly. 'I don't know. If a woman can change, why can't a man do the same?'

Sade laughed. 'Babe, are you kidding me? Conventional wisdom says when it comes to men, you really can't teach an old dog new tricks.'

'As an economist, you should know that "conventional wisdom" lasts for about a month. I think men are just as capable of taking a different course in life as women. Just as you hear of some reformed prostitute or drug addict turning over a new leaf, so too do you hear of a former alcoholic deciding to change his ways for the sake of his family,' Winston said. 'You see, Sade, the problem these days is that women are being depicted as these faultless Amazons with superhuman powers. This is just another PC trend spurred on by those wily feminists.'

She put the carrots into a pan of olive oil and wiped her hands on her apron, looking up at Winston.

'I hope you don't let any women's magazine editor hear you say all that stuff. It's very caveman-like, and besides, what's wrong with women enjoying their moment in the sunshine for a while? We've been the underdogs for long enough. Please pass me the grater,' she said, preparing to make the salad.

She continued, 'If you're telling me that a half century of female worship is a passing trend, you can't mean that the two thousand years that you guys plundered the earth were justified and that the status quo should remain unchanged forever. You men have had your years of glory and you did a sad job of it too. Maybe it's time we claimed the next few centuries; we might even manage to reverse global warming!'

'*Neh*. You're mad. Then we'll have to end up hosting emotional intelligence workshops on a daily basis, sharing and caring all the time. Nothing will get done. The international spectator sport will be watching reruns of *Oprah*. No! Someone please help.' He gagged dramatically.

She slapped him playfully with a washcloth. 'I think I might need to apply for a divorce,' she joked.

Again, her phone rang. This time it was Linda.

'Hey girl, how's it going?'

It was weird how Linda was starting to be such an attentive caller. Usually one could go for months without hearing from her. This turning thirty thing was like a contagious epidemic with adverse effects on people.

'Linda, I just got a call from Dikeledi. Guess what?'

'What?' she asked, bracing herself for the worst.

'Your Tswana friend has finally proposed. Apparently, he just popped the question. Isn't that amazing? You can imagine Dikeledi is just beside herself with excitement.'

'Wow. Wow,' said Linda, sounding shell-shocked.

'Yeah. That's what I also said. I think we should go out mid-week to celebrate. She's wanted this for like, centuries.'

'I know, I know. Wow. Um, so I'll call you midweek so we can make arrangements to go out, okay? Bye now,' she said hurriedly.

After the phone cut off, Sade looked at Winston with a puzzled expression.

'She sure sounded weird. Sometimes I wonder how God wired that girl.'

Winston laughed. 'Let's just hope all the lights are still on,' he said.

Sade couldn't resist. 'The lights may be on, but is anyone home?'

They both giggled, enjoying the shared jibe. Such moments were too rare not to treasure.

Chapter 24

LINDA

What was Linda to do? That bastard Tebogo! How could he? What an oxygen thief! How was she going to relay the news to Nolwazi? Nope. She was not the one who would break it to her. Nolwazi would be devastated.

In a daze, Linda grabbed her Bob Marley bag, twisted her dreadlocks into a ponytail, put on jeans, tekkies and a casual T-shirt and got into her Jeep. She did not know where she was going. She just needed air.

After driving around in circles for a while, she found herself cruising in the direction of Woodmead. Since she was in the area, she decided to pay her mother a visit. Guiltily, Linda realised that she had begun avoiding these visits of late. Her mother's condition was beginning to weigh heavily on her. Linda hated seeing her so weak and lifeless.

Her mother had been a doctor and she doted on Linda. Their bond was made closer when her father, a popular television and stage director, Floyd Mthimkhulu, had suddenly left her mom for a French actress called Monique. Her father's company had co-directed a collaborative television drama supported by both the South African and French governments. The French had flown in their own crew and cast to work with South African actors and technicians. Monique was one of the supporting French actors.

After countless excuses about working late and promoting the high-profile project, he and his lover had finally dropped the bombshell. The couple had called Linda's mother and had asked to meet with her at the Parktonian Hotel, which is where they undoubtedly spent many a steamy night. The meeting had been brief and business-like. With patronising alacrity, they had apologised to Linda's mother for having 'fallen in love', but explained that it was something beyond their control. The moment they had seen each other, each felt like they had met a soulmate and . . . blah, blah, blah. The main reason they wanted the meeting had been clear: Floyd wanted a quick, painless divorce.

At the time, Linda was in her final year at high school. Floyd's relationship with Monique had been a defining moment in Linda's life and she had sworn she would never see her father again, which was easy since he had left within months of his divorce from her mother to stay with Monique in the South of France. The move seemed to have bolstered his career, as Europe provided vast opportunities for television directors, especially those who were as multilingual and egotistical as her father.

Although Floyd had written a collection of letters and postcards since, Linda had never bothered to respond to any of them. For her, the alliances in this battleground were clear: she was Lunga Mthimkhulu's daughter and Floyd was Monique's husband and they would never meet; they lived in different worlds.

Floyd's actions had completely eroded Linda's trust in men. This was exacerbated by the fact that prior to his affair with Monique, Floyd had been an attentive, albeit relatively absent, father. When he had been around, Linda had simply basked in the glory of his attention. He would spoil her, take her to meet with some of the glamorous celebrities he worked with, and gloat about his 'smart daughter'. Although she would never admit it, her father was the reason she chose to study film-making in the first place. How ironic that it was his career that had brought him together with Monique.

At first, Linda had not noticed anything amiss about her father, especially because the family had been thrust into a deeply traumatic medical emergency around the time that his affair with Monique began.

Their family doctor had discovered a malignant <u>tumour</u> in Lunga's left breast. At first, Floyd had been the model husband: taking her mother to every consultation, insisting on enlisting only the best treatment for her and generally being a reassuring presence for both <u>Lunga</u> and the then eighteen-year-old Linda. It was only once her mother had undergone treatment and the cancer had gone into remission that he started acting noticeably differently.

Once <u>Lunga</u> had been given the all-clear, Floyd simply avoided her. He seemed to regard her good health as a get-out-of-jail-free card for his bad behaviour. Things worsened once <u>Lunga</u> went back to her medical practice.

Floyd started spending less time at home, suddenly becoming more devoted to 'his work', but Linda knew about her father's vanity and his sometimes-desperate attempts at eternal youth. He had probably viewed her mother's ill health as a descent into decrepitude that must be avoided at all costs.

Linda called her mother's phone to announce that she was at the gate. A few minutes later, Uncle Phuti, her mom's companion of eight years, came to open it. A mild-mannered, taciturn man with non-descript features, Uncle Phuti was a wallflower compared to the exuberant, flamboyant Floyd. Linda's father was the type of man that could not be ignored. He walked with the confidence of a man who was aware of his extraordinarily good looks and his imposing stature.

When Uncle Phuti first came into her mother's life, Linda was already at varsity. The first time she met him she assumed he was a librarian, or at least had something to do with libraries, but she later discovered he was a director of a Chapter Nine Institution, which sounded like some dreary organisation aimed at accommodating everyone under the rainbow as per the South African constitution. She found Uncle Phuti nice, but mildly boring. Linda suspected that her mother had chosen to be with him precisely because he tended to wilt away into the background, whereas her dad had always wanted to claim centre stage.

In spite of being with Uncle Phuti for eight years, her mother still kept her own residence, even though they spent a lot of time together. Linda knew that after the break-up with her father, her mother wished to maintain some semblance of independence and so the question of marriage never seemed to surface during their lengthy courtship.

'Hi, Uncle Phuti. How's she holding up?' Linda asked as she stepped out of her car.

Uncle Phuti shook his head without much enthusiasm. 'Linda, I really wish I could say her condition is improving, but she's not really doing well. I'm not sure if she's getting enough care here. Maybe she would be better off in a hospital,' he said as they entered the home's open-plan area. Linda's heart sank. Her mother's cancer had recurred a year ago and she had been on treatment for months, spending most of that time in hospital beds, which she'd hated. Once she was done with chemotherapy, she'd insisted on convalescing at home.

It pained Linda to see her mother suffer like this, especially since she had dedicated her own life to saving others. As she trudged upstairs, she wondered, not for the first time, what would become of her if her mother passed away.

When she finally got to her mother's bedroom, she found her half asleep, battling to open her eyes for Linda's sake.

'Oh, my precious baby. Is that really you? I haven't seen you in months,' her mother said as Linda drew closer.

'It hasn't been months, Mom. I was here three weeks ago. How are you feeling?'

'Could be better . . . could be worse.' She laughed quietly. She always tried to see the humour in everything. She used to call the situation between her ex-husband and Monique 'the French Revolution' and Monique's official name in Lunga Mthimkhulu's residence was 'the French'.

'I missed you. I was talking to Uncle Phuti; he says you're not doing so great. What's the matter?'

'Nothing. You know how he is. He worries too much; doesn't get out much. Tell me something, have you heard from your father lately?' she asked unexpectedly.

Linda looked at her mother like a bull that had suddenly spotted a blazing red flag. '*Hhawu*, Mama. Why are you asking me about him? You know I don't like talking about that man.' Then she sighed. She could not help but notice that listening to this simple protest was a struggle for her mother. Something about her was too frail today. At fifty-five, she looked like a woman ten years older. Linda found this quite alarming.

'He's your father, lili girl. You have to make amends with him before it's too late. When I'm gone, you will have nobody. One of the greatest mistakes that Floyd and I made was to only have one child. Of course that twit was worried about what another baby would do to my figure. I guess that's why Monique never gave birth. But I digress. I worry about you, my little sweetheart. The thought of you being left alone in this world kills me.'

'Come on, Mama. Please don't talk like that. You're not going anywhere. Besides, I'm not alone. Your sister, uAunt Nosisa, is like a mother to me, and my cousins, well, they're annoying at times, but they're all right. And then there are my friends, who are an absolute pillar of strength and, of course, there's you! As long as you're still alive, I'm fine,' she said in a panicked tirade. Linda hated it when her mother forced her to contemplate a world without her.

Her mother looked at Linda with glassy eyes. 'You may not like to hear this, but you're a whole lot more like your father than you'd ever admit. Like this thing of yours with Lehumo. I know you broke off the engagement. That's exactly the kind of thing your father would do. I don't want you to be alone in the world. I know that you're very independent, but you can't keep breaking up and making up with people. In the end, they'll start believing it's a game you're playing with them.'

How did her mom know about her break-up? Was it one of her friends who'd betrayed her?

Then she suddenly remembered mentioning it to Uncle Phuti when he last asked after Lehumo. Argh! She could strangle that old man!

Linda had never realised how much insight her mother had into her life, but she was definitely *not* like Floyd.

'*Hhawu*, Mama, I come to visit you and you just pour coals of fire over my head. What have I done to deserve this?'

'I'm tired, Linda. I'm really tired. Baby, let me go to sleep for a while. Will you stay on?'

She looked at her mother. Her eyes were already closed; she was so frail and Linda could tell she was suffering. 'God, please don't take her away,' she said silently. Although Lunga was no longer quite her old self, Linda knew she would feel lost without her.

Chapter 25

Nolwazi

Nolwazi looked at her belly and frowned. It still looked so flat. Was there an actual baby in there? She still struggled to believe it. She was lying on her sofa trying to focus on the eight o'clock news, but her mind kept spinning back to Tebogo and his unforgivable treatment of her. He'd been ignoring her calls, making her feel like some pathetic stalker but she couldn't help herself. He'd managed to accept Dikeledi's child so why couldn't he be as welcoming of her baby? When she finally managed to get hold of him, he'd asked her if she'd come to her senses about getting an abortion.

She'd dropped the phone on him in frustration.

She fidgeted with her tummy and took a deep breath. She looked at her Samsung phone as it lay silently next to her on the sofa.

This is it, she thought. It's now or never. She'd given him an ultimatum as he'd clearly left the ball in her court. She took the phone and scrolled down on her phone contacts until she got to Dikeledi's number.

She sighed, closed her eyes and made to dial Dikeledi when her mobile buzzed.

It was Sade.

'Lwazi, you're the only one who hasn't phoned to congratulate uDikeledi. I just spoke to her now. Haven't you heard the news yet?'

Nolwazi muted the TV. Whatever the anchor woman was saying about the state of the world today could not be as important as anything relating to Dikeledi right now. All of a sudden, a bad premonition gripped her.

'No. What is it?'

'*Shoo!* I'm so glad to be the one telling you this. I thought good news travelled fast, but clearly Linda doesn't think so, otherwise she would have told you!' she enthused.

'What? The suspense is killing me, Sade. Come on.'

'Okay. uTebogo finally proposed to Dikeledi! He did it this afternoon! Isn't it amazing? I mean I know we all have reservations about Tebogo, but I really think those two were made for each other. I honestly can't see either of them settling down with anyone else, especially after all these years, hey?'

Nolwazi was speechless.

'Lwazi . . . are you still there?' asked a confused Sade.

'Um, um. *Ja*. Wow. Um, that's amazing . . . I agree. After all these years,' she said. Her voice sounded like that of an insincere radio DJ, blabbering in the distant background.

'*Ja*. So anyway, I told Linda that we must all go out and celebrate. This is history in the making. I'm sure Dikeledi's broken some kind of Guinness World Record, like for longest bride-in-waiting or something,' she cackled.

'Yeah, sure. You guys let me know when. Listen, Sade, I think someone's knocking on my door. I better go get that. Tell Dikeledi I'm really happy for her,' she said, and quickly put down the phone.

Zombie-like, she went to her bedroom, shut the door, grabbed a pillow and wailed into it. She hoped never to surface again.

Chapter 26

LINDA

Linda finally decided to give Nolwazi a call, two days later than she'd intended, after a full day shoot in Soweto. What had seemed like a straightforward, almost too PR-like story had turned out to be much more disturbing. She was doing a piece on the booming tourism trade in Soweto. As she dug deeper, she was disappointed to stumble upon an exploitative culture of using children to try and milk as much cash from tourists to the area as possible. She worried that if the trend continued it would become a trap for sex tourists – paedophiles who roamed around lenient avenues where they could freely exploit young children by paying them for sexual favours.

She was deeply disturbed by the shoot and her own thoughts following the filming and she desperately needed to just chill with a friend, although she doubted Nolwazi would provide the kind of mindless chatter she needed.

Displaying uncharacteristic cowardice, she hoped someone had already broken the Tebogo news to her.

After two rings, Nolwazi picked up. She was still at work.

'Hey, Linda. *Unjani?* You obviously heard the news?' she asked. After the past couple of days, Nolwazi did not have much fight left in her. She was just depressed – a submissive, nothing-I-can-do-about-it sort of depression.

'Yes. Listen, how about I meet you in Rosebank in half an hour? We can have coffee at Nino's or something.'

'Okay. That sounds okay, but let's not go to Nino's. Let's meet at Primi Piatti instead.'

Later, as Linda parked underground at The Zone shopping mall, she saw Nolwazi's silver Toyota Conquest in the parking bay opposite hers. She was glad Nolwazi had come early. At least it meant she was up to meeting with her. As she went up the escalator, the orange, hip, factory-like interior of Primi Piatti confronted her. Her spirits rose. She liked the young waiters' orange overalls that optimistically proclaimed, 'Work is love made visible'. If only those freelance camera operators she worked with felt that way.

The restaurant had a relaxed, rustic ambience with wooden benches, varnished brick walls and splashy branding with colourful lettering that gave off a carefree and youthful vibe. Their menu was equally spartan, offering less than ten variations of pizza options.

It suited Linda's 'less is more' attitude to everything.

As she passed the first table in the restaurant, she saw Nolwazi in a head wrap that towered over her face, made even tinier by the red headgear. She was sipping a latte. This was a good sign. Like Linda, Nolwazi usually drowned her sorrows in alcohol when she had run out of ways to make them disappear. It suddenly struck her that her coffee-drinking state was all the more commendable because she was, astonishingly enough, about to become a mother.

Linda put down her over-laden bag, self-consciously tugged at her dreadlocks and sat down to join her friend. The waiter came over to their table and asked for Linda's drink order.

'I'll have a glass of white wine please,' she said, anxious to gauge Nolwazi's mood. Once the waiter left, she said, 'So, was it Sade or Dikeledi who told you?'

Nolwazi shrugged. 'Does it matter? The die is cast, isn't it? Not much I can do about it either way,' she said morosely.

'Well,' said Linda as the waiter placed her glass of wine on the table, 'what are you going to do about Tebogo? He's still the father of your child.'

'That bastard!' Nolwazi cursed him, rolling her eyes. 'This has to be the single most stupid thing I have ever done in my life. And you know what the worst bit is?'

'What?' asked Linda, wondering if things could possibly get any worse.

'At work, Ephry's singing my praises. I'm getting to create more and more of my own designs. I just finished off six bridesmaids' dresses for Khanyisile Mbali's wedding. Everybody's raving about them. Ever since that incident with Aldo Mabuza's emergency dress I'm getting the sort of credit I've been yearning for for years! Instead of enjoying this break I'm now stuck with bearing the child of my friend's husband! I really wonder why things like this always happen to me, you know. I must have a big sign that says "Loser for sale, press here to enter".'

'But, babes, you're no loser. It's great that things are picking up at work, and it's not as if you guys do serious manual labour. Your work is all about creativity, which is good, since I hear most gifted people are at their peak when they are pregnant anyway. You could probably work right through to your ninth month. Come to think of it, you should just forget about that creep and focus on your baby and your career. Sometimes the universe is in control of whatever shit we may think is flying off the radar. I don't think it's a coincidence that you're getting all this kudos at this specific point in time, you know.'

Nolwazi looked at her and tried to put on her most cynical face, although she wanted to buy into what Linda was saying. 'Yeah, yeah, yeah, Miss New-Age religion.'

Just then, two good-looking banker types came into the restaurant and grabbed the table next to them. One of them was a tall, light-skinned guy with dimples, a short haircut and muscular shoulders. He wore a pink Yves Saint Laurent shirt, gold cufflinks and form-fitting formal pants. Linda could not help but take a second look. She liked guys who were light in complexion. She thought it went well with her own darker tone, and she definitely fancied corporate-looking types after having dated one too many artists.

Nolwazi, careful not to raise her voice, said, 'If you look at him any harder, he's going to melt from all those hot vibes you're sending.' They both laughed.

Linda leaned towards her. '*Shoo* . . . he is quite hot though, hey?'

Nolwazi stole a glance at them again. 'Hmm, if I had to choose, I'd go for the shorter, darker guy.'

Just then, the shorter of the two men turned towards them and said, 'Excuse me, are you ladies dining alone?'

Nolwazi raised her hands, guru-like, and said, 'No, we're having dinner with our two spiritual guides who would rather remain invisible for now, thank you.' Convivial laughter all round.

'Well, do you mind if we join you?' asked Linda's good-looking chap.

Linda shrugged nonchalantly. 'Don't see any harm either way,' she said.

As the gentlemen took the other two seats at the table, Linda seized the opportunity to assess the object of her desire. She was quite tall herself, so it was important that the guy's height be at least above average. The stranger had a hulking quality to him, which she liked. It was very rare for her to date (or find) guys her height or taller.

After the introductions, Linda was glad to hear her suspicions confirmed. The two were investment bankers who worked a few blocks from Nolwazi's company. They chatted on gaily then, joking like old friends.

Two hours later Nolwazi was ready to call it a night. 'Well, guys, it's been epic. Just that I have an early morning tomorrow,' she said, drumming her hands for emphasis.

Kennedy, the one who had been flirting with Linda the entire time, said, 'Well, if you guys are going, I'll have to close all the doors in this place and lock everybody up until I get Linda's number.'

Linda was glowing. 'Well, for the sake of my fellow patrons, I guess I'd best give it to you right now, mister,' she said. She rattled off her number to Kennedy, who prudently programmed it into his phone.

Miles, the shorter of the two, gave his business card to Nolwazi and asked her to write her details on a piece of paper from his shirt pocket.

After scribbling her number down, Nolwazi warned, 'I hope you don't walk around with pieces of paper to get women's numbers.'

'No way. It's destiny . . . I just knew I'd meet someone special today.'

Nolwazi and Linda both stood up.

Kennedy said, 'So Linda, when is the best time to call?'

She hated it when men asked this question. Did they assume she was married or something? Or maybe a call girl of some sort?

'I'll be entertaining my regular clients till ten, thank you very much.'

Is that what they expected to hear? Besides, how does one answer that sort of question? If you say 'any time', you sound too eager, but then again, if you said something like, 'between eleven fifteen and midnight', it would not bode well for any signs of good mental health either.

She shrugged as she made to leave. 'Dude, call when you wanna call.'

As they were paying for parking, Nolwazi said, 'Linds, the little get-together that's planned by Sade – the one to celebrate the proposal – I just can't go there, hey. I'd feel . . . I can't even begin to imagine how uncomfortable it would be for me to join you guys.'

Linda took her ticket from the machine and nodded. 'Geez, I can imagine, hey, although they'll start wondering about your behaviour.'

'Look, I'll phone them, both of them, and explain that I'll be working late, which, by the way, is true. All you have to do is back me up in case they start asking weird questions.'

Linda hated this whole situation. She hated how it made her feel complicit in Dikeledi's betrayal. Hated how it made her feel like she had to choose between two friends that she loved . . . hated how it made her question Nolwazi's decency . . . and her own, as she was now starting to feel like a co-conspirator of sorts.

Half the time she wanted to be 'bitchy Linda' and scream at Nolwazi for her stupidity, but at the same time, she felt for Nolwazi just as she did for Dikeledi.

They were both casualties of love. No. Not casualties of love but casualties of the poisoned chalice that was Tebogo. The same Tebogo who reminded her of her own father with his easy charm and his devastating effect on women.

She really despised the man.

'Nolwazi, you can't keep running away from this forever. Somehow, Dikeledi's going to find out. I don't know who the best source would be . . . between you and Tebogo, I mean.'

'I haven't had time to think about that. The worst part is, I gave Tebogo an ultimatum on Saturday night because he was leading me on to believe that we could be some sort of item. When I was dumb enough to buy his story he said he wanted me to have an abortion and he'd support me throughout. What I had thought he was saying was that he wanted us to keep the baby and stay together. Amazing how much I've learned to deceive myself, hey?'

Linda could only look at her with sympathy.

'Anyway,' Nolwazi continued, 'it appears that I scared Mr Makwetla into a proposal. I said to him that if he didn't tell Dikeledi within twenty-four hours, I would spill it, so guess what he did? He must have woken up that Sunday morning with his jogging shoes on to look for the first open jewellery store.'

Linda was in shock. 'Ha! So he reckoned if he proposed you'd soon hear about it and, by that time, you'd be too guilt-ridden to burst Kedi's bubble.'

'Yup,' said Nolwazi as she slid her key into her car door.

'So that's it? That's how he gets away with this?' asked Linda, now fully realising the enormity of the situation. She flashed forward to dinner at the 'Makwetlas' with Dikeledi, Tebogo and their three and a half kids. And her, Sade, and Nolwazi sitting around the dinner table pretending that everything was okay.

The vision made her want to start a world war.

How had she become caught up in this web of lies? She loved Dikeledi just as much as she did Nolwazi. It was unfair that she was part of the collateral damage in this nightmare.

'No, Nolwazi, we must do something. This isn't fair on Dikeledi. Can you imagine the weight of this betrayal? It's not only Tebogo who's at fault – you and I are complicit in the fuckery of it all! His proposal is just going to commit her to a life of misery!'

Nolwazi shrugged. 'I don't know, Linda. I'm not in the best position to deal with this. After all, I'm the one who betrayed Dikeledi, if you look at this objectively. I think I should just focus on me and my baby for now. I'll cross the other bridges when I get to them,' she said conclusively as she opened the car door.

But Linda stood firm. 'No! You and Tebogo are equally at fault. You can't just walk away and hope the situation will resolve itself,' she said, folding her arms in protest.

'But what am I supposed to do, hmm? If I tell her about this mess, I'll only look like I'm trying to destroy their relationship. There's no way she'll believe my intentions are honourable. And if I were in her shoes, I wouldn't believe me either. Think about it. I'm the idiot who allowed herself to get knocked-up by her friend's baby daddy. In what universe do I get away with telling her what to do?'

'Fuck. I fuckin' hate this! All you grown-ups are full of shit. I'm dealing with so much shit with my mom and her situation and no one fucking cares. I can't believe you people got me involved in your stupid, incestuous mess!' Linda said as she walked away, fuming.

Nolwazi stepped out of the car and ran towards Linda. 'Linda, wait!' she said, running after her recalcitrant friend. But Linda's strides were quick and firm.

Nolwazi half walked, half ran towards her. Finally catching up with her by Linda's car, she touched her on the shoulder as if Linda were a delicate thing that could break any moment.

'Linds . . . I'm so sorry. I didn't know. What's going on with your mom?'

Linda shrugged her off. 'It doesn't matter. No one cares anyway.'

'I care, Linda. Please tell me what's wrong?'

Linda shrugged again, fighting off tears. 'Nothing. It's all the same. She's dying. What else is there to say?'

Nolwazi felt herself drowning in shame. Of course, Linda needed her. She knew about her mother's condition, but for some reason she had assumed that Linda was coping. As Linda always did.

She never complained about anything. If anything, she always seemed to be the one with the upper hand in all situations. But maybe that was her crutch. Linda never wanted to show weakness.

Nolwazi now realised that maybe she was supposed to read between the lines. After all, nobody wanted to face the prospect of losing their parents. Especially if they were as close to them as Linda was to her mother.

'I'm so sorry I've been such a shitty friend. I was so wrapped up in my own drama that I haven't even checked in on you or Sis Lunga in a while. Please forgive me, buddy? I promise I'll make it up to you,' she said as she leaned in to embrace Linda.

She was surprised by how weakly Linda surrendered to the hug. It tore at her heartstrings to realise how self-absorbed she'd been. She made a silent promise to do better. After all, actions spoke louder than words. The situation with Tebogo was a sobering reminder of that.

Chapter 27

Linda

Linda, Dikeledi and Sade were on their second bottle of wine at the News Cafe in Sandton, celebrating Dikeledi's engagement. The atmosphere, typical of the News Cafe franchise, was young, cosmopolitan, noisy and boisterous, and the girls were in good spirits and enjoying the evening, all the while poking fun at each other.

'Linda, do you remember that geeky guy who liked you when you worked at that production house? What was it called again?' asked Sade.

'Oh no. You mean my first job?'

'*Ja*. You were into a serious phase of weird men at that time. I remember I'd just returned from working at KPMG in Durban and I was looking forward to seeing you guys again.'

Linda squirmed, knowing what was to follow. 'Then you arrived with him at the airport to pick me up in that beat-up old Golf of his and he kept on holding on to your arm like you were gonna run away.'

'I know. He was plenty creepy. But you know what the worst thing about him was?'

'What?' Dikeledi and Sade asked in unison.

'He used to kiss me inside my nostrils. It was so weird . . .'

'Ew, yuck, man!' Sade squealed in delighted disgust. She actually remembered this well, which is why she had regurgitated the tale in the first place. She still enjoyed the telling of the story straight from the nostril-owner's mouth.

'Inside your nostrils how?' asked a perplexed Dikeledi.

'Like literally, fishing for the holes in my nose and sticking his tongue in.'

'Ew!' they screeched, fascinated by the gory details.

'But Sade, you had your fair share of weirdos too. Like that guy who kept stalking you in Durban. That's why you quit that job, isn't it? Didn't you say it's the same guy who once rocked up on campus; the one who was threatening to kill you?' Linda recalled in wine-inspired detachment.

An uncomfortable silence descended on the table. Sade and Dikeledi looked at each other quickly and Sade downed her glass of wine.

'Guys, I need to go to the bathroom,' Sade said stiffly.

After Sade had left, an eerie cloud hovered in the air. Dikeledi looked at Linda as if weighing up what to say. 'Linda. That guy . . . we're not really supposed to talk about him. He's . . . he's just somebody who's a nasty stain on Sade's past. I mean, especially now with Winston. I get the feeling that there are certain things that Sade wants buried forever. There's something about her relationship with Winston that tells me she doesn't need to revisit things like that, okay? It's complicated.'

Linda was completely lost. She vaguely remembered that after the guy had been held in custody by campus security he'd been sent to a nearby mental hospital. She had not been there to witness the harassment of Sade but apparently he had been badgering her throughout the Easter break.

Sade and Dikeledi, who had been honours students at that stage, had decided to spend the Easter holidays in their shared digs in Cape Town instead of going home to Durban; Nolwazi had gone home to the Eastern Cape, while Linda had stayed with her mother in Woodmead. Although there had been a lot of rumours about what the guy did or did not do to Sade, Dikeledi and her friend had been very scant with the details to Nolwazi and Linda. It seemed there was more to this guy than met the eye because years later he had managed to locate Sade at the management consulting firm where she worked, and had caused a scene there too, which later forced Sade to relocate to Gauteng.

As Linda sipped her drink, it suddenly occurred to her that there were more secrets in this shared friendship than any of them were willing to admit. She wondered how long before the Pandora's box would spill open, destroying their comfort zones forever. She shuddered at the thought.

Sade came back to join them, seemingly confident that the distasteful subject had been put to rest. 'So, Linda, are you sure Nolwazi's telling the truth when she says she's working late? I mean, do designers do things like hike up their billable hours?'

Linda rolled her eyes. 'How do I answer that question, Sade? Ask it differently, minus the management consultant BS.'

Dikeledi intercepted the impending tiff with a small laugh. 'You know what she means, Linds. Nolwazi's been acting shady lately. Locking herself up in her room on her birthday, not calling to say congrats on my engagement, and now this? Something's obviously up. Spill it.'

Linda put on her best poker face, suddenly feeling nauseous at the very mention of Nolwazi from Dikeledi's mouth.

Things had been tensing between her and Nolwazi since their confrontation at the parking lot at The Zone. To her credit, Nolwazi had been trying to make amends. She'd even brought over chocolate cake from Lunga's favourite bakery the last time she came to visit.

Linda's mom had always liked Nolwazi. A fashionable woman in her youth, Lunga's chats with Nolwazi were peppered with references to what was happening on local and international runways; a topic that Linda neither possessed nor desired to possess a lexicon for.

But now, as always, when she was with Dikeledi and Sade, she felt an odd duty to protect Nolwazi.

'Okay, okay. You know Nolwazi with her low self-esteem issues. She's doing great at work, that's why she's so scarce, but if she were to tell you that, she'd feel like she's boasting or something. I mean she's getting these great gigs, like that socialite Khanyisile Mbali's wedding.'

'The shameless one who's married some rich gazillionaire twice her age?' offered Sade.

'The one and only. Lwazi just finished creating this amazing ensemble of dresses for that chick's bridesmaids and I think she's brought in a tidy sum for her company. Plus, the bridal dress, which was designed by Ephry, and Nolwazi's bridesmaids' designs, will be featured in upcoming bridal editions of three major women's magazines.'

'Wow,' said an excited Dikeledi. 'This is great. A toast to Nolwazi, the reluctant genius.'

They all raised their drinks.

'Damn. I didn't know we had such talent right under our noses. I feel guilty now that I had my wedding dress designed by Sun Goddess,' said Sade.

'Well,' said Dikeledi, 'Nolwazi can still design our bridesmaids' dresses.'

Linda did not like where this was going.

'And I definitely want her to design my wedding dress,' said Dikeledi, rather inevitably, now that Linda thought about it. She wished she could yank her foot out of her mouth right at that moment.

'Umm,' Sade began, 'about the whole bridesmaid thing. You guys, you've been my best friends forever, and Kedi, I've known you for practically all my life, so you are like a sister to me.' She paused, then sipped her wine for Dutch courage.

She looked away from them briefly. 'You guys don't really take all that bridesmaid stuff seriously, do you? I mean, we're empowered women; we don't need our friendship to be defined by stuff like that, right?' she asked unconvincingly.

The other two had no idea where she was headed with this.

Linda shook her head and said, 'Sade, what's going on?'

Scratching the back of her head uncharacteristically, Sade could barely look them in the eye. 'It's just that . . . at church, we have certain rituals, and . . . and standards that we have to abide by. The maid of honour has to be somebody from my cell group and Winston and I have discussed this extensively. The people at church are the ones who take centre stage in matters like this, but you guys will sit with me at the main table, and everything will be just great,' Sade explained with a fixed smile and tensed shoulders, looking like a well-programmed Stepford wife.

The other two could not believe their ears.

'Sade, you are a sister to me. What do you mean I'm not going to be your maid of honour? No one knows you better than I do. This is insane. This will be your biggest day and you're prepared to share it with strangers? I've never heard of anything like this. That church of yours must be some damned crazed cult!' raged Dikeledi, who was usually more restrained.

Linda just looked at them. Either way, she was glad she didn't have to wear one of those frequently hideous bridesmaids' dresses. No reflection on Nolwazi's designs intended, but she knew that with Sade's sometimes poisonous streak, she was definitely going to ensure that she outshone her bridesmaids. A sure-fire way for her to do this would be to pick some shocking colour like yellow, which had no chance in hell of making a pretty wedding frock. So as far as the church cell groupies were concerned, she could only say, let them enjoy it. Relief was Linda's middle name right now.

'Listen, Kedi,' Sade continued, 'I'm not betraying you or anything. You guys will be right there with me at the main table, just a few seats away. If I need anything, I'll just slip in between you and share my panic! It's not as bad as it sounds. Winston and I are very active in the church; if we defect from its norms it would raise a lot of eyebrows. In the long term, we want our children to be an integral part of the church community. You see, it's our faith that binds us together so if we mess up on that front, it would feel like we're allowing the wheels to come off early in the game. Please, please try to understand.'

Dikeledi, whose sweet nature could never be faulted, had folded her arms in quiet protest, but Linda could see the thin sliver of ice between her and Sade thawing rapidly.

Finally Dikeledi shrugged. 'I guess with all the sacrifices I've made for my man, I can hardly judge you for your cultish behaviour,' she said with a smile.

Sade bumped against her playfully. 'Thanks, Kedi, I knew you'd understand – but my church is definitely *not* a cult!'

Chapter 28

Nolwazi

Nolwazi had been stewing on Tebogo's diabolical engagement to Dikeledi for months. Meanwhile, her belly seemed more eager than ever to make its presence felt.

As she lay down on her bed, distractedly watching Linda's award-winning documentary on her laptop, she once again pondered her life and the miserable situation she was in. She'd been to the obstetrician for her five-month ultrasound scan yesterday and had come back home feeling teary about the solitude she felt on her maternal journey. Linda had accompanied her to two of her scans, but of course she could not expect her to play the role of a full-time Tebogo proxy; she had her own troubles to worry about.

She'd managed to avoid more than three invitations from the girls but realised that the jig was finally up for her; she could not come up with any more excuses. All four of the girls were gainfully employed; a fashion designer could only have so many work-related excuses for not showing up for her friends.

But the thought of smiling along while Dikeledi gushed about her engagement to Tebogo made her stomach turn. Not because she was jealous of Dikeledi. No. She had long passed the phase of yearning for Tebogo's love. All she could think of now was how Tebogo had manipulated Dikeledi to get his own way in this situation. What was she to do?

She felt like bolting like a wild horse. Running away. From her friends. From Tebogo. From life as she knew it.

But no. Why was she being such a coward?

She leaned over to the side pedestal next to her bed and grabbed her phone and scrolled down to Tebogo's number. She couldn't believe she'd managed to restrain herself from texting him for three whole months, but why was she letting him get away with such criminal behaviour? What he was doing to both her and Dikeledi was unforgivable.

She stopped for a moment and thought about what she was about to do. Then she smiled ruefully and texted.

Congratulations on your pending nuptials.

That should put him on the spot.

No response for almost an hour. She'd been checking while trying to pay attention to the documentary.

It satisfied her to think he was sweating buckets about how he would respond to the text.

Finally, he replied . . .

Thank you!

The nerve! What the hell was wrong with this guy? She typed quickly.

Fuck you!

Then '. . . *Tebogo is typing*'.

Then . . . Nothing.

A void. A dark silence. Nothing at all.

She wanted to kill him! At the very least, she'd expected him to offer an explanation; no matter how lousy it could be. But this was it. Just 'Thank you'. She felt like a total idiot.

Chapter 29

LINDA

Linda came out of her mom's feeling encouraged. Her mother's condition seemed to be improving, although the doctors were cautious about giving too optimistic a picture. They had sat and chatted for almost an hour and her mom seemed to be in a good mood, even though the doctors had prescribed another round of chemotherapy with morphine to help her deal with the pain.

The only explanation she could think of for Lunga's upbeat mood was that her doctor had agreed to her getting the treatments at home. Linda noticed some weirdly naughty glances between her and Uncle Phuti, which sparked an inappropriate but fleeting curiosity about their sex life.

It was only later, when she realised she had left her phone and had to drive back to the apartment, that she discovered what the naughty glances were about. She found Uncle Phuti rolling a joint of marijuana while Lunga smoked hers languidly with her eyes closed.

'You guys!' she said, scolding them as if they were naughty teens.

Lunga laughed as she cleared the smoke. 'Stop it. Cancer's no joke, child. At least let me enjoy my spliff.'

She looked at her mom with her clean-shaven head, then at the man who'd devoted his heart to her, and just appreciated the love that she felt at this moment: for her mother and for this gentle man who'd showered her mom with such joy and devotion over the years.

Linda laughed and went over to kiss both on the cheek then went to get her phone from her mother's bedroom.

As she stepped in the car to go to work, Linda checked her phone and found several missed calls listed. She saw that one was from an overseas number – her father. What did he want? Every time she thought about that man, her blood boiled. She knew he'd probably left some cheery message, as if the fact that she never returned any of his calls had absolutely no impact on him. Sometimes she could not believe that this was the same man who used to carry her on his shoulders when she was younger; the same man who'd bought her tampons for her first period – they had once been so close. What had happened to him? Had he always been this shallow and selfish? Maybe she had been too young to notice back then.

Before listening to the messages, she went to a small cafe and ordered a tuna sandwich and flavoured water. She wanted to fuel up before going to the office.

The first message was from Kennedy! The guy she'd met with Nolwazi months before. Mmm, that boy was seriously gorgeous. He wanted to know if she was free for dinner on Wednesday. Man, and it was only Monday! She had to count an entire two days before seeing him again.

Her favourite part of a relationship was the beginning. She liked the whole butterflies-in-the-stomach, getting-to-know-you-better phase; but why was she so hopeless at staying the course? She didn't need to pay a psychologist to know that part of her man problems probably had something to do with her father. Speaking of which, she thought, she'd better listen to the rest of the messages.

Sure enough, there was the familiar, cheery voice: 'Hey, baby girl, I heard from your Uncle Jabu that your mom is not doing well. Please call me, precious. I want you to know that your old man still cares a great deal about you. I know I haven't always been the perfect dad, but don't shut me out now; I'm the one shoulder you can cry on at a time like this. Please call me.' And then he started singing, 'I love you, *je t'aime, je t'aime*, darling Linda.'

Why he always felt the need to include some crappy French in his messages completely escaped her. Was he high? Did he have any clue how annoying that was? A permanent reminder that he'd left her and her mother for that French woman!

She was not going to return *that* call, but she certainly wanted to speak to Kennedy. She dialled his number.

After the first ring, he answered. 'Let it ring a bit. You don't want to seem too eager,' she said, deliberately sounding serious.

'Umm, no, I was actually just finishing another call when your call came through,' he said. Was he a touch nervous?

She laughed. 'Just joking. Don't sweat it. How was your trip to Nigeria?'

She was elated that he'd finally returned from his seemingly eternal work trip. She had tried not to think about him after their first meeting at Primi and when he sent her sporadic messages while he was away, she decided to take a casual approach to their friendship.

'Fine. You know how it is. Those of us in the not-so-creative fields don't enjoy ourselves as much as you glamorous types do. Sometimes I wish I could have superpowers that allow me to do different jobs every day. Like one day I'm a schoolteacher and the next day I'm a movie star, or even better, a big-shot TV producer like you.'

'Spooky. How do you know what I do? And, by the way, I'm not a big-shot producer, just part of the working class. So, are you a stalker?' she asked, enjoying teasing him.

'Hey, I'm no stalker. I think you mentioned it the night we met or in one of your texts and besides, I googled you. Joburg is a dark and murky place. I try to get to know about the type of people who keep walking around my head after spending a mere two hours with them.'

She liked that. So, he'd been thinking about her. Well, she had been thinking about him quite a bit since that day at Primi Piatti too. 'No wonder I'm so tired. All that walking inside your head's done me in,' she said, happy to be cheesy with him. For now.

'Anyway, listen, I need to get cracking on some work stuff but consider me in for Wednesday, okay?'

'Great. It's a date. Cheers hey.'

'Bye,' she said, before hanging up.

◆　◆　◆

Two days later Linda was getting ready for her big date with Kennedy. Why was she so nervous preparing for a date with this guy? She didn't remember ever feeling like this with Lehumo, or anyone else for that matter. Scary!

She'd slipped out of work at four to get her dreadlocks washed and styled at a salon. She then rushed home, saw a sexy lingerie shop on her way and decided to stop and buy a matching lingerie set; not that she was planning on letting him see so much, but she was feeling very sexy and wanted to exude femininity. When she got home she showered, put on some subtle make-up and donned her favourite date outfit: a sexy strappy black top, skinny jeans and killer heels. She did not like wearing dresses on the first date – she did not want to seem like she was trying too hard.

She got into her Jeep, put on some Barry White and sang loudly to the music all the way to the restaurant where she was to meet Kennedy for dinner.

When she reached her destination, she looked in the mirror once more, sprayed on some Tommy Girl and stepped out of the car as gracefully as possible, in case he was watching.

She found him already seated, looking at the menu. 'Hey there,' she said, when she arrived at the table.

He looked up and smiled. *Oh my gosh.* He actually looked better than she remembered. He was wearing a crisp white shirt with cufflinks again, and she noticed that his teeth were almost as white as his shirt. Ah . . . *men* . . . Alleluia.

She sat down, and they started chatting, awkwardly at first, but, once the food arrived, they started to loosen up.

'So tell me, Linda . . . you are very pretty, funny, smart and interesting. How come you're still single? Are Joburg guys that blind?' he asked, as he took the glass of red wine the waiter offered him.

Linda was cutting into her kingklip and paused. It was nice that he thought she was pretty and all the other stuff, but was it appropriate to talk about Lehumo right now? Maybe not . . . but then, what if this was the beginning of something? She was smart enough to know that honesty was the best policy. Especially after having come out of an engagement to someone she had realised she did not love.

She shrugged in what she hoped seemed a casual gesture. 'Well, there was someone fairly recently, but it didn't work out. We were not really compatible.'

'Oh. Had you guys been dating for a while?'

She nodded.

'So when did you realise you were not compatible?'

Now it was her turn to sip her wine. 'We were actually engaged, but we realised that the relationship was not really going to work.'

It now dawned on her how shoddy the whole Lehumo break-up had been. The fact that she could not share the details with this beautiful stranger was a sure sign that she had been unfair on Lehumo.

'Guilt, where did you get my number?' she wondered in pure panic.

Kennedy was quiet for a while, as if he was allowing this bit of news to sink in. 'I hope I'm not being too forward, but who decided that it wouldn't work – you or him?'

Now she was getting annoyed. Was this a date or the Spanish Inquisition? Couldn't the guy give her a break? A bit of room to breathe?

'*Ag*, man. You know, I don't think I'm really ready to talk about it . . . not that I'm still hurting or anything,' she added quickly, suddenly realising that Kennedy might misinterpret this to mean she was still not over her ex.

He shrugged. 'Okay. I can understand that. An engagement is quite a big thing. I'm sure there's a lot you still need to process,' he offered.

She nodded, suddenly feeling awkward. She wiped her mouth with a napkin and excused herself to go to the ladies' room.

When she got to the bathroom, she looked at herself in the mirror and started to feel waves of panic. She'd blown it. She'd never thought about how this engagement thing might crop up in a conversation with a new (and staggeringly attractive) suitor. Admittedly, her actions towards Lehumo were not exactly noble – okay, maybe they were a bit churlish – but her mom had always warned her against settling for the sake of it. She did not want to wind up in an unhappy marriage. She'd done both her and Lehumo a favour, damn it!

Then why was it so difficult to explain to Kennedy? Because women did not walk out on men. It was supposed to be the other way round. Like her dad and the way he'd walked out on her mom. What a warped world. Okay. She needed to go back out there and salvage the situation before that gorgeous man ran for it.

A few minutes later, she was back at their table. She sat down and resumed eating.

'So tell me about you. Anyone special in your life in recent times?'

He shook his head. 'The last time I was in a serious relationship was two years ago. She left to go and live in the States. I've been sort of travelling light ever since – in terms of relationships, that is. My work has become very demanding; there's a position I'm vying for, and to get it, I must put in serious hours. Don't let that put you off though. I think I'll be hearing some good news in a month or so.'

She smiled knowingly. 'I know what that's like. I'm a bit of a workaholic myself, but I'm also trying to slow down these days. Those annoyingly wise people always say that when you're about to die, you won't be saying, "I wish I'd spent more time at the office."'

He toasted to that. 'I hear ya. It's funny though, with people our age in Joburg. Have you noticed how everybody's just pushing themselves to death? Is it the big chase for the luxury car or the house at the right address?'

She shrugged. 'It's never been about that for me. I love the work I do. Seriously, don't look at me like that,' she said, as he rolled his eyes teasingly. 'I really enjoy it. I get to meet different people, get steeped into their lives for a few days, really get to know them and have empathy for them. It's almost like having the ability to do different things every day.'

He laughed. 'Okay. So what do we call you? Super Linda?'

'Nah. Wonder Woman will do just fine,' she said, beginning to enjoy herself.

She liked this guy. She felt it in her gut. She was terrified that maybe, just maybe, this was the first time she had ever really liked anyone.

'You know what would be really nice? There's this friend of mine in Hartbeespoort who owns a nice little boat. Maybe we could go boating with him sometime. Since we're both workaholics, what say we look at each other's busy schedules and see if we can squeeze in a Saturday outing? How is this Saturday afternoon?'

She grinned. 'Okay.'

Her heart was screaming with elation. After all that awkwardness, she'd passed the first round. Phew!

Chapter 30

Nolwazi

It was the day of Sade's wedding and Linda (with Nolwazi next to her) drove her Jeep through the picture-perfect grounds of Avianto, a wedding venue in Muldersdrift that inspired even the biggest cynic to daydream about exchanging vows with a tuxedoed groom.

The Tuscan-style building was offset by sprawling yards of impeccably manicured greenery, well contrasted with the blooming azaleas, roses and lilies. The tall, bold trees completed the scene of an ideal garden wedding.

Sade had been wise to choose her birthday, the twentieth of October, to host the wedding, because the sun shone so brightly it was as if the hand of God had extended a blessing to the Khumalo–Gumede union. And of course, Winston would never forget their wedding anniversary.

'I'm definitely showing, aren't I?' asked a nervous Nolwazi, as she roamed her hand over her slightly swollen belly. Her slender frame still looked gym-trim but the now six-month-old bump was difficult to conceal even in the flowing bare-back red and gold chiffon dress. Despite choosing something that would not hug her figure, the fruit of Tebogo's seed refused to stay hidden.

'Look, if I were you, I would start thinking of a story for all the questions you're gonna get about whether you've gained weight or not, and, of course, knowing someone as straight-shooting as Sade means you are highly likely to get the direct "are-you-preggers" question.'

'Oh, it's her day today. She can't afford to spoil it on my account. Besides, isn't she supposed to be the new and improved version of her former self?' she asked, brushing her eggshell belly with mounting worry.

'Humph,' groaned Linda, 'I don't know about that. All I'm saying is: brace yourself, my dear little lamb.'

'Linda, you do realise that you're not really comforting me right now?'

'Babes, this is a pregnancy; it's not going anywhere so you might as well angle it into your daily conversations because people are not going to pretend to be blind to that big, bulging tummy. You must start thinking of a standard answer to the questions. Maybe just own up that your secret lover knocked you up and then upped and ran away. It's a common enough story. If it weren't, those American country singers would be out of work.'

Nolwazi digested this for a while. She looked at herself in the passenger mirror. With a sigh, she realised that she looked better than she had in ages. Her face was slightly rounder, making her look more feminine and at peace with herself. She liked this. So far, being pregnant was not as bad an experience as she had anticipated, except for the morning sickness. She had to admit that Linda had been a wonderful source of support over the past few months, although she could try and ease up on the tough-love thing. Maybe it was time, though, for Nolwazi to face up to reality. Although she was far from forgiving Tebogo for what he had done, she was less hard on herself about the overall situation. The one thing that was really helping her cope was the wonderful turnaround that was occurring in her workplace. She was now treated as a fully fledged designer, and, as Linda had said, her creative spark was at an unbelievable peak.

Thankfully though, Nolwazi had been spared the discomfort of designing Sade's odd bridesmaids' dresses because one of the ladies at Sade's church had offered to do them for next to nothing. Sade claimed that since she was not so close to these ladies, she might as well spare a penny where the opportunity presented itself. They all found this aspect of her wedding extremely bizarre but decided to keep mum, lest they offend Sade and her husband-to-be.

As they joined the bevy of luxury German cars in the parking lot next to the chapel where the wedding party was, Linda looked at her watch once more and bemoaned the fact that they were at least an hour late, thanks to Nolwazi's dilly-dallying about which outfit would make the dreaded bulge less obvious.

They scurried into the quaint chapel – joining the last pew – where the ever-flamboyant, larger-than-life Pastor Franks of the New Revival Fellowship presided. This pastor was like none that Linda had ever seen. Being an Anglican girl herself, she was used to the subdued, almost grave priests from her church. On the few occasions she had accompanied Sade to the New Revival Fellowship, she had observed that Pastor Franks looked more like a rock 'n' roller who was about to go on tour than a man of the cloth.

Today he had abandoned his customary jeans and cowboy boots for a rather dashing, all-white, Hugo Boss suit. Pastor Franks certainly practised what he preached. As much as he often motivated his followers to go out there and be the best that they could be, he certainly lived up to this credo. His collection of properties was only outmatched by the Porsche, Rolls-Royce and Harley-Davidsons parked in his garage.

The fact that the man himself was presiding over the Gumedes' wedding was a significant barometer of Sade and Winston's standing in their popular church. Members of the New Revival Fellowship were mostly from Jozi's elite nouveau set, and the congregation that had gathered in the tiny chapel glistened with the golden faces that usually inked up the society pages of local tabloids. Much to her surprise, Linda noted not one but three celebrities among Sade's bridesmaids, who were distinctive in aquamarine and white satin dresses. Linda enjoyed a private grin. Although not as garish as she had expected (which must have had something to do with the celebs using their considerable social leverage to fight the good fight), the dresses still looked like they were better left to the experts to wear.

Linda was beginning to question the whole church-standard requirements for bridesmaids story that Sade had fed her and Dikeledi months earlier. She knew Sade loved to be perceived as high society these days – a trait she seemed to share with her beloved, perfect fiancé – so could it be that Linda and the other girls' status as Sade's closest friends had been usurped by the power of celebrity?

Somewhere inside Linda was a young girl who still yearned for the wild, unassuming, take-me-as-I-am Zulu buddy she had immediately clicked with at varsity. Where was that girl today? She had to admit she missed her. Looking back, she could not believe that once upon a time, she and Sade were the closest among the four. It would be heart-breaking if Sade had indeed become that cynical: swapping friends for celebrities. That would be sinking to new depths. Suddenly she thought of her father, the 'beautiful people's person', as he used to call himself. Maybe she and Sade were switched at birth. Looking at the medley of high-powered businessmen, the odd pot-bellied politician and the collection of celebrities, it suddenly occurred to Linda that Floyd would take to this scene like a duck to water.

'Where's Dikeledi?' whispered Nolwazi.

Linda looked around, struggling to locate her. 'I don't know, but I think this part is almost over so we'll probably see her when we step out.'

Just then, the pastor proclaimed, 'You may now kiss the bride,' and Sade, who looked resplendent in her traditionally inspired white dress, planted a lingering kiss on her new husband who cut a dashing figure in a black designer tuxedo.

As the guests erupted in a wave of ululation and praise, Tumi, a prominent gospel singer, burst into song with a traditional wedding ditty. The rest of the congregation joined her as they accompanied the newlyweds out of the church towards the large white marquee set up on the lawn.

As the throng walked in rhythmic step following the Gumedes, Nolwazi felt someone touch her arm. When she looked up, she saw Dikeledi standing next to a decidedly uncomfortable Tebogo. With them was Phemelo in a white fairy dress, which, as she remembered, was how Linda had described Phemelo when they'd seen her at the shopping mall. A lump of panic formed in Nolwazi's throat.

'Hi, Dikeledi! I was looking for you inside the church; where were you guys sitting?' she asked, offering Dikeledi a perfunctory hug.

'We were in the front row. What time did you guys arrive? I hope Sade didn't notice how late you were.'

Thankfully, Linda appeared behind the party of four. She kissed Phemelo on the cheek. 'Look at you! You're so gorgeous.'

'Thanks, Aunty Linda,' she said shyly.

'Hi, Tebogo,' she said, hoping to sound as icy as possible.

'Hi, Linda. Let me leave you ladies to your women's stuff. Phemelo, let's go and talk to Preston there. Give your mom and her friends some air, okay, angel?'

'Okay, Daddy,' she said enthusiastically. She loved being glued to her father's side.

Nolwazi looked at them together and felt a pang of jealousy.

Linda took both Nolwazi and Dikeledi's hands. 'So, it's one down and three to go, guys. One of the team has been permanently dispatched to that eternal institution of marriage.'

'Hmm, don't count on me sticking around the single girls' club for too long,' proclaimed Dikeledi, holding out her left hand to show off the gleaming engagement band. 'This ring is my exit strategy, girls.'

'Let me see it again,' said Linda, taking hold of Dikeledi's wedding finger. 'It's gorgeous,' she said, her voice lacking enthusiasm. 'At least Tebogo finally made good.'

For a split second Nolwazi did not know what to do, but then Sade appeared, all smiles and warm hugs. She really did look like a fairy-tale princess.

'Oh yes! My best friends! I've missed you guys so much! I must show you the seats allocated to you on my VIP table. Come with me,' she gushed, holding Dikeledi and Nolwazi by the hand, with Linda trailing behind them.

Best friends. VIP table. Oh lawd, thought Linda, rolling her eyes.

The interior of the marquee was tastefully decorated. Flower centrepieces blended elegantly with gold organza overlays draped over cream tablecloths. The entire tent was draped in gold and white with tie-backs and fairy lights that added detail to the decoration. As guests entered the venue, four violinists were already playing, setting the scene for a classy and romantic wedding.

A long table, also adorned with a cream tablecloth, was set out at the front of the marquee for Sade's VIP guests. Twenty covered and decorated chairs were lined up behind the table. Sade sat her friends at the far end of the table as the guests started trickling in.

'Guys, you see what I mean when I said you'd be by my side throughout. Winston and I will be sitting in the middle there, so whenever you want to come over and chat, please feel free to do that,' she said.

Linda rolled her eyes. She noticed that their seats were about six places from Sade and her husband. She calculated that the Barbie bridesmaids, along with their Ken dolls, would probably be sitting at either side of the wedded pair. Meanwhile, the other two ladies showered compliments on Sade about her dress and praised the venue.

'Do you know Mafikizolo's been booked to perform a few traditional love songs later today when we all start to unwind?' she asked an enthralled Nolwazi and Dikeledi.

'Wow? I love that group. How'd you manage to secure them? Hey, *wena*, you're full of surprises,' said Dikeledi, visibly impressed.

'Let's just say I know people who know people.' Sade winked, then did a double-take as she gaped at Nolwazi's belly.

'Lwazi, are you pregnant?'

'Oh, here we go,' mumbled Linda.

'What? No, no, I'm not,' stuttered Nolwazi.

'You are too! Stand up, let me see you . . . I swear, she's pregnant. Dikeledi, don't you see it?'

Dikeledi was amused. She could not imagine Nolwazi being pregnant. 'Come on, *wena*, Miss Bride, Nolwazi's just picking up some weight. It's natural when you turn thirty. In fact, it's a very common and healthy trend. Nolwazi, don't let this one get to you. It suits you. You look more content and comfortable in your own skin.'

Sade just kept staring at Nolwazi's stomach. '*Hhayi!* I know a pregnant woman when I see one. Look at you – you even have that gorgeous glow! Linda, what do you think?'

Linda just looked at her. 'Don't you see you're making Nolwazi feel uncomfortable?'

'Lwazi,' Sade persisted, 'you're not uncomfortable, are you? Please stand up for me. I want to see if I really am just being a nasty old cow.'

'Sade, stop it!' said Linda.

Suddenly Nolwazi spoke up. 'Linda, it's fine. They might as well know the truth; it's inevitable anyway. You're right, Sade. I am pregnant.'

Sade clapped her hands. 'You see! I knew it. Now tell, tell. Who's the father?'

Without warning, Tebogo emerged from nowhere, Phemelo in tow, and hovered above them. 'Sorry to interrupt you ladies, but babes, where's the car keys? I need to fetch my camera.'

Sade pushed his leg away playfully. '*Hey wena*, Motswana. You're interrupting something crucial here. As the bride around here, my time is seriously limited and I need to hear this so you're just gonna have to wait,' she said, and turned back to Nolwazi. 'So, babes, who is the father?'

Nolwazi looked up at Tebogo and immediately felt sick. 'Excuse me, guys. I need the bathroom,' she said, as she rose with one hand covering her mouth as if she were fighting nausea. Linda followed her.

Dikeledi looked at Sade, and then at Tebogo. 'She seems upset. *Wena*, Sade, can't you, for once, be more sensitive? She's obviously not ready to talk about it,' said Dikeledi, folding her arms and casting an accusatory look at her friend.

Sade shrugged. 'I didn't know that's how she was going to react. It's a natural question to ask under the circumstances. Tebogo, do you think I was wrong to ask? Everybody's turning me into a wicked witch on my own wedding day. Was I wrong, Tebogo?' she repeated, pleading for affirmation.

Tebogo looked very uncomfortable. 'Hey guys, this is women's stuff. From my experience, it's best not to get involved. Babes, car keys, please,' he said urgently as he extended his hand to Dikeledi.

Dikeledi did not budge. 'No, Tebogo, you were here to witness the whole thing. I mean, Sade asked that question right in front of you, for crying out loud, even though it was clear that Nolwazi was too embarrassed to even admit to the pregnancy in the first place. I really think you've crossed the line, Sade, and I'm not going to pretend I'm okay with it.'

'Really, Kedi? On my wedding day? Why are you guys being so mean?'

'You always do this, Sade. Deflecting from issues when they're staring you in the face.'

Tebogo wanted the whole scene to come to a rapid and final close. 'Kedi, it's okay. It's Sade's day. Just let it slide, please, baby. This is not who you are.'

Dikeledi looked at Tebogo then at Sade. She knew she'd had quite a bit to drink, which was not her style, but she was wholly unhappy about a lot of things that had been happening around her. With the wine spurring her on, she continued.

'No, Tebogo, I'm sorry, but Sade is my best friend and quite frankly I don't understand what's happening at this wedding. I don't understand why some women we don't know are bridesmaids. I don't understand why I'm not the maid of honour. I don't even understand why my friend is pregnant and hiding it. None of this makes sense. It just feels so very fake. All of it. I thought I knew all of you but nothing about this day feels genuine to me. I'm sorry, Sade, but I can't keep pretending all of this is okay anymore.'

Tebogo looked abashedly at Sade and wished the ground could open and swallow him whole.

As he wondered how to respond to this tirade, Sade started crying. 'So you're saying I'm a selfish, cold-hearted bitch? Thanks for letting me know. Thanks for telling me that on my wedding day. You're a really great friend!' she said, scrambling for a tissue, which Dikeledi whisked out of her bag and handed her icily.

Some of the people who had already taken their seats started whispering. Since this was all happening at the front of the marquee, they could not help but wonder what was making the bride look so crestfallen.

Winston came over, concern on his face. 'What's the matter, baby? Who's done this to you?' he asked as he looked accusingly at Dikeledi and Tebogo. Sade just offered him her hand and they quickly disappeared, away from the gathering crowd.

Chapter 31

NOLWAZI

Nolwazi examined herself critically in the bathroom mirror as Linda came out of one of the lavatories. As she washed her hands, Linda kept looking at her to make sure she was okay.

'I could drop you off at home if you're too uncomfortable to face everyone, you know,' she offered, drying her hands under the automatic hand dryer.

Nolwazi shook her head. 'No, I'm okay,' she sighed. 'At least it's out there. After what happened, I doubt that even someone as callous as Sade would ask me the baby-daddy question again.'

Linda grabbed her bag and said, 'Hmm, you'd be surprised.'

Rummaging for something in her bag before stepping out, Nolwazi said, 'Linds, would you give me your car keys? I think I left my make-up bag in the car.'

Linda hesitated. 'Do you want me to come with you?' she asked, fishing the keys out of her bag.

'No, I'll be fine. I'll meet you back in there. Don't worry about me, man,' she emphasised, seeing the concern on Linda's face.

'Okay. I'll see you inside then.'

The parking lot was almost completely deserted. Nolwazi enjoyed strolling to the car with nothing but the dazzling green lawn ahead of her and the bright sunlight warming her exposed back. She finally located Linda's Jeep and clicked the remote to open the front door.

After searching for the brown make-up bag, she found it under the passenger seat. As she sat up to fix her face in the car's rear-view mirror, her dress riding up her thighs, she realised that someone was standing next to the car, watching her. To her irritation, it was the last person she wanted to lay her eyes on.

'Tebogo, what are you doing here? Shouldn't you be in there with your fiancée?'

He pushed the slightly opened door wider, to allow him more room to stand closer to her. 'Nolwazi, listen, we need to talk. I mean, I feel really lousy about this whole situation. I never thought it would turn out like this.'

Nolwazi did not know what to do with him. She just wanted him to disappear. 'Do me a favour, and leave me alone, okay?' she said, trying to remain cool and aloof by applying powder on her face, all the while looking in the mirror.

'I just want us to talk for a few minutes. Please step out of the car. Let's just talk about this thing. I don't want you thinking I'm this bad guy for the rest of your life. I mean, we all make mistakes; it's just that there is a lot at stake for me here.'

Nolwazi closed the lid of her powder box and threw it into the make-up bag. She sighed heavily, looked around to see if anyone was watching, and stepped out of the car. 'What do you want from me, hmm? You want me to say, sure it's fine. Go to your fiancée and I'll just be the idiot walking around with a tummy full of something that doesn't have a father? Mmm? Is that what you want, Tebogo?'

He moved closer to her, but Nolwazi noticed that he had pushed the door even further back to make sure they were concealed. 'Listen, Lwazi, I'm not a bad person. I offered a solution that I thought could work, but you must know that by not taking it, it means you are making your own decision about this. I can't—'

With all the force she could summon in her slender arm, Nolwazi threw a whopper of a punch across Tebogo's face before he could continue any further. 'Just leave me alone, you dog!' she screamed and rushed back to the marquee.

Chapter 32

LINDA

Linda was sitting next to Dikeledi, watching the maid of honour, Palesa, sashay around the room. She wore a low-cut dress that emphasised her generous cleavage. Linda noticed something odd when Palesa went to stand next to the groom; her bosom was at eye level to Winston, who was seated. She noticed how Palesa straightened her posture so that her breasts seemed even bigger. Linda nudged Dikeledi. 'Uh-oh. Bunny-boiler alert.'

'What?' asked Dikeledi.

'Look,' said Linda, moving her head in the direction of Palesa and Winston. 'The maid of honour seems to have more maid in her than honour. She's been thrusting her boobs at Winston for the past five minutes, and Winston does not seem to mind the view at all.'

Dikeledi laughed uncomfortably. 'No, man. Winston only has eyes for Sade. That's his varsity buddy.'

Linda shrugged and rolled her eyes. 'I dunno. If my husband's varsity buddy were to sway her boobs like that at him, I'd give her breast-reduction surgery faster than you could say "nip and tuck"! Look at her . . . she's even pouting. *Hhayi*. Where the hell is Sade?'

'There she is, chatting to her Uncle Themba. She doesn't seem to have a care in the world, and neither should you,' said Dikeledi dismissively.

'Well,' said Linda, who was still eyeing Winston and Palesa, 'looking at her, and how she keeps lingering around him, touching his shoulder and being the genuine seductress, I say there's more to this than meets the eye.'

Dikeledi was silent, deciding to ignore Linda. The journalist in Linda was forever looking for drama. It sometimes surprised her that Linda had chosen to focus on documentaries. She'd have been an excellent tabloid journalist. In any case, Dikeledi had no time for Linda's theatrics.

She was worried that she had been too hard on Sade about Nolwazi and the phony bridesmaids . . . especially since it was Sade's wedding day. Even if she'd elected to rent a bridesmaid from outer space . . . it was okay. A wedding day came only once in a lifetime, she surmised, ever the peacekeeper.

'Why is Sade not coming over to speak to us? You know, I attacked her about how she treated Lwazi with the whole pregnancy story. I even complained about the fake bridesmaids. Do you think she's still mad at me? She cried, you know? I mean, she actually cried – on her wedding day! What kind of a friend am I?'

Linda looked at Sade, happily socialising with the guests. '*Hhayi wena.* You're just worrying yourself. Since when did Sade start crying when she's reminded about her bitchiness? She knows herself. I don't think that's what was making her cry,' said Linda.

She pointed at the celebrity bridesmaids. 'You see that? And that there?' she said, now pointing at Palesa, who was laughing at something that Winston had said. 'That's what's making Sade cry. Because when you live a fake life, it soon catches up with you. I'd cry too if I suddenly realised that I'd betrayed my friends over some plastic people whose intentions I did not know,' Linda remarked, sipping her champagne.

Dikeledi tried to take comfort in Linda's words though she knew that when Linda got tipsy, she bitched about everything. Anyway, Dikeledi was now growing concerned about where Tebogo may have disappeared to.

Just then, Nolwazi walked in, looking a head taller. 'Hey, guys,' she said, flashing a winner's smile at them.

'Well, hello. You obviously met a tall, dark and handsome hunk on your way here. After all, that's what weddings are about,' remarked Linda.

'Tall and dark, yes. Handsome . . . I'm not so sure,' she said mysteriously.

Dikeledi was intrigued. 'Did you really meet someone so fast? I mean, you were only gone for fifteen minutes.'

Nolwazi grinned. 'I don't kiss and tell.'

The other two ladies just oohed at this piece of news. Linda could not wait to corner Nolwazi for more details.

Just at that moment, Mafikizolo got up to perform one of their popular Afro-pop songs. Dikeledi sprang up with enthusiasm. 'I just love this! I'm gonna go get Tebogo to dance with me,' she said, her new shoulder-length weave bouncing along with her as she sought out her man.

After dancing with Tebogo, an exhausted yet exhilarated Dikeledi went out to the ladies' room to freshen her make-up. She left Tebogo dancing humorously to a *pantsula* song with Phemelo, who always seemed to have the latest dance moves down pat. That's when Dikeledi saw him . . . or she could swear it was him: the ghost that had haunted Sade's life since high school. It *was* him standing in the parking lot, smoking a cigarette and looking at the marquee with deep concentration. He should *not* be allowed to be here! Dikeledi ran back to the marquee to get Tebogo.

'You have to help me with something, Tebza. You remember I told you about that guy who harasses Sade?'

'*Jislaaik*. The Zulu guy. Is he here?'

'Yes, and baby, he's crazy. He'll definitely cause a scene. You have to get the security guards to get rid of him. He could ruin everything for Sade. Literally,' she said, making sure he got the point.

Tebogo ran out and quickly summoned two burly men from the security company that was assisting with the event. Dikeledi followed them, determined to ensure that the dreaded Malusi would not ruin Sade's wedding day. By the time the security guys got to the spot where the man had been standing, he had vanished.

'He's gone, baby. I saw him getting into a Honda,' said Tebogo.

'Are you sure? That man is nothing but trouble. I shudder to think of the damage he could cause.'

Tebogo wanted to check up on Phemelo. 'I don't know why you and Sade stress so much about this guy. He's just another nut job. Go back in there and enjoy yourself,' he said as he went back into the marquee.

Dikeledi needed some time alone. She was not going to tell Sade about what had just happened; it would completely ruin her evening.

Meanwhile, Linda could not wait to hear about Nolwazi's happy new mood.

'So, what happened out there?'

Nolwazi grinned like a Cheshire cat and folded her arms. 'Tell me something, Ms Mthimkhulu, when did you become so nosy? You usually think your life is so interesting, you hardly ever bother about your neighbours' dirty laundry.'

'Tell that to Dikeledi. She said I should be a tabloid queen.'

Nolwazi laughed. 'Come to think of it . . .'

Linda nudged her playfully with her elbow. 'Shut it.'

Smiling, Nolwazi gestured with her finger for Linda to lean closer to her for a piece of gossip. 'I punched him! It felt so good, I could do it again and again. You know, I've never punched anyone before in my life? If I'd known before how good violence was, I would have used it a long time ago!' she exclaimed.

Linda was enthralled. 'You punched the bastard?' she shouted with glee, banging her hands on the table. A few people around turned to look at them, worried that they'd missed out on a crucial bit of wedding drama.

'Shh, not so loud,' Nolwazi cautioned. 'I think my work here is done.'

Linda's phone rang. With champagne-induced zest, she sprang up from her seat and left the marquee so that she could hear her caller properly. She was delighted to see that it was her banker friend, Kennedy.

They'd been out on three dates together, although they hadn't yet done the deed. All that crap about the third date being the sex date was just women's magazines trying to get women to act like a bunch of sheep. Not that she would have minded, but Kennedy seemed all about taking it easy, which was fine with her . . . for now.

'Hey, stranger. How's the weather in London?'

'Depressing. I can't wait to get home. How's your friend's wedding?'

'Dunno. Kind of sucks like a lemon but everybody's still in one piece. When are you coming back again?'

'Tomorrow. I miss you. Can you pick me up from the airport?'

Although she was tipsy, she felt cornered. Why did she have to pick him up from the airport? Were they married or something? She would be nursing a hangover tomorrow. There was no way she could be at the airport at— Oh, he had not said what time his flight would be landing.

'What time?' she asked quickly.

'At six in the evening. Look, I can get a friend of mine to pick me up if you don't think you'd be up to it. I just . . . I just sort of missed you. I wanted to see that gorgeous face first thing when I landed,' he said.

Hmm. He was quite a little charmer, wasn't he? Linda thought, the champagne making him sound about a thousand times sexier.

'Okay, no worries. I'll pick you up. Enjoy what's left of London, milord,' she said, and put the phone down without thinking. She was too excited.

Chapter 33

Nolwazi

Six months later

Nolwazi looked at her daughter once more, playing with her tiny little fingers, breathing in her innocent baby aroma. She was the most beautiful thing she had ever seen. Dikeledi was on her way to see the baby for the first time and, for some reason, Nolwazi could not help but worry that her friend would immediately see through her well-kept secret the minute she laid eyes on Siphokazi.

Her baby had Tebogo's round eyes and curved cheekbones, as well as his sharp nose. She was still very light in complexion, like most babies, where Tebogo was more toffee-coloured, so Nolwazi hoped that, at least, would stay the same, so that it drew attention away from all the other obvious ways she resembled her father.

Nolwazi had worked right through her pregnancy. She had developed her own signature design style, which was lauded for its unique use of unconventional pairings of material to pull off a striking, unforgettable look. She had managed to raise her profile through the magazine coverage that she and Ephry shared for the Khanyisile Mbali wedding and had made enough waves to reach her relatives in the Western Cape. Her cousin Ntombi had called her and even tried to entice her into opening a shop in Cape Town where the demand for chic African garments was high and the competition was lower.

At first, Nolwazi had dismissed Ntombi's idea, but the more she thought about it, the more it started to make sense.

The love triangle involving her, Tebogo and Dikeledi caused her many a sleepless night, and the burden of keeping such a big secret from her close-knit group of friends made her feel duplicitous. She was frustrated with Tebogo's attitude towards her and her baby. He capitalised on the impotence brought on by Nolwazi's obvious desire not to hurt Dikeledi and just continued with his life as if Nolwazi and her child had nothing to do with him. She'd never felt so powerless in her life.

After speaking to Ntombi about the prospects in Cape Town, she flew up to the beautiful coastal town with baby Siphokazi and spent a week staying with her cousin while also exploring the fashion scene.

Fortunately, Ntombi, who worked in PR in the fashion industry, was the perfect companion during her fact-finding mission. By the end of the week, she had become emboldened about making plans to root herself in the beautiful city. She also believed that the fresh air and the languid lifestyle by the coast would be beneficial to her and her daughter. Cape Town's relaxed pace suited her sensibilities far more than busy and buzzy Johannesburg.

She was planning on leaving Joburg within the next three months. She was not sure how she'd managed to keep such a heavy secret from prying eyes, but the pressure was too much for her in Joburg. Thankfully, her mother was supportive of her plans and as she had had a financial windfall of sorts – her company had granted its employees dividends from shares invested through an employee benefits scheme – she had loaned her enough money to tide her over for the first few months of her new business.

Nolwazi heard the buzz of the intercom. That must be Dikeledi. She wrapped Siphokazi in a beautiful white cotton baby quilt and kissed her protectively once more before going to open for her guest. Dikeledi was at the door with Phemelo by her side.

'Ooh, I can't wait to see the baby!' Dikeledi enthused, rubbing her hands in anticipation.

'Hey, you're looking well. Come through to the bedroom. She's in her cot.'

The three of them walked to the bedroom. 'Can I hold her?' Dikeledi whispered.

Nolwazi nodded.

Phemelo said, 'Hmm, she's so cute, Mom. She's got a strange mark on her face like Daddy's.'

Dikeledi laughed. 'I'll be sure to tell him that. She's just adorable. You must be so proud, Lwazi,' she said warmly.

Nolwazi was still reeling from Phemelo's innocent observation. 'Thanks. Do you guys want something to drink? I've got juice and assorted biscuits, or tea if you want,' she said, moving towards the open-plan living area.

'I'd love some tea and biscuits,' said Phemelo.

'I think I'll have the same,' Dikeledi replied.

Nolwazi went into the kitchen while Dikeledi and her daughter followed with the baby. They sat on the couch facing the kitchen where they could sit in full view of Nolwazi.

'Listen, I'm sorry it's taken so long for me to come and see the baby. I spent two weeks in Durban at a conference and I was just inundated with work on my return,' said Dikeledi.

'Oh no, don't worry. I've hardly noticed the passing of time. This little one has been keeping me busy,' responded Nolwazi.

'So why are you uprooting to Cape Town and robbing us of a chance to bond with this gorgeous angel, *maar wena*?' asked Dikeledi, gazing at the baby.

'I don't know,' shrugged Nolwazi. 'I guess I need a change of scenery. Joburg is a bit too hectic a place for me to raise my baby.'

'Really?' asked Dikeledi, standing up to go and talk more intimately with Nolwazi in the kitchen. 'Lwazi, are you sure this has nothing to do with the baby's father?'

Nolwazi looked down as she poured steaming hot water into the three mugs she had set on a tray with biscuits. 'No . . . I mean, he's probably part of the reason, but I just feel this place is too much for me. I'm just a simple Xhosa girl from the Eastern Cape. I can't stand Joburg's fast pace much longer. Besides, I think in the Cape I'll relate more with the people, and there are many more opportunities for me to make a name for myself in design circles there than here. Abo, Stoned Cherrie and all the rest have pretty much taken over the market, so it's that much harder to break through here,' she rationalised.

Dikeledi looked at her with concern. Nolwazi had lost weight dramatically after childbirth, which she worried was probably not good for the baby. Maybe it was from breastfeeding, but she felt sorry for Nolwazi, carrying such a heavy burden on her own. The baby's father must be a real bastard because she had never heard Nolwazi mention him throughout her pregnancy and they'd all given up trying to get the truth from Linda about his identity because, after the wedding fiasco, neither she nor Sade dared raise the question again.

Since Nolwazi was leaving, maybe she'd be willing to talk about him. After all, she was obviously leaving all remnants of him behind.

'Tell me something, Nolwazi . . . the baby's father, has he tried to make any contact with you since Siphokazi was born?'

Nolwazi took the tray laden with tea and biscuits to the lounge and shrugged. 'You really don't want to know about this guy. I've pretty much accepted that I made a huge mistake. I guess if the trade-off was having a healthy, beautiful baby, I did not do too badly,' she said, hoping to dismiss the topic.

As they sat down to drink their tea, Phemelo kept staring at the baby. Suddenly overcome by paranoia, Nolwazi scooped her daughter from Dikeledi's arms, worried that Phemelo would make another uncanny observation about Siphokazi's likeness to her own father.

'Let me take her back to her cot. I don't want her to get too restless,' she said quickly.

When she came back, she found Dikeledi still concerned about what she considered to be Nolwazi's rash decision to go to Cape Town.

'Seriously, Nolwazi, I'm worried about this move of yours. I mean, have you really thought about all the implications? You've just had a baby and have been thrust solidly into the role of single mother. If you move to a place where you'll be all alone, without your friends' support, you could put yourself at risk of a serious emotional breakdown. I mean, I'm sure you've read up on postnatal depression. Don't you feel like you're risking your emotional well-being by moving to a new environment?'

Nolwazi had expected that Dikeledi would come up with some psychological angle that would depress the living daylights out of her. 'Look, Dikeledi, it's really sweet of you and all to be concerned, but I'm a grown-up mother who can make sound decisions for herself. I've put a lot of thought into this. And besides, the reason I chose Cape Town is because I have a lot of good people there – some old contacts from varsity days, and quite a few relatives. Remember, it's Xhosa land there, so I'm definitely not going to be lonely. In fact, I'll be staying with a cousin of mine who's gonna help me look for a decent place and store premises where I can run my design studio from.'

Dikeledi sipped her tea and nodded. 'Well, it sounds like you've really thought this through. For what it's worth, I'm really going to miss you. You're a wonderful friend and I couldn't have dealt with those two drama queens without your sobering presence.'

Nolwazi struggled to stave off guilt-ridden tears. She hugged Dikeledi. 'I'm going to miss you too. I really wish I could have been more open with you about what I've been going through.'

Dikeledi hugged her back, warm and tight, and then withdrew from Nolwazi and faced her. 'But, babes, why haven't you been able to do that? You know I'm a good listener. I wouldn't judge you. Is he married? Is that why you're scared of telling me about him?'

Nolwazi could not help but let the tears roll freely down her cheeks.

Phemelo, ever her mother's daughter, rushed to the bathroom to get some tissues for Nolwazi. She grabbed them absent-mindedly and wiped her tears away. 'It's more complicated than that really. Maybe one day I'll be able to talk to you about it. I guess I really disappointed myself, so I first need to get over that, before I can share it with anyone.'

Dikeledi hugged her again. 'You poor, poor baby,' she said, holding her tight.

Of all the men in the world, why did she have to have fallen for Tebogo? Dikeledi was such an amazing person . . . how on earth was she ever going to reveal the truth to her?

As she held on firmly to Dikeledi's embrace, she felt a strong conviction that the move to Cape Town was indeed the best decision for her, under the circumstances. She simply could not continue living a lie.

Chapter 34

LINDA

It had been months since she'd started going out with Kennedy and Linda had, amazingly, not looked for excuses to break up with him. Okay, there was that day he was late for their date . . . oh yes, and that time he introduced her to that female colleague – the too-good-looking one who could not seem to get her hands off him. On both occasions, Linda had come up with some pathetic excuses about how they probably needed to 'slow it down' but Kennedy saw through her. He seemed to have a knack for doing that. Earlier in their relationship, he had asked her to partake in something that Linda still felt both extremely good and a bit uncertain about.

It was on their fourth date, when he had returned from London after Sade's wedding, that he had taken Linda to his house for the first time. Linda had been visibly nervous. It had been a very hot day. Kennedy had given her a tour of his house, and had told her more about himself than he had on previous occasions. When he'd completed his matric, he'd gone backpacking through parts of Europe and Asia before coming back to South Africa to study for a degree in commerce at Wits University.

His house contained an interesting mixture of items from different countries, an ode to that time of his life. He had a Zen-inspired lounge: a long, elegant carpet decorated with Mandarin characters, low tables and cushions, all of which gave a feeling of tranquillity. In the room where they sat after the tour, there were Asian paintings on the wall, and a little stereo played the most beautiful, calming, exotic music she had ever heard.

He had prepared a quick pasta meal for the two of them, which he served with a bottle of Cabernet Sauvignon. They relaxed for a while and chatted casually, but Linda, for some reason, still felt very nervous and clammy. She had known where the date was going, but her stomach had literally trembled at the thought of being with Kennedy. She could not understand what was going on with her.

After he tried to get her to relax, Kennedy finally said, 'You know something, Linda? I've been observing you over the past few weeks since we started seeing each other. You're great in every way but you always seem to be holding something back. You refuse to let your guard down, and I'm not really sure where that's coming from.'

She put her glass of wine down and felt embarrassed because her hands had started trembling. If this was how people acted when they were in love, she did not want to be part of it. It was ridiculous. How could another human being have so much power over her? Maybe this was the onset of some deadly virus. She was certainly feeling feverish.

Before saying anything, she laughed nervously, as she tended to when she was not in control of a situation. 'I don't know. You sure you didn't pick up some voodoo spells in your many travels, because I don't usually behave this way. I don't even know why I'm so nervous,' she said, feeling a bit shy.

'Okay, I have an idea!' Kennedy said, dashing off to the bedroom.

A few minutes later, he brought out a dozen gel candles and started placing them around the small, relaxed room. After lighting them, he turned off the main lights so the candles cast a comforting ambience around the room. When he was done, he inspected his work and then rubbed his hands together. 'Okay, now take your clothes off.'

She looked at him incredulously. 'What?'

'Stand up and take your clothes off.'

'Yikes. You sure are weird. Are you high?'

He laughed, a quick but resolute laugh. 'I'm serious. Trust me. You take off your clothes, I'll take off mine. This is not a sexual thing. Just do it. Have some faith. You'll see where I'm going with this.'

She still wasn't sure about it. How weird was this guy? Sure, she had, up until that moment, fully intended to sleep with him, but what in the world was he up to? Well, he hadn't shown any signs of mental illness until that point, so she decided to go along with his idea. But she did put her phone where she could see it. Maybe his travels had turned him into a member of a cult that got women to strip naked, kidnapped them and . . .

Oh my gosh! He was naked. Thirty seconds later she was naked too.

'Now what?' she asked, feeling ridiculous and self-conscious. Thank God she'd been going to the gym.

'Sit down on one of these cushions, and I'll sit on the opposite end. You have to sit cross-legged, you know, yoga style.'

She shook her head and thought, I wonder where they made him.

Sitting down, she hugged herself, as if it would protect her from the situation. They were stark naked; the only thing separating them and protecting their dignity was the long, low coffee table. She felt uncomfortable sitting on the cushion, but decided to accommodate the man's strange requests.

'Okay, I want you to breathe in and tell me something you've never told anyone before.'

'Oh . . . is this truth or dare Adam-and-Eve style?'

'No. No dares. It's not a juvenile game, it's just two people trying to build a circle of trust around each other . . . if both parties are willing, that is.'

She gave it some thought. It seemed like a very dangerous idea. If you let a man know all about you so early on, chances are he could end up using your weaknesses to destroy you.

'I don't think I'm ready for this game. I don't really go around trusting people I've just met.'

'Ouch,' he said, pretending to hold his heart with his hand. 'Wow . . . and I thought you really wanted to get to know me. So, if you don't trust me, why do you even want to be with me? Or maybe you're just passing time, trying to get over your ex-fiancé? Is that it?'

She shook her head vigorously. 'Are we allowed to drink wine as part of this session?'

'Nope. No wine,' he answered seriously.

'Okay, okay. You go first. Tell me something about yourself that nobody else knows.'

He was quiet for a while, as if he was seriously pondering what to say. Then he put his hands together, prayer-like, and began. 'Well, about fifteen years ago, when I had just completed my matric, I walked in on my mom and my gran talking in hushed tones. They weren't aware of my presence, but I could clearly make out what they were saying, and their piece of news literally blew me away.' He paused, blowing air through his hands. 'They were saying my real dad had just died and were debating whether to tell me about it or not.' He sighed.

'Before that point, I had no idea that the man I grew up calling my father was actually a surrogate. It turns out neither of them were my biological parents and I'd been adopted. You see, I grew

161

up being the golden boy in the family, or so I thought. I was my parents' only son and I worshipped the ground my dad walked on, so I lived to be like him one day – I even intended to study medicine so I could also be a doctor . . .'

'My mom is a doctor as well . . . Sorry to interrupt. I just thought that was a weird coincidence. Please continue.'

'Anyway, I was gutted. The shock of it made my whole world feel like it was crumbling. I felt like I had been living a lie . . . the worst cliché in the world, huh? After that, I wanted to run away from my family; just cut loose and find the real me, not the make-believe child that they'd created. I was very angry.'

'Geez, that must have been really painful. I know how terrible it can be for a teenager to have to start reconstructing their sense of self. I kind of went through something like that. How old were you then, about seventeen, eighteen?'

He shrugged. 'Yeah. Thereabouts. That's when I decided not to go to Medunsa, which is where I was gonna study medicine, and opted for backpacking instead. My dad gave me a credit card to see me through, and my mom kept sending me money throughout my eighteen months of travel. I did a lot of soul-searching. I was heartbroken. Even got mixed up with drugs when I was in Amsterdam, but one of my younger sisters, who I've always been close to, used to call and rap me over the knuckles. Can you believe it?'

'Was she also adopted?'

He shook his head. 'I was the only one. They had thought they couldn't have babies so they adopted me, but afterwards, they had decided to go for fertility treatment and give it another go. The result was my twin sisters. The irony is, I was the one people used to say looked like my dad. The twins don't look like either of our parents. They look more like my grandmother.'

'Talk about a twist of fate. So how are you now? With your family, I mean?'

'We kissed and made up . . . to some extent. There was no point keeping all that anger inside, you know. Although my relationship with both my parents has never been quite the same. I still feel like a fake sometimes, calling them my parents.'

Linda nodded thoughtfully, feeling empathy towards the man.

'Okay, no need to brood. Your turn.'

She emitted a long sigh and fidgeted with her hands, her eyes cast downwards.

'Where do I start? I *hate* my father. I hate that he walked out on my mom when she was barely recovering from her illness. I hate that he's a fake wannabe white man, wannabe big-time French director. I hate his friends, the letters he sends me, the work he's done . . . I hate the fact that I chose the same career as him, and,' she said, starting to feel out of breath, 'I hate that I love what I do because it means I love something that's a part of him.' She shrugged with an air of resignation. 'And that's me. In a nutshell. A woman walking around with an awful lot of resentment. Sometimes I worry that it will never go away. It's gonna turn me into this horrible person, which I probably am already but don't know it.'

She took a deep breath. She had never articulated her feelings quite like this to anyone. Usually she just pretended her father was dead, which suited her fine, because then she could avoid dealing with the pain of disappointment that accompanied any thought of him. Much to her dismay, she realised that she wanted to cry. Oh no. There was no way this guy was going to see her cry.

'Okay,' he said, deciding to alleviate the mood a little. 'I can see this has taken a lot out of you. Can I share something lighter? You do the same . . . if you're up to it.'

She nodded, scared that her voice might betray her. She was half disappointed that he had not offered to hug her, or any of the other warm gestures people resort to at times like these.

'I lost my virginity at the grand old age of twenty-two,' he said, looking at her for a reaction.

'No way!'

'Way!'

They both laughed.

'What was wrong with you? Are you one of those late bloomers, or did someone hook you up with some plastic surgery? I mean, I can't believe a guy who looks like you could start so late. Was it a religious thing?'

He laughed in a self-deprecating manner. 'I was just slow with girls . . . and very shy. Even during the backpacking period. I met a lot of girls, some of whom were really wild, but I just couldn't make it to the goal posts.'

'So you never scored. *Ag* shame,' she said, beginning to enjoy herself.

He threw a cushion at her. 'Hey, it's funny but not *that* funny. Your turn to embarrass yourself.'

'Okay, okay. When I was a kid, I used to enjoy eating battery acid from cars.'

'What? Were they starving you at home?' He chuckled.

'No, I just enjoyed it, till my mom caught me doing it. She went ballistic! Told me my stomach would rot from the stuff and I'd turn green. Never tasted battery liquid since.'

'And not a moment too soon. I'm not really into green girls.'

They both laughed. She looked at his shiny eyes, his muscular, toned body, and his gorgeous charming smile.

'Okay, I think we can put our clothes back on now,' he announced.

She stood up, and went over to him. She started kissing him tenderly, feeling the soft moisture of his tongue. She desired him like she had never wanted anyone before.

They made love slowly. They touched and stroked each other gently as if they had all the time in the world. The haunting music in the background felt like part of the lovemaking act, as if it were specifically made for that moment. Linda could not take the anticipation anymore. She wanted to feel him inside her, wanted to believe that this really was someone she could trust. By the time he entered her, she felt herself surrender completely to him. When she finally climaxed, she felt that she was lost inside him. But it felt good. And it felt safe.

Chapter 35

SADE

Sade was on top of the world. The doctor had finally confirmed it – they were pregnant! She booked off early from work and set about cooking one of Winston's favourite meals: pasta and salmon in a thick, creamy mushroom sauce.

She phoned Winston's secretary to find out when his last meeting would take place. Six o'clock, Sade was told, and it was scheduled to last about an hour. Great! That would give Sade time to prepare a romantic atmosphere so she could surprise him with the announcement.

This pregnancy was so different. Not like the other time . . . no, she would not think about that. She had been young and naive. She had panicked. At least God had given her a new lease on life. For a long time she had thought her punishment would be infertility. She had taken a gamble by marrying Winston, even though she feared she was infertile, but here she was: miracle of miracles. Pregnant! Hallelujah! She felt like shouting it from the rooftops. She had been forgiven; she really had managed to find redemption after all these years.

Three months ago, Winston had left the management firm he had worked for after being offered a CEO position at a larger competitor firm. His star was rising, and they had already discussed the fact that should she get pregnant, Sade would stop working until the baby was in nursery school. Sade, who had previously thought herself a career woman, was surprised at how much the idea appealed to her. After all, Winston was earning more than enough to take care of both of them. Since they had sold her property and were now staying in Winston's equally cosy home while they searched for their dream house on an equestrian estate, they had a lot of cash floating around. Besides, she had built up an impressive portfolio of investments since she had started working, so money was certainly not a challenge in this home.

She sighed happily, envisioning a hassle-free pregnancy that included floating in a sea of spa treatments, Lamaze classes, yoga, easy exercise at the gym, shopping for baby clothes, manicures and pedicures, all the while being spoiled rotten by her husband. Hmm, she sighed, sipping her orange juice with gay abandon as she hummed her favourite tune, life could not possibly get better.

By ten o'clock Winston had still not arrived. Panicking, Sade tried him on his mobile for the fifth time. It was still on voicemail. What in the world was the matter? Was he okay? She hoped he had not been in an accident. Oh God, please don't let anything happen to him, she pleaded.

This was not like Winston at all. She tried his secretary's mobile phone once more.

'Hello, Mrs Gumede,' responded the perennially patient Madeleine.

'Have you any idea who he was meeting with? Do you have their numbers? I can't get hold of him because his phone is off. Madeleine, my husband is not one of those men who . . . who does this sort of thing. You have to give me the numbers please!'

Madeleine sounded hesitant. 'Well, it's his business associates. I'm not sure if Mr Gumede would appreciate it if we bothered them so late about domestic issues. I . . . I just mean, maybe he went somewhere after that meeting,' she stuttered.

'Listen, you . . . you *secretary*. I'm pregnant. I need my husband. You give me those flipping numbers or else I'll make sure you never sit behind that shiny mahogany desk of yours again . . . ever! Okay?' Sade yelled, trying her best to avoid swearing at the woman.

'Okay, okay. I'll give you the numbers but please don't be disappointed if they can't help you,' she said firmly, an air of smugness in her voice.

'Bitch,' murmured Sade, as she took down the numbers.

She called the first gentleman's number. After three rings, he answered.

'Hello. Is that Mr Townsend?'

'This is he. Who am I talking to?'

'Mr Townsend, my name is Sade Gumede. I believe you had a meeting with my husband, Winston, earlier. I'm really sorry to bother you so late but I can't get hold of him. Are you with him by any chance?'

'Oh no, Mrs Gumede. Our meeting wrapped up a few hours ago. I'm sure your husband got delayed somewhere. I wouldn't fret too much about it. He should be on his way soon. At least he's a teetotaller so you don't have to worry about anything serious,' he assured her.

'Okay, okay. Thank you, Mr Townsend,' she said, absent-mindedly.

Where was Winston? Maybe there was something on at church? Something that she'd missed? Perhaps that would explain why his phone was off. Sade took a shower to distract herself. From now on she was going to take extra care with her health to make sure there would be no complications.

While moisturising herself with lotion, she heard the front door open. Thank God, she sighed, donning her bathrobe. He better have a good explanation.

'Sade! Sexy Sade,' shouted an odd-sounding Winston.

As he swaggered through the lounge, he knocked over her favourite vase. She quickly ran out of the bedroom to inspect the damage.

What was going on here?

'Hello, sexy Sade,' he said, dragging her forcefully with one arm.

'Winston. What's wrong with you? Have you been drinking?'

He hiccupped. 'Me?' *Hiccup.* 'Drinking?' *Hiccup.* 'Hell, no. I don't drink, sexy Sade. I don't drink. Remember? Remember who you married? Sober, trusting, stupid Winston!' He spat out the words, and suddenly hit her across the face with such force that she fell to the ground.

'What? What's happening? What's wrong with you?' she gasped, sprawled on the floor and in shock.

He came to her and grabbed her braids with one hand, twisting them roughly to and fro, as if playing with a rag doll, then he punched her in the face violently.

'Poor, stupid Winston. Sleeping with the town whore! How everyone must have laughed behind my back!' He straddled her. 'Guess how my day went, honey! Guess how my meeting went today!' he said in a faux-cheery tone. 'Today I had a meeting with some top clients, including one with a name that I'm sure, from your collection of many, many boys' names, you'll remember!' he announced, now sounding like a demon-possessed maniac.

Then he grinned sardonically. 'This man . . . his name is Sello Mkhize, you see. He says to me he went to UCT. So I say, "Really? Which year?" And he says, "Between ninety-three and ninety-seven." Then I say, "Do you know Sade Khumalo?" And he gets this stupid, stupid grin on his face, like a guy who's just had the best orgasm in the world. And he says, "Who could forget the campus mattress?" Is that what they called you? Were you everybody's Sealy Posturepedic?'

Then Winston started singing the Sealy Posturepedic advertising jingle, all the while twisting and turning a clump of Sade's braided hair. 'It's a Sealy! It's a Sealy Posturepedic feeling! That's the feeling you gave them, hey, Sade? Hey, baby? Hey, sexy Sade, who doesn't want to screw her own husband until "the time is right".' He punched her across the jaw repeatedly until she was bleeding through her gums. Then he got up. 'Stand up,' he commanded.

She struggled to her feet. Shame, shock and confusion blinded her. As she stood, he took off his belt and lashed it against her violently. Ignoring her crying pleas, he pinned her to the ground and pulled open her gown, exposing her naked body. He pulled down his zipper with such urgent violence that Sade thought he'd ripped it off his pants. Then he opened her legs forcefully and spread them wide like an animal forced to give birth. Still singing his maniacal jingle, 'It's a Sealy Posturepedic feeling,' he thrust himself into her shocked, dry opening until she was bleeding. By the time he was through with her, his taunting chime had turned into his own pathetic, alien sobs.

Chapter 36

LINDA

Linda hated the piece that the broadcaster had commissioned her to work on. Why was she producing so many street-life documentaries lately anyway? Just because she'd scooped an award on her piece on the homeless, it seemed she'd been typecast into rough-edged Linda. She was sick of it. The grime, the depression, the hopelessness . . .

Yes, she was certainly most sick of the hopelessness. It had reached the point where she had started to feel like the voyeur who sucked on the underdog in exchange for applause from her peers for her so-called fearlessness. Quite frankly, the work did not feel fearless at all anymore. It felt downright parasitic.

She remembered how Deon Venter's face had lit up in that production meeting. 'Linda, I think our viewers need to be treated to a day in the life of a Hillbrow prostitute. I'm serious, man,' he'd exclaimed, as he saw her rolling her eyes to express the sheer lack of imagination that she thought came with such a suggestion.

'Deon, don't you guys get enough of prostitutes when you see them on your regular Friday night sojourns?' she'd retorted irritably.

Her boss, Warren, had looked at her with panic when she said that. This was, after all, the chief commissioning editor at the SABC she was talking to and he could easily scrap their entire contract in a heartbeat. But she knew better. They needed them. Their production company, Static Frequency, produced the best and longest-running current affairs programme on air. *On Cue* had been a viewer's favourite almost since its debut broadcast.

Thinking back on the meeting earlier, she frowned as she revved her beloved car into fourth gear. She had no clue where she was going . . . something that was occurring far too often. She checked the time. It was already eight o'clock. Maybe she could grab herself a quick Nando's meal, although she'd read somewhere that it was not good for the figure to eat after eight. *Ag*, those women's magazines again. To hell with them! They always wanted to tell you how to live your life: what to eat, what to wear, when to wear it, how to have sex. She needed Nando's chicken and she needed it now. Extra hot, she thought, smiling.

Decisively, she stopped by her local Nando's eatery – only to bump into Lehumo, who had a tall, stringy woman attached to his arm. Uh-oh. Why did he look like he'd lost weight? And why, oh why did he actually look . . . sort of . . . *good*? Linda was wearing her 'working uniform' of old Levi's (emphasis on old), a loose-fitting black jersey that was not at all flattering, a white top and her canvas sneakers. Her dreads were loose and she wore no make-up.

Meanwhile, the tall carrot stick hanging on Lehumo's arm was dressed to the nines in stilettos, skinny jeans, a fashionable little handbag and a skimpy top, which emphasised her figure. As they stood alongside each other, ready to place their orders, Lehumo said, 'So, how've you been? It's been a while.'

She nodded and tried her best to act cool and smile. 'I'm good. Just busy, you know . . . the usual.'

He placed the order: a full chicken and chips. For the two of them? wondered an amazed Linda. And she was worried about eating after eight, she thought, flabbergasted.

After placing their order, Lehumo turned back to her and introduced the carrot stick. 'This is my girlfriend, Shanice. She's a model.'

Ah. She was a model, was she? And where did they get a name like that? Shanice? Like the 'I love Your Smile' singer . . . wait a minute. Did they even make Shanices in South Africa?

Shanice extended her long, manicured nails in greeting. 'Nice to meet you. You must be Linda.'

That felt good. So at least he'd talked about her. Okay, all was forgiven. 'Hi, Shanice. Pleasure to meet you. Listen, guys, I don't mean to be rude. Let me just place my order quickly. I'm starving.' They politely let her go forward, visibly holding hands.

Having placed her order, she wondered whether to turn around and attend to the waiting couple, or whether she should dash outside and pretend to make a call. Out of the corner of her eye, Linda saw Lehumo whisper something intimately into Shanice's ear.

Okay. Time to call a buddy. She turned around, said, 'I gotta make a call,' and stepped into the chilly night air. Thankfully, her phone rang. She sighed. Thank God for cell phones, she murmured, looking up. You could always rely on them for rescue missions. When she looked down at her phone, she saw that it was Kennedy. *Jislaaik!*

She'd been avoiding him. She was not sure why. Maybe she liked him too much, and he was sort of . . . not really there enough, or at least, he seemed ambivalent lately. He'd made an excuse when she had asked him to attend the awards ceremony where her documentary was recognised for excellence a few months back. He was always citing work pressures, but she knew how men were. For a man to turn down accompanying his fairly new girlfriend to such an important event meant only one thing: *he's just not that into you,* as the book said. She was nobody's fool. Rather suffer loneliness than cling to someone who didn't care.

173

'Hello,' she said flatly.

'Hey, Linda. Why are you avoiding me?'

'I'm not avoiding you. I've been busy . . . just like you.'

'You're being childish.'

'Really? Am I? Is that what it's called when I do as you do?'

'Oh, man. Linda, when are you going to stop being so confrontational? I told you, I've been busy with a major project the past few months . . . I even got you to meet the client.'

Yes, the one who couldn't seem to keep her hands to herself. Her greedy little paws kept touching him . . . client indeed! Humph!

'Are you telling me you still think I was avoiding you? I don't know what to do with you anymore,' he said, sounding exhausted.

She liked him. She felt bad about avoiding him, but she was terrified. She took a deep breath. 'Okay, look, let's just start with a clean slate. When do you want to hang out? I'm free on Friday.'

'Friday's great. We can go to Mike's place. He's having a house-warming party. You like Mike, right?'

That sounded good. Mike was a big social animal so there'd be lots of people there. At least it would get them out of this self-absorbed, relationship-driven, boring stuff.

It was Wednesday. She wished she had just asked him to come over. She really liked being with him but, for now, it was just going to have to be her and her Nando's chicken.

Chapter 37

DIKELEDI

Dikeledi had decided to find herself a hobby after realising that she'd spent ten years worrying about Tebogo's failure to propose. Now that he had finally done the deed she had nothing left to do with her fretting time. Maybe she had become addicted to all the drama associated with the old Tebogo. She'd read about those kinds of relationships plenty of times in psychology textbooks. They were termed 'co-dependent relationships', where the abuser was addicted to a specific vice – in Tebogo's case, women – and the victim was addicted to the thunderstorm that came with someone like that. She had to admit it was a relief to finally focus on herself. Aside from the inevitable backdrop of family expectations, *lobola* negotiations and wedding arrangements.

She saw an advertisement on the campus noticeboard placed by a dance studio that offered lessons for everything, ranging from the samba and the cha-cha right down to classic ballroom dancing. Impulsively, she took out her cell phone and dialled the number printed in bold red on the advert. She was told that they were situated in nearby Rosebank, a mere ten minutes from campus. She immediately signed up for her first lesson, scheduled for the next day – Thursday. Excited at the prospect, she smiled as she hung up, only to find a tall shadow standing next to her. When she looked up she found Professor Kwame smiling down at her.

'It's the first time I've seen you look so excited. I'm sorry, I couldn't help but stand here to see what's making you smile to yourself like that. I thought maybe one of your students had done you proud.'

Shyly, she smiled back and said, 'Humph, it'll be a cold day in hell when that happens. It's this ad. It caught my eye. I haven't done anything fun in a long time.'

'Ah,' he said, nodding jauntily, 'that makes two of us. Have you signed up? I happen to have joined them last week. I went for my first lesson last Thursday. It's quite something.'

A slight panic overcame her as she worried about the awkwardness of seeing him at the dance studio. She had started to develop a mini crush on him, which was surprising since Tebogo really was acting like the model husband . . . or husband-to-be.

But lately, like all the other women, she had taken to observing Professor Kwame when she thought he wasn't looking. She loved the way he carried himself, and the way he wore those tailored suits as if he worked in a big corporation instead of teaching economics to a bunch of unappreciative students. Increasingly she had started to enjoy the rich baritone of his voice, which tended to lull the listener, like a cosy, warm blanket wrapping itself around you slowly as he spoke.

The strong pull towards him was a great surprise to her, yet she couldn't help herself. Maybe she had been walking around with a lump in her throat, waiting for Tebogo to decide on the fate of their relationship for so long that she had not stopped to smell the roses . . . or rather, the scent of other men's cologne?

She laughed to herself. She was still certain that Tebogo was the one for her. She now realised that throughout Tebogo's messy affairs, she'd never considered that there could be another man with whom she could enjoy life and have the great romance that she'd dreamed of since she was in her early teens. It was strange to her how the proposal seemed to have trivialised all her worries. Now that she had his ring on her finger, there was an anti-climactic quality to the whole situation. After all, she'd almost choked on her engagement ring . . . though she never wanted to entertain whether that was a bad omen or not.

Anyway, she reckoned she deserved a harmless office flirtation. After all, she was never going to act on it.

'So you're going again tomorrow?' she ventured.

'Yes, and I hope you've signed up too. It would be an absolute pleasure if I could steal you as a partner before those octogenarians pick you out.'

She laughed and made a face. 'Exactly how old is the average member of this dance shindig?'

He scratched his head, suppressing imminent laughter. 'Let's just say you and I will probably be the only members who still chew with our own, original, God-given teeth,' he laughed.

She elbowed him playfully. 'Oh, I'm sure you're exaggerating.'

He shrugged. 'Well, let me see you there tomorrow and you can judge for yourself. Dress accordingly because I'll definitely only have eyes for you . . . not that you'll have much competition.'

She laughed. What a flirt! 'Hmm. One day you'll be old and grey yourself so don't be so smug,' she said, as she started strolling towards the lecture hall. She had a class in five minutes, she noted, looking at the wristwatch Tebogo had bought her last Valentine's Day.

The professor walked with her. 'You've a class right now?'

'Yes. Industrial psychology two. Everyone in that class looks like they are just taking it as an extra credit. The students are about as enthusiastic as a five-year-old who's just been forced to watch the news. I don't know why I bother. I wish I could inject some excitement into that bunch.'

'Well,' he said, stuffing his hands in his pockets, 'why don't you do what I do?'

She looked up at him, half smiling. 'Which is what exactly, Professor?'

'I just strip down naked and let them enjoy the view.'

She giggled. 'So how's that working for you?'

He paused, as if contemplating this. Finally he said, 'No . . . no. It works for them,' he said, with mock seriousness.

Chapter 38

SADE

Sade lay shivering on the left side of the bed that she had shared with Winston for more than six months. She felt as if she'd been ravaged by a wild animal. Her face was swollen, and she could barely rise from the bed without a part of her body screaming out in pain. This was her side of the bed, she tried to remind herself, although on this cold morning she could not have felt more lost anywhere else in the world.

The dark, masculine figure resting next to her had the smell of the familiar, but nothing about him felt real to her. Who was this man? When he awoke, what would he say? Where did this man, who was pretending to be someone that she knew so well, come from? Winston's looming figure heaved a deep sigh, looked like it was stirring back to life, then rested again.

What am I going to do? thought Sade. I'm married to an abusive man . . . Am I? Really? She had always thought this was the kind of thing that happened to some poor women in the townships. No . . . this was a mistake. Was she dreaming? Maybe he was just upset . . . and drunk. Of course! He does not drink, she thought. The news was too much of a shock to him. Why did she have to go and lie about her past?

But had she really lied? Does omitting certain things about one's past amount to lying? Everyone did it, didn't they? Besides, she was a completely different person now, so why was she supposed to revisit such an unsavoury period in her life?

She looked at him again. He seemed so menacing, like a monster about to strike at any moment. This was her husband, for crying out loud. Last night had been so terrifying. He could have harmed the baby. Oh my God! The baby.

Sade touched her stomach and suddenly she had the urge to run to the bathroom to examine herself – to check that everything was okay. She had bled last night, and it was so horrifying, it reminded her of that incident in high school. The one she and Dikeledi were never supposed to talk about.

That's why she could not tell Winston. It was too close for comfort. History was repeating itself in the worst way possible. She was being punished for her sins!

As she stood up, wild with panic, Winston woke slowly and glanced at her, as if he'd woken next to a stranger. 'Sade, what's going on? Why do you have that crazy look in your eyes?'

'I have to go to the bathroom now. I have to go. I hope she's okay, Winston, I hope . . .' she cried, then ran to the bathroom.

He followed her abruptly, but found that she had already locked herself in. 'Sade, what's going on?' he banged on the bathroom door. 'Baby, you're making me worried.'

'We have to go see the doctor now, Winston. Our baby might not have survived . . . she or he might not have survived last night.'

With savage, desperate force, he banged the door again. 'Sade, open up now. Open up, baby. I don't understand what you're saying,' he wailed. This was only the second time she had ever heard him cry – both times within twenty-four hours, and for very different reasons.

Slowly, she opened the door. Standing there exposed, with her blood-stained gown open, her braids covering her bruised face like a wild, demented woman, she said, 'Winston, I'm pregnant.'

Within seconds, Winston was frantically searching for clothes for her to wear, rummaging through the drawers to locate the car keys, and in a few minutes, they were at Sade's obstetrician's consulting rooms.

The doctor was surprised to see the usually organised and efficient-looking Sade standing in his waiting room looking like a typical abused woman. She had made no effort to hide the bruising. Was it deliberate, or had she not had the time to make an effort? Dr Mzilethi was even more surprised to see her equally harassed-looking husband with her.

He led them into his consulting room. 'It's good to see you, Mr and Mrs Gumede. I gather Sade here has shared the happy news with you, er . . .'

'Winston. The name is Winston. Um . . . yes, my wife did tell me the good news, but we're very worried. You see, she tripped on the stairs early this morning so we're worried about what might have happened to the baby,' he said, speaking rapidly.

Sade could not believe how easily the lie rolled off his tongue. He sounded like somebody who had done this sort of thing before. Suddenly a cold chill went down her spine. She was going to call her mother after this.

The doctor nodded with sympathy. 'That must have you two in a lot of distress. Look, let me examine Sade in the consulting room. How far did you fall on the stairs?' he asked, looking at Sade. By the look in his eyes, Sade knew he could see through her husband's lies.

She looked down, while Winston attempted a response.

'Um, it wasn't a very hard fall. I'd say less than a metre. Look, Doctor, I'd really appreciate it if you examined her as soon as possible. It would really kill me . . . I mean, it would really kill *us* if anything's happened to the baby,' he finished.

Dr Mzilethi rose and took Sade by the hand. 'It's okay, Mr Gumede. Let me run a quick scan to see how things are looking. I can understand and sympathise with your anxiety. Just sit here and try to take it easy. I'll get one of my assistants to get you a glass of water. Let's just pray that it's nothing too serious,' he said gravely.

Winston nodded, drumming his fingers.

A while later, a sombre-looking Sade emerged, walking along-side the doctor. She was relieved that her baby was fine, but she could not bring herself to share the relief with Winston. She was still in shock about the way he had savagely attacked her. She had read up on women in abusive relationships and knew that once they started, abusers tended to repeat their violent behaviour. But the altercation had come out of the blue; was it possible that Winston had only reacted out of pain and anger?

She could not reconcile a world in which a man that she so loved could turn out to be an abuser, but she was in too much shock to decide one way or the other.

Would she have to leave him? She swallowed a thick lump in her throat. She was not sure she could bear a life without him but if he was an abuser, there was no way she was going to raise a child with him.

'Well, Mr Gumede, I have good news. Nothing seems to have happened to the foetus. From this scan here, it looks like you two have a perfectly healthy seven-week-old baby,' he said, handing over the scan to a now-grinning Winston.

Beside himself with relief, Winston stood up to hug the doctor as if he had just saved the baby from the jaws of death. 'Thank you so much, Doc. Thank you. May the good Lord bless you! You don't know how relieved we are,' he gushed.

Then he hugged Sade passionately. Like the old Winston.

When they got to the car, he rushed to open the door for her and then settled into his seat.

They were both silent for a while.

'I'm sorry, I'm sorry, I'm sorry. I don't know what came over me. I will never ever cause you harm. I would never want to hurt you or our child, please believe me Sade.'

She just stared ahead, unable to so much as look him in the eye.

When she finally found her voice, it was cool and firm.

'If you ever so much as raise your hands to me again, Winston, it'll be over, you hear me?'

'Yes. I understand, baby. I promise this will never happen again.'

Chapter 39

LINDA

It was a cool Saturday afternoon, and the air was rich with melancholy. The girls were about to bid Nolwazi a final farewell as she sailed off to her new life in Cape Town. Linda had decided to treat them to a surprise edited DVD of their lives and times together. She had spent hours in an editing suite in Randburg on Friday night going through footage that dated from varsity through to birthdays, break-ups, house-warming parties and the inevitable blowing of first pay cheques. After a few hours of viewing the footage, she had been glad she got to spend some time alone in the editing suite before Kennedy had joined her towards the end of her emotional ten-year audio-visual journey.

She had been surprised to see how fresh and young they had all looked and sounded back then when they were all doing their final year, because that's when she had started filming them as part of her TV practical course. What had also shocked her were some of the glaringly obvious nuances in their relationships, which they had been so blind to back then.

In one clip, Tebogo was poking fun at Dikeledi about a new hairstyle, and then while all the other girls assured her that it wasn't so bad, there was a shot of Nolwazi looking at Tebogo expectantly as if to say, 'I think you're right, it doesn't suit her'. Then her expression changed quickly as Tebogo leant over to kiss Dikeledi, and said, 'This is not your best hairstyle in the world, bunny bear, but I love you anyway.' The others gushed over this sweet sentiment while Nolwazi looked on despondently.

Linda had decided to edit that bit from her video montage.

When Kennedy had finally joined her with a chicken maestro pizza, her eyes were red from nostalgic tears.

'Ah, shame, all that lost youth. Don't worry, Linds, if you stick with me, you'll feel young forever.'

She had leaned into his warm, ginger-smelling sweater. He was wearing the cologne that always gave her a feeling of comfort, and made her feel a strong, passionate pull towards him. 'It's just so sweet, you know. To share your life with a good mix of people and to stay loyal . . . okay, loyalish, towards each other for so long,' she had said sadly.

'So, how are you going to cope with Nolwazi leaving? You guys are clearly closer to each other than you are to the other two.'

She had looked up at his light brown eyes. He looked so caring, concerned. He was a sweetheart. How could she ever have doubted him? He'd been honest with her from their first date. Was she developing those insecurities women have in relationships? She hoped not. She never had viewed herself as the jealous type.

'I don't know, hey. And those two have moved in a direction that I'm completely unfamiliar with. The marriage thing will make them have even more in common with each other than with me.'

He had taken her by the hand and pressed the stop button on the muted DVD. 'I might not be much to look at, but at least you still have me,' he had said in his usual self-deprecating manner. He had kissed her gently and she had responded with a lonely, hungry ferocity.

Before long, she had been on top of him, feeling incredibly powerful and a bit possessive over him. She had suddenly had an urge to feel at one with him, secure in the knowledge that he would be there for her. A lot had been weighing on her mind lately – her mother's health, Nolwazi's departure . . . Ah, the love of a good man was all she could hold on to.

He had responded just as ferociously. He had gripped her bum and pressed her onto him with masculine force. They had been completely oblivious to the fact that they were at a place of work.

After their passion-fuelled bout of lovemaking, she had said, 'Flip, I think they've got cameras in here.'

He had looked around. 'Linda, you're in the film business. How could you be a victim of your own trade?' he had asked with rising panic.

'When passion calls sometimes . . . well . . .' She had shrugged.

'Are you serious? Aren't you scared of what your colleagues will say?'

She had laughed. 'I'm joking, genius. I've used this editing suite for aeons. You think I'd trade my reputation like that? Heck no! Not even for you, my gorgeous friend,' she had said, kissing him playfully as she grabbed the DVD.

On Saturday, while she waited for the other ladies, she reminisced about her encounter with Kennedy the previous night. She smiled with delicious contentment. He was really something special. Unlike anyone else she had ever been with. He sort of . . . understood her. Kennedy was a breath of fresh air because he never came on too strong. He seemed to understand the idea of pacing oneself, taking it easy and not rushing to some sort of bleak finish line.

A knock on the door pulled Linda out of her reverie. She looked through the peephole. It was Nolwazi. Linda opened the door with her arms outstretched.

'Oh, last hug. Parting is such sweet sorrow,' she said dramatically, throwing her head back.

'Yeah well, I will certainly miss you too, oh strange one,' said Nolwazi, pushing the baby in a stroller.

Linda had long declared herself a non-baby person, but with Siphokazi she occasionally attempted to play the role of an appreciative aunt. 'Okay, settle in and let me prep you about what's to come,' she said.

Nolwazi closed the door behind her. 'Look, with the whole Cape Town move coming, I think I've buried my demons. Dikeledi and Tebogo were probably meant to be together. She clearly loves him, warts and all, so who am I to rob her of that fantasy?'

Linda just nodded and went over to the lounge. She sat lazily on her leather settee and said, 'So you're crossing a bloody mountain so Dikeledi can live under the false illusion that Tebogo could possibly, remotely, prayerfully be a decent person? The point is, she's still about to marry someone who has no qualms about sleeping with her friends. I'm sorry to put it so crudely but you're not doing her any favours.'

Nolwazi just nodded irritably. 'Okay. Can we just not talk about this whole situation? I plan to spend my last days relaxing with my three best friends before moving, so I don't need to be reminded of the circumstances surrounding this. I think about it enough already as it is.'

There was another knock at the door. Sade and Dikeledi had arrived in one car. Dikeledi carried with her two bowls of salad and Sade brought grilled chicken, rolls and chakalaka.

'Since Linda is hosting, we were worried that there'd be too much booze and too little food,' said Sade as she set the chicken and rolls on Linda's dark-wood dining table.

Dikeledi walked in and looked appreciatively at the placemats and scented candles set out by Linda. 'Humph. Looks like someone aimed to surprise us.'

Linda grinned. 'I may have set out the table but all I've got is some grilled lamb chops, steak and Greek salad, so your efforts haven't been wasted, ladies. And, of course, I'll start us off with my choice of Cabernet Sauvignon to set the mood. I've also got a surprise for you girls, which will be revealed much later,' she said, taking the salads from Dikeledi and placing them on the dining table.

Sade smiled. It had been almost two months since the incident with Winston. Although the wounds had healed, she still felt guarded around him, but was determined not to let her feelings show to the entire world. She'd spoken to her mother about the beating but quickly retracted her confession when her mother wanted to call a family meeting between Winston and her people. She could not afford the source of Winston's consternation to be revealed. It would shame her family and taint her reputation forever.

For Winston's part, he'd been contrite about the incident, constantly reassuring her that he had acted out of shock, jealousy and rage, and that such violence was completely out of character for him.

He had agreed to go to couples' counselling at church and so far, it seemed as if they were both committed to overcoming this ugly incident in their marriage.

'Well, you're not the only one with a surprise for the evening,' Sade said, smiling nervously.

Baby Siphokazi started wailing. 'Oh, poor baby, give her to me while you get her bottle,' offered Dikeledi.

Nolwazi whisked a warm bottle of milk from the baby flask that she took out of the cute pink baby carrier bag and handed it to Dikeledi, who was skilfully lulling the baby.

They all sat down at the dinner table while waiting for Linda to finish laying everything out. In a few minutes, everyone had dished up a light meal and had a glass of red wine in their hands. Sade opted for a glass of grape juice.

'So, Nolwazi, are you nervous about the move?' asked Sade, drinking her juice in her slow, elegant way.

'No, not really. Actually, right now, I'm quite excited, believe it or not. I'll be staying with my cousin Ntombi in Newlands for a while and then she'll help me look for a place that'll be close to my shop. I've already called up a few contacts and it's amazing how helpful everyone is.'

'*Shoo!* It's quite daunting though, hey. Starting over . . . at thirty-one!' mused Sade.

Linda drank her wine while reflecting, 'I think I actually envy you, hey. Imagine a chance to start a brand-new life in a new city. You're really brave to be doing this, Lwazi. All power to you,' she said, toasting Nolwazi.

Dikeledi looked at Siphokazi, whose bright eyes were staring back at her. She kissed her. 'I just love babies, you know. Now that Tebogo and I are going to be settling down, I'm seriously thinking about an addition to the family.'

Linda instinctively glanced at Nolwazi.

Sade said, 'Which brings me to my news for the evening . . .'

All three pairs of eyes now gazed at her expectantly.

'Guys, I'm pregnant.'

They all stood up to hug her.

Glass in hand, Linda said, 'Hmm. Brother Winston sure don't waste no time, right?'

The others laughed merrily.

'Well, I'm so glad to hear the good news . . . but you actually look like you've lost weight. Don't starve the poor child, *wena*,' remarked Nolwazi.

'Look who's talking. You hardly even showed throughout your pregnancy,' Sade retorted.

'Ha! Says the woman who cornered me into admitting my sins,' said Nolwazi good-humouredly.

'*Wena ou*. You're the only one who's still a virgin here. Three mothers . . . man, you must do something,' said Dikeledi, addressing Linda.

Linda shook her head. 'Count me out, guys. First I have to find a sperm donor who's willing to risk creating some complicated bohemian child who'll be born with dreadlocks.'

'By the way, Linds, how's it going with Mr Gorgeous Kennedy?' asked Nolwazi.

'Yes, Linda. And when are you making it official with him? He's perfect for you!' said Sade.

Linda looked up and suddenly she felt like a shy seventeen-year-old. 'Guys, Kennedy and I are taking it easy. It feels like something special, which is different for me, you know? I mean it's now almost a year so there's something we're doing right but I really don't want to spoil it . . . for now. Besides, he still has to pass the acid test.'

'Oh, please remind me again what the acid test is,' asked Dikeledi.

'Well, it's like this: if I'm walking in a shopping mall with the guy and this gorgeous creature of a woman passes by, I check to see if my guy's gaze follows her . . . even though I know that she's exactly the kind of girl he'd be in to. If he doesn't, he passes the acid test.'

They laughed.

'What kind of ridiculous test is that?' asked Sade. 'Almost every man on this planet would fail it hands down! *Wena*, you've got impossible standards. You'll stay single forever.'

'But every woman has some sort of acid test. Mine is the man's hands. If I meet you, and I like your smile, your style or whatever, but am not really sure if you pass my first assessment, I look at your hands. There are guys with long fingernails . . . a definite no-no in my book. How's he gonna . . . you know?' offered Nolwazi.

'*Ja*. I think I'm with you on that one, Nolwazi,' said Dikeledi, 'I mean, I once went out on a date with this guy in high school. His fingernails were all neatly cut, but then his pinkie finger had this long nail with red nail polish on it.'

'Ew!'

'Aha! I once got asked out by this cute Zulu soccer player and I was thinking, you're so cute, are you sure all the women won't kill me when they see us together? Then he asked for my number. When he took out a pen and paper, I noticed his fingers. They were black with greasy oil. It turns out the guy was also a part-time car mechanic. I could just imagine those greasy fingers all over me. Needless to say, the dude never got to oil any part of my body,' declared Linda.

They all doubled over with laughter.

The girls went on chatting till the early hours of the morning, while repeatedly rewinding scenes from Linda's DVD. Unbeknownst to them, it would be the last carefree evening they would share together in a very long time.

Chapter 40

NOLWAZI

A year later

Nolwazi was at her boutique, which had been up and running for a year now. She was chatting amiably with a young blonde client who had become a regular at the shop, when a good-looking black couple strolled in. She noticed the man first: tall, with glasses and a smooth, dark complexion. For some reason she'd always been attracted to guys with glasses. Maybe it was the air of intellectual armour that the glasses projected. This young woman was certainly lucky to have hooked up with such a good-looking brother.

She subconsciously stole a glance at herself in the mirror. She wasn't looking too bad today. At least all the stress of starting a new life was dissipating with the growing popularity of her store. This was due in no small measure to the fashion show that Ephry had organised for her to showcase her work alongside his. It had been a grand affair, hosted at the Cape Town convention centre. It spread the word of Nolwazi's Afropolitan Designs – an amalgamation of African authenticity and cosmopolitan flair. Capetonians had lapped it up and she'd been busy almost from the first day she'd opened her shop.

The good-looking young man approached her and said, 'Excuse me. You must be Nolwazi. I read all about you in the *Cape Times* a few months back. Won't you help this Eurocentric, colonised sister of mine get some real style by showing her something that will look fabulous on her?' he asked.

Ooh . . . such gorgeousness! But probably out of her league. Too perfect!

'It would be my pleasure. What's your name, darling?' she asked the curvaceous stunner on her brother's arm.

'I'm Charlotte. Don't listen to my brother. It's not a matter of being colonised; it's just that I'm most comfortable in my jeans and sneakers.' She shrugged, offering a friendly, gap-toothed smile.

'Okay. Then I've got something perfect for you, which you'll feel absolutely comfortable in,' Nolwazi said, taking her through the Afropolitan Designs streetwear section, which included flattering A-line skirts and funky tops.

Charlotte disappeared into the fitting room with a number of items.

'I'm Simphiwe, by the way. Like you, I've just moved to Cape Town from Joburg to join my partner . . . he's originally from here,' the good-looking man said, speaking quickly. Then he laughed. 'You probably think I'm some kind of stalker, telling you things about yourself without us having spoken a word to each other before, but like I said, I was pretty impressed by that article on you.'

'Are you also into design?' she ventured.

'As a matter of fact, I am . . . in a way. I'm an architect but I have an appreciation of the aesthetic, hence I'm drawn to creative people like you.'

Nolwazi was caught by surprise. This man was certainly forward, no mincing of words. Yet he even sounded gorgeous. Why was Cape Town like this? And why were so many of the good guys gay? One thing was certain . . . his partner was one lucky guy.

I'm going to be a nun if I stick around this town, she thought. Charlotte, whom Nolwazi had momentarily forgotten about, emerged looking like a foxier version of herself.

'Wow! Welcome to the twenty-first century, my sister!' said Simphiwe with transparent admiration.

'It is kind of a cool look, isn't it?' asked Charlotte, seeking affirmation.

'You look gorgeous. It is so you,' concurred Nolwazi.

'That's it then. I'm taking it. Charge it to my big brother's account,' Charlotte said, heading back to the fitting room.

Simphiwe waited patiently for Charlotte to re-emerge with the clothes.

'Wish I had a big brother like you,' said Nolwazi as she went behind the counter to prepare to ring up the sale. She suddenly felt comfortable with him. With no hope of him being attracted to her there was no need to act coquettish.

He shrugged. 'I've got three little sisters and she's my favourite one by far. Bright as a jackal and cute as a button. She plans to be a journalist one day.'

'Nice,' nodded Nolwazi.

'I could adopt you as one of my little sisters too, if you want. I could start by taking you out for coffee one of these days.'

She nodded. 'That sounds nice. It's not like I've got this swinging social life here anyway,' she confessed.

'Cool,' he said, taking out his wallet as Charlotte came out with her new clothes.

Nolwazi rang up the sale and folded the clothes into plastic bags. Her assistant was off sick today, so she was the general dogsbody for the day.

Before parting, Simphiwe said, 'I'll come round during your lunchtime tomorrow for that coffee. You do have someone helping you here, don't you?'

'Yes.' She smiled. 'She's just off sick today but hopefully she'll be in tomorrow.'

'Fabulous. See you tomorrow then, around one,' said Simphiwe. And off he went with his cute little sister trudging along behind him.

Chapter 41

SADE

Sade braced herself for another outbreak of Winston's temper. She kept holding on to the fact that he'd not been physical since the first incident . . . maybe she needed to enrol him into anger management. It seemed he had a lot of unresolved issues from his past. She really believed that if she got him the help he needed, he would go back to the Winston she had fallen in love with.

But now all her hopes were dashed.

The ghost had reappeared. Right at her front door this time. How did security let him in? Just when things were beginning to change. How could he come here? How did he find her? Worst of all, how would Winston react? She dared not think about that!

'Sade! Open the door! I want my baby! *Kunini ngikufuna Mthakathi ndini!*' he roared.

It was a Sunday morning. She, Winston and baby Ntokozo were preparing to attend the morning Mass. Winston served as an usher for both morning and evening church services these days, so their Sundays were frantic, but they both enjoyed it. Nothing brought them closer as a family than attending Mass together. Something about these simple morning rituals made Sade feel like she was truly saved. She and her family had given themselves to Jesus.

She had been humming her favourite tune, when this racket had suddenly manifested itself outside her own living room! Why, Lord? Why now? It was him. She would recognise that maniacal voice anywhere. She rushed quickly to get the door, wanting to deal with the situation before Winston cottoned on to what was happening. This was the man who had forced her to leave Cape Town, made her leave her first cushy job in Durban and now . . . now . . . no! She would not allow him to ruin her life again.

She realised she'd left her car keys and ran back to the bedroom to grab them. Although she had stopped working almost as soon as she discovered she was pregnant, Winston had made sure that she retained her creature comforts.

'I just need to get something at the shops quickly, honey,' she said, rushing towards the living room without waiting for an answer.

As she stepped out of the door, there he was. He looked dishevelled; his beard, which had speckles of premature grey in it, had grown even longer. His eyes were red, wilder than the last time and more bitter. His breath reeked of alcohol. How had they let this man in? She was definitely going to file a complaint with the body corporate.

'Malusi, what are you doing here? Why don't you just leave me alone, for the love of God?' she pleaded, desperation and panic written all over her face.

'Ha, ha, ha!' he laughed, pointing at her like a small child. 'Ha, ha, you . . . you've found God, hmm? Where's my child, you bitch? You know I'll always find you. No matter where you go. *Mna*, I just want my child. Where is he, hmm?'

Sade looked around in wild panic. '*Lalela*, let's go in my car and discuss this, okay? I can't talk here. It's not even my house.'

He pushed her towards the door. '*Hhayi wena s'febe!* You think I'm stupid, man? I know you live here, I know who you're living with and I know you're pretending to be a goody-goody, born-again Christian, man. You swine! Where's my child?'

'Please, Malusi . . . can't you see what you are doing to yourself? You need to go back to the hospital where they can take care of you, please. *Mina,* I still care about you. You're just destroying yourself. Come with me, please. You've got a degree; you should be doing something with your life. You just need to take your medication and then you'll be okay again. Please, let me take you somewhere. We can even . . . we can even just talk, please.'

He stood firm. 'Where's your husband? I want to talk to him. I heard that you didn't kill his daughter. So why? What's so special? *Mina,* why am I not so special? Hmm? Mr Husband!' he called out. 'Hubby! Come out here! I want to do a deal with your wife! Come out!'

Sade pushed him with as much force as she could summon, but he was too strong for her. He just kept mocking her.

'Mr Husband! Come out! I have a surprise for you about your born-again, goody two-shoes wifey! Come now.'

Her next-door neighbour, an elderly gentleman, came out.

'What's this racket? Sade, are you okay?'

She shook her head. 'Please, Mr Wilson. Please call security. This man is demented.'

'*No!* Liar! Bitch! She killed my baby, this one. Imagine. She was only seventeen years old. She killed my own baby, now she wants you to believe she's a good person. Fuck off, man!'

Just then, every fragment of time slowed down for Sade as Winston, like an uninvited intruder, stepped out of the house.

'What in the name of the good Lord is going on here?' he asked.

'Ah, so you're the lucky bastard who ended up with Sade . . . the beauty queen of Umlazi, *huh?* Nice. Not bad, lovey. You didn't do too badly considering your history.'

The neighbour, Mr Wilson, was still standing on his side of the fence, hands in his pockets. He could not take his eyes off this little suburban drama that was playing itself out on a chilly Sunday morning. Winston, ever aware of his neighbours' perceptions, decided to steer the drama inside closed doors.

'Come, come, whoever you are. No need to cause such a spectacle so early in the morning.'

Sade shook her head rapidly. 'No, no, Winston. This man is crazy. I know him from my childhood. We have a baby in the house, Winston. We can't let him in.'

Winston suddenly looked at her panicked expression, stepped into the house and moved towards the telephone. When he turned around again, the deranged man had a butcher's knife to Sade's neck.

'Now listen here, little sissy boy! Drop that damned phone and let me in! I have some business with your wife. If you drop the phone, I'm not gonna hurt her; if you don't, I'll slit her throat with this knife. Believe me, she deserves it!' he said, pressing the blade to Sade's neck.

For a split second, Winston did not know what to do but he hoped that Mr Wilson, who had gone back into his house, was still watching or had at least called the police. He looked into the man's blood-red eyes and saw that he meant everything he said.

'Okay, okay, but if I let you into my home, what difference will it make? I mean . . . I hope you're not going to harm my wife, because, as God is my witness, I will kill you with my bare hands.'

At this, Malusi pushed the blade so that a trace of blood appeared from a small cut on Sade's neck.

'All I want is for you to hear me out. Then you can decide for yourself if your so-called wife is worth all this effort. Maybe afterwards, we can share some notes . . . if you know what I mean.' He winked.

Winston, so accustomed to being in control, let the stranger in and stared back at Mr Wilson's house. He saw Mr Wilson's shadow from behind his lace curtains, closed his eyes in exasperation and mouthed the word 'help'.

The moment he allowed the stranger into his home, he regretted it. Sade looked heartbreakingly helpless. He swore he would never allow her to be in this position again. What kind of a man was he, unable to help his wife while she was held at knifepoint by a deranged lunatic?

'Li-listen, my brother. I'm not crazy or whatever this woman wants you to think. I just want my fucking son, you know! That's all I want. Did she tell you what she did? Hmm? Did she? Sade, do you want to tell him, or should I tell him?'

Sade was now breaking down, thick tears covering her face. At least the baby was asleep upstairs, she thought, looking at the blue and white baby monitor placed at Winston's knee. Winston was sitting down like a man in prison. His hands were shaking, his glasses had gone hazy. He was sweating. She prayed to God for forgiveness.

'Ok, Sade, my sweetheart. I think, at least Brother Winston here deserves to know what he's dealing with . . . I mean, after all, he's entrusted his life to you, right?' the crazy man said.

'*Broer*,' said Winston as calmly as he could muster, 'what do you want from us? Do you want money? Food, jewellery? What? Please tell me. Let's just give you what you want, and we'll all forget this happened. We'll go back to our lives and you'll get whatever you want. I swear, I won't do anything to you. I won't even report you. Please, let my wife go.'

'*Ag* shame, *Ta* Winston. Tsk, tsk, tsk. I feel for you, my brother. I feel for you. No, don't worry, you're not alone. I think I was once like this. Exactly like you. We're talking about a beauty queen, here. Everyone wanted her . . . but,' he said, spitting into Sade's face, 'I'm the only one who discovered the evil within her.'

Finally, Winston relented, hoping this would make the man go away. He opened his hands with resignation. 'Okay, brother. What is it that you want to tell me so much – so much that you would put so many people under such strain on a Sunday morning of all days?'

'Ha, ha!' Malusi laughed, this time sounding even more demented, almost merry. '*Hhayi*, Sade. *Yinduna le*. A real man. You always knew how to pick the good ones, but you corrupt us. Look at me. You know where I'm from, *baba*? My family is rich! *Ja*. I see that look on your face. You don't even believe me. Ask her. This one – your wife. She can tell you. Back home, we owned butcheries, petrol stations, everything. Even today, there's some of it left.' He sighed, suddenly sounding tired. 'But . . . your Sade destroyed me and everything I had. We were seventeen, both of us. In love . . . *shoo*, you couldn't touch us. In fact, you couldn't touch her! I would kill you . . . with my bare hands . . . just like you now, I guess. Can you believe she could make a man do that at seventeen?' He shrugged and then laughed mockingly.

'Anyway, I can see she's got you the same way. The same spell, but *beware*. She's dangerous,' he said, grabbing her by the scruff of her neck and sitting down on one of the couches, still with the knife fixed against her neck. 'It's a long story, that's why I'm sitting down. Not because I'm tired, in case you're starting to have some funny ideas.

'So, I was telling you, *Ta* Winston . . . can I call you *Ta* Winston? Because I respect you. I can see you're a little older than me and Sade here. *Ag*, you're not responding but it's okay. I'll call you *Ta* Winston anyway.

'Sade and I, we go back a long way. So there we were, in love, always together, making plans for varsity. It was even my idea that we should both go to UCT, you know that? Did she tell you? Humph. Then, around February in our matric year, she tells me she's pregnant. *Ja*. I can see you don't believe me, but it's true. *Ne*, Sade? Isn't it true, my sweetie?' he asked, looking at her.

Sade's face remained frozen with the same terrified expression, but now her eyes seemed haunted.

'Just nod your head, bitch, or else I'll slice you right in front of your husband,' he whispered to her with malice.

Reluctantly, Sade nodded.

'That's a good girl. I used to like her. She'll surprise you. Just out of the blue, do something like this. Like nod, when you ask her to . . . or even give you your first blow job. Does she still do that? Jeez, she used to be good at that, hey?

'Anyway, I digress now. Where was I? Oh, *ja*. The pregnancy. *Mina*, I'm a Zulu boy. I'm not scared of things like that – teenage pregnancy. I mean, my family could afford it. Besides, she could have just stayed away from school for a few months, then we would get married and she would go to university *mos*. It's not unusual. University is not for single people only. So, you know this one, *mos*. She agreed to my plan. She does that sometimes – agrees with something – meantime, she doesn't mean it!' he screamed and then spat in her face again.

Winston stood up and said, 'That's enough. I've heard your story, now get out of my house before I call the police.'

'You're lying, *Ta* Winston. You do want to hear what happened. After all, better the devil you know, right?' he asked, and winked at Winston again. 'Don't worry. It's almost over. Here's the best part: so we agree to keep the baby, and then I go to the village to talk to my uncles about this matter between me and Sade. I go for about two weeks, and by that time she's in her seventh or eighth month. She's at a boarding school, a good one, in Inanda. When I come back, the news is all over town. You see, we never told anyone but our families about the pregnancy. She was so small, and only seventeen, she never even showed. So when I get back to Inanda, I hear that a baby was found in one of the toilets of the girls' dormitories. Can you believe it? A dead baby in the girls' dormitories, *wena, Ta* Winston.' Then the man suddenly stopped speaking. He let go of Sade, dropped the knife onto the floor, and crumpled into a large human bundle, his body shaking with grief, filling the room with the haunting sound of a grown man crying.

He did not say anything after that. He just stood up and left.

Chapter 42

Dikeledi

Dikeledi was still thinking about her last dance with Professor Kwame. It was hard to believe that after more than a year of attending the dance class, they had suddenly almost kissed last night. What was she to do? Maybe it had something to do with the fact that, after proposing to her, Tebogo had not done anything further to show his commitment to her except, of course, by letting her move in with him – which was inevitable in any case. For months he had made excuses about not having enough money to pay off the rest of the *lobola*, and now, he was busy 'working late' so that he could pay off the balance of his *lobola* and save up for them to get a decent home. As if they needed such a thing. His three-bedroom cluster was more than sufficient.

Was he trying to compete with Sade and Winston's opulent lifestyle? Those two were in a completely different league. Winston earned a six-figure salary; he could afford to live on that fancy estate, with all the trappings of a modern upwardly mobile couple. Besides, Dikeledi had never desired an ostentatious lifestyle. For her, having a devoted husband and a beautiful, close-knit family would always be enough. Which was why it was so ironic that she almost had a devoted husband, and she almost had a stable family life, but she was still somewhat . . . unhappy. Something was missing, but she could not put her finger on exactly what it was.

Her phone buzzed. It was a text message. Probably Tebogo working late again.

Enjoyed the slight flutter of those soft, sweet lips.

Oh goodness, it was the professor! If Tebogo ever came across this, Dikeledi would be dead meat, but, as if it were some forbidden fruit, she could not keep from looking at the message again. She felt a smile playing on her lips. She thought of him, holding her by the chin, as if afraid she'd withdraw from him. She remembered thinking, I need to stop this, before feeling his lips join on to hers. She wanted to pull away, but it was so hard. It was as if she were under his spell. But her senses quickly returned to her and she did pull away. For some reason, though, the warmth of his lips on hers never quite left her. Was she really falling for this man? No. She knew what this was: it had to be infatuation. Tebogo was her one and only. Wasn't he?

'Mom, I'm finished with my bath but I don't have a towel. Please bring it!' shouted Phemelo.

Dikeledi stood up reluctantly. Why couldn't Tebogo be half as attentive as Professor Kwame? Then maybe she wouldn't think about the professor so much. Distractedly, she fished a fresh towel from her wardrobe and went to give it to Phemelo.

It was already half past eight. Where was Tebogo? She'd grown tired of phoning to check on him. She knew that she was already playing the role of the nagging wife, which was unfair; she did not even officially qualify to carry the title of 'wife'. After all, the only thing she had to prove her status was an engagement ring, which had been sprung on her on the day that she was going to quit this hollow relationship. It was funny how she increasingly referred to that day as such. The main thing she remembered these days was that had he not chosen that fateful day to propose, she would have really left. What was going on with her?

She tucked Phemelo into bed and switched off her bedroom light.

Just then, the front door lock turned.

'Hello . . . anybody home?'

It was Tebogo. At least he was not so late tonight.

'Hi, babe. I'm so hungry I could eat a horse. I was putting the final touches on my Gidane case. Baby, if I win this one, you don't know. All our troubles will be over,' he said, taking the plate of food she offered him.

'What troubles? We don't have troubles, Tebogo. You're speaking as if we're living in a shack or something.'

'Dikeledi, there's nothing wrong with being a little ambitious, you know. This lecturing thing of yours is keeping you out of touch with what's happening out there in the real world. Look at your friends. They are making serious waves, and they are fulfilled. They drive nice cars; I also want to see you driving a nice Beemer instead of that old Honda, babe. More importantly, Phemelo must go to the best schools and get a degree and grow up enjoying a good quality of life so that she doesn't have to be impressed by some older man who promises her heaven and earth. She must be accustomed to the good life so that she's nobody's victim. You don't know how vulnerable young women are these days.'

Dikeledi looked at him, unimpressed. 'And I suppose with your vast experience with young women, you would know exactly how vulnerable they are, hence you want to protect your own daughter from men like you.'

Tebogo was stung. He dropped his knife and fork and stared at her for a long time. 'Kedi, exactly what is going on with you these

206

days? You're judgemental, bitter even. Nothing I do or say seems to please you. What's wrong, baby? What's missing?' he asked.

Dikeledi did not know what to say. Suddenly she felt guilty for jumping on him when all he was saying was that he had their daughter's best interest at heart. Lately, she found little to appreciate in Tebogo. Was it because someone else had started dominating her thoughts?

She went over to him and started massaging his shoulders. 'Babes, I don't know what's going on with me. You know, before we got engaged, I had this idea that I needed to go away and just be by myself because so much was going on in my head. Besides, ever since varsity I've never really been by myself. You're always there, and I think I've lost touch with myself. I think I need to take a break; nothing too hectic, maybe a long weekend somewhere . . . away. I just need time out.'

He pulled her by the hand and sat her on his lap. 'Are we okay? Are you having doubts about us?'

She shook her head, although she was struck by how unconvincing she must have looked. Why was she having doubts? Is this not what she'd been waiting for all these years?

Tebogo sighed with relief, oblivious of Dikeledi's inner turmoil. 'Because I've never felt more committed to you than I am right now, Kedi, I swear. I know before I was this lousy player who did not appreciate you and my daughter, but the long hours I'm keeping are not about girls, believe me. They are just about me wanting to build a solid foundation for my family. To provide for the two of you and maybe another little one later,' he said, kissing her gently while rubbing her left nipple through the flimsy top she was wearing.

After allowing herself to be lost in him, she stopped and looked him in the eye. 'Will you love me enough and trust in us enough to give me the space that I'm asking for? Just a weekend, some time on my own?'

His big round eyes stared into hers. 'You're not seeing anyone, are you?' he asked, laughing at the preposterousness of the question. He had never seen Dikeledi so much as look at another man in all the time they had been together.

She jabbed him in the shoulder. 'Are you mad, *wena*? I don't have time for such things,' she said, kissing him fondly. 'But I'm glad you're a little bit jealous. I don't remember ever giving you a reason to be.'

He bit her lower lip and kissed her with great tenderness. 'I trust you, my sweet wife-to-be. You can take your break but give Phemelo and me enough notice so we can plan something that will make you regret ditching us,' he said.

'Oh, you're the best. Thanks, love. Now let me show you my appreciation,' she said, leading him slowly to the bedroom while taking off his clothes along the way.

Just after their bout of lovemaking, Dikeledi's phone rang from the lounge. She sprang up to fetch it, worried about who would call her so late in the evening. When she got to the phone, she heard Sade's worried voice on the line.

'He was here, Dikeledi . . . yesterday morning. He just showed up on my doorstep! You don't know what a nightmare it was. Now Winston knows everything!' she said, her voice choking with tears.

'What? You mean . . . do you mean Malusi?'

'Yes. I don't know when this nightmare is going to end. I thought if I changed my life and chose to be closer to God, this thing would just disappear; that I would be forgiven and start on a clean page. But it's not going away, Dikeledi, it's not,' she moaned hysterically.

'Is Winston there with you now? How did he react?'

There was a long pause. 'Well, I guess . . . you know Winston is a family man, and he's a good Christian. He certainly did not believe me to be capable of all that Malusi was saying, but there's a lot of tension in the house, Kedi. I wonder if my marriage will survive this. Imagine being divorced after only one year of marriage!'

Dikeledi was in shock. Malusi cast such a dark shadow in Sade's life. Dikeledi had tried to protect her from him since high school. The first time Malusi was admitted to a mental institution was through Dikeledi's assistance. Nobody believed the torture and harassment that Sade claimed to be enduring from a boy so popular in the township nearest to their boarding school.

Malusi was from a well-off family, so all the girls wanted him, but he was obsessed with Sade almost from the first day he laid eyes on her. He had wanted to marry her, but Sade panicked about how society would perceive her once it was discovered that she had been pregnant while in high school. Sade was extremely vain at the time. She had refused to allow anything to mar her reputation as the most beautiful girl at the school and in her neighbourhood. A baby was the last thing she had wanted, despite Malusi's insistence that he would stand by her throughout the predicament. She had opted to have an abortion, an act that sent Malusi completely off the rails. Malusi had been looking forward to fathering her child, regardless of his young age, but Sade had felt trapped and immediately knew she was too young to see the pregnancy through. When Malusi's psychosis seemed to threaten Sade's life, Dikeledi had agreed to testify that the threats and the pictures of dead babies that were constantly dropped off at Sade's dormitory room were the product of Malusi's disturbed mind.

Whenever Malusi had seen Sade around town, he had chased her and threatened to stab or throttle her. He would shout at her in public, calling her a murderer or a baby killer . . . even claiming that she left their baby in the school toilets when she was eight months into her pregnancy. In truth, Dikeledi had accompanied Sade to a women's clinic, and she had had the abortion done there when she was eight weeks pregnant.

Since then, Malusi had been periodically in and out of mental hospitals.

'Can I come and see you tomorrow, Sade? You sound edgy,' she offered.

'No, no. Eh . . . no. I just needed to talk to you. You're my sister; you're the only one I can talk to about this. I'm just glad he hasn't involved my parents. Imagine my father's reaction. He would make me relive the whole ordeal. I mean, Dikeledi, at least you understand I was only seventeen years old. I was a different person then!' she cried.

'Shh. Don't berate yourself, sweetie, please. Take some sleeping tablets and relax. Your baby needs you to be strong right now; don't lose your cool. I wish you'd allow me to come and see you. I know how Malusi rattles you. Please let me come through. I'll swing by your house during my lunch hour. I know you want to give Winston the sense that you guys can wade through this alone, but it's a very sensitive issue.'

Sade was quiet for a while. 'I don't want to bother you, Kedi. It's not like you're the one who killed your own baby, you know.'

'Stop it, Sade. I'm coming by your house tomorrow, okay? End of story,' she said, and put the phone down.

Chapter 43

SADE

The next morning, Sade was shaky, nervous and neurotic. She had changed Ntokozo's nappy and given her the first morning bottle. Even though she was no longer working, she and Winston had hired a nanny, Sibongile, who stayed with them during the week, but left over weekends.

Ntokozo was sleeping fitfully upstairs while Sade kept putting on heavy make-up to hide the bruises that Winston had inflicted on her after Malusi's visit. As she applied foundation below her right eye, the area most bruised by Winston's thunderous blows, she wondered whether this was how the rest of her life was going to unravel. A vivid image of Winston's face right after Malusi had left their house flashed through her mind. He had turned into the man she had last seen over a year ago, when he had first stumbled upon her scandalous past.

She knew, deep down, that he would never forgive her. Malusi's revelations had turned her into a monster, a demon in Winston's eyes. In a way, she understood why he would be reviled by her. There she was, acting like the good Christian, yet she had committed murder. That was what Winston called her – a murderer, a baby killer.

She was willing to serve her penance, but surely God would forgive her. Surely Winston would one day see her for the woman she had become instead of the woman she had left behind. After his last temper tantrum she had tried to explain this to him, tried to plead with him to help her overcome her transgressions. Although it was difficult, he had seemed to be willing to help her build herself up again in God's eyes. She was thankful that Winston was willing to give her a chance.

Her wristwatch showed ten minutes to twelve. Dikeledi would be arriving soon. She could not bear any of her friends knowing that Winston was sometimes abusive. Of course, it was occasional. She did not want her husband judged by incidents that she had only brought on herself. She knew well enough that had she not had such a murky past, Winston would never have raised his hand against her . . . ever! She winced at the thought, and broke down again, spoiling all the handiwork she'd done to fix her face.

Feeling pathetic, she went to wash her face and started all over again. Foundation, powder, more powder, mascara, blusher. Finally she convinced herself that she had managed to hide all traces of yesterday's assault.

After she and Winston had sat down to talk about how Sade could make amends for her past, he had broken down and asked her to forgive him for having lashed out at her like that. Sade prayed that there would be no more skeletons coming back to haunt her. She really did not want to turn Winston into a monster. She wanted her old Winston back.

Thirty minutes later, Dikeledi was at her door. She'd brought some bran muffins with her to soothe Sade's nerves. She knew they were Sade's favourite.

Sade opened the door with a wide, if strained, smile and hugged her best friend. After holding on tightly to each other, Dikeledi finally withdrew and held Sade at arm's length.

'How've you been? Seriously?' she asked with concern.

Sade turned her head and started acting busy. 'Sit down while I make some coffee. Thanks for the muffins,' she said as she busied herself in her immaculate, ultra-modern kitchen.

'Where's your helper? Can't she make us the coffee? I only have forty-five minutes left; I need to sit with you right here. I can't afford to waste the time.'

'Don't worry,' said Sade from the kitchen, 'I'll be done in a minute. I'd already set the espresso machine so it won't take too long. How are things at the varsity?'

Dikeledi watched Sade from her seat in the lounge. She was acting nervously; she seemed too frantic. Something was definitely wrong.

'*Hhayi,* man, *wena*. Come sit with me or else let me join you there.'

A few minutes later, Sade was in the lounge with two steaming cups of coffee on a tray with milk and sugar. 'Okay, Hitler, here I am. Don't fuss over me. I know I sounded a bit rattled on the phone last night, but I was just panicked. The wound is not so raw anymore.'

Dikeledi sipped appreciatively on her coffee and bit into her muffin, which she had covered generously with peach jam. 'Hmm. Nice. This is pure indulgence. Now I see why you insisted on making the coffee yourself. It's coffee-bar perfect.'

'*Ja*, it's weird how I've become so domesticated since I quit my job. I can cook anything now, from gourmet meals to *umnqcusho*, and *mala mogodu*! You should see whenever Winston brings one of his colleagues over for dinner – he just fawns over me cos I've become incredibly good at making him look good.'

Dikeledi was slightly bewildered. As much as she was all for marriage, she could not believe that Sade was actually turning into a full-time, happy housewife. For a second, she had a wild image of herself preparing *mala mogodu* for Tebogo's white-collar criminal clients and some drunken judge. She shuddered visibly.

'But, *sweetie*, are you fulfilled? When you look in the mirror, do you still see Sade staring back or do you sometimes feel like it's someone else?' asked Dikeledi.

Sade was annoyed at the question. Who did Dikeledi think she was, practising her cheap psychology on her? If she was that good, she'd be running a successful practice instead of teaching disinterested first-year students. 'Why do you ask me that? Are you implying I'm some kind of impostor?' she demanded, hands on her hips and an ugly twisted expression on her face.

For the first time Dikeledi noticed Sade's heavy make-up. What in the world for? It wasn't as if she was going anywhere.

'Darling,' she said, extending her hand and placing it on Sade's, 'I'm not attacking you. In fact, I'm being a bit selfish because I'm talking about myself. The other day I told Tebogo I'm going for a weekend break . . . to find myself. I've been feeling a bit afloat lately.'

Sade felt uncharacteristically envious. Such a request would be regarded with outright suspicion in her household. 'Tebogo actually said yes? That's unbelievable. I don't think Winston would agree to such a thing in a thousand years.'

'Why? Is he the jealous type?'

Sade shrugged. 'I suppose you could say that. He really did not take too kindly to Malusi's allegations, hey. I'd never seen him so mad. He terrified me . . . absolutely. I just hope he never has to go through that again. I really love him, Kedi. I don't want to lose him.'

Dikeledi felt uneasy. There was something she could not put her finger on. There was something about how Sade constantly cast herself as the culprit whenever something went wrong between her and Winston. Of course, there was no denying her past but it was not like Sade to play the victim to the extent that she did with Winston. It seemed that in Sade's eyes, Winston was faultless. But then again, the little that Dikeledi knew of Winston did seem virtuous. Almost too perfect, now that she thought about it.

'Listen, Sade, from what I've seen of Winston whenever he's around, there's very little chance of him leaving you anytime soon. The man absolutely adores you. Besides, where in this world is anyone ever going to find another Sade? Hmm? You're just too special, too . . . I don't know . . . intriguing for any man to just let you go like that. I mean, for my part, I've never seen someone reinvent herself like you've done. You could give Lady Gaga a serious run for her money!' she said, flashing a fire-warm smile.

Sade fought back tears. She hugged Dikeledi, feeling blessed in the knowledge that someone believed in her with such unbridled conviction. 'Thank you, friend. Thank you so much. And listen . . .' she said, holding on to Dikeledi's hands, 'I'm sorry about the wedding.' Her tears were running freely now.

'No, man, you've got nothing to be sorry about. That was your day, *wena*!'

Sade shook her head. 'I know what I did. You don't need to defend me, Dikeledi. If I could do it all over again, I would have you there as my maid of honour. I'm so sorry for not doing the right thing. I'm a bit crazy and stupid sometimes.'

Dikeledi was shocked and touched at the same time. 'It's okay, Sade. I was a bit hurt at the time, but I was such a mess myself with Tebogo and his girlfriend stories. I'm not sure if I'm overstepping the mark here, but I've noticed how you've changed since you met Winston. Listen, Sade, Winston is not a perfect person, or a perfect man; no one is. I know he's great and everything but it sometimes seems like you've got him on this pedestal, like he's someone who can't do any wrong, but you really have to cut yourself some slack too, otherwise he'll end up not respecting you. The relationship can't just be about him.'

Sade looked at her with a frown. 'Look, with all due respect, Kedi, you're my friend and all, but I don't really appreciate you judging Winston without really knowing him. That man is the best thing that's ever happened to me. I don't know what you mean about placing him on a pedestal. Unlike other guys he doesn't go around screwing everything that walks. He's a man of God, who is deeply committed to his family. If I love him for that, then please don't punish me for my sins,' she said sarcastically, pulling her head back disdainfully.

Dikeledi was left blinking at her, shocked at the defensiveness of her tone. 'Oh. So because I'm "stuck" with someone who "screws everything that walks", I'm not allowed to comment on your perfect husband? Well, Sade, once you see your perfect Winston's true colours, don't come running to me for help cos, quite frankly, I'm tired of nursing your wounds while you do nothing but act superior all the time!' she said, as she marched out the door.

Chapter 44

LINDA

Linda looked at the glossy invitation for the umpteenth time. She could not believe it had been delivered to her office. This was done to make sure that she got it in case she had relocated her residence.

> The Rikhotso and Mokwena families cordially invite you the wedding of Lehumo Rikhotso and Shanice Mokwena.

She shook her head. Lehumo had certainly recovered from their break-up. Suddenly she was struck by how cold she had been throughout the incident. She wondered how Lehumo recounted the tale to those who cared to listen. Since that fateful day she had met one or two of Lehumo's friends and they had treated her with the disdain usually reserved for hardened criminals.

What if her relationship with Kennedy was destined for a similar disastrous denouement? She certainly had a shocking relationship track record. Was she merely an overgrown child posing as an adult? Why was it that she seemed to court disaster whenever she was involved with the opposite sex? Her mother, who was now critically ill, exacerbated her worry by constantly asking her when she was going to settle down. Perhaps she was right after all. Maybe she was just like her father.

The phone on her desk jolted her out of her torturous reverie.

'Hi, Linda. It's Deon. Did you see today's paper?'

Not now Deon, she thought. 'Umm . . . no. What's the story?'

'Do you remember that story you did on Dineo Fakude? The one I suggested?'

Of course. How could she forget? Deon had been mighty pleased with himself for having suggested that Linda produce 'a day in the life of a Hillbrow prostitute' for her company's current affairs programme *On Cue*. The documentary had an unusually high audience rating and was subsequently rebroadcast three times due to viewer demand. 'Yes, Deon, of course I remember Dineo. Is she in the papers?'

'Get today's *Reporter* and call me after reading the front page,' he said, promptly hanging up.

Suddenly feeling an adrenaline rush, she rose up from her desk, grabbed her bag and headed for the corner cafe. Before she could even get there, she saw an A3-size *Reporter* poster screaming in bold type:

On Cue prostitute found dead.

Oh no. Poor Dineo. Trust the tabloids to tap into the publicity that her documentary had generated. She went into the cafe, grabbed the paper and hurriedly whipped out a five-rand coin to give to the cashier. Ignoring the thick fish-and-chips smell that usually revolted her, she walked back to her office while reading the shocking front-page news story.

Dineo had been found in a dingy hotel in Hillbrow with deep strangulation marks around her neck. Predictably, everyone in the hotel claimed not to have witnessed her coming in. Nobody knew if anyone had been with her. Quite simply, nobody was talking.

218

She hurried back to her desk and immediately called Deon. 'Poor girl. Did you hear how she was murdered? Jeez, Deon. You want us to take on this story, don't you?'

'Well, we discovered her,' he said, as if Dineo were some choice meat that they had heroically stumbled upon.

'Last time I checked, being strangled in a seedy hotel did not make for *SA's Got Talent.*'

'Hmm, Linda. Watch that tongue. Your contract is due for review in a few months' time, you know.'

'Yes, yes, so you keep reminding me,' she retorted.

On Cue was the most highly rated current affairs programme on the channel; there were minimal chances of it being scrapped. Although, in her industry, egos were sometimes in charge, so she made a mental note to behave . . . at least until the contract was renewed.

'Listen, I think you should get your crew to go back to Hillbrow and talk to some of Dineo's friends. Find out what the feeling is on the ground, hit all the right spots. Once you turn on that Mthimkhulu charm that you reserve for your sources, I know you can find all the angles that everyone else is missing. Maybe you can add more kudos to that wall of fame in your office.'

'*Ja*, look, I know it's a sexy story, Deon, but it sounds like a pretty dangerous one to me as well. Just give me a day or two to sleep on it, please.'

A pregnant pause followed. Finally, Deon said, 'Okay, twenty-four hours. Think about it. And remember, this is the kind of thing that's made your show stay on air so you don't want to tempt fate here, hey.'

She could almost see the silly smirk on his face as he said that. Bloody Deon.

Chapter 45

Dikeledi

Dikeledi was looking at the pictures on the website of the lodge that she had booked for her weekend getaway. She clicked on the image of a woman lying down like the Queen of Sheba as a masseuse rubbed hot stones down her back. Hmm, she smiled, closing her eyes in dreamy anticipation.

Just then Professor Kwame entered her office. 'Penny for your thoughts, lovely lady,' he said.

Startled, Dikeledi swung her chair around to face him. '*Eish*, Prof. When are you ever going to stop sneaking up on me like this?'

He swaggered further into her office and looked at the screen. 'Riverview Spa Resort – prepare to be pampered!' he read out loud, then whistled. 'Impressive,' he said. 'You certainly know how to spoil yourself. Are you going there with your family?'

She looked up at him, not for the first time noticing the way he looked at her. Always with a very slow, seductive gaze. 'Nope. This is me finally taking time out on my own. Just to relax and find my centre. Have you ever felt like that? A need to get away from everyone, just to rediscover yourself again?'

The professor shrugged. 'Well, of course. I think we all need our own space from time to time. Perfectly normal. Although I'll be fantasising about joining you all weekend long,' he added naughtily.

'Then maybe you should join me,' she heard herself say, and instantly regretted the words.

'I'll take that as an invitation.'

'No, no, no. I was only joking,' she replied, covering her face like a bashful child.

'Well, you don't know my plans for the weekend. Maybe I'll accidentally bump into you,' he said, studying the computer behind Dikeledi with intent. 'Hmm . . . www.riversidespa.com. Okay, see you around,' he said jauntily, as he left her gaping after him.

Alone again, Dikeledi panicked. What if he meant it? Part of her found the idea titillating. The other part prayed that he did not mean it. Either way, this professor was becoming dangerously adept at pressing the sort of buttons that Tebogo had had sole propriety of for years. She smiled to herself, imagining the prof lying next to her on a massage bed. Tsk. This was so out of character. She had never met someone with such a powerful sexual aura. Maybe it was a Ghanaian thing. From what Linda had said of her own escapades with the men from the north, these brothers certainly possessed a sexual prowess that belonged in a class of its own.

She suddenly felt like a virgin again. Considering that she had only been with one man all her life, the prof would probably find her too inexperienced. Maybe that's why Tebogo sometimes ran into the arms of other women, she pondered sadly. Then she laughed at herself. When did she move from fantasising about a soul-searching weekend to considering the sexual prowess of Ghanaian professors? Really! She just needed to get a life.

Chapter 46

SADE

Sade returned from her boxercise class feeling drained and exhausted. The class had come out earlier than scheduled, so she was looking forward to getting home and relaxing in a hot bath before preparing dinner for her and Winston. As she pushed through the predictable traffic so synonymous with her residential area, she sighed and tuned the radio to the Classic FM traffic report.

Apparently a truck had overturned on the highway not far from Winston's workplace. She considered calling to warn him about it but thought better of it. She wanted to have enough time to spruce up for him when she got home. She was feeling terribly randy and looking forward to being with him. She noticed that her abs were becoming tighter, thanks to the toning exercise she had been doing. She couldn't wait to put her fabulous new body to good use.

Her relationship with Winston had started improving after they had attended couples' counselling classes again at church. Winston had seemed keen to work through their problems, and neither of them wanted to see the relationship end in divorce. Occasionally he would seem glum and moody, sometimes grilling her about her past, but she was glad to see that he was working hard at controlling his violent temper. What seemed to bother him more than the abortion were the revelations about her promiscuity at varsity. There had been one night when he kept her up for hours, demanding that she tell him exactly how many men she had slept with and what she had done with them. He had wanted graphic details of sexual positions, how many times and where.

His obsession with her sexual history was like a cruel tormentor that always seemed to visit their bedroom. Winston was becoming increasingly insecure, sometimes grilling her about her passion for the gym. Who was she seeing there? Why did she go to the gym when he was perfectly happy with her body? Who did she want to impress? She prayed steadfastly that this new, ugly side of their relationship would also pass.

The thing about Winston was that he was terribly complex. One minute he seemed like a ticking time bomb on the point of exploding into the violent man she had encountered, and the next he was the personification of a prince. Winston had taken her and their daughter to Disneyland, something she had never thought she would experience in her lifetime. He certainly knew how to dole out the charm when he felt like it. Throughout the trip to Florida, he had acted like the perfect husband and father. He had even talked about adding another bundle to their family, which had raised Sade's hopes about their relationship.

As she opened up the automatic garage door, she realised, to her mild disappointment, that Winston's car was already parked in its usual spot. She drew in a long, deep breath, grabbed her gym bag and opened the kitchen door. She steeled herself in anticipation of yet another lecture from Winston about how she was obsessed with her body and how she should be sitting at home with Ntokozo instead of showing off her body to the men at her gym.

Did he really expect her to be content with staying indoors all day? The gym only took about two hours of her time each day.

Besides, what were they paying Sibongile for, if she could not afford even two hours in the day to herself?

Much to her surprise, she heard muffled sounds coming from the living room. As she approached the room, she saw one of Winston's shoes thrown carelessly on the floor. When she entered the lounge area, she was shocked to find Winston and *her* maid of honour, Palesa, caressing each other in *her* living room.

Horrified, she dropped her gym bag onto the floor. Hands flailing in the air, she screamed, 'What in the world is going on here? What is this slut doing on my brand-new leather couch?'

The couple quickly got up and tried to grab whatever items of clothing they could to cover themselves. 'Baby, I'm sorry. It's not what it looks like. I swear,' said Winston.

'Not what it looks like? What are you talking about, Winston? You made me give up my friends so that this bitch here would stand beside me on my wedding day; meantime, you're screwing the living daylights out of her! How dare you? How dare you humiliate me like this?' she raged.

Palesa stood up, and was shamefully zipping up her jeans and putting on her shoes when Sade approached her, fuelled by aggression. Before Palesa knew what was happening, Sade had yanked her up by her weave and slapped her on both sides of her face.

'*Hey wena*. Where do you think you're going, you disgusting home-wrecker? Sister this, sister that, acting like a good Christian, whereas all you are is a slut who sleeps with other people's husbands. *Sies!*' She spat at her. 'Get out of my house, you bitch!'

Winston stood up. 'Okay, Sade. I know you're upset but there's no need to treat her like that. How is she going to look at us in church when you're acting like a common *bitch*, beating other women up like this? Baby, you're a lady. That's why I married you. Please try and act like one.'

'What! Are you mad? Do you hear what you're saying? I want a divorce. That's what you're trying to do anyway, isn't it? That's what all this is about. You want to break me until I ask for a divorce, don't you? Well, guess what, you're getting it!' she screamed, as she went upstairs to check on her daughter.

Minutes later Sade was back downstairs to find Palesa gone and Winston sitting on the couch looking despondent. All the arrogance and cockiness had been wiped away.

'Where's my daughter?' she asked her husband.

'Our daughter? Sibongile took her for a stroll in the park.'

She laughed derisively. She felt like a vampire. She wanted to jump on Winston and suck the lifeblood out of him. She had never been so disgusted. 'How convenient. So when it suits you, Sibongile must take our daughter out so you can fuck the woman you forced me to have as my maid of honour. Well, I can see that she's a maid all right. How much did you pay her to do what she was doing here?'

He stood up and grabbed her by the arm, twisting it painfully. She froze, rooted to the spot, and looked him in the eye with deadly intensity. 'Go ahead and hit me. Do it. When we get to the divorce courts I'll make sure you never see Ntokozo again. After all, I'm sure the courts won't be convinced that you'll manage to resist hitting her since you've become so fond of bashing me around.'

Right then he stopped and looked at her fearfully. He shook his head. 'You can't be talking like this, Sade. You can't be talking about divorce so early in our marriage. You know . . . you are the one who's doing this to me. You're turning me into something I'm not, and I'm scared, baby. I'm really scared.'

'Oh, you'd rather I postponed it for later? And what, Winston Thamsanqa Gumede, exactly am I doing to you? I did not take out your dick and stick it into that woman!'

He slumped onto the couch and covered his head with his giant hands. 'Baby, I'm sorry. I really don't know what's come over me. I love you, Sade. I've never loved any other woman more than I love you. Sometimes I feel like it's driving me crazy, this whole idea of loving you so much. I end up doing stupid things. When I heard about the stuff you did in the past . . . it made me feel like less of a man. Like all these men . . . all these faceless sinners, have contaminated your body.

'Sister Palesa . . . she is nothing like you. I have no feelings for her whatsoever, but lately I have been feeling so weak. I feel like I'm competing with all your former lovers . . . and . . . and I'll never catch up.'

Sade threw her arms up in the air. 'What are you talking about, Winston? This will never work! If you've decided to go on some kind of sexual rampage because you want to even out the score between us, then what am I doing here? Must I sit here and wait for AIDS to get me while you try to "catch up"?'

Winston looked up from the couch and shook his head, tears in his eyes. 'Please, Sade, please forgive me. I'm trying my best to deal with something that is completely foreign to me. When I asked you to become my wife, you were an angel in my eyes. The things I discovered about you . . . they did not make me love you any less, but they were too much for me to deal with. Too much to take in . . . You don't understand.

'I've always seen you as my ideal woman. Beautiful, principled, intelligent, God-fearing . . . You were all these things and more . . . much more. But the discovery, Sade . . . the discovery about your past . . . it almost broke me. It really did,' he said, covering his eyes.

Now he was crying in a way that she had never thought him capable of and it broke her heart. She went over and put her hand on his. She had never felt such tenderness for anyone, but she feared her love for him would destroy her.

'Winston, it doesn't have to be this way between us. I don't know how much more I have to repent for what I did in my past but if you keep throwing it back at me like this, I am going to have to start all over . . . without you. I've matured so much spiritually since I committed myself to God, but your behaviour makes me feel like I'm regressing. This has to stop, or else I will leave you.'

He was quiet for a long time, as if taking in everything she was saying. He held her hands and looked into her eyes. 'I'm sorry. Please give me one last chance. I'll do anything to keep you, Sade. You don't know how much you mean to me.'

She sighed. She hoped they could overcome all these obstacles. Secretly she hoped this incident would mark the end of the worst for, surely, he had finally evened the score.

Chapter 47

Nolwazi

Nolwazi was running late for her appointment with Simphiwe, whom she had grown close to over the past few months. She had never met anyone as stylish and debonair as this man. She cursed her luck that he was not interested in her in the way she wished he would be. As she checked her bag once more to ensure that she had the two theatre tickets he'd secured for them, she shook her head, once again berating herself for fawning over a gay man.

'Only I would go and fall for someone who has no interest in my entire gender; you'd think I'd learned my lessons about unavailable men after that disaster with Tebogo,' she murmured to herself.

As she prepared to step out the door, her phone rang. She was surprised to see it was Linda. Linda had seemingly resorted to her old ways of rarely keeping in touch. Nolwazi was somewhat disappointed to note that the attentive Linda she had left behind in Johannesburg seemed to have faded into oblivion, replaced by the self-absorbed Linda of old. With mild irritation she remembered that she had left several unreturned messages for her. Some friend!

'Hi, Linda. What's up?' she asked, trying to hide her general disappointment with her.

'Hey you. I'm fine. Listen, I'm really sorry I haven't had a chance to get back to you, but I've been swamped with work. How's the pregnant city?'

'I think you mean the mother city. It's fine.'

'Well, it does take nine months for anything to happen, so since I'm yet to hear anything exciting coming from there, to me, it's still very much pregnant.'

They both laughed.

'You're crazy, you know. I was mad at you for not calling but trust you to get me laughing when my intention was to punish you with a severe cold shoulder.'

'*Ag*, shame, man. You know how it is. I'm not exactly a great one for a long-distance relationship, but it doesn't mean I've forgotten about you. How are things going at the boutique?'

An involuntary smile played on Nolwazi's lips. 'Quite good, actually. These Cape Town ladies are loving Afropolitan Designs. I'm actually flying to Italy in a month's time to check out the fashion scene there and to get some new fabrics for the store.'

'Nice. Now you're the globe-trotter.'

'*Ja*. Simphiwe's actually the one who suggested it. He's incredibly stylish and has contacts I'd sell my granny for. He's hooked me up with a number of people I'll be meeting with when I get there.'

'Who's Simphiwe? The gay guy?'

'The one and only.'

'Lwazi, you seem to be spending an awful lot of time with this man. Have you taken a vow of chastity? I mean, yes he sounds amazing, but you should try and hook yourself up with some undercover lover as well. The body needs nourishment, you know.'

'I'm actually glad to be doing all these fantastic cultural things with Simphiwe. Besides, half the men in this town are gay anyway.'

Linda sighed. 'Only you would fall for one though. Anyways, don't be a stranger. I should try and scrounge up some leave so I can come there and check out the local fare, introduce you to some sexy boys so we can get rid of that chastity belt.'

Nolwazi was nonplussed. 'After what happened last time I unlocked the belt, I think I'm better off flying solo.'

'Hmm, never has a better point been made. Geez, babes, I'm so glad you can joke about that stuff now. Have you heard from the slimeball since you moved?'

There was a brief, uncomfortable pause. 'Nah . . . don't want to hear from him either. Actually, can we never talk about him again . . . as in ever?'

'You got it,' Linda said quickly, cautious not to spoil the light-hearted mood.

Wanting to cut the conversation short, Nolwazi looked at her watch. 'Oh my gosh! I'm late – as usual. We're going to the theatre. Gotta run!'

'Okay, enjoy!'

As Nolwazi ran through the door, she collided with her German friend and neighbour Eva, a tall, buxom, friendly blonde who had moved into the apartment next to Nolwazi's a few weeks after Nolwazi had settled in. They had immediately struck up a friendship at the launderette downstairs from their first-floor apartments, and had been revolving through each other's doors ever since. Eva was an exchange student studying her master's in political science at UCT. This further strengthened their kinship as Nolwazi was fascinated with the idea of someone over twenty battling it out with the young and fabulous varsity set in Cape Town.

'Ouch! That really hurt,' Eva shrieked in her distinctive German accent. Nolwazi had literally bumped into her nose when she had opened the door.

'Oops! I was in a bit of a hurry, and I really didn't know you were there. Are you okay?' she asked, touching Eva's red, scrunched-up nose.

'*Ja.* But be more careful next time. I'm a struggling student; my parents don't send me enough pocket money for me to afford a nose job.'

Nolwazi dragged her in by the hand. 'Let me get you some ice.'

'No, I'm fine. I swear. Where's the baby?'

'She's gone off with my cousin Ntombi. I'm going to the theatre with Simphiwe.'

'Really? That sounds nice. What are you guys watching?'

'*Rent.* It's finally playing at the Baxter Theatre and I'm so looking forward to it. Oh my gosh, look at the time! I really have to go . . . Listen, do you want to come with?' she asked, realising once more how lonely Eva's life probably was. She hardly ever socialised with anyone.

'You think Simphiwe won't mind?'

'Oh, please. Let me call the theatre and see if they've any more tickets available.'

After a few minutes on the phone, Nolwazi confirmed that they could still get a ticket for Eva.

'Can I go like this?' asked Eva, looking critically at her fashionably torn jeans and her white UCT sweater.

'Mmm. Maybe ditch the sweater but the jeans are all right,' said Nolwazi. 'In fact, I've got just the right leather jacket to show off those boobs of yours.'

Within ten minutes their cab pulled up at the theatre parking lot, where an impatient-looking Simphiwe stood looking at his watch.

'You're late,' he scolded, sounding uncharacteristically irritated.

'Sorry, sorry. I hope you don't mind Eva joining us. I thought it might be fun, especially when we go out for drinks later,' she said flippantly.

For a moment Simphiwe looked confused. He appraised them carefully; they looked like two naughty schoolgirls. They were actually holding hands and staring at him with stupid grins on their faces, as if waiting for approval. He sighed. 'Okay, okay. We've wasted enough time already. The play is about to start.'

As they walked in, Simphiwe and Nolwazi assumed their seats in the front row, which had been secured thanks to Simphiwe's friend who was a set director on the play. Eva had to sit further back.

Nolwazi kept stealing furtive glances at Simphiwe, trying to detect whether there were any traces left of his irritation. She felt a bit guilty about inviting Eva without checking with him first. She had not really expected him to react; after all, he had met Eva before and they had seemed to hit it off. Simphiwe, however, seemed impervious to her attention. He was fixated on the stage and didn't utter a single word throughout the production.

After the play, they went to an upmarket lounge and ordered drinks. They sat on a brown suede couch that was tastefully lit by the bar's low-hanging lamps. This was Nolwazi and Simphiwe's favourite hangout.

'So what did you think of the play?' asked Nolwazi, directing the question at both her friends.

'Mmm, I liked it. I've seen *Rent* before in New York. I prefer this version. Maybe it's just better vocals, I'm not sure,' volunteered Eva.

'Did you see the sets? They could have been better. I think there was not enough attention paid to detail. I know my friend designed it, but it looked a bit like a rush job. It did not completely suit the ambience of the play.'

Nolwazi smiled to herself. She liked how passionate he was about design and aesthetics. There was literally nothing she disliked about Simphiwe.

She noted that for a fleeting moment at the theatre, she had almost been tempted to interpret Simphiwe's annoyance at her showing up with Eva as a sign that maybe he had wanted it to be just the two of them.

'I thought the set was fine . . . beautiful, actually, but then again, I'm no architect,' said Eva, flashing a smile.

Just then, a young white man with scruffy features passed by their couch and asked if he could buy Eva a drink.

She grinned playfully. 'Sorry, I'm with her,' she said, pointing at Nolwazi.

Flushed with embarrassment, the young man left. The two girls had a good laugh about it.

Nolwazi said, 'Seriously though, does he think I'd let some guy run off with those sexy boobs?'

They both doubled up laughing. Simphiwe was the only who did not get the joke.

Chapter 48

Linda

As she left the seedy hotel in order to go to yet another of Hillbrow's dingy venues, Linda prayed that the text message she had just received was not a fluke. After three weeks of endless chasing, she was starting to lose patience with Dineo's story. First, she was tired of hanging around the dark holes of this neighbourhood, and second, there were no new leads, despite Deon's insistence that *On Cue* could break the case.

She walked hurriedly to meet the potential 'source' who had sent her the message asking her to meet them at the Summit Hotel – a renowned, albeit rundown, strip club that featured strippers for a much cheaper price than the mushrooming strip joints in the northern suburbs.

On her arrival she was greeted by a menacing-looking bouncer whose arms were tattooed with sketches of nude women in various sexual positions. His thick forearms were folded to show off the artistic work done on his body and his black mesh top exposed his exaggerated muscles. If he had been anywhere else in the world aside from at that door, one would still have been able to discern his vocation.

'What you want?' he asked, his Nigerian accent coming out thick and clear.

'I'm here to meet someone.'

'Are you a cop?'

'Don't embarrass me, okay? So I happen to like women . . . shoot me. Last time I checked, it wasn't a crime.'

The bouncer laughed. 'We cater to everyone here. Best fun under the African sun, guaranteed,' he said, winking.

'Can I get in or what?'

'Two hundred cover charge.'

She whipped out two crisp hundred-rand notes and handed them to him.

'Enjoy,' he said, laughing once more.

She shook her head, grimacing over what she had to put up with in pursuit of this story.

As she wandered into the place, her phone pinged. It was a text message from Kennedy.

Despite herself, she could feel the corners of her lips lifting as she knew it was probably a naughty message from her boyfriend.

Don't forget to sign us up for pole dancing lessons.

He knew how frustrated she was with the story and had been trying to cheer her up with random ridiculous texts. She responded quickly.

The doorman says they're looking for male strippers. You can finally quit that job you hate.

His reply came within seconds.

Please send a list of all my special qualities. I'm ready to go for it NOW!

She grinned and put her phone back in her bag. She really liked him. A lot.

As she looked around the joint, she was surprised it was still lit with eighties-style disco lights. The peeling wallpaper told stories of neglect and poor taste. A musty stench added to the overall effect of seediness that screamed from every corner of this 'hotel'.

Only three other patrons were present to enjoy the show: one old white man with a thick beer belly that threatened to fall on the floor, and two skinny men who seemed more intent on their conversation than on watching the show on stage.

She whipped out her phone and sent a text message to her source. 'I'm here,' she typed, but already a young woman, no older than eighteen, was approaching the bar chair where Linda was sitting rather uncomfortably.

'Hello. You the lady from that show.' It was more a statement than a question.

Linda nodded while she assessed her. The woman's face had black bruises, as if someone had punched her or knocked her against something. Although she looked young, she had a world-weary face and dead eyes.

The young woman sat down next to Linda, her shoulders hunched. 'I'm going to be very brief,' she said, her eyes downcast, as if she were afraid Linda would film her face if she looked up. 'The man who did this to me, my face, that's the same man who killed Dineo. He's a John. One of the not-so-regular ones. He comes here maybe once in six months; sometimes a whole year passes without us seeing him. He's violent – likes to slap the woman around – but he pays well. It's part of his whole thing . . . you know . . . part of his kink.'

Linda nodded sympathetically.

'So we're all scared of him because there are rumours that he's someone powerful, you know,' she said, now looking up at Linda.

'Powerful how? Politician? Drug lord? What?'

The woman shrugged. 'That's the thing. People don't say who he is exactly. They just claim he's powerful and they say it in hushed tones. You don't know how paranoid this place can get sometimes. Everyone looks like they're watching their back. My suspicion is he's with one of the drug rings . . . or else, like you say, maybe he's a hotshot politician with powerful connections. I'm not really sure.'

'So you know what he looks like? You'd be able to point him out to the police?'

The woman shook her head vigorously. 'I don't want anything to do with the police. As it is, my record stinks. The last time they held me I had to give some cop a blow job just so they would release me, but I think officially I'm still supposed to be behind bars. Besides, it's too much trouble. If I'm seen talking to cops, it'll get to that man. He's just trouble . . . big trouble. So I decided to talk to you instead. Maybe you can carry this forward for us. We're all scared. Some Johns can be very evil. We need to wipe them out. Teach them a lesson and show them that we're not helpless here. We also know people,' she said, lighting a cigarette.

'Okay. So how do I trace him? How do I find this guy?'

'Well, he drives a silver Merc, though sometimes he shows up in a BMW. I don't have the registration numbers, but here,' she said, taking out a piece of paper and scribbling something down, 'if you call this girl, she'll give it to you. She was best friends with Dineo. Sometimes he'd book the two of them together. Apparently, he was into some really kinky stuff, but those two are . . . *were* the only ones who could handle him.' She sighed.

'Did he ever tell you his name?'

'Name? They call him Mustafah. He calls himself that too but I don't know if it's his real name.'

Chapter 49

DIKELEDI

Dikeledi was enjoying the long drive . . . alone. She sighed. How long had it been since she had done something like this, just for herself? To her surprise, she realised that she had never done anything purely to satisfy her own needs. As she pushed her foot further down on the accelerator, her life flashed in front of her eyes, the way people claimed it did when they were about to die; yet death was the furthest thing from her mind. How had she been living all this time? Like someone on probation, that's how. It felt as if all her life she had lived as if she owed somebody something. As if within a hair's breadth, somebody would walk up to her and say, 'That's it, your time's up. You were not good enough. You are the weakest link.'

She sped up even more. Her little Honda was now doing 140 kilometres an hour. Why was she such a pathetic wet blanket? Take the argument she'd had with Sade a few weeks ago. Sade was obviously in the wrong, but as usual Dikeledi was the one who'd ended up being made to feel guilty. If Sade could not face up to the fact that her husband was not perfect, clearly she had something to hide, either from herself or from the rest of society. In fact, by protecting Winston's 'untainted honour', Sade was only drawing attention to his imperfections.

For instance, Dikeledi was Sade's closest friend, but Dikeledi and Winston had not, in the three years since she'd first met him, said anything beyond mild, affected greetings to each other. What kind of a husband could not be bothered to get to know their wife's closest friends? Humph! Even though Tebogo wasn't perfect, he was always friendly and warm towards everyone. Maybe that's what made Sade jealous. She had obviously realised that being stuck with that cold fish was not the boat of bliss she'd thought it would be.

Dikeledi was beginning to calm down and, by the indication of the road signs, she was also drawing nearer to her getaway. What joy! For the next two days she would only switch on her phone if she had to call Phemelo, otherwise, it would be a weekend of unbridled selfishness and, for a change, the word didn't make her cringe, which meant she was already a step closer to losing her martyr label.

She arrived at the Riverside Spa Resort to find a beautiful place, far removed from the rest of the world. It personified old-world charm, with a classy exterior surrounded by sprawling greenery from the top of the highest tree to the perfectly manicured lawns that covered the compound like a luxurious green blanket.

As she stepped out of the car, a short young woman in a white uniform branded with the resort's logo welcomed her. She had come down to meet her in the parking lot and introduced herself as Cecilia. She had a strong Zimbabwean accent and brilliant white teeth, which gleamed when she smiled.

'Hello. Welcome to the Riverside Spa Resort. We aim to please, so let me know if you need anything. You don't need to register at reception. You are Dikeledi Langa, right? We have all your details registered already on our system, even your ID photo, which is why I knew exactly who you were! Come with me,' she said, as she helped Dikeledi with her bag. 'I'll take you to your room.'

Dikeledi was impressed. This was exactly the kind of break she needed.

On the way to Dikeledi's room, they passed a few bucks and a long stream that seemed to whisper ancient secrets as they walked around it. She smiled, thinking how lovely it would be to come here with a lover. To her mild shock, she thought of Professor Kwame.

Cecilia was chattering amicably as they approached her room – a gorgeous setting with a double bed surrounded by classic Victorian-style curtains and mirrors that gave the place a warm, old-world feel.

'This is you,' said Cecilia, placing some of Dikeledi's luggage on a stand by the cupboard. 'If you need anything, dial nine for reception. If it's something very specific, ask for me,' she said, flashing her dental masterpiece once again.

'Thanks. I'll do that,' said Dikeledi as she settled in.

Dikeledi took off her clothes, which felt sun-drenched, especially in this fresh atmosphere, and got into the shower. There was a minibar in the room, so she helped herself to an ice-cold glass of Chardonnay after showering. Within minutes, she drifted off to sleep.

By the time she awoke it was already dark outside. She stared at the grandfather clock opposite her. It was seven o'clock. How long had she been sleeping? She sprayed water on her face, and put on her brand-new shorts with the feminine chiffon top that she had bought only two days before. Feeling like a queen, she applied a bit of lipstick and mascara and some French perfume. She grabbed her tiny bag and swayed towards the dining area.

As she entered the restaurant she saw a familiar figure sitting by himself and studying the menu. She froze. After what seemed like an eternity, she straightened her shoulders and sidled up to where the gentleman was sitting.

'And what, may I ask, are you doing here?'

He looked up, an exaggerated look of surprise on his face. 'My, my, my. What a great coincidence,' said Professor Kwame.

She put her hands on her hips and shook her head.

Professor Kwame laughed. '*Eish*,' he said, the South Africanism sounding odd coming from his lips. 'I'm in trouble now.' His face displayed a huge grin.

She shook her head again. 'What are you doing here, Professor?' she asked icily.

Her pulse was racing. Had she been leading him on? Seeing him here made her feel cornered. Maybe she'd bitten off more than she could chew. She felt like turning around and bolting back home to her safe, 'normal' life. Despite the professor's easy demeanour, she could not bring herself to thaw.

He raised his hands and with a resigned air, said, 'I come in peace . . . seriously. If you feel I'm intruding on your time out, you could always ignore me, you know. Pretend I'm not even here.'

She fumed, feeling like a deer caught in the headlights. 'You know what, actually, I'll do just that,' she said, and went over to sit two tables away from him as if to erect a barrier between them.

They both continued with their dinner, all the while pretending to ignore each other. After Professor Kwame had polished off his meal, however, he walked up to her table.

'Okay, I'm a fool. I admit it. I just came here on a whim, partly because I needed the break but mainly because I was hoping . . . I wasn't even sure because you never confirmed it, but yes, I came here in the hope of seeing you.'

She looked up, her round eyes still blazing with accusation. 'Why?' she asked, looking around to see if she had said this too loudly; her legs were shaking underneath the table.

'Why? May I sit . . . to explain?' he asked, sounding like a humbled teenage boy rather than the dashing figure that dazzled the female fraternity at their shared workplace.

She nodded, but the fierceness in her eyes remained.

'Well, one reason is that I honestly needed a holiday. I'm serious. Seeing you perusing the Internet for a getaway catalysed my own need to go on this vacation. Since I can be a bit lacking in imagination, I decided to choose this place because I saw the website on your PC,' he said, hoping that he sounded convincing enough. When he realised that she was still regarding him with the same stony glare, he continued. 'Okay, the other reason, of course' – he chuckled in a self-deprecating manner – 'is that I obviously hoped to bump into you. And, may I add, I hoped you'd gradually forgive my being so forward.'

A stony silence followed, then finally, Dikeledi said: 'I hope you're not expecting anything to come of this.'

He feigned a hurt expression. 'But, Dikeledi, of course not. Although I would love for us to take advantage of this beautiful resort and this great weather by going for cocktails by the lake. I've checked, they serve them till late. I can't think of a better way to start a long weekend.'

She smiled then, her dimples making attractive little dots on her face. 'Okay. I guess I might as well loosen up. I'm gonna go to my room and get something to put over my shoulders in case it gets a bit chilly. You know how cold it can get when you're near water.'

'All right, I'll go grab some cigars and I'll wait for you in the foyer.'

When Dikeledi got to her room, she found herself giggling with girlish gaiety. The wine she had consumed clearly had something to do with this heady feeling. Oh, but he certainly was quite gorgeous. And that voice . . . even Barry White would be green with envy!

Hmm. She looked at herself in the mirror. I definitely need more lipstick, she thought. And more perfume, she decided. She opened her suitcase to find something that would keep her warm without detracting from the sexy top that showed off her cleavage to its best advantage. Then she closed her eyes, did the sign of the cross, for some indiscernible reason, and left to join Professor Kwame.

By the time she reached the foyer, he was already standing up in anticipation of her arrival. They walked leisurely towards the *lapa* alongside the lake. The moon glimmered with a serenity that made them feel more intimately drawn to each other. The cool whispering of the water was their only companion as they approached their destination. They did not say much to each other but the atmosphere felt loaded with unspoken words.

When they reached the *lapa* they settled on two high chairs and were vaguely surprised to find a barman waiting to take their drink orders. They had almost forgotten that other human life awaited them at the cosy bar area. Professor Kwame insisted they order a cocktail and, both being partially shy due to the unexpected intimacy of the atmosphere, they settled for the most tame-sounding drink . . . Sex on the Beach.

Professor Kwame began to regale Dikeledi with anecdotes from his beloved Ghana, sharing unbelievably funny tales about the antics that he and his friends used to pull in their adolescent years in their attempts to charm females. Meanwhile, Dikeledi kept ordering more cocktails until the professor finally asked, 'Dikeledi, exactly how many times have you had Sex on the Beach?'

Now completely tipsy, Dikeledi did not notice the double meaning. 'What do you mean? Are you saying I'm a prude? I've had sex on the beach dozens of times . . . in different positions even. Certainly more than you . . .' *hiccup* '. . . and at more beaches!' *Hiccup*.

The professor laughed. 'I wasn't accusing you of being sexually infantile, Kedi,' he said, an amused smile playing on his lips. 'I was just worried that perhaps you've had too many of those cocktails.'

Now she was not only insulted but embarrassed. 'You know what? I think you're right, Kwame. And I can see you're making fun of me. I'm going to my room.'

'Wait. What's your room number? I'll walk with you.'

'I'm perfectly fine, thank you.'

'No, I'm serious. It's quite dark and it is a long walk. I'm in room twenty-one.'

That was the room next to hers. Had he orchestrated that too? Bloody stalker.

'Don't worry, I'm a big girl. I'm gone,' she said, and she marched back towards her room.

After walking around in circles for more than ten minutes, she realised that not only was she sobering up, but she had also managed to get lost in what had seemed to her like a rather small resort.

She wanted to cry. Bloody Sex on the Beach. Bloody Professor. *Sies!*

As she walked over a small bridge that she had not seen before, she tripped and almost fell into the water, twisting her leg on the crude wooden structure.

'I knew I'd find you eventually,' a voice said behind her. Professor Kwame helped her up and flung one of her arms across his shoulders. 'You are in no condition to walk alone, woman,' he said.

She kept quiet throughout the walk, limping slightly and feeling like a complete fool.

When they got to her room, she gingerly took out her key, and tried unsuccessfully to unlock the door. Professor Kwame opened it for her. She collapsed onto the bed, and immediately closed her eyes.

He brushed his lips against hers, and whispered, 'Goodnight, my perfect angel.'

In spite of her inebriated state, she could not help smiling to herself.

Chapter 50

LINDA

Linda received the news about her mother's passing at the worst place possible. She was at a grocery check-out counter when the call came through from the hospital. Her beloved mother had lost her life at ten fifteen that morning.

She stood frozen to the spot.

'That'll be three hundred and fifty rand, ma'am,' said the cashier. Linda stared into space. 'Ma'am. I said that'll be three hundred and fifty.'

For what seemed like an eternity, she could not make up her mind whether to pay for the groceries or to leave without them. 'My mother just died,' she said to nobody in particular, and walked, zombie-like, to her car.

Once in the car, Linda could not move. Somebody passed by her and greeted her with a smile, but she was not sure who the person was. She managed to say hello without realising that her mouth had even opened.

After ten minutes of vegetating in the car, she finally managed to drive to her mother's house. Once there, she found the only person she knew would share the same level of grief that she was feeling. Uncle Phuti was sitting in the lounge staring at a framed picture of Linda's mother. When he saw Linda, he rose and embraced her.

'She knew it was coming soon,' he said. 'I got the news while I was on my way to see her. We'd established this pattern, you see. Every morning I'd go to the hospital, and tell her how my day had been . . . not that anything much happens in my life without her around . . . you know your mom with her spunk!'

There was a smile on his lips and tears in his eyes. 'I've been so lucky. A lot of people my age never get to experience love the second time around. Your mother . . .' He caught his breath. 'She was an exceptional woman. A beautiful woman with the soul of an angel and the strength of an Amazon,' he said, now allowing the tears to run down his face.

Linda held on to him. 'I know. I know. What are we going to do, *buti* Phuti? What will we do without her?'

Chapter 51

SADE

Sade waited anxiously in the domestic arrivals lounge at OR Tambo International Airport. Despite the tragic circumstances of their reunion, she was looking forward to seeing Nolwazi again. It had been more than a year since they had last seen her. She had come to visit with the baby on her way to Joburg Fashion Week. She had looked amazing – glamorous in the understated way that only a designer can pull off.

Ntokozo was fussing about the doll they had left in the car. Sade fixed her eyes on the gate to see if her friend had come through yet.

'Mommy, Mommy. Dolly! Dolly!' pouted little Ntokozo straining against the straps of her pushchair.

'Not now, Ntokozo. Let's wait for Aunty Lwazi first, okay, baby? Just a few more minutes,' she said, tying up a stray red ribbon on Ntokozo's dress.

'There you are,' a confident voice announced behind her.

She stood up. 'Look at you! Stylish as ever,' she said, admiring the fusion of a bright-orange A-line skirt, her trademark head wrap and a tiny top that just revealed her toned midriff.

'I have to live the brand, babe,' said Nolwazi, turning around to show off her design.

'And look at Siphokazi. What a grown-up little madam,' Sade said, addressing the now twenty-month-old little girl standing next to Nolwazi. She whispered surreptitiously into Nolwazi's ear, 'You'll never tell us who her father is, will you?'

Nolwazi just smiled mysteriously and shook her head.

'You're so wicked.'

'Our friend Linda once advised me that an occupational hazard of turning thirty is acquiring some allure . . . a sense of mystery; so I guess I've got that pegged.'

'Well, just beware of secrets. You can never bury them forever no matter what. In my experience they have a tendency to come back and bite when you least expect them to.'

Nolwazi murmured her agreement. She was not very comfortable with this subject. 'Look at this cute little thing . . . and my gosh Sade, her pushchair probably costs the same as my car!' she said, deflecting from the topic.

'Yeah . . . it's probably time for an upgrade,' quipped Sade.

'I'm never getting rid of my beloved Conquest.'

They both laughed.

Sade looked forward to having some company at home, something that Winston would never have permitted before. His guilt over the affair with her maid of honour had turned him into a compliant little lamb. After Sade had threatened to leave him, he seemed to have been jolted out of his jealous scourge; Sade, with her unfailing optimism – at least when it came to the subject of Winston – hoped that would be a permanent state.

When they arrived at the house, they found that Sibongile had a light meal ready for them to eat before they headed out to Linda's house to support their grieving friend.

Chapter 52

DIKELEDI

Ever since her weekend outing Dikeledi was feeling disorientated and completely off-balance; the exact opposite of the effect the weekend was supposed to have induced. Although a part of her was glad that nothing physical had transpired between her and Kwame, there was another part that absolutely longed for the man. She could not spend more than five minutes without an image of his beatific smile warming her heart, or a memory of his soothing, masculine voice cracking a small private joke between them.

She looked forward to going to work every day, if only for the sheer indulgence of seeing him. They had even gone as far as developing a tradition of going out to lunch at a restaurant near campus on Wednesdays, when their schedules colluded to allow them that time together.

After her spat with Sade over Winston's perfection, or lack thereof, she had decided that for once she would not be the one to initiate a reconciliation with her best friend. If she had learned anything from the weekend trip, it was that she had a weakness for pleasing people. Since then, she had decided to assert herself with her fiancé, her seniors at work and the friends who'd made it their duty to take advantage of her overly accommodating nature.

Despite all this soul-searching, nothing had prepared her for the shock of hearing about the death of Linda's mother. She knew that Dr Mthi, as they had been fond of calling her, was the bedrock of Linda's existence. Although she always carried on like the blasé, carefree life of the party in their little circle, Linda's one weakness, if it could be called that, was her complete loyalty to her mother.

It seemed that she attributed everything that was good about herself to the close relationship she'd had with her mother. Dikeledi remembered how Linda used to always go on about her during their days at varsity, clearly proud of the almost sisterly relationship they shared. She never ceased to remind them what an amazing character her mother was.

When Dikeledi had heard the news, it had felt like being informed that her friend had lost some important human faculty, like the ability to see or walk. It was as if she instinctively knew that Linda would never be the same again.

Since then, Dikeledi had been at Linda's side, helping her to take care of funeral arrangements, calling all the relatives, some old friends and close acquaintances of Linda's mother, who had been a very popular doctor, especially from the days when she had run her practice in Soshanguve.

Now Dikeledi was on her way to Linda's again, to go over the final details of the funeral, which was to take place the next day.

While she was there, more guests poured into the doctor's apartment. As per custom, Dikeledi, who had been intermittently assisted by an uncharacteristically tense Sade over the past few days, would prepare tea, coffee and scones for the guests who had come to pay their last respects. Being the closest female relative to the deceased, Linda was required to sit on the mattress in the main bedroom as a show of mourning for her mother. With her were her mother's two sisters, Nosisa and Ntobeka.

Dikeledi needed to go home to check on Phemelo and Tebogo so she was anxious for Sade to arrive with Nolwazi so that they could relieve her. She was exhausted, not only because of the physical activity, but also due to the fact that a lot was weighing on her mind, and she had nobody she could share most of these thoughts with. Sade was too aloof to act as any kind of confidante and, as much as she knew Linda would relish any mention of a romantic interest in anybody other than Tebogo on her part, she was obviously not in the right frame of mind to discuss such matters. It was sad to see all the fire in Linda's eyes extinguished. Not even Kennedy's constant visits and words of comfort unburdened her; nor did her father's attitude bring Linda any solace from her grief.

All of Linda's friends were shocked to discover that her father would not be attending the funeral. Apparently, he had called and left a long message on Linda's phone, explaining that he had heard the news too late and could not secure a flight to South Africa at such short notice. He had sent a fat cheque 'to assist with the funeral arrangements' and had left a number of messages that only served to upset Linda even more.

Dikeledi heard a knock on the door. It was Kennedy. The poor guy seemed at a loss as to what to do in this situation but she knew that his presence meant a lot to Linda, even though she probably had not said anything to him.

'Hi, can I have a word with Linda? Is she all right?'

'Okay. I'm glad you're here. I need to go and check on Phemelo. Let me go get Linda for you.'

A few minutes later, a despondent Linda emerged, wearing a *doek* as a traditional sign of reverence. She had lost a little bit of weight over the past few days and her eyes looked sunken, probably from all the crying she had done. Dikeledi left them together in the empty kitchen.

They both sat down on the yellow chairs around Dr Mthi's quaint little kitchen. Linda's shoulders were hunched and her eyes were downcast.

'*Sthandwa sam*'... how are you today? I brought you something. Just to cheer you up,' Kennedy said, rubbing her shoulders.

She was quiet, as if she had not heard him, then said, 'I just want it to end, Kennedy. I really can't cope with this, you know. I thought I'd be strong, but without my mom . . .' She shook her head, as if the pain of uttering those words was too much for her.

Kennedy took her by the hands. 'Do you remember that day we went to visit your mom together? She was so spirited, you could have sworn she was someone in great health, the way she kept poking fun at you, saying I must watch out for your stubborn temper.'

Linda smiled. 'Yes, and she kept on remarking how good-looking you were . . . then she almost spoiled it by saying my dad was good-looking like you.'

'She had a forgiving heart . . . I could tell. And she really loved you, called you her special lili girl.'

Now Linda smiled. 'I can't believe you remembered that! I will really miss her. You know, she wrote me this little letter. I found it on her bed before they took her away. She told me to be strong, and asked me never to give up on people. Of course, I know who she was talking about . . . but I don't know if I can ever reconnect with my father . . . and that makes me really sad.'

'Don't worry, *sthandwa sam*'. We'll get through this together. I'll be here for you. Anything you need, I'm here, okay?' She just looked at him.

'I mean it, Linds. I really love you and I know you're feeling all alone right now, but it doesn't have to be that way. Right now, the most important thing for me is to make sure you get through this.'

Finally she nodded and kissed both his hands. 'Thank you. I love you so much. And I'm really glad you're here. I'd probably be falling apart if it weren't for you,' she said. And she meant every word.

Chapter 53

LINDA

The funeral was a sombre affair. Relatives, colleagues, friends and old patients who had been treated by the good doctor all gathered in their Sunday best to bid the last farewell to Dr Lunga Mthimkhulu. The sun shone brightly, showing off a jovial light while those gathered at the cemetery looked down respectfully as the priest recited the final eulogy for Linda's mother.

Under the family gazebo, rows of red and yellow plastic chairs were laid out and fully occupied by the Mthimkhulu family. Linda had steeled herself against displaying any emotion, but every time she thought of her father a black cloud of fury would envelop her. Why hadn't he even bothered to come? The man had the gall to lie to her about not being able to get a flight and then had further patronised her by sending her money, as if money could take away the gaping hole in her heart! How cruel. His only daughter! The man was heartless.

When the tears formed again in her eyes she let them run freely, crying for the fact that she had long ago lost a father and was now also without a mother. When this reality hit her, she almost choked on her tears until she looked at Kennedy. She took a tissue from her small black purse and wiped her eyes and nose, trying to regain her composure. She watched Kennedy for a long while, looking at the outline of his lips from where he was standing with the rest of the crowd at the cemetery. He cut such a fine figure; she wished she was standing next to him, leaning on his strong shoulders.

What was she going to do now that she was all alone in the world? For the first time in her life she wished she had settled down earlier, so that instead of standing under this tent, all eyes fixed on her with naked pity, she could have been there with a supportive husband . . . and maybe one or two children. She sighed. She made a silent resolution to start thinking more seriously about her life; she probably needed to settle down.

She looked on as the pallbearers helped to settle her mother's casket six feet under, as they say. A phrase so loosely used, almost with a dark humour attached to it, but now here it was. Her mother, the most caring soul she had ever met, was going six feet under. She wept again, in spite of herself; she was such a pathetic display of emotion! Her Aunty Nosisa materialised with more tissues and a reassuring arm over her shoulder. It was going to take her a long while to adjust to this.

After the funeral, all the guests gathered at the local church hall for a full traditional meal. Usually the catering would take place at the deceased's home, but because Linda's mother had stayed in a security complex it was decided that it would be too disruptive to invite all the guests there. Linda was relieved that she would not have to deal with droves of people streaming into her mother's house throughout the day. She could drift off silently to one of the rooms until the few remaining guests had finally retired back to their homes.

Having nibbled absent-mindedly on her food, she left in one of the funeral directors' cars and found her three best friends waiting for her at her mother's house. Other relatives who had come from the Eastern Cape had also arrived at the house. She could not wait for everybody to finally leave, get back to their lives at last, and leave her in peace. It suddenly occurred to her that poor Uncle Phuti must have felt quite lost throughout the week. Despite his intimate relationship with Linda's mother, his status was not recognised because he and Linda's mother had not tied the knot, and Dr Mthimkhulu's family had met him only on very few occasions.

Linda was relieved to see him in the townhouse, poor man, sitting having tea with her three friends in the lounge. They were the only people who knew how close he was to her mother, because aside from the fact that most of Linda's relatives lived far away in the Eastern Cape, her mother had also been a very private person – especially since Floyd's departure had had tongues wagging, even long after he'd settled himself comfortably in France.

Chapter 54

LINDA

The next day Uncle Phuti was the first to bid farewell to Linda. They stood together on the front porch of Dr Mthimkhulu's modest townhouse and looked out at the little patch of garden that Linda's mother had grown lovingly when she had first moved into the place. Holding Linda's hand, Phuti said, 'I'm going to miss her, Linda . . . and I'm really going to miss you too.'

Linda extended a warm hug to this quiet man whose humility and love had encouraged her mother until her last day. She was grateful for his presence in her mother's life.

'Uncle Phuti, please do not become a stranger to me. You were like a father to me over the past couple of years, you know. I hope you don't mind me calling you every now and then. I think you're the only person who truly understood my mom, and the past few years . . . well, you definitely added a special glow to her life.' They hugged again.

'I'll never stop being in your life, my sweet one. You're all I have left to remind me of your mother, you know,' he said, holding her hands.

Just then Dikeledi stepped out onto the porch to join them. 'Sorry for interrupting you, Linda, but your aunts are also about to leave.'

Linda hugged Uncle Phuti once more and saw him out. It struck her that there was a lot of dignity in this unassuming man. She smiled as she watched him leaving and said a little prayer of thanks for him having been in her mom's life to the very end.

Her aunts were already packing the last of their luggage into the car. They both fussed over her.

'Linda, whenever you need anything, anything at all, just call, okay?'

'I will, Aunt Nosisa.'

They both then lectured her and her friends about looking out for each other. After many words of advice, they too finally drove out, hooting as they went.

Linda and Dikeledi stood outside and waved them off.

'*Shoo!* I never thought this moment would come,' sighed Linda, as she watched the Toyota sedan drive off with Aunt Nosisa at the wheel.

Dikeledi turned to hug her. 'Shame, it was a bit too much for you, wasn't it?'

Still holding on to Dikeledi, Linda said, 'I'm so glad you guys were there for me throughout all this. Especially you, Kedi. You've been like my warm security blanket. At every turn I felt comfortable in the knowledge that you were there for me. You must also thank Tebogo for me . . . for his patience. You've spent more time in this house over the past seven days than you have at your place!'

Dikeledi laughed. 'Hey, I actually did, hey? Serves him right. This way, he'll learn to appreciate me. You know what they say about absence making the heart grow fonder.'

Just then Kennedy came out of the house. As he strode up to them, Linda just looked at him and started smiling.

'Babes, I need to steal you for a second. Do you wanna come in?' he asked, his shoulders looking tense.

Linda made a face and walked up to him. 'Nothing serious, I hope,' she said, as she went into the house with him, Dikeledi trailing behind. Linda and Kennedy went upstairs to her mother's bedroom. Kennedy sat down on the bed and gestured for Linda to sit next to him. He held her hands and kissed her on the lips. '*Sthandwa sam*,' he said, looking her in the eye.

Uh-oh. Is he going to propose? thought Linda, her mind whirring in a slight panic. Not now . . . not now, of all times; is he nuts?

'*Sthandwa*,' he said again, 'I spoke to your father. He called on the landline a few minutes ago, begging to talk to you but I know you're still not ready for that.'

She kissed him. 'Good. I'm in no mood to deal with that despicable man.'

'But, baby, I promised him that I would talk to you about making amends with him. He's your father, for better or worse, and I know deep down you still love him, so please—'

Linda stood up and flailed her arms in the air. 'What? Is that what you called me up here for? And what are you now, his trusted messenger? I can't believe you! Where is your loyalty, Kennedy? I warned you, the man is a snake-oil salesman. He thinks he can use that silver tongue on anyone. I can't believe you fell for it! I thought you were one person who understood. I thought you knew where I was coming from. You are so unbelievable!' she fumed, storming out the door.

As she descended the stairs, more drama was unfolding.

'And how long were you planning to keep this from me, you bitch?' she heard Dikeledi's voice.

This was not good. She had never heard Dikeledi call anyone a bitch – at least not to their face. What was going on here? Where was the peace and quiet Linda was hoping for? Slowly she

259

continued down the stairs and saw a sight that instantly revealed what had transpired.

Nolwazi's face was streaked with tears, Sade was looking at her with disgust, and Dikeledi had her hands on her hips and was glaring at Nolwazi confrontationally. She felt like climbing back up the stairs, but Sade, who was looking in her direction, had already seen her.

Sade butted in, 'Nolwazi, who the hell are you? Do we even know you? How could you do that to a friend? And then you managed to keep this from everyone for what . . . over two years? *Shoo!* she said, smacking her hands together.

As Linda reached the lounge to join the trio, she stood quietly next to Nolwazi, as if to provide some comfort to her. Kennedy was now behind Linda.

Dikeledi turned around. 'Linda, please tell me you didn't know anything about this.'

With instant cowardice gripping her, Linda said meekly, 'About what?'

'Ladies, what's going on here? Linda's been through a lot. Whatever this is about, maybe you guys should discuss it later?' Kennedy said, motioning towards Linda. He held her by the shoulders, but she shrugged him off.

Dikeledi raised her hands. 'I am sorry, Kennedy, but this cannot wait. My sanity is at stake here. Linda, please tell me you did not know that this heifer here has been screwing my man behind my back . . . managing to fool all of us into feeling sorry for her single-mom status when, in fact, she is the original man-eating whore!'

Nolwazi took her bags and said, 'Can I go now?'

Before any of them could see it coming, Dikeledi threw a slap across Nolwazi's face, catching her off-guard. Down went Nolwazi's bags and before she knew it, another slap came from her infuriated friend. Kennedy tried to defuse the situation, but Dikeledi was having none of it.

'Listen here, *wena*. You're not going anywhere until I'm done with you,' she said to Nolwazi. 'I don't know why you chose to do this to me instead of anyone else here in this room, but I think I've a pretty good idea. For years you people thought I was your doormat. Always asking for favours, making offhand comments about me and my relationship with Tebogo, all the while knowing I'd just sit there and take it without fighting for myself. I've had it. Nobody is leaving this room until I say so. All of you sit down now!'

Kennedy pleaded with her to be calm, but all she said was, 'I'm sorry, Kennedy, but this has nothing to do with you so before I lose it, please . . . just sit down!'

Terrified, they all sat, timid as little kindergarten pupils. 'Now, you first, Linda. Did you know about this?'

Linda looked down, shamefaced. She wished there had been another way for Kedi to find out, but the die was cast. Kennedy wrapped his arm around her. This time, she did not shake it off. 'Um, look, Kedi, to tell you the truth . . .'

'Did you or did you not know about this?'

'I-I . . . sort of did. But . . .'

Dikeledi regarded her with an expression that Linda knew she would never forget. The defiance that Kedi had displayed only a few moments before was replaced with a look of betrayal, disappointment and even resentment.

Dikeledi nodded, as if she were beginning to understand a deep, unwritten code that she was somehow not surprised to have cracked. 'Right. Right. And you, Sade? How long have you known about this?' she asked, this time looking a little more stoic, as if she understood that she wasn't to expect anything from the people in the room.

Sade just shook her head and sighed. She shrugged. 'I'm as shocked as you are, Kedi. I really had no idea that Nolwazi gave birth to Tebogo's baby. No idea at all,' she said, as if hearing herself say the words made them all the more shocking.

Dikeledi was silent for a long while, just staring into space, her hands on her hips. She nodded intermittently but said nothing.

'Well, now I know who my friends are,' she said finally, and, with that, she strode out the door.

The four who were left in the room sat in stony silence.

A few seconds later Sade said, 'Nolwazi, I don't want to see you in my house again. I need you to collect your things along with your daughter and I want you to leave.' She picked up her car keys and her bag. 'I hope it was a really good screw, one worth destroying a lifelong friendship for,' she barked as she also marched out the door.

As Nolwazi sat in shamefaced horror, Linda put her arm around her. 'You're obviously welcome to stay with me for as long as you need to. You don't need to go through this on your own,' she said.

Nolwazi was still quiet, then she started weeping. 'What was I doing, Linda? What was I thinking? I feel so dirty . . . I'm nothing but a cheap traitor, and I'd somehow convinced myself that I'd never tell anyone.'

'Um . . . let me go and . . . get something,' Kennedy said, eager for an escape.

'How did they find out?' Linda turned to Nolwazi with big eyes.

Nolwazi shrugged. 'I don't know what I was thinking. I guess with your mom passing and the solidarity we were sharing over the past few days, especially with Sade, you know, staying with her and her family, I guess I felt the need to share the secret. I was tired of her making little comments about Siphokazi's paternity and I guess the weight of betrayal was weighing heavily on me,' she said quietly.

'Anyway, Sade was just commenting on how great the past few days have been and how she felt closer to me than anybody. She felt we'd connected somehow and she'd confided quite a few things about her relationship with Winston, which I'm sure she wouldn't tell anyone else . . . so, I don't know. I just felt she was opening up to me so I thought I'd share something with her as well. Anyway, Dikeledi walked in on me telling Sade about me and Tebogo.'

Linda suddenly understood. '*Jislaaik* . . . you really shouldn't have told her. You know Sade; she would have told Dikeledi anyway. They share a lot, even though they've been distant towards each other these past few days.'

Nolwazi shrugged. 'I guess I didn't realise there were lines of division in our little circle. I took it for granted that the four of us were all friends; I didn't realise there were these cliques within the circle.'

Linda couldn't believe how naive Nolwazi was, but she kept quiet.

After a while Kennedy came back downstairs. Linda had completely forgotten about him, but suddenly felt a magnetic pull towards him. She realised that all that had happened was too much for her. She had long anticipated the penny dropping about Tebogo; she just did not expect it to happen so soon after her mother's funeral. She could only hope that she had not lost a life-long friend too.

Chapter 55

Dikeledi

Dikeledi left Linda's mother's house in a daze. A swirl of emotions drummed through her head so that she could barely focus on the road. It took her almost half an hour to realise that she had taken a wrong turn and was now in an unfamiliar part of town. Before she knew what she was doing, she had stopped at a small convenience store and bought a packet of cigarettes and a box of matches. Although she had never smoked in her life, she found herself saying 'Dunhill Special Mild' when the store attendant asked her which brand she wanted.

Within minutes she was back behind the wheel on the unfamiliar road lined with cars; a young couple held hands, while another couple looked engrossed in conversation. She looked at four teenage boys chasing after each other while teasing a small boy with a Mohican haircut. She watched an old man sitting by the fish and chip shop strumming a happy song on his guitar and she wondered how the world could look so normal when her life had fallen completely off its axis.

Suddenly her phone came to life. She gritted her teeth, instinctively knowing that it was Tebogo calling. Bastard, arsehole, prick! *Fucker!*

She considered not picking up, but then thought better of it. She needed to confront this bastard face to face. She wanted to show him that she was no longer going to be his fool. No way. It had been too long.

'Hello,' she said calmly.

'Hey, *mntwanam*. When are you coming home? This place is falling apart without you.'

She paused. Mr Smooth. She really hated him right now. 'I'll be there in about thirty minutes,' she said, dragging on the cigarette slowly, contemplatively.

'Okay. I've got a special day planned for you. You've been caring for Linda all week; I think it's time for you to get pampered,' he said jovially.

'I'm coming,' she said, and put down the phone.

She breathed in, dragged on her cigarette again, got tired of it, and threw it out of the window. How could this have happened? she thought. Her head slumped down on the steering wheel. When she looked up again the old man with the guitar was standing at the window of her car.

'Hey lady, are you okay, man?'

She gazed at him, then sudden tears streamed down her face.

'No, no, don't cry. Don't do that. A pretty young lady like yourself? Don't cry. You're just like my daughter. Always crying. Man trouble, man trouble all the time. Take it easy, man. Just take it easy, okay? Look at me. All I got is my guitar, my sweet voice and my good looks. You see me crying?'

She faced him, really seeing him for the first time. He had only two front teeth, a grey scraggly beard and a full head of snow-white hair. His clothes were tattered and torn, yet his face was full of sunshine.

Suddenly she felt silly and self-conscious. Why was she still crying over Tebogo after all these years? It struck her that all Tebogo's prior indiscretions were compass points leading to this destination. She should have seen it coming. After all, this man had cheated on her almost all her life. It had to take something this big to make her realise her own folly in trusting him; she'd been living in a fog of deceit and refusing to see the truth for what it really was. This old man was right. It was time she took it easy. She needed to give herself a permanent break from this vicious cycle of emotional abuse. She simply needed to get rid of Tebogo.

She turned to the old man with a brave smile and said, 'Thanks, *baba*. I'll try. I'll try and take it easy.'

He strummed his guitar gaily and gave her a big, twin-toothed grin. 'That's my girl,' he said, and strolled back to his corner.

With renewed purpose, she drove home, trying not to think about what she was going to say to Tebogo. She focused only on the fact that she was leaving. There was absolutely nothing to debate.

When she finally arrived at the whitewashed cluster, she opened the remote-controlled gate and drove slowly into the carport. She got out of the car, took her bag, went to the front door, took a deep breath and entered her house.

'Take it easy,' she murmured to herself.

'Is that you, Mom?' Phemelo's voice reverberated sweetly, pulling at her heartstrings.

'I'm sorry, baby,' she said quietly to herself, for the first time really thinking about the ramifications of what she was about to do. 'It's me, love. Come over here and give me a big hug.'

Phemelo ran to her from her bedroom and soon got swept up in Dikeledi's arms.

'Did you miss me?'

'Of course, Mom. Did you bring me something?'

'Oh. Sorry, I didn't. But maybe we'll do something special at the weekend. Just you and me, okay?'

Phemelo nodded, kissing Dikeledi on the cheeks.

'Where's your father?'

She shrugged. 'I think he's taking a shower.'

'Ok, baby. Let me go upstairs and wait for him. Listen, don't you want to play with Lindiwe from next door for a little bit? I have something very important to talk to your daddy about.'

She pulled a face. 'No. I was enjoying playing with my dolls, Mom.'

'Oh, pretty please? I'll get you something really big when we go shopping this weekend.'

'Like a phone?' Phemelo bargained.

She paused. She was desperate. 'Yes. like a phone.'

Phemelo started skipping up and down. 'Yeah. I'm getting a phone! I'm getting a phone! Wait till I tell Lindiwe!' Then she went to fetch two of her dolls and she was out the door.

Dikeledi sighed. She worried how all of this was going to impact on Phemelo. Bloody Tebogo! He would never learn to keep his pants on!

She strode upstairs with a weary gait. When she got to their bedroom she found him drying himself as he walked out of the en-suite bathroom. He turned around as soon as she walked in.

'How's my favourite *chérie*?' he asked cheerfully, walking towards her for a kiss.

She stopped him in his tracks. 'Tebogo, it's over. I've had it. No more.'

He looked flabbergasted. 'What are you talking about? Is this a joke?' he asked incredulously, half laughing.

She glared straight into his eyes, her face an impassive wall that gave away nothing. 'I know about you and Nolwazi.'

Suddenly, Tebogo looked like he'd been slapped in the face. He slumped down on the bed and stared at the floor. 'Oh. So she finally told you,' he murmured, as if to himself.

For an eternity, neither of them spoke. Then he went down on his knees, towel wrapped around his waist. A desperate man. With his hands together, prayer-like, he begged, 'Please, Kedi. I swear it was a one-off thing. I was stupid. I'm really, really sorry. I've changed so much since then. You know it yourself that I'm a new man. That . . . that mistake showed me how important you and Phemelo are to me. Come on, it was more than two years ago. If I could turn back the clock, believe me I would do everything differently. I swear.'

She kept shaking her head. 'Tebogo, this is not open for debate. I'm leaving you and I'm taking Phemelo with me. You've turned my life into one big insult and I'm tired of it. If I think back to your pathetic proposal, I realise that it must have been at more or less the same time that that slut of yours discovered she was pregnant. No wonder you haven't married me yet. You only proposed to deal with your guilt. Your excuses about setting a wedding date are just further proof that you will always play me at one level or another. I'm your convenient idiot, someone you're always going to enter-tain yourself with by playing games. I've had it.'

Tebogo was silent, worried at the calmness of her tone. There was a definite finality to it. 'But, baby, what about Phemelo? Are you really willing to sacrifice her happiness for something that hap-pened two years ago? I mean, even Nolwazi has moved on with her life. She's probably living it up in Cape Town. Is she really worth our misery?'

Suddenly, Dikeledi turned towards him, her fury now unleashed. 'Don't you dare patronise me with your manipulative tactics! If you ever cared about Phemelo, you wouldn't be sleeping with my friends! You never even bothered to use a condom . . . God knows what kind of diseases you may be exposing me to! I'm moving out at the end of the month but if you dare touch me at any time during the period we're staying together, I swear I will kill you,' she said and took a long breath in.

She looked at him and shook her head. It suddenly occurred to her that she had stopped loving this man some time ago, and all she had needed was an excuse to leave. She sighed and went into the guest room. Oddly enough, after releasing all that fury she found herself smiling quietly. What was it she felt? Relief? Yes. After all these years she had miraculously stopped loving this man who had caused her so much pain. What a relief that she did not need to explain herself to him, especially since he'd undergone his sudden personality makeover. What an ironic turn of events: his infidelity had given her the escape she'd needed.

Chapter 56

Linda

Linda decided to immerse herself in her work after facing the melancholic weekend of confessions, bereavement and drama. She woke up on Wednesday morning, her first day back at work, full of drive and energy. If there was one thing that gave her a sense of normality it was her job. At times like this she simply thrived on it.

As she walked into the production offices of Static Frequency she found a bunch of sunflowers waiting for her on her desk. A sweet welcome-back note was attached to the plastic wrapping of the flowers from all her colleagues. She smiled and thanked everybody at the top of her lungs. The team of sixteen in her open-plan office was a fairly warm but conscientious one. They seldom had time for social niceties, especially Linda, who was famed for her workaholism. She took in the scene around her and was glad to realise that here, at least, it was business as usual.

Riaan, her favourite cameraman, was not at his desk as per custom. Deon and Phumla were locked up in the meeting room just opposite her and she could see them discussing some or other project with deep intensity. Lynette, the production manager, who sat opposite her desk, was ordering ten cars for a new client's commercial. The buzz in the office was the perfect antidote to the soap opera that had been playing itself out in her life. She took out her iPad and scrolled down to find the number of the stripper who she had been told was the last person to see Dineo alive. She had tried to call her twice before she heard about her mom's passing, but the stripper's phone was off on both occasions.

Just as she was about to dial the number, a call came through to her extension. It was Kennedy. She had forgiven him his faux pas with the trying issue of her father, and she knew the message had sunk in.

'Hey, babe. How's the first day back at work?'

She smiled. 'I'm just trying to settle in. I received a bunch of flowers from the guys in the office. So *shweet*. I'm so glad to be back. I was really getting tired of staying home.'

'I'm sure the rest did you some good,' said Kennedy.

To which Linda would have liked to ask, 'What rest?' but decided better of it. She was beginning to feel a bit like a whiner, so she let it go. 'Are we still meeting later tonight?' she asked instead.

'Yeah, sure. I'll be knocking off a bit late. Maybe around eight, but I'll sleep over at your apartment . . . and I've a surprise for you.'

'As long as you're not pregnant,' said Linda, 'it's all good. See you later, *sthandwa sam*'.'

On to the next piece of business, she thought, dialling the stripper's number.

After a few rings, a woman picked up. 'Hello?'

'Hello, is that Zodwa?'

'Who's looking for her?' The voice sounded like it belonged to an older woman. Her mother maybe?

'Umm . . . my name is Linda Mthimkhulu. I got Zodwa's number from a friend of hers named Primrose. Is she there?'

'Hold on,' said the woman.

After a few minutes someone else came on the line. The voice sounded raspy and weary. 'Hello? What do you want?'

'Zodwa, my name is Linda. I got your number from Primrose and I was a friend of Dineo's. I really need to talk to you. It's very important. I know about the man. I want to help.'

There was a long pause. 'If you know about him then what do you need to talk to me about? Who are you anyway, a cop?'

'No, I'm not a cop. I work for a television programme. We are the ones who did the story on Dineo and a couple of other girls. Do you remember that?'

'Oh. You. I remember. After that programme some of the social workers came to help us with some stuff. That was okay. But I am not part of that life anymore. I'm trying to stay as far away from it as possible so I can't help you.'

'Surely you don't want Dineo's killer to get away with her murder just like that? Please, Zodwa. I won't take up more than thirty minutes of your time. I won't even bring any cameras and I swear I'll protect your identity. I'm legally bound to do so if that's what you want.'

'Hmm,' Zodwa said sarcastically, 'and what are you going to get from this? Praise from your colleagues?'

'It's not about that, Zodwa. You knew Dineo. You knew how desperate she was to get out of that life. Nailing this guy will be a tribute to her last wishes. These are the kind of guys who endangered her life on a daily basis. Please, do it for her. Do it for the other girls out there who could end up like Dineo.'

Zodwa was quiet for a while, and then with a resigned air she said, 'Okay. I give you two hours to get here before I lose my nerve to go ahead with this – that's condition number one. Number two: no cops, no colleagues, no one else comes with you. If I so much as see another figure lingering alongside you, I'll disappear. This is not something I want to get involved with . . . any more than I already have.'

'Deal. Where do you want me to meet you?'

'Do you know Soweto very well?'

'Yes, I know my way around.'

'There's a place called Sakhumzi's. It's not that busy during the week. Meet me there at twelve. If you're a minute late, I'm gone . . . Oh, and be prepared to buy me a drink. God knows I need one.'

'Okay, great. Thanks!' said Linda, scribbling the details down. Maybe this would be her lucky break. And on her first day back at work!

She grabbed her car keys and rushed to join the M1 South highway to Soweto. She did not want to lose a moment now that she had started to appreciate the real prospects of this story. Deon may not be the most charming man on the planet, but usually his worst suggestions tended to land her with the very best of stories. The adrenaline was kicking in and she was completely lost in the moment.

Chapter 57

Nolwazi

As Nolwazi drove from the airport to her apartment complex, she felt physically and mentally drained. Poor Siphokazi did not understand why her mother was barely paying her any attention on the journey back home. The little girl kept herself busy playing with her Hello Kitty doll until she got bored, then tried playing with her mother's hair, much to Nolwazi's irritation.

As Nolwazi carried the luggage into the house she was slightly disappointed to see her friendly neighbour Eva coming downstairs to help her with the lifting.

'Hugs please. I missed you,' said Eva, a wide smile lighting up her face.

Nolwazi offered a weary hug back, although she would have preferred to bolt the door, never to surface again.

'You look tired. How was Johannesburg?'

Nolwazi grumbled, 'I guess it was okay, all things considered,' she said, as she walked up the stairs, child in tow.

Eva followed them, carrying one of Nolwazi's suitcases. 'You packed for a month-long holiday; what's with the excess?'

Nolwazi was not in the mood for conversation.

They finally reached the top of the stairs. Nolwazi opened the door to her cosy two-bedroomed apartment, hoping that Eva would get the message and disappear, but she was far too eager for some idle chatter. She plonked the suitcase down and settled on Nolwazi's favourite couch.

'How did Linda handle her mother's funeral? Did she cope?'

Before leaving for Johannesburg, Nolwazi had filled Eva in on the travails of her colourful Joburg friends. She sighed and finally gave in. Clearly, Eva was not letting up.

'She managed okay. Linda's a strong girl . . . besides, she has this gorgeous boyfriend who was at her side throughout the whole thing. Funny to think of it now, but I was there when they first met at a Primi Piatti.' Nolwazi shook her head in wonderment. 'I'd have never guessed it would end up this serious,' she said offhandedly.

'Wow . . . I thought Linda was the commitment-phobic one? So what else has changed since you left Johannesburg?'

Just then, Siphokazi grabbed Nolwazi by the sleeve. 'Mama. I want sleep.'

'Okay, pumpkin. Let me tuck you in,' Nolwazi said, and went into the child's bedroom.

Once she'd settled Siphokazi, Nolwazi realised she was feeling clammy in her travelling clothes, so she went to change into a sleeveless top and shorts before going back into the living room.

'Good. You don't look so uptight anymore. So, tell me more. What happened when Linda saw her dad with his white woman?'

Nolwazi fixed herself a glass of orange juice and offered one to Eva. 'You just love the fact that she's white, don't you? Anyway, you'll be disappointed to hear that neither her dad nor his little floozy showed up.'

Eva shrugged. 'That must have been tough. What kind of a person is her dad anyway? You know, mixed couples are interesting.

I mean, there are all these cultural issues to deal with . . . maybe this French girl didn't think it was such a big deal not to show up at the funeral, but obviously, according to African custom, this is a major social blunder.'

'*Ja*, well, Eva, the last thing I want to do is analyse the cultural nuances of Linda's dad and his French mistress,' said an exhausted Nolwazi.

'Party pooper. You South Africans are so hung up on this racial stuff,' she said, twisting a lock of her blonde hair.

'I didn't start with the racial stuff. Besides, I'm too wiped out to debate Linda's dad's love life. I just hate bloody Joburg. I was in such good spirits before going to that place.'

Eva could see that something was bothering Nolwazi but she sensed her friend did not want to talk about it. She had always been cagey about her Johannesburg life, especially about her reasons for leaving the place. 'I haven't been to Joburg, you know, and you make it sound so bad. I think I'll limit my South African experience to this peaceful town,' she said, crossing her legs lazily.

'Yup, you'd best do that,' Nolwazi said, stifling a yawn. 'I'm so tired.'

In the blink of an eye, Eva was up. 'Okay, I can take a hint. But I'll be knocking on your door sometime this week to invite you out for drinks. Get over your Joburg hangover, okay?'

'Hangover is just right. I need to get over that place for good.'

Before Eva was out the door, she stopped and said, 'Oh, and by the way, your "husband" was here, pining after you. Why didn't you call the poor guy while you were in Joburg?'

For a minute, Nolwazi was confused. So much had happened in Johannesburg that she had almost completely blanked out her entire Cape Town existence. 'Simphiwe was looking for me?'

'Of course he was. He's lost without you,' Eva said dramatically, pretending to swoon. She winked mischievously and then she was gone.

After seeing Eva out, Nolwazi checked if there was any alcohol in her fridge. She found a half-empty bottle of vodka, mixed it with orange juice, then slumped herself onto the couch. She tried to reflect on the events that had transpired during her trip to Joburg. Feeling sentimental, she replayed her time at Sade's house, enjoying the girlish camaraderie they had shared while they prepared for Dr Mthimkhulu's funeral. She went over the heart-to-heart talks they had had and wondered again about how surprised she'd been at discovering a new, more vulnerable side to Sade, whom she had always secretly feared for her unshakeable confidence. She was shocked once more about the revelations of Winston's infidelity.

It had taken so much for Sade to confide in her about this issue. She knew that Sade had always strived to reflect a perfect life and, for a long time, Winston had been her ideal companion to shine this brilliant light to the rest of the world . . . until he turned out to be a dog, just like any other man. When Sade had broken down about her anxiety over the results of the AIDS test that the couple were awaiting, Nolwazi could only offer her a shoulder to cry on. She had felt compelled to open up about her own secrets, something she now deeply regretted doing.

As she finished the last drop of her vodka and juice, she mumbled, 'I've got no friends. Nobody loves me. I'm obsessed with a gay man. A perfect ending to a perfectly dreary existence.'

Chapter 58

SADE

Sade had not made love to Winston since the maid-of-honour incident. He would be back from work soon and she felt a tingling sensation as she waited in anticipation for him. The HIV tests she had insisted they take after catching him in flagrante delicto with Palesa were in the left drawer of the dresser. They were both relieved the tests had come back negative, although Sade was annoyed that Winston had not been confident of the results. Clearly it meant he had been sleeping with the wench without a condom.

Sade had lectured him about his infidelity while a remorseful Winston swore that he would never stray again, this time without making up the excuses that had begun to irk Sade. Considering the incident had happened four months ago, she felt that her sexual well had been kept dry long enough. Winston had displayed model-husband behaviour throughout this period so perhaps it was time to forgive . . . if for nothing else, at least to take care of her carnal desires. Damn! She was thirty-one years old; she needed to get her groove on.

She checked with Sibongile to see if she had put Ntokozo to bed. Satisfied that the baby was sleeping, she ran a hot bath with aromatherapy oils and gave her face a quick home-made facial.

After her bath she took out the racy lace lingerie she had bought during her afternoon shopping trip – a red two-piece La Senza number. Then she put on a silky red gown that barely hid the sensuous lingerie underneath. She sprayed on the Issey Miyake perfume that Winston had bought her a month back and then tied up her long dark hair before proclaiming herself ready for the seduction game she wanted to play with her husband.

A few minutes later she heard Winston's key turn in the front door. She lay on the bed, pretending to read a book. When he came into the bedroom, he looked at her with blazing-hot desire, before cracking a wide smile.

'Hello, gorgeous. You smell wonderful,' he said, putting his jacket on the chair next to the bed and bending down to kiss her.

She looked up at him and returned the kiss, full on the mouth, slowly exploring his lips.

'Is the little one asleep?'

With her eyes still closed, focused firmly on Winston's lips, she nodded, 'Hmm-hmm.'

He threw his tie off and hungrily started kissing her all over, playing with her breasts, touching her everywhere, and finally entering her. They both held on to each other until they climaxed in unison.

He kissed her again, on her forehead, her lips, her ears. Marital bliss.

Chapter 59

LINDA

Linda drove up to Sakhumzi's and was pleasantly surprised to find that in the outside *lapa* of this inviting, warm restaurant there was only one other patron. She decided to take a seat on one of the wooden benches in the far corner. Sakhumzi's epitomised township charm with its urban flair and brown, rustic chairs. It was famous for its location on Vilakazi Street, the only street in the world to have served as a residence for two Nobel Peace Prize laureates: Nelson Mandela and Archbishop Desmond Tutu.

Before sitting down to order a drink she went inside the restaurant to see if the girl had arrived. There was nobody there except three waiters and the manager. Linda went back to sit outside and ordered a rock shandy while she went through the mental list of questions she had made on the drive over. It was important for her not to scare the girl away. Zodwa was so crucial to the story, the last thing she needed was for her to develop cold feet.

She checked the time; it was eleven thirty and the girl had said to be there no later than twelve. Linda was not taking any chances.

After downing the whole glass, she started looking around for any sign of Zodwa. Getting paranoid about her showing up, she decided to call the girl again.

No answer. Frowning, she called a waiter over and asked if a young woman had been there earlier.

The waiter, a young man with a small scar on his chin, shrugged and said, 'Nope. You're the only bourgeoisie who can afford to come here so early during the week, sister.'

She looked at him with a puzzled expression. Was he trying to chase business away or what?

As she wondered about the waiter's offhand comment, she heard a small voice behind her saying, 'Hi. Are you Linda?'

When she turned around, she saw an incredibly thin woman of about twenty with wispy hair and a tortured yet pretty face. She wore jeans that looked two sizes too big for her and a red sweater, despite the searing heat of the golden Soweto sun. She noticed that Zodwa had a strawberry-shaped birthmark on her left cheek.

'Hi. You must be Zodwa. Thanks so much for coming, *sisi*. Please sit down,' she said, with as friendly a smile as possible.

Zodwa looked nervous. She kept tugging at the ends of her jersey while looking around as if she were expecting somebody to pounce on them. 'Can I order a drink?' she asked, fidgeting.

'Sure, of course,' said Linda encouragingly.

'Thanks,' Zodwa said, gesturing shyly to the waiter to serve them. 'Can I have a Hunter's Dry, please?' She was silent for a while, as if she had forgotten the reason for this meeting.

'Hot day, hey?' said Linda, trying to get the conversation going. How pathetic, she grimaced. Of all things, I had to talk about the weather.

The girl shook her head absent-mindedly. 'When you're going cold turkey, all days are the same. Doesn't really matter,' she said, still looking around her.

The drink came and Zodwa seemed relieved to see the chilled cider on her table. She put aside the glass that the waiter had brought and drank straight from the bottle instead. After a long sip she closed her eyes and said, 'Hmm, that feels good. It's been a while. My mother . . . she's so strict I'm not even allowed to touch anything. She doesn't get that alcohol and drugs are not the same thing. Imagine,' she said, laughing humourlessly, 'being deprived of all your vices all at once. It's inhumane, man.'

Linda nodded offhandedly, neither agreeing nor disagreeing. 'Are you on a programme . . . for rehab?'

Zodwa laughed derisively. 'A programme? No way, man. With my kind, there's no time for such luxuries. First of all, the dealers would be the first ones to know where to find you while you're on your so-called programme. Plus, I can't afford that shit. I just want out of the lifestyle. Plain and simple. It's all about me. I'm not as weak as most of those girls, *mina*. I can turn it on or off as I like. Don't need a programme.'

Linda nodded and ordered another rock shandy. 'Listen, you can order food if you like. I've already had breakfast.'

The other woman looked at her appraisingly. 'Hmm. You really want this story, *ne*? Do you have two hundred rand for me?'

Linda was annoyed. She hated it when people thought they could get money off her in exchange for information, but since she was dying for this lead, she just nodded. 'Maybe I do. Let's see. I don't want you to screw around with me, Zodwa. For me, this is not just a story, whether you believe it or not. You may be strong enough to have options about choosing the lifestyle, but I spent some time with those girls and I know that most of them don't have an easy way out. They're stuck in that cycle, so the least we can do is try to protect them from the monsters who take advantage of the facelessness of the profession.'

Totally unimpressed, Zodwa drained her bottle of Hunter's Dry. 'I'm going to order another one.'

Linda rolled her eyes. She was starting to think this was going to turn out to be a waste of time.

When her second drink arrived, Zodwa sighed, weaved her fingers together and said, 'Okay, lady, I'm going to tell you the story quick and straight. Don't ask me too many questions because I do not talk about this . . . period. Not even to my mother. When I'm done telling you the story, you give me two hundred rand . . . make that three hundred. I'm not going to lie, but I'm never going to repeat it, so you'd better be listening good, okay?'

Linda nodded, not bothering to protest about the sudden price hike.

'Dineo was the kind of girl that all the Johns liked because, for enough money, she would do anything . . . I mean anything. Just name the fantasy, she'd be down with it. Anything from threesomes, foursomes, dildos, S&M, white men, Arabs, anything, she did it . . . as long as the money was right.

'So anyway, round about two years back, this good-looking man – tall, dark in complexion – starts coming to the hotel where our pimp had set up. He says he wants a girl that can go on the wild side with him, so Antonio, the Nigerian guy who's running that hotel, calls me and Dineo down to see this John. He was all right. Looked clean, so we both wanted him, especially because we saw his car keys – the guy drove a Beemer. We knew that sometimes these ones were the high rollers. Antonio called us bitches and asked the guy to choose. Surprise, surprise, the guy chose to get down with both of us.

'So we went upstairs to room 301 in that hotel. Antonio calls it the penthouse, but shit, the place is no penthouse . . . but by Hillbrow standards, I guess it passed. It was certainly good enough for the guy.'

Linda interrupted: 'Sorry, Zodwa. What's the name of the hotel?'

Zodwa looked at her, opened her mouth, then hesitated. 'You did not hear any of this from me,' she said with a stern look.

Linda nodded. 'I know, I know,' she said anxiously, dying for the information.

'It's called The Towers.'

'Okay. Continue,' said Linda.

'Anyway, we usually don't bother asking these Johns their names – it's all lies anyway – but Dineo seemed to be taken by Mr Man so she asked what we should call him and he said, "Mustafah". I knew it was bullshit cos you could tell he was South African and there's barely any South African black men going around with names like that,' she said, then stopped. 'I need a cigarette. Can you please give me twenty bucks so I can ask the waiter for a box?'

Linda took out her wallet and fished out a twenty-rand note.

'Thanks, you're a sweetheart,' she said, and called the waiter to get her cigarettes.

She sipped on the Hunter's Dry as if she were taking an official break until her additional needs were catered for. Linda was spellbound by her behaviour. She was afraid that if she spoke, this unpredictable woman would simply stand up and leave. So she decided to wait it out. She could tell that Zodwa was not one for small talk in any case.

When her cigarettes arrived, Zodwa asked for a match and dragged on her cigarette long and hard. She sighed. 'I've missed this,' she said dreamily. After taking another gulp of her drink, and smoking energetically, she continued.

'So this John . . . Mr Mustafah' – she spat out his name like it was poison – 'he liked me and Dineo, and he liked what he called S&M – you know, bondage games. He'd tie one of us up or watch us tie each other up; spanking, fucking – the works. I didn't get it, quite frankly. I don't think Dineo got it either, but she was good with clients, especially this guy. I mean, it was like she really wanted to please him, and I think she did please him cos he kept coming back for more. Sometimes he would ask for her only, sometimes he'd ask for the both of us, but he was always secretive. I remember one time he came and he had forgotten to take off his wedding ring. So I started asking him about his wife. I was high that day so I said, "Prince Mustafah, what does your wife think about you fucking around with us whores here?"

'Shit. I've never had someone beat the crap out of me like that. *Sies*, I hate that fucking guy. The whole week, my left eye wouldn't open and I had a burst lip. Imagine this beautiful face with a burst lip. I just hate him. So, after that, I wanted my revenge. I was gonna find out who he was and I was going to spill it to his wife,' she said, and took a drag of the cigarette. 'I didn't care. I hated the lifestyle, you know. So anyway, one time he comes to ask for me and Dineo, maybe a month later. What does he care? I'm a whore anyway; I don't have feelings so obviously he figured I'd forgotten all about the bruises he gave me. Although I was broke at that time, I told him to fuck off and I went to go smoke some weed with some girls in another room upstairs while he went to room 301 with Dineo.

'There're these games he likes to play. He calls it "asphyxiation". The most disgusting thing you could ever experience. The guy is like those white Johns: into seriously kinky shit.' She leaned her elbows on the table. 'To be honest, I think it's the kinky shit that killed Dineo. This asphyxiation game is what he'd play – where he lets you tighten the scarf around his neck while you're busy fuck-ing him or he tightens it around you. But with him, when the belt or scarf gets really tight, almost to the point of strangling him, it makes him come – and boy does he come. Sick, sick, sick,' she said, and then spat as if recoiling from witnessing the act. She dragged on her cigarette some more and, for the first time, Linda noticed the dark circles around Zodwa's eyes. The woman looked as if she had not slept for months.

'Anyway,' she continued, 'Dineo pretended to get off on it too. That night, they went into 301, did their thing, and then next thing, I go looking for Dineo cos another sicko John wanted the two of us and Mustafah's hour was up. I can't find her in her room. When I get to 301, I find Mustafah gone, and I find Dineo's dead, naked, strangled body sprawled across that dirty, stained carpet. The stupid guy left the belt hanging around her neck so, just then, Antonio comes in, looks at the scene, and knows exactly what's happened. He said Mustafah had left in a hurry and given Antonio a thousand bucks.

'So, I know Antonio. He's one smart Nigerian. He's obviously cut a deal with Mustafah to keep quiet about the belt and the evidence, and he's probably earning a monthly salary for his silence.'

'And what about you? I don't understand. Why don't you come forward with the information? You were already set on exposing him, so why don't you go ahead and do it?' Linda asked, excited about the possibilities presented by this testimony, if it were all true. It just seemed too easy.

'Because Antonio said if I tell anyone – and he's said this to all the other girls – we are all dead meat. And trust me, I don't want to mess with Antonio. That's why I left. Besides, I found out what the guy does . . . there's no way I'm messing around with someone that high-powered. So, sister,' she said, as she stood up, preparing to leave, holding her hand out for the R300 she had asked for, 'you did not hear any of this from me.'

'Just one last thing, please,' said Linda. 'Your friend that led me to you . . . Primrose . . . she said you've got the guy's licence plate. Please at least give me that.'

Zodwa shook her head. 'I'm sorry, lady. I don't know what you're talking about,' she said, taking the money. In an instant, she was gone.

Chapter 60

Nolwazi

Nolwazi and Eva were dressed to conquer the world, or at least in this case, two gay men. They had taken a bet on who was going to score the highest points under the gaze of Simphiwe's ever-stylish eye. Nolwazi had decided to go for one of her own creations: a strapless brown-and-white traditional *Sesotho dress* that hugged her tiny waist and flowed down to just below her knees. She teamed this with a pair of brown stilettos and accessorised it with beautiful beads and round ivory earrings. Eva went for a simple but elegant black dress and tied up her blonde mane, leaving little curly wisps of loose hair to flatter her oval face. She wore diamanté earrings and a diamond pendant choker and threw on a blood-red pashmina for good effect.

As usual, Simphiwe had chosen a refined Italian restaurant that was frequented by an older, sophisticated crowd of professionals. They were meeting him and his partner, Anthony Ransom, whose acquaintance they had not yet made.

When the women arrived at the restaurant, they saw the two men sitting prominently at the centre table. Spago's was almost full and had a convivial, yet upmarket atmosphere. A pianist was playing Frank Sinatra classics, and large crystal chandeliers hung on the ceiling, adding to the overall glamour and elegance of the general ambience. Nolwazi was relieved that she and Eva had decided to glam up for the evening. She did not want to disappoint Simphiwe, knowing how much he praised her eye for detail to anyone who cared to listen.

When they got to the table, both men stood up to greet them. Simphiwe gave both her and Eva a warm hug while Anthony air-kissed them with gusto.

'May I just say you ladies both look divine,' said Anthony, clapping his hands with relish.

Simphiwe laughed, covering his face. 'And this, my dear friends, is my larger-than-life partner, Anthony,' he explained.

Anthony grinned. 'It's my distinct pleasure to finally meet you two. I must say, Simphiwe has spoken volumes about both of you . . . especially you, Lwazi. He just won't stop! I was almost getting jealous. Nolwazi this, Nolwazi that. Well, now that I've met you, of course, I can see what he was on about,' he said generously.

Nolwazi beamed. 'Believe me, Anthony, the admiration is mutual. Your partner happens to be a very talented and charming man,' she said.

'Don't I know it,' he said, winking.

'Right, what would you ladies like to have for starters?' asked Simphiwe.

'I'll try out the snails, and then for the main . . .' said Eva.

'I'd suggest the stuffed chicken florentine, it's absolutely fabulous,' said Simphiwe, obviously familiar with the menu.

'Sounds divine; I think I'll have the same,' said Nolwazi, noticing that Anthony was looking at her with an appraising eye.

Anthony ordered a bottle of red wine, and then toasted both ladies for their outstanding appearances. 'So, Eva,' he said, 'I hear you're a master's student at UCT. How's the student life treating you?'

Eva grinned. 'Much better than the working life, I can tell you that much. I'm beginning to worry I'm going to be one of those perennial students. I just find the idea of pushing paper behind a desk a bit daunting,' she said, sipping her wine.

Simphiwe laughed. 'I hated varsity. All I did was read books, get sloshed, read books and then get sloshed again. It's all a bit of a blur actually. I don't even know how I made it.'

Anthony had started telling them about a project that he and Simphiwe were working on that involved designing the plan for an upcoming restaurant in Camps Bay, and once the two architects started talking shop, the ladies began to feel a bit left out.

Simphiwe said, 'Sorry, ladies, for boring you, it's just that we've a major presentation to the client tomorrow, so . . .'

'All work and no play makes you boys a bunch of dull cats,' said Nolwazi, to which Eva added, 'Hear, hear.' The two men laughed.

'Okay, please forgive us. We'll make it up to you two. Remember it's only Thursday night and we still have the whole weekend to get through. After our presentation, which, by the way, I'm sure will be a monumental success, we'll take you two out on Saturday to celebrate. How's that?' asked Simphiwe.

'Great,' said Nolwazi. 'On one condition.'

'What's that?'

'Absolutely no shop talk.' They all drank to that.

After settling the bill, Anthony and Simphiwe left in Simphiwe's Audi Roadster while Nolwazi and Eva went searching for some more night-time action. As Nolwazi slid into her car, she waited for Eva to get in and sighed before starting the engine.

'I'm a bit depressed,' she admitted frankly.

'Don't tell me you're jealous of Anthony. He's quite the man,' Eva said.

Nolwazi grumbled, 'Isn't he just?'

Eva suddenly realised that she was serious. 'Lwazi, listen to yourself. You are jealous of a gay man. Simphiwe already has a partner, so don't do this to yourself.'

Nolwazi started driving.

'Where are we going?' asked Eva.

Nolwazi shrugged.

'I know. There's a nice spot popular with students in Mowbray. It's cool. We can get completely sloshed without worrying about what anyone thinks,' suggested Eva brightly.

'Great. Show me the way, my German navigator,' she said, getting into the swing of things.

Twenty minutes later they were at Codes, a dingy, crowded student hangout.

'Let's go order some drinks,' said Eva, taking Nolwazi by the hand.

The music was loud and raucous, mostly European house music, which they both liked. They started swinging to the beat while drinking their ciders. When Nolwazi went to the bar to order more drinks, she literally bumped into a tall guy with diamond studs in his ears and a sexy tattoo on his muscular arm.

'Oops, sorry,' she said, giggling.

He turned to her, and she immediately noticed that he had the sexiest lips ever to grace earth. 'I don't mind,' he said, looking at her with a seductive gaze.

'Don't mind what?' she asked, feeling incredibly flirty.

'Don't mind you bumping into me,' he said.

All of a sudden, she had a wild idea. She wanted to kiss this guy. Heck. She was going to kiss this guy. After all, he was probably a student; he looked young enough, and she was never going to see him or any of the other people in the club again. Ever.

'Kiss me,' she said.

Before she knew what was happening, his sexy lips were on her, and boy, was this young one a good kisser. Mmm.

She didn't know how long it had been since they had started locking lips when she felt someone tug at her. Who could be so cruel as to interrupt this? Did they have any clue how long it had been since—

'Nolwazi,' she heard Eva hiss.

Oops. She managed to rescue her lips from the young one but still said, 'Gimme a sec,' before turning to face Eva.

Eva dragged her outside. 'What are you doing?'

'You told me to stop pining over Simphiwe so I'm getting my groove on with a guy who looks like Usher. Tell me what's wrong with that.'

Eva looked at her and then started to giggle. 'Okay. As long as you know what you're doing.'

Nolwazi was incredulous. 'Do you know how long it's been?'

'I was wondering how you were surviving without.'

Nolwazi was already darting back into the club. 'Look who's talking,' she shouted.

She found her mystery man sitting at the bar. Clasping her Brutal Fruit for courage, she went back to talk to him. 'You still here, stranger?'

'Waiting for you. Nobody else is interesting.'

Ah yes. They started dancing until a sexy R&B song began playing. He squeezed her closer to him and held her as if there was nowhere else he wanted to be. He whispered in her ear, 'You're so sexy. Look at you, with that tiny waist, and that cute little ass,' he said, squeezing her bottom.

Mmm. She was melting. She wanted him.

'Let's go outside,' he said.

'Okay.'

Before she knew it they were in his small, messy student digs, tearing each other's clothes off. Her threw her onto his bed and tore open a condom wrapper. Within moments they were grinding ferociously against each other.

The boy may be young, but he sure knows what he's doing, she thought.

After a ten-minute rest, they were at it again. By the time they were through, the furthest thing from Nolwazi's mind was Simphiwe.

Chapter 61

DIKELEDI

Dikeledi was sitting in the campus cafeteria when her colleague and friend Seipati arrived with a tray laden with lasagne and a glass of Coke, and asked if she could join her.

'Sure,' replied Dikeledi with half a smile.

Seipati enjoyed her food almost as much as she enjoyed conversation. She was one of the oldest members of the faculty and was by far the most popular. Although she loved to chat with her colleagues, she was trusted not to betray confidences and so most people warmed to her.

Dikeledi ate her Caesar salad slowly, her thoughts suspended in a maze of frustration. She could not bear living under the same roof as Tebogo any longer and her tenants were pleading for a two-month notice period, which turned out to be in the lease agreement that Tebogo had made them sign. Although it had seemed like a good idea at the time, she deeply regretted not being able to move back into her old apartment. She hated the insincere pleading she had to endure from Tebogo on an almost daily basis, but, more alarmingly, she realised that somebody else had stolen her heart long before the news about Nolwazi broke, yet she was ill-prepared to start dealing with the very real feelings she harboured for Professor Kwame.

'You don't look well lately, Dikeledi. I'm sorry if I'm sticking my nose in, but is everything okay?'

Dikeledi looked at the woman sitting next to her, wishing she could gush out all the frustration she was feeling. Instead she said, 'I need a place to stay. Things are not well between Tebogo and me.'

Seipati picked the last bit of lasagne off her plate and said, 'How long do you need a place for?'

Dikeledi shrugged and said, 'Well, I suppose for about two months. My apartment is rented out to a couple who have a two-month notice period. They have already served the first two weeks, but I can't stand living in close quarters with Tebogo. It's driving me crazy.'

Seipati smiled. 'Well, I think I've good news for you. It really helps to talk because I'm flying to the States this weekend on a month-long lecturing tour at Howard University. I'd be happy to loan you my apartment while I'm gone,' she said.

Seipati was a consummate traveller, never staying at one academic institution for longer than two years. She rented one of the apartments subsidised by the university. Dikeledi almost burst into tears. She was flooded with relief at the prospect of seeing the back of Tebogo for good.

She stood up to hug Seipati. 'My gosh! Thanks so much, Seipati. You truly are a lifesaver. You don't know how miserable I've been. That man has done so much to me, I truly could not stomach the thought of living with him for a whole month longer. I really owe you one.'

Seipati just smiled. 'Well, you could do me one favour.'

'Anything.'

Seipati laughed naughtily. 'My apartment is directly opposite Professor Kwame's and I've been trying to get that man into my bed for the longest time. I don't think I'm really his type but if you could shag him on my behalf, I'd be happy to enjoy it vicariously,' she said, giggling uncontrollably.

Dikeledi laughed along but was terrified that Seipati's joke was cutting too close to the bone.

Chapter 62

LINDA

Linda's heart was racing. The information supplied by Zodwa about Dineo's murder was enough for her to rope in her friend Sergeant Eddie Mokgotlwa of Hillbrow Police Station to follow up on the lead. When she arrived at the office, she immediately got on the phone to call him.

His mobile phone rang, and then disappointingly went to voicemail.

'Eddie, please call me; it's urgent. I've got a serious lead on the Dineo Khubeka case.'

She sat at her desk, fidgeting with her fingers while thinking who else needed to hear the new information. Deon would get overexcited if he heard the latest developments. Linda was very careful about how she managed leaks on stories that had ramifications for the criminal justice system. She was not as overzealous as Deon, who would want to play detective on a story like this. Her relationship with some members of the police force was a symbiotic one and she knew Sergeant Mokgotlwa would be the best person to help her use the evidence available as speedily as possible, and would respect her wishes as far as managing the flow of information to the rest of the media was concerned.

While she logged on to her computer to see if she could discover something from the Internet about The Towers Hotel in Hillbrow, her phone rang. The caller ID showed that it was Sergeant Mokgotlwa.

'Hi, Sergeant. Thanks for getting back to me so soon. Listen, I have some information about Dineo's case that I think could be critical. Meet me in Yeoville at The Shades restaurant in Times Square and I'll fill you in. I think I've got someone you could question about the case and this man probably has enough evidence to help you nail the sick bastard who killed that girl.'

Sergeant Mokgotlwa agreed to meet her in downtown Johannesburg immediately, so she grabbed the keys to her Jeep and scurried quickly out of the office.

She bumped into her boss, Warren Smith, on her way out.

'Watch it, Linds. What's the hurry?' he asked, looking at her with mild curiosity.

'Hot new lead on the Dineo case. Don't tell arsehole Deon,' she said breathlessly, and was gone.

When she got to The Shades, she asked the bartender for a Miller Draft. Her nerves were on edge. Sergeant Mokgotlwa arrived with his young partner, Constable Sipho Madlopha, for whom Linda harboured a passionate dislike. Constable Madlopha had once leaked information to the *Sunday World* before Linda could flight it on her show, contravening the deal she had struck with Mokgotlwa. Madlopha was young, ambitious and hungry for publicity. Linda did not address him directly but said to Mokgotlwa, 'What is he doing here?'

Looking at her expression, Mokgotlwa decided to send the young constable on an errand involving another case they were working on in Hillbrow. 'Be back in forty minutes, Madlopha. We've a long day ahead.'

Constable Madlopha said, 'Don't you think I should sit in on this meeting? I'm working the case too, you know.'

Sergeant Mokgotlwa threw him a fierce look. 'Are you refusing to follow my orders? That case with the Mbalula brothers is equally important so you better step on it, rookie!'

Madlopha took the car keys to their marked police van and left despondently.

'Okay, Eddie, listen. I met with this young sex worker earlier and she gave me what I think could be critical information relating to your case,' Linda said, and breathed while she waited for the waiter to place her Miller Draft on the table.

'Drinking so early? Are we developing a bad habit here, Ms Mthimkhulu?'

'*Ag.* You guys do it all the time. I'm very edgy. There's something about this story that's really started to feel personal to me. Maybe it's because I genuinely believed that Dineo would eventually make it out of the skin business.'

The sergeant shrugged. 'Or maybe you have real empathy towards the underdog.'

Linda took a long swig of her beer. She put her phone on silent, and said, 'Okay, here goes. Apparently, The Towers, some seedy hotel in Hillbrow, is run by a pimp called Antonio and he uses it mainly to carry out his business ventures. The last time anyone saw Dineo alive was when she was with one of her clients, a man who goes by the name of Mustafah. This Mustafah is a prize piece of work. A black man into S&M games, bondage, all sorts of crap. Anyway, he likes strangulation with objects like belts, scarves, ties, the works, and, apparently, he was with Dineo, playing one of these games, when, presumably, the game went horribly wrong. There's something called "asphyxiation", which involves tying somebody up around the neck until one or both parties climax. I'm not sure of the exact mechanisms of the game but this was one of Mustafah's favourite ways of getting himself off. According to the woman I spoke to – who was more than once involved in threesomes with Mustafah and Dineo – this is what killed Dineo. This is why there were no other signs of violence or bruising on her body. The bastard choked her to death. And get this: Antonio still has the belt that was used to kill Dineo. He's keeping it as blackmailing collateral against the guy, who's either a drug dealer or some kind of big businessman.' She breathed out.

'*Shoo*. That's quite a story,' said the sergeant, surprised as always at Linda's speed of delivery whenever she came across ground-breaking information. He respected her investigative skills and wondered once more why she was not working for the police service. 'So how reliable is your source? You sure this is something I can work on?'

'Well, if you think a sex worker can make up a story like that, maybe she deserves a career in Hollywood. Look, she was very emphatic about keeping her identity secret because she is scared of this Antonio and, for my money, I completely believe her story. Another girl had corroborated half the facts already. Look, Eddie, you know where The Towers is. All you have to do is get a search warrant, go looking for this Antonio there, and force him to produce the evidence. I'm sure there's enough dirt on his previous record to coerce him to hand over the object used to kill Dineo.'

Sergeant Mokgotlwa laughed. 'So, you're suggesting we should blackmail him into releasing the belt?'

Linda drank the last of her beer, shrugged and said, 'It's not like you haven't done it before.'

Chapter 63

Nolwazi

Nolwazi stared at her petite Samsung phone again. Thirteen missed calls from the young man with whom she had shared a night of unbridled passion. What was wrong with kids these days? The boy, Thabiso, who could not have been older than nineteen, was relentless in his pursuit of her, yet she wished to leave all memories of their encounter behind, like remnants of a disgraceful affair.

She had a meeting scheduled with Simphiwe because she wanted to transform the entire look of her boutique in order to lure more customers to her business. She dropped Siphokazi off at the nursery she attended near her shop then rushed to Afropolitan Designs for her meeting.

When she got there, she found her two assistants busy attending to customers. She put her bags in the small office attached to the store and followed up on online orders. Her business was amassing overseas clients who regularly trawled the Internet looking for unique buys like the ones she had to offer. As she added to the list of online purchases on a separate worksheet, she heard Simphiwe's voice as he joked with her assistants. She immediately took the notes she had prepared for their meeting and walked out of the office to meet him on the shop floor.

He hugged her and complimented her on her new hairstyle; she had long, neat, shoulder-length cornrows.

'Let's grab a coffee at Angelo's next door,' she said.

When they arrived at the coffee shop, she took out her notes and made a little presentation to Simphiwe.

'I've been thinking about how to get more customers into my shop, and I think I've come up with a solution, although it's a bit unconventional,' she said, whisking out the amateur floor-plan sketch she'd drawn to show her vision to Simphiwe. 'You see, I want to turn my boutique into a little coffee-shop-stroke-boutique by creating a really funky, modern interior with a combination of warm tones and striking colours, like silvers and reds, to lure customers into the shop. The look of the coffee shop should be art deco with minimalist, sophisticated lines. On the one side you've got the dining area, a small space of no more than three or four tables and on the other, you have the boutique, so that customers can enjoy their coffee and then browse through the clothing racks to look for something to their taste.'

Simphiwe folded his arms contemplatively. 'Aren't you worried about them getting your clothes dirty, once they finish having coffee with . . . say croissants or muffins or whatever?'

'Well, all I need to ensure is that it's a standard in the coffee shop that customers wishing to view garments must wipe their hands with wet wipes before moving to the clothing area. I think that will be easy to manage. I also want to change the mirrors in the fitting rooms to have the most flattering lighting so that the overall mirror image makes the clothes say "Buy me". Remember, I have very sophisticated ladies coming to my store; people who already have money to spend on designer wear.'

'So why exactly are you introducing this dining aspect to your boutique concept?' he asked matter-of-factly.

Nolwazi remained confident. 'Well, the point is to create a talking point about the store; it's a unique concept, I haven't really seen it anywhere. Also, women these days are busy. They don't have enough time to fit everything into their schedules so, this way, if a woman wants to meet with a friend for coffee plus squeeze in some shopping time, she can accomplish all of that in one sitting. Lastly, some women are intimidated by exclusive boutiques. This way, I'll be bringing a new type of client into the store.'

Simphiwe was now nodding his head with enthusiasm. 'Okay. I can see this now; I think it could fly,' he said, leaning against the table with concentration. 'What I'm going to do for you over the next three weeks is to draw three different plans for your shop according to what you're telling me. I'm going to throw in an Asian-inspired element to one of my sketches to see if we can pull off an East-meets-Africa look, because I see a lot of potential in the use of striking colours to give your boutique-coffee shop a unique flair.'

'Wow. I can't believe this. When I went to Italy, I met with this fabric supplier with the most gorgeous, gorgeous Eastern fabrics. The line that I'm working on for Joburg Fashion Week has a whole haute couture selection that's based on exactly that theme. It's an explosion of colour that, if done right, will definitely blow the fashion critics off their seats. I'm talking silk kimonos in eye-catching Ndebele patterns, A-line skirts in bold Eastern prints . . . you won't believe how good the sketches are looking.'

Simphiwe raised his cup. 'To great minds.'

'To great minds,' Nolwazi sang back with a huge grin.

After her session with Simphiwe, Nolwazi went to pick up Siphokazi from nursery. Nolwazi's cousin Ntombi was taking Siphokazi to a playdate with one of her own mommy friends so Nolwazi was in a rush to get her to Newlands on time.

She managed to meet Ntombi at the gate of her townhouse. The small child hopped from one car to the next, after kissing Nolwazi goodbye.

'Thanks, Ntombi, for doing this. Please bring her back before twelve tomorrow. I'm visiting the aquarium with her.'

'My friend is so thrilled. Her daughter is almost the same age as Siphokazi so hopefully the little ones will entertain each other while we finally catch up properly.'

Nolwazi laughed.

'You guys better keep them occupied otherwise you'll have your hands full,' she said.

Ntombi gave her the thumbs-up and drove off.

Just as Nolwazi wondered what to do with the rest of her Friday, Eva called. 'Let's go for drinks somewhere on Long Street. I've had the worst Friday ever. I handed in an assignment late and I'm worried I'm going to be in huge shit,' she explained.

'Okay. Let's meet at Ziyawa, that upstairs reggae pub near that surf shop you like.'

Half an hour later Nolwazi parked her car opposite Ziyawa and saw Eva crossing the street from the opposite end. She waved at her and Eva quickly came towards her parking spot.

'Made it on time, I see,' said Nolwazi as she fished out her army cap from the messy back seat of her car. She liked to look cool whenever she was in the midst of the reggae crowd, for reasons she could not explain. When she rose to close the back door, she saw her young Usher lookalike facing her car directly from the opposite side of the street.

'Duck,' she said, pulling Eva down with almost masculine force.

'What?' asked Eva, who was now cowering behind Nolwazi's car alongside her panic-stricken friend.

'Shh!' whispered Nolwazi.

'Okay, but can you explain why we're hiding behind your little car instead of enjoying Friday drinks?'

'It's that boy . . . Usher, from last Thursday.'

'Your one-night stand?' asked Eva incredulously.

'Don't call him that. He's weird. He leaves me messages every day. He's mad. He should be in an institution. He seems to think we've got a relationship.' Eva peeked out to see if the offending man was still in view. 'He's just stepped into the travel agency on the other side of the road.'

'Are you sure?' whispered Nolwazi.

'Why are you whispering? Do you think he can hear us all the way up the other end of the street?' Eva giggled.

Nolwazi just rolled her eyes. 'Are you with me or against me? Check again to make sure he's gone.'

Eva, who was tired of crawling behind the Toyota stood up and said, 'The coast is clear, Nolwazi.'

Nolwazi stood up with relief. 'That boy needs to disappear from Cape Town. I'm glad he's going into that travel agency. I hope he goes to a land far, far away from here. Now quick, let's run to Ziyawa before he comes out again!' she said, running up the stairs to safety.

Chapter 64

DIKELEDI

Temporarily living opposite Professor Kwame turned out to be a laboured and awkward affair for Dikeledi. How was she to explain the coincidence without sounding as if she had schemed her way into being at close quarters to him? Although she'd seen him twice at work in the week of her move, she had not managed to summon up the courage to tell him that she would be staying in the apartment directly opposite his door for a few weeks.

Tebogo had refused to let her take Phemelo with her, citing the unfairness of the adjustment for their daughter. After arguing at length about the matter, they had finally reached an agreement whereby Phemelo would move back in with her mother once Dikeledi's apartment was ready for resettlement. Dikeledi worried that Tebogo's legal background could lead him to use this temporary set-up against her, should he decide to fight for Phemelo's custody, so she took the step of ensuring that they both went to the police station to sign an affidavit stating that this was a temporary arrangement agreed to in the best interests of the child.

She feared Tebogo's rampant bitterness over the separation. He had taken to drinking more alcohol when he came back from work, a trend that worried Dikeledi more than his ability to be a support for Phemelo during his interim custody of her. She had decided to drop by as often as possible whenever she came from work in order to ensure that her child was being well taken care of. She was tired of fretting over her separation from Tebogo. She had even managed to lose three kilograms over a period of a month. Not even her Planet Fitness membership had managed to rack up such astounding results.

As she dragged the last of her bags into the compact apartment, she heard a knock on the door. She went to open it, wondering who could be looking for her . . . or for Seipati. As she opened, she was slightly elated to see Professor Kwame's face, looking pleasantly surprised.

'Hi, Dikeledi. I'm looking for Seipati. I wanted to say goodbye to her before she left for the States,' he said, barely managing to hide the smile on his handsome face.

Dikeledi raised her eyebrows subconsciously. The knots in her stomach were making it hard for her to breathe. Here he was, the object of her fantasies, barely a few inches from her. The thought that she would be a mere door away from him for the next few weeks made her breathless. She sighed to ease her breathing. 'Um, I'm afraid Seipati has already left. She took off two days ago already . . . Some neighbour you are!' She grinned.

He shrugged. 'That's a pity. It's a constant struggle with Seipati. If I'm too friendly she rewards me with a bit too much attention.'

Dikeledi screwed up her face. 'No need to share the dirty laundry with me, brother. After all, you're supposed to love thy neighbour.'

For some reason, the professor seemed to find this extremely amusing. After laughing himself into a stupor, he said, in between grins, 'Well, if you were my neighbour, I could easily bring that saying into practice. What are you doing here anyway?'

As he stood there, with his hands tucked in his pockets, Dikeledi had the crazy urge to invite him in . . . and see what would happen. 'Well, as luck would have it, I am your neighbour. Temporarily, anyway.'

The look on Professor Kwame's face was that of a child in a theme park. His eyes danced with joy. 'Are you serious? May I welcome you then to this modest den of academics by inviting you to dinner at my house . . . at seven?' he asked hurriedly.

Dikeledi always wondered why Professor Kwame never asked about her personal circumstances. Did he not want to know why she was staying opposite him all of a sudden? Was he not concerned about the circumstances that would bring an engaged woman to stay in a one-bedroom apartment off-campus without her family? This is what she feared the most about him. Perhaps he really was nothing but a playboy who was out to score whenever he got the chance. Surely if he had feelings for her, he would at least be curious about her personal life? The man was danger personified . . . and yet, she could not resist him. Caution be damned! She was going to take a chance with him.

After all, what had all her caution achieved so far?

Chapter 65

LINDA

Linda was anxious to hear some feedback from Sergeant Mokgotlwa but she had left him several unanswered messages over the past week. She wondered why he was being so unresponsive. She knew that the case he was working on, which involved the infamous Mbalula brothers, was quite pressing, as it had been in the news for over a year. It involved racketeering, drug trafficking and child pornography. Clearly Dineo's story was not exactly top of his list. She played with the idea of calling Constable Madlopha to see if he had any news, but when she imagined actually having a conversation with the arrogant rookie, she immediately decided against it.

As it was a Saturday, she allowed her mind to drift back to Kennedy. He had told her to be ready at twelve because he wanted to take her somewhere. It all sounded very mysterious, and she hated surprises, especially from boyfriends. They had an uncanny ability to read her completely wrong and now she wondered what Kennedy had up his sleeve as she recalled some of the blunders that Lehumo had committed every time he had planned a surprise for her. She remembered the time when he had decided to buy her spiky red stilettos and a red dress that clung to every inch of her body, making her look like something from a porn site. The brother had spent a couple of years hanging out with her at soccer and rugby matches, pubs and all sorts of macho places, yet he expected her to whip out some sexy-mama persona from thin air?

She looked out of her window and watched Kennedy park his Jaguar in the visitor's parking bay. He had with him a bunch of her favourite flowers: lilies. She sighed. That was exactly what her mom used to bring her when she visited her at her university residence. This brother had her pegged. She went to the mirror to tie her dreadlocks into a neat ponytail, put on some glossy lipstick, and adjust her sexy, denim mini skirt, which she wore with comfortable flip-flops.

When Kennedy came through the door, she planted a slow, sexy kiss on his lips before taking the lilies and placing them in the glass vase on her coffee table.

'How are you, my honey?' she asked, taking him by the hand.

He grabbed her by the waist and led her into the bedroom. Slowly, he started to take off her clothes while kissing her on the lips without stopping.

She loved the feel of his skin on top of hers. Nothing made her feel more connected than having Kennedy inside her. She wished they could spend the whole day like that, just locked into each other – no conversation; enough words passed between them through the ancient language of lovemaking.

They dozed off lazily for a few minutes afterwards until Kennedy said, 'Wake up, *sthandwa*, we need to go somewhere.'

Linda was lazy after making love. 'Nooo. Why?'

Kennedy was already getting dressed. 'I told you I wanted to show you something.'

Linda moaned. 'You're no fun at all. Always doing something. Can't you just be like a Buddhist monk and be still?'

He slapped her playfully with his T-shirt before putting it back on. 'If I were a Buddhist monk I wouldn't be able to give you the kind of good lovin' that you're getting, babes.'

Linda stood up. 'You make a good point. Okay, I'll get ready. Where are we going anyway?'

'Come on,' he said, grabbing his keys. 'I told you it's a surprise.'

Once they were in the car, Kennedy started driving in the direction of Northcliff, where Linda worked.

'Tell me you're not taking me anywhere near my slave station.'

'Relax,' was all he said.

After meandering through the hilly side of the leafy suburb, they ended up in front of a property under development: a large estate with roomy clusters that boasted modern exteriors. 'I've bought this three-bedroom cluster here with an upper and lower terrace, balconies in all the main bedrooms and a little swimming pool, right over here,' he said excitedly.

Linda was mystified. Where was all this going? 'This is gorgeous, baby. I could never fault you when it comes to good investments,' she said as enthusiastically as possible.

'D'you like it?'

'Who wouldn't? It's stunning,' she said, this time quite genuinely.

He grabbed her by the waist and kissed her, then looked into her eyes. 'So would you mind moving in with me into this gorgeous piece of real estate?'

'Um, um . . . well . . . what? You want to do *vat en sit* with me?' she asked, hoping to duck the issue for a moment.

He went down on his knees. 'If you want to get married then I'll be more than happy to,' he said, grinning.

'No, no, no. Stand up. No need to get ahead of ourselves now,' she said, panicking. She was thinking fast. On the one hand, she did not want to lose Kennedy. Truth be told, she had no reason to break it off with him, even though he was behaving like an idiot with all this commitment stuff. Maybe, just maybe, she could live

310

with him under one roof. After all, they were practically playing revolving doors between each other's apartments already.

He stood up before she could say a word and put both his hands on her shoulders. 'Listen, *sthandwa*, I'm as scared as you are here, okay? I've never done anything like this, but I'm crazy about you and I don't want to lose you. I'm not the man who is going to rush you into anything you don't want. It is your very independence that I love about you, but I feel that we need to make some sort of commitment towards each other, otherwise one of us will stray without the other even paying attention.'

Linda groaned. 'Baby, I know what you're saying but what if this whole commitment thing changes everything? What if you start getting bored with me? Dating someone and living with them under one roof are two totally—'

'Yes. They are two totally different things and I'm ready for it. I mean, I already know you don't snore, so that's a big plus . . .' he said, trying to bring some light-heartedness into the topic.

She smiled.

'Listen, Linds, I love you and you mean the world to me. You don't have to marry me if you're not ready but . . . we have to start thinking about solidifying what we have otherwise we'll start taking each other for granted. I, for one, would love to wake up to the sight of you every day. Nothing would make me happier than that.'

She had tears in her eyes. 'Okay,' she whispered. 'I love you. I'll move in with you.'

Chapter 66

Nolwazi

Nolwazi felt ebullient at the prospect of finalising plans for her business with Simphiwe. Over the past few weeks, she had seen his inspired creativity come alive and they had already made considerable headway in completing the design for the boutique coffee shop. He had recently renovated his apartment, so she looked forward to meeting him there to go over the colour scheme of the restaurant. He had also selected fabrics for the decor and furnishings of the store, so she wondered what this style giant had in mind for her.

On entering Simphiwe's apartment, Nolwazi was accosted by the glistening surface of a circular table in fuchsia pink. The walls and curtains were a warm oyster colour, which offered a neutral backdrop. He had also reupholstered his couch in a light brown and had thrown brown and pink scatter cushions to offset the circular table. On each side of the couch were two chairs in different designs, but both contrasted well with the colour scheme. The overall effect was surprisingly tasteful, yet unique.

He was carrying a crystal glass and bottle of champagne when he invited her in and he filled the glass, a wide smile on his face. 'Good evening, Lwazi. No Eva tonight?'

She went in and took off her jacket, careful to hang it on one of the hooks by the door. She flashed him a smile. 'Now why would I bring Eva to a business meeting?'

He feigned disappointment. 'Oh. So this is a business meeting . . . how disappointing.'

Nolwazi sat down and sipped her champagne, while Simphiwe slipped in a Michael Bublé CD. The Italian pop classic 'Quando, Quando, Quando' started to play and Simphiwe sang along.

Unable to resist, Nolwazi jumped from the couch and sang along with him. They continued dancing, each repeating lyrics in an impromptu karaoke session. When the song finished, they collapsed back onto the couch, Simphiwe grinning while holding his glass and Nolwazi lost in thought.

Once again, Nolwazi was struck by how comfortable she felt in this man's company, realising how much she enjoyed being alone with him. Sometimes they would both sit in contemplative silence, each deep in thought, dreaming up some artistic tower of beauty, which they would then turn to share with the other. They were twin spirits in many ways. She sighed. Perhaps it was for the best that he was gay. At least they did not have to worry about sex rearing its ugly head and complicating matters.

He looked at her and smiled, drawing closer to her on the two-seater couch.

'What are you thinking about?'

She shrugged. 'I'm just amazed at how well we get on with each other. I actually don't remember ever being as comfortable with a man as I am with you.'

He was silent for a while, playing with his glass. 'What's the deal with you and men anyway?' he asked, surprising her.

'What do you mean?'

He took off his glasses, and she realised he had deep brown, almond-shaped eyes, almost like hers. 'Stop me if I'm being too personal, but . . . what happened to Siphokazi's dad? I mean . . . when exactly did you discover you were . . . you know?'

She was puzzled. 'You mean when did I discover I was pregnant?'

'Um, yes, and . . . how did you get pregnant? I mean, did you do it the normal way or . . . or did science maybe help you along?'

'Science? What are you talking about? Of course I had her the normal way . . . you know, man and woman get together . . .'

'So when did you find out that you are . . . you know, the way you are?'

Nolwazi was completely lost. What in the world was this man on about? Was there some nasty rumour circulating about her? What did he mean about her being the way she was? She would be mortified if Simphiwe knew that she had slept with her best friend's boyfriend.

'Look. I don't know what you are talking about, Simphiwe, and, as I told you when we first met, I generally don't talk about Siphokazi's father. I have my own reasons.'

He nodded. 'Okay, I understand. Do you want a refill?'

'I'd love one. This champagne's divine. What is it?'

'It's Veuve Clicquot. Anthony introduced me to it. It's his favourite. Fabulous, fabulous drink.'

She watched him as he went to the kitchen to refill their glasses.

'So how's it going with you and Eva?' he asked, still busy with the champagne.

'Fine. We're like two peas in a pod. She's just the greatest thing ever, that girl. Her carefree spirit rubs off on you. I think she's absolutely irresistible.'

He came back with coasters and set the glasses down on the fuchsia-pink table. 'Well, she's one lucky woman to have you, that's for sure,' he said, silently toasting to Nolwazi.

She laughed. 'The way you say it implies we're a couple.'

He paused with his glass in mid-air. 'You mean . . . you guys aren't a couple anymore?'

Now Nolwazi was almost falling off the couch. 'Me and Eva? Are you mad, Simphiwe? No!'

Now it was his turn to be shocked. 'You're not? But you guys are always holding hands and hugging and you're inseparable. Then there was that incident where you told some guy to back off from your girlfriend . . . what was that about then?'

She could not believe he was being serious. She held him by the hand, smiled and said, 'I'm sorry I overreacted about you thinking Eva and I are a couple. I mean, being gay yourself, I can see why you might think that but the truth, my dear, is that I am a fully heterosexual woman.'

It was his turn to look at her and laugh. Once he started, it seemed as if he would never stop.

'What's so funny, Simphiwe? What's so funny?' She started tugging at his sleeve, but he could not stop laughing.

Finally, he said, 'Nolwazi, what in the frigging world gave you the idea that I was gay?'

'What? You're not gay?'

He shook his head. 'Nope. Not since the last time I checked.'

Then they looked at each other, cupped their mouths and could not stop laughing as they realised how foolish they had both been all this time. They laughed and laughed, until suddenly they found themselves kissing.

When they stopped and realised what they had just done, Simphiwe looked at her tenderly, touching her face. 'How foolish we've been. I couldn't ask you out for so long because I was convinced you were into women.'

Nolwazi closed her eyes, sighed, laughed, and then became serious again. She found that she was shaking with emotion; she could not get the words out properly. 'I've wanted to be with you since the first day we met. I don't know when I started convincing myself you were gay. This is the most ridiculous thing ever! You know, when I met you, I was still reeling from the disaster of my relationship with Siphokazi's dad. I think it was convenient armour for me to think of you as a gay man. That way I was able to let my guard down with you without worrying that you'd hurt me.'

They kissed again and, overwhelmed by the Herculean comedy of errors they had created, started to laugh once more.

'I'm so glad you're straight. So glad. Fabulous news! Whoopee!' screamed Simphiwe who poured more champagne.

'A toast,' he said, as he handed Nolwazi her glass. 'To two of the world's dumbest smart people.'

'Hear, hear!' said Nolwazi.

Chapter 67

LINDA

The call finally came on Wednesday afternoon, just when Linda was about to give up on Sergeant Mokgotlwa's investigative abilities. It was a grey day with pregnant clouds threatening to release torrents of angry rain. Linda dreaded such days because they had a way of turning her mood to a dull, deathly monotone. She had been staring pensively at the clouds through her office window, wondering what else the day had in store, when she was roused out of her thoughts by the violent ring of the phone.

'Linda. I have good news,' said the sergeant in his booming baritone.

Linda stood up from her desk anxiously, cradling the phone next to her ear. At least the forces of human will seemed to be triumphing over the dark clouds outside her window.

'We've got a match for the prints we lifted from your Nigerian friend's prized belt. By the way, his real name is not even Antonio, but that's another story for another day. You are going to be gobsmacked when you find out who this guy is . . .'

'Really? Does Constable Madlopha know that you've got a match?'

'Of course he does; he's working the case.'

'Please, Sergeant, if it's somebody prominent, don't let him run off and inform the entire paparazzi. This is my story; I led you guys to this breakthrough,' she said possessively. She could feel the veins throbbing in her neck. She was so excited at the news she could barely keep still.

Sergeant Mokgotlwa sounded irritated. 'When did I ever not keep my end of the deal?'

'Hmm well, you remember that *Sunday World* leak? You think I don't know it was Madlopha who told them about my lead?'

'Okay, okay. I'll take care of the little guy. Now, do you or don't you want to know who our Mustafah is?'

'Bated breath, my friend.'

'Okay. It's a guy called Winston Gumede, some hotshot CEO of an international management consulting firm. He was in the news recently about pulling off some high-profile merger of two banking groups and . . .'

Linda did not hear anything the sergeant said beyond the mention of Winston Gumede's name. Sade's Winston? This was a mistake. Surely it was just a huge mix-up.

'Sergeant. Stop. Did you really just say Winston Gumede? It can't be. I know that man personally. It just can't be him.'

'Well, we're going to his office right now to read him his rights. Forensics don't lie, Linda.'

'No, no, wait. Can't you just hold it a bit? I mean . . . I'm serious, Eddie. This has to be a mistake. The guy is a born-again Christian. He's devoted to his wife . . . I know these people very well. If you are in any way mistaken, this is going to have huge implications for the police. You guys will not hear the end of it. You will have the biggest lawsuit in the history of the police in this country. The man is enormously powerful. He consults for the biggest wigs in the country and the world. You will be taken to the cleaners if this is not accurate.'

The sergeant was silent on the other end of the line; meanwhile Linda's mind was racing. She hoped her argument was convincing. She needed to stall, and she was absolutely sure that Winston was the wrong man. He may not be the most engaging of personalities but she knew him enough to be convinced that he was incapable of this crime.

'Linda, let me read you a description of this Winston from one of the sex workers we interviewed, as well as your Antonio. Tell me if your guy fits this description,' the sergeant said, with a confidence that unnerved Linda.

She breathed in and said a silent prayer. She hoped this was all a nightmare that would soon be quashed by the reality of daylight.

'Mustafah is about one point eight metres tall, wears square-rimmed glasses, is softly spoken, wears expensive suits and drives a BMW.'

Linda scrunched up her face and dropped back on her swivel chair. How could a good story go so wrong? Now she was caught between her professional responsibilities and her loyalty to Sade. Here it was in black and white. Sade's Winston was into hookers and kinky sex and now he was about to be charged with murder.

She needed to gather her wits about her. Damage control. She must ensure that she softened the blow for Sade in whatever way possible.

Chapter 68

DIKELEDI

As Dikeledi walked into Professor Kwame's house, she inhaled the enticing smells that wafted from the kitchen. He was preparing a Ghanaian speciality tonight: Kentumere – an exotic mix of kippered herring and spinach cooked in palm oil. Ever since she'd moved into Seipati's house, she and the professor had taken to treating each other to cultural dishes; it was an exercise they found deliciously exciting, especially because it forced them to be in close contact with each other – passing a fork here and assisting each other with cutting something else there. They loved the communal aspect of sharing these mundane tasks together yet, at the same time, exploring such an intrinsic part of each other's identity.

'Penny for your thoughts, my lady,' said the professor, rousing her out of her reverie.

She tasted the morsel of food he'd perched on a fork for her.

'Mmm. This is . . . different,' she said.

'Good different or . . . ?'

'Oh please. You're practically a qualified chef. I've yet to taste anything you've made that doesn't resemble something out of a five-star restaurant.'

He clapped his hands in delight and, for a moment, Dikeledi wished she could freeze the image: this big man wearing a colourful apron made in *kente* cloth, looking so content, so happy. She smiled, thinking that she had not felt so calm in years.

Her relationship with Tebogo had been filled with tension and turmoil. She had always had to be on the lookout for any signs of infidelity, never feeling relaxed that he was hers and hers alone. Yet with Kwame . . .

They were locked in a lingering kiss now, completely out of nowhere. He laughed and did a little dance. 'You think too much . . . that's your problem.'

She drew him in and enveloped him with her arms, kissing him back slowly. 'You're right,' she said.

'You know what you should do?'

She shook her head, her eyes twinkling in anticipation. 'What?'

'You,' he said, pointing a finger at her teasingly, 'young lady, should marry me, that's what.'

She laughed, enjoying what she thought was a delightful joke. 'Please tell me why a broken-down love cynic like me would want to marry anyone at this point?'

He looked at her in a way that made her uncertain if he was actually deadly serious or joking, then he shrugged. 'Because you know it would be good for you.'

He went back to stirring the meal he was preparing. She took a fork and dipped it back into the large skillet with the now simmering Kentumere.

'Mmm. Spinach, fish and tomatoes . . . all the things that my mom said are good for me.'

He laughed. 'Yes indeed.'

Chapter 69

SADE

Sade was watching an old episode of *Oprah* featuring her favourite gospel singer, Kirk Franklin. He sat on Oprah's star-washed couch, bathed in the media mogul's studio lights. Sitting next to him was his pretty, petite wife. Sade held the TV remote with her mouth ajar, raising the volume. The gospel singer was confessing to an addiction to porn and his wife was actually holding his hand supportively while attesting to the scandalous revelation. The singer admitted that this had been a persistent problem at odds with his faith, but that he had realised the error of his ways and had prayed for God's support and protection from this affliction.

Well, thank God for that, but still . . . Was Sade actually going to continue playing this man's music? She felt very disappointed in him. Was he not supposed to set an example for the likes of her? How was she to strengthen her faith if those who led the way were so flawed as to be addicted to something as deviant as pornography? It was people like this man who led to the backsliding of born-again Christians. She had always maintained that for her to stay on this path she had chosen she must surround herself with those who walked in the light of God, undeterred by outside influences, including the media.

But then again, how bored would she get?

Perhaps it was time she went back to work. It had been two years since she stopped being a salaried member of society and she was beginning to feel useless. Her mind had always been sharp and cried out for new challenges. She was even beginning to feel jealous of Winston's career trajectory. He was a regular feature in the business publications in South Africa. A wunderkind of sorts . . . black boy makes good on the financial markets. She needed to prove herself, not in opposition to her man, but just to remind herself that she was also an intelligent woman. Lazing around all day had long lost its initial lustre.

As she planned how she was going to present her case to Winston, her phone buzzed. She saw that it was a private number. Assuming it was Winston calling from his office, she answered casually, 'Hello.'

A pause, then the voice on the other end said, 'Hi, Sade. It's Linda.'

She had not heard from *her* since the revelations of Nolwazi's betrayal. Sade knew it was not Christian-like to hold a grudge against Linda, especially since it was Nolwazi and not Linda who had committed the deed with Tebogo, even though the fact that she had kept this secret from her and Dikeledi was unbelievable.

'Hi, Linda, how are you?' she asked, suddenly aware that she had not asked how she was coping with her mother's death after that fateful day of revelations.

'I'm fine. Just fine, and you?'

'I'm okay. How's Kennedy? I hope he's been making things easier for you.'

For a moment, Linda was quiet, not understanding what Sade meant by this comment. She too had just realised that she had not spoken to Sade since Nolwazi's confession two months back. 'He's great. We're moving in together,' she heard herself say.

Sade was unimpressed. It was against her values to move in with a man before marriage, but then again, Linda was Linda. What more could one expect? 'So, what's up?' she asked.

'Sade . . . we need to talk. It's very urgent. It's something I can't discuss over the phone with you. I need to tell you this now . . . as soon as possible, before you hear it elsewhere,' she said, the words tripping over each other, her voice suddenly panicked.

Sade was wearing jeans and a halter-neck top – her stay-at-home gear – and she was not in the mood for one of Linda's dramas.

'What is it about? Winston's about to come back from work and the nanny's taken Ntokozo to a play date down the road. I can't just up and leave . . .'

'Trust me, Sade, you will thank me for this. It's very important.'

'Linda . . . I hope you're not messing around with me. I don't live the kind of lifestyle where I can just drop everything at the ring of a phone call.'

'Look, just come to Sergio's, that coffee shop I took you to next to my office. Trust me, it's very important.'

'Okay. It better be,' said Sade stubbornly.

Before driving off to Northcliff, Sade tried Winston on his mobile phone. It was on voicemail, so she left him a brusque message saying she was having a quick meeting with Linda. She also called her child's nanny to alert her that she would be out for a short while. She then grabbed the keys to her Mini Cooper and started feeling mildly jubilant about this outing. It had been a while since her life had even the slightest frisson of intrigue so at least she had something to look forward to aside from the drudgery of daily domesticity. Whatever Linda had to say obviously had to do with one of their two mutual friends; quite frankly, she had no time to entertain Nolwazi's pathetic life and its accompanying fault lines. If the emergency concerned Dikeledi, however, she would be more than willing to rally around her.

324

When she veered towards the restaurant parking area, a slow trickle of rain washed over her windscreen. She breathed in and parked her Mini smartly opposite the front entrance of the coffee shop. Thankfully, Linda's Jeep was already there. She ran up the stairs to avoid the drizzle and mentally calculated how long she had so that she could make it home on time to ensure Winston had a warm dinner waiting for him. She sighed once more at the realisation of how much of a homemaker she had become. Yes, she definitely needed to chat to Winston about going back to work. This level of domestication was an affront to all the education that her parents had invested in her.

As she walked into Sergio's she saw Linda. Her shoulders were scrunched up and she had the expression of someone who had just witnessed a death. Something was definitely not right.

Sade sat down, wiping off traces of rain from her bare shoulders. '*Shoo*. I didn't expect to be accosted by rain coming here . . .' she began conversationally.

'I'm sorry . . . I mean, I'm sorry for the rain.'

Sade laughed. 'Last time I checked, Linda, you were not God. No need to apologise about the rain of all things,' she said jovially.

Linda smiled weakly. 'Geez. I'm sorry . . . I mean, sorry for saying that,' she said, and then waved to the waitress to take their orders.

The waitress came over with a broad, friendly smile. Linda had been to Sergio's a number of times but nobody had ever attended to her that quickly or with such a broad smile. Sade ordered a caffè latte while Linda asked for an Irish coffee. Then they stared at each other, like strangers linked by a quiet discomfort from the past.

Sade shrugged and gestured with her hands. 'Well, can you please tell me why you had to drag me from *Oprah* to come all the way here?'

Linda was quiet. She kept on looking down, avoiding Sade's gaze.

'Hellooo . . . earth to Linda,' Sade implored.

Just then the waitress arrived with their orders. Linda was gobsmacked by the efficiency of the place on this day of all days. Couldn't they drag everything out for as long as possible? She was ill-equipped to deal with this situation, she realised. When did life become so serious? Why did Sade have to go and get married to this bloody Winston anyway? Why did Deon talk her into doing the story? If she had not done this story everybody would be in a coddled universe, safe in the knowledge that their world was a beatific, peaceful and embryonic place that shielded one from all the filth and the dirt that surrounded them. They could pretend that they were a decent bunch with normal, perfect, so-called black-diamond lifestyles. Now this . . . How in the world was she to tell her friend that her born-again Christian husband was some sort of S&M psycho-murderer?

'So . . . Linda . . . I'm waiting,' said Sade, sipping her caffè latte. She looked at her watch. It was five thirty. Winston would be home in half an hour.

Linda still looked tongue-tied. She was drinking her Irish coffee and staring outside as if she had never seen the rain before. Finally, she placed her glass down on the table gently, as if it would break, weaved her fingers together and leaned forward. She looked more serious than Sade had ever seen her. Suddenly Sade had the urge to laugh.

'Sade, what I'm going to tell you will probably turn the world as you know it inside out. It has to do with your husband,' she said.

Sade looked at her with a queenly disbelief. Linda knew nothing about Winston. In fact, she had no authority to speak about her husband, so this little announcement was to be taken with some measure of scorn. She folded her arms with an imperious attitude and looked at Linda impassively. 'Yes?' she said, in as balanced a tone as she could manage. She was irritated that Linda, with her lifestyle, would believe herself fit to comment on Winston or anything else that pertained to Sade's world.

'Sade, I've been doing a story . . . actually, a follow-up to a story I did long ago on this young woman called Dineo Fakude.'

'Yes . . .' said Sade, her irritation mounting. She remembered this Dineo to be the sex worker in the piece that Linda had won some sort of award for. It was so crass, this whole journalism business; that someone could be glorified for going around following a sex worker's life as if it were something to be lauded.

For a long time, they looked at each other, the wedge of silence drawing them further from each other. How could Linda sit there and mention Winston's name in one breath and a sex worker's name in another? Suddenly, the image of Kirk Franklin sitting on Oprah's couch confessing to his porn addiction struck at the very core of her heart; she felt as if she did not want to breathe again. Her head drummed and she became momentarily numb. What devious plot had Linda hatched to crumble her already imperfect world? What kind of a mockery was this?

'Linda, I don't think I want to hear this!' she said, grabbing the keys from the table aggressively.

'There's a chance it might be on the news tonight . . . I've done all I can to prevent that,' said Linda, already imagining Deon taking some of the material her team had captured and giving it over to the news crew. She had tried her best to embargo the information but Winston, although not a famous man, was familiar enough in financial circles for this news to cause quite a few waves. The possibility of Deon holding on to the material until tomorrow's broadcast of *On Cue* was highly unlikely. He would want the SABC chiefs to know it was *his* programme that broke the story . . . and he would want the acknowledgement on the most watched show on TV: the evening news.

When Linda mentioned the evening news, Sade froze. Already she could feel something sordid and dripping with scandal slithering into her life and spitting venom into her very existence. Slowly, she put the keys back on the table and sat down. She hated Linda at this moment, for she knew that she held an important part of her future in her hands.

'Okay. What is it?' she asked, sinking further into her chair.

'Sade, I'm really sorry about this but, at any moment now, Winston will be held as a suspect for Dineo's murder . . . and the evidence is stacked strongly against him. There's a cop who's been working this case, he's a friend of mine, and he's really good at what he does. It looks like Winston's fingerprints are all over the object used to strangle this woman . . .' She let the sentence hang.

Seeing Sade's shocked expression, she continued, hoping to allay her fears. 'Look, it was an accident, by all accounts. It looks like they were playing . . . they were playing some sort of game,' Linda continued, embarrassed to reveal her knowledge of Winston's sexual fetishes. She assumed that Sade probably knew of Winston's S&M fetish but that she would prefer to keep it private. She did not want to go further into the details but only wished to exhibit the fact that whatever happened had not been premeditated, that her husband had committed a fatal mistake.

Sade shielded her face by arching both hands to cover it. 'Linda, I don't know what games you're talking about. Tell me,' she said, eyes closed, as she brought down both hands, 'tell me what games you claim my husband was playing with this . . . with this *prostitute*.' She breathed the word out as if it were poison, but her eyes remained closed, and her hands were now on the table.

Linda cleared her throat, completely uncomfortable in the situation. 'Well . . . um, apparently Winston liked to tie up these girls and . . . and, um, you know, it was something that . . . that aroused him, so—'

'Jesus Christ!' Sade exclaimed, as if unaware that anyone else was with her.

Linda stopped. 'Look, I really can't go on with this story, Sade . . . I feel really uncomfortable,' she said, tentatively.

Suddenly Sade opened her eyes and glared at Linda with fiery hatred. 'Well, you brought me here, didn't you? You probably couldn't wait to see my reaction. I know you've been silently mocking me . . . mocking my Christian beliefs! You wanted this to happen so that your devilish ways could triumph over my religion! I know it!' she shouted, attracting the attention of the waiters in the restaurant.

It was Linda's turn to be shocked. How could Sade say these things about her? She had never mocked Sade's beliefs . . . not in terms of embracing God. She had relied on her own faith to guide her through the loss of her mother. The only thing she had a problem with was the way in which material aggrandisement was such a strong feature at Sade's church.

All the waiters were looking at them, as if wary of the next move in this unfolding drama.

'No, Sade. That's unfair,' she said, suddenly wanting to protect her position.

'Oh, is it? You think I haven't seen you rolling your eyes every time I talk about my church or my God? You are just a typical messenger of the Devil . . . ready to break up anything that's made in the name of our Lord,' she said, standing up to leave.

Linda grabbed her arm.

'Let me go, you frigging heathen. I curse the day I ever met you!'

Linda still held on to her arm. 'Sade, you're in denial. In a few hours your husband will be exposed as a man who not only frequents brothels in Hillbrow but one who's been arrested for murdering a sex worker. You have a choice: to do something proactive about this, or just to stay in your blissfully ignorant state. Now, I know you once said something about Winston's mom or somebody being related to the broadcaster's head of news. I would normally not advise something like this as it's against my professional ethics . . .' She paused. 'My suggestion is that you try and prevent footage of your husband being handcuffed and taken into police custody amidst flashing cameras until you've had a chance to absorb all of this stuff and deal with it in a way that minimises the damage to your family,' said Linda, still gripping Sade's arm firmly.

Sade looked at her with venom, her arm hurting from Linda's grip, her teeth clenched in protest until finally, she managed to pull away and settled back down on her chair with quiet defiance. She sat in a prayer-like position for a long while, mulling over her options. Finally she decided to turn her anger into something constructive, because she now realised that time was no longer on her side.

Resignedly, she dialled her mother-in-law's number and calmly explained to her what had just transpired. She alerted Winston's mom to the fact that they needed to speak to her cousin, who was head of news at the national broadcaster, in order to ensure that the footage bearing Winston's story would not be shown on the news that evening. Her mother-in-law was hysterical, but Sade stayed cool and told her to remain likewise as they needed to try and save the family name.

When she'd finished the call, Sade was quiet and contemplative.

'What are you going to do now?' asked Linda.

'Please call your cop friend and find out what's happening,' a now composed Sade asked.

Linda nodded and made the call. 'Sergeant, what's happening with the Gumede case?'

'Where are you, Linda? Your crew is crawling all over the place here. They're attracting too much attention. I thought you'd be here . . . you know how I hate dealing with them when you're not here.'

'Is Deon Venter there?'

'Of course, he is. What's he doing here anyway? Isn't he supposed to be some kind of pencil pusher? This is ridiculous. I don't want to work with you TV people anymore. Now all of Gumede's staff have come down to witness this bloody circus. I'm struggling to get the guy into the police van.'

'Is he cooperating? Don't manhandle him or anything.'

'Dammit, Linda! Why aren't you here to control your people?' he asked, and then cut her off.

Sade was looking at Linda anxiously. Suddenly she felt like she had just lifted the curtain and taken a glimpse for the first time at the real Winston Thamsanqa Gumede. So, all along, she had been running away from her demons, when the real demon resided right under her nose. All that time he wouldn't touch her, he must have been trawling Hillbrow's dark and murky dens, looking to pleasure himself with sex workers. When he accused her of sleeping around in her past, he was doing much worse in the present.

She had forgiven his relationship with the maid of honour, only to find that there was still more to uncover about the 'perfect' Winston Gumede. She shuddered, thanking God once more that he had not infected her with HIV, although she needed to go and get checked for other STIs to be sure. This man was unbelievable. The devil incarnate! The archetypal wolf in sheep's clothing – that's who Winston Gumede was. Now she asked, 'So where are they taking him?'

'They're fetching him from his office. At least Sergeant Mokgotlwa didn't mention anything about a news crew, although all the crews probably look the same to him. He'll probably be taken to the Hillbrow holding cells. Do you guys have a good attorney?'

'I'll get him a good one . . . then I'll divorce him. I've had it with that bloody bastard,' she said, much to Linda's surprise.

Epilogue

Linda, Sade, Nolwazi and the many guests that were assembled outside the church hall laughed as they waved off Dikeledi and Professor Kwame's marital chariot: a black PT cruiser adorned with balloons, bells and whistles, and a 'Just married' sign. It was all very corny and sweet at the same time.

Phemelo had been the flower girl and had looked remarkably like her mother – all dimples and an illuminating smile. Sade had caught the bouquet but then proceeded to throw it in the bin, causing raucous laughter all around.

It had been three months since Winston had been arrested for the murder of Dineo Fakude. The saga had turned into a perfidious scandal the likes of which had not been seen before in Gauteng financial circles. Sade had served Winston with divorce papers, but had to wait for the trial to unravel before they could finalise their official separation.

Her family had been flabbergasted at her reaction, but once the lurid details of Winston's brothel visits had been laid bare in the national papers, even her father had started to rally around her.

She had also been continuously challenged by her church about not standing by her man, but the group that was lecturing her on this matter eventually shut up when she asked them if they would stand by a man who not only frolicked with sex workers, but with church members like Sister Palesa as well.

She continued to find her strength through the support of her fellow churchgoers and her faith in God, but she no longer sought refuge from her past by hiding behind her religion. If she had learned anything from her experience with Winston Gumede, it was that nobody under God's sun could claim to be perfect.

Nolwazi, who had flown up from Cape Town with Simphiwe, had been nervous that the subject of her and Tebogo's affair would once again surface to cloud over the day's event. She was relieved to find that everyone was too preoccupied with the excitement of the wedding to take that thorny walk down memory lane. Besides which, Simphiwe, with his glasses and his intelligent air, was probably daunting enough to ensure that everyone was on their best behaviour.

However, Nolwazi noticed that Dikeledi kept a significant distance from her. Throughout the event, she only spoke to Nolwazi when she had needed someone to fetch Professor Kwame's mother from the guesthouse she was staying at. Since Sade and Linda were both knee-deep in wedding preparations, Nolwazi was the only one who was free to pick up the groom's mom – an errand she took up with much relish. She was very eager to make amends with Dikeledi and would have driven to the North Pole had Dikeledi asked her to.

Nolwazi and Simphiwe had been enjoying their new relationship as if they were teenagers who had just started dating. They had set tongues wagging amongst their circle of friends. When it was first revealed to Eva, she had almost collapsed from sheer shock. She and Nolwazi still joked about their lengthy gay theory, which had crumbled in a cloud of pink dust.

Linda and Kennedy were a happy pair who had officially moved in together and had adopted a puppy in order to help them deal with their commitment issues. They had decided that if they managed to live peacefully with the pet dog for over six months, then they'd start thinking about babies . . . maybe.

Kennedy was steadfastly working on convincing Linda to go with him to visit her father in Europe. He still believed her animosity towards her father was the source of her relationship fears. Linda surprised herself by starting to warm to the idea. She knew this had more to do with placating Kennedy than her wanting to make amends with Floyd. She planned to surprise Kennedy by going to France with him later in the year. One of her documentaries had been shortlisted for the Cannes Film Festival and her father, as always, would be there. She reckoned that Cannes would probably provide a good backdrop for her and her father to make an attempt at civility towards each other. Their shared passion for filmmaking would probably serve as an antidote to any misgivings or misunderstandings.

As Dikeledi and Kwame drove down the street towards the venue they had booked for their wedding reception, the professor leaned towards Dikeledi and whispered, 'How I wish we could press the fast-forward button and find ourselves in our hotel room, already.'

Dikeledi giggled pleasurably. 'You're insatiable. Aren't you exhausted from all the wedding preparations?'

He kissed her passionately. 'I can never get enough of you. You know that.'

Twelve hours later, Kwame and Dikeledi enjoyed a well-deserved rest after a marathon, passion-fuelled lovemaking session.

'It was worth it,' said an exhausted Professor Kwame.

'What was worth it?'

'The long wait . . . all those months of suppressed sexual chemistry. All the days when I longed for you but felt unseen by you.

It was worth it. I'm the happiest man alive, right at this moment,' he said.

Dikeledi sighed. She could not describe how he made her feel. It was almost other-worldly. She felt like she had transmogrified into a magnificent goddess.

She smiled secretly to herself as she turned to cuddle her Ghanaian prince.

Life *is* beautiful, she thought, before drifting off into a peaceful slumber.

GLOSSARY

Urban South Africans mix different languages in their daily speech because of the cosmopolitan nature of Gauteng, the province where Johannesburg is located. South Africa has eleven official languages, and the speech of urbanites blends most of these languages, as you will discover when you read the book.

So, to help those readers unfamiliar with South African dialect, I have put together a list of words and phrases that my characters use in the book.

ag – an exclamation

baba (isiZulu/Xhosa) – father or a respectful greeting to older man

broer (Afrikaans) – a friendly form of address

buti (isiZulu) – brother

cluster – a unit on a housing estate

doek (Afrikaans) – headscarf

eish (South African, colloquial) – used to express a range of emotions, such as surprise, annoyance, or resignation

hey wena (isiZulu/Xhosa) – hey you

bhawu (isiZulu/Xhosa) – Oh my word!, used to express anger or shock

bhayi (isiZulu/Xhosa) – No

bhayi wena s'febe (isiZulu) – No, you bitch!

Induna – (isiZulu) Chief

Ipapa (isiZulu) – hardened porridge, a staple accompaniment to meat dishes

jislaaik (Afrikaans) – expression of shock or surprise

Jozi (isiZulu) – Johannesburg

kente – Ghanaian handwoven cloth

kunini ngikufuna Mthakathi ndini (isiZulu) – I've been looking for you for a long time, you witch

kwerekwere (slang) – foreigner (derogatory)

lalela (isiZulu) – listen

lapa – courtyard

lobola (isiZulu/Xhosa) – the traditional bride price or dowry

lona basadi maar (Setswana) – you women, though . . .

maar wena (slang) – but you . . .

mala mogodu (Setswana) – tripe and offal

mina (isiZulu) – me

min' emnandi kuwe, min' emnandi kuwe – (isiZulu) happy birthday to you, happy birthday to you

mna (isiZulu) – me

mngani wami (isiZulu) – my friend

mntwanam (isiZulu) – my boy

mos (expression, Afrikaans) – affirmation

nana (Setswana) – baby/my baby

neh (expression, slang) – right

nina (isiZulu) – you (plural)

nkosi yam' (isiZulu) – oh my God

nogal (Afrikaans) – moreover

pantsula – South African street dance

shoo (slang) – an exclamation

sies (slang) – expression of disgust

sisi (isiZulu) – sister

sthandwa sam (isiZulu) – my love

tekkies – trainers

tokoloshe – a mischievous mythical spirit

umnqcusho – samp and beans

unjani (Xhosa/Zulu) – how are you?

vat en sit (Afrikaans, colloquial) – cohabitation by an unmarried couple

varsity – university

wena (isiZulu) – you

wena ou (isiZulu) – you, my friend

yoh – exclamation

yinduna le (isiZulu) – this man is a chief

A NOTE ON SOUTH AFRICAN SEASONS

South African seasons differ from European and US seasonal ranges. For reference, below is the South African seasonal split:

Spring: September, October, November

Summer: December, January, February

Autumn: March, April, May

Winter: June, July, August

ACKNOWLEDGEMENTS

I would like to thank Victoria Oundjian and the rest of the Lake Union team for their unwavering faith in my work and their patience as we worked away to update this proudly and loudly South African book for the enjoyment of readers across the globe.

The world of the book is one that is made all the richer for the horizons it opens for the reader, so we worked hard to ensure that new readers of my work get to experience modern South Africa without getting lost in some of the quirks that are unique to the southern tip of the African continent. We hope that you will enjoy the rollercoaster ride!

Special thanks to Celine Kelly for her detective-like editorial observations; *The 30th Candle* is all the better for her wonderful inputs. I would also like to credit Gillian Holmes for her hawkish eye. All writers deserve an editor with such precision.

All of this would not be possible without my wonderful agent, Aoife Lennon; she is pure stardust!

And finally, thanks to you. I hope you enjoy *The 30th Candle*, whatever age you are.

ABOUT THE AUTHOR

Photo © 2022 Nicolise Harding

Angela Makholwa was born in Johannesburg, South Africa. A qualified journalist, she cut her teeth reporting on crime stories in the 1990s. The case of a real-life serial killer went on to inform her debut novel, *Red Ink* – the first South African crime novel with an African female protagonist. Her writing has gained her critical acclaim and several literary award nominations, including the 2020 UK Comedy Women in Print Prize, for which her novel *The Blessed Girl* was shortlisted.

She is a keen yogi, reader, occasional dancer and a juggler of businesses – as well as writing novels, she currently runs a public relations agency.

Follow the Author on Amazon

If you enjoyed this book, follow Angela Makholwa on Amazon to be notified when the author releases a new book!
To do this, please follow these instructions:

Desktop:

1) Search for the author's name on Amazon or in the Amazon App.
2) Click on the author's name to arrive on their Amazon page.
3) Click the 'Follow' button.

Mobile and Tablet:

1) Search for the author's name on Amazon or in the Amazon App.
2) Click on one of the author's books.
3) Click on the author's name to arrive on their Amazon page.
4) Click the 'Follow' button.

Kindle eReader and Kindle App:

If you enjoyed this book on a Kindle eReader or in the Kindle App, you will find the author 'Follow' button after the last page.